Seven Brides for Beau McBride

AMY BARRY

ATRIA BOOKS

New York · Amsterdam/Antwerp · London · Toronto · Sydney · New Delhi

SEVEN BRIDES FOR BEAU MCBRIDE
First published in Australia in 2025 by
Atria Books Australia, an imprint of Simon & Schuster (Australia) Pty Limited
Level 4, 32 York St, Sydney NSW 2000

10 9 8 7 6 5 4 3 2 1

New York Amsterdam/Antwerp London Toronto Sydney New Delhi
Visit our website at www.simonandschuster.com.au

© Amy Matthews 2025

All rights reserved. No part of this publication may be reproduced,
stored in a retrieval system, or transmitted in any form or by
any means, electronic, mechanical, photocopying, recording or
otherwise, without prior permission of the publisher.

ATRIA BOOKS and colophon are trademarks of Simon & Schuster, LLC.

This book is a work of fiction. Any references to historical events, real people,
or real places are used fictitiously. Other names, characters, places, and
events are products of the author's imagination, and any resemblance to
actual events or places or persons, living or dead, is entirely coincidental.

A catalogue record for this
book is available from the
National Library of Australia

ISBN: 9781761631078

Cover artwork: Alissandra Seelau
Map: Josie-Lynn O'Malley
Printed and bound in Australia by Griffin Press

The paper this book is printed on is certified against the
Forest Stewardship Council® Standards. Griffin Press holds
chain of custody certification SCS-COC-001185. FSC®
promotes environmentally responsible, socially beneficial
and economically viable management of the world's forests.

Praise for *Seven Brides for Beau McBride*

'Sweet, hilarious and totally delicious, *Seven Brides for Beau McBride* is the perfect book to escape into. I adore this series!' **Hannah Grace, international bestselling author of *Icebreaker***

'What a delight to be back in Bitterroot with the McBrides! True to form, Amy Barry brings us hijinks, hilarity and a wonderfully sweet love story that had me smiling from start to finish. With a cast of characters who will have you laughing, sighing and swooning—*Seven Brides for Beau McBride* is a keeper!' **Elizabeth Everett, *USA Today* bestselling author of *A Lady's Formula for Love***

'*Seven Brides for Beau McBride* is the sparkling, swoony, and laugh-out-loud funny romance we all need right now. The perfect tonic for these turbulent times. You'll be smiling all the way through.' **Mimi Matthews, *USA Today* bestselling author of *Rules for Ruin***

'Bless yore beautiful hide, Amy Barry. I'm in seventh heaven after devouring the latest McBride adventure. Ellie and Beau are adorably unputdownable!' **Amy Andrews, *USA Today* bestselling author of *Nothing But Trouble***

'A jewel of a novel. It had me snort-laughing and swooning all at once. The perfect romantic escape from today's troubles that I didn't know I needed. Please can I request the TV series!' **Tess Woods, bestselling author of *The Venice Hotel***

'Thank goodness there are so many McBride siblings, what a delight to be back in the glorious chaos of Buck's Creek, Montana: I love it here. Author Amy Barry has hit her stride with her third instalment of this beloved series, a pitch-perfect epistolary romance … There are mistletoe kisses and stolen moments, a Christmas dance and a marauding bear. Pure, joyful, hilarious escape.' **Clare Fletcher, author of *Five Bush Weddings* and *Love Match***

'Oh, Beau McBride. Swoon! The latest McBride adventure is a grin-inducing, impossible to put down, irresistible romantic romp … with enough steam to warm a cold Montana winter. I'm head-over-heels for this series!' **Amy Hutton, author of *Love from Scratch***

Also by Amy Barry

KIT McBRIDE GETS A WIFE
MARRYING OFF MORGAN McBRIDE

In memory of Lucy,
the best writing cat there ever was.

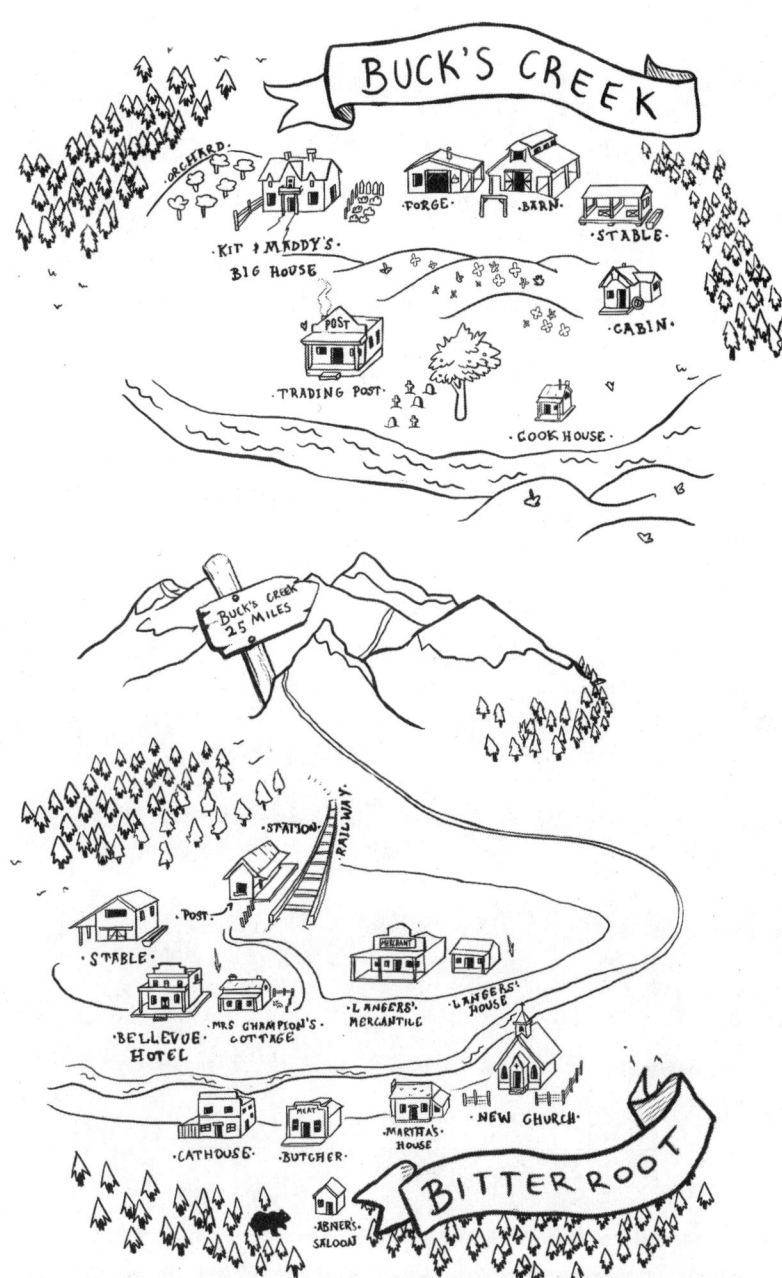

Prologue

Buck's Creek, Montana, 1887

Junebug McBride had sworn on her life that she wouldn't advertise for any more unwanted mail-order brides for her brothers. Over the past two years she'd ordered up two separate brides—one for her brother Kit and one for her brother Morgan—and she'd caught all kinds of hell for it. Mostly because no one had known she'd done it until the wives had turned up in Buck's Creek, expecting a hitching. If there was one thing Junebug had learned about her brothers, it was that they didn't appreciate having women sprung on them. But while they'd bullied her into promising no more unwanted brides, no one had said a darn thing about *wanted* ones.

Junebug's brother Beau was actively interested in matrimony, which changed everything. Thank goodness—because she needed more help around here with all the wretched women's work. As if men couldn't launder and cook, Junebug thought darkly.

Even though she'd ordered wives for her eldest brothers Kit and Morgan, Maddy was banned from doing any of Junebug's chores, and Pip was off honeymooning with Morgan. It was high time Junebug got a proper wife. One who'd do some of the damn work around here.

It had been a flat-out delight to find Beau raiding her stockpiled editions of the *Matrimonial News*. Well, maybe not at first. At first, she'd been incensed that he'd dared to touch her things. And it was extra vexatious because her things had been hidden, damn it. What kind of man went rifling through a girl's secret hiding place?

"What in hell are you doing?" she'd exploded, catching him red-handed up in the loft of the trading post. He was lucky she hadn't crammed him full of buckshot.

He snapped the newspaper open, completely at ease with his blatant thievery. "What does anyone do with the *Matrimonial News*? I want to find a woman."

Junebug felt like he'd whipped the ground out from under her. "You what?"

Beau had settled into reading on a pile of old hides. "I'm a red-blooded man, ain't I? And there ain't no women up here, so I thought I'd see if I could order one up. And then I got to thinking about all the ads in here. There's plenty of women already looking for husbands. I don't need to do anything but pick one."

That was Beau in a nutshell, wasn't it? Too lazy to even write his own damn ad.

Beau was her third oldest brother, after Morgan and Kit, and full of airs now Morgan was away and Kit had moved into the big house with his wife. Beau had always been irritating but he was extra irritating now that he thought he was the man of the cabin. He'd taken to bossing her and their brother Jonah around something awful. And he did it so breezily, like they should be *glad* of it. Junebug blamed the women of Bitterroot, who treated him like some kind of minor deity just because he had a pretty face. This is what came of people melting at his feet all the time. He thought Junebug should take his orders with melty gratitude—when in fact she just wanted to kick him most of the time.

Junebug was the only unmarried girl in Buck's Creek and she wasn't melting over anyone, least of all her idiot brother. But the meagre clutch of women in Bitterroot, four hours ride down the mountain, spoiled Beau something rotten. It was a shame none of them were marriageable. Junebug would put up with their spoiling of Beau if they did it while washing a pot or two. But they were all too old, too young, or too disreputable for wifedom. Junebug wasn't entirely sure what made a woman disreputable, but she knew it had something to do with working in the cathouse. It was a crying shame disrepute and marriage were mutually exclusive, because those cathouse girls sure were fond of Beau and would probably marry him in a heartbeat. And then Junebug could put 'em to work making the morning bread . . .

Her brothers ate bread faster than she could bake it so she baked more bread than a girl should reasonably be expected to. Beau was well into his twenties now and if he'd lived anywhere else he'd be safely hitched with a nice amenable wife kneading all that dough. But no, they had to live up a mountain in a town of seven people, all of them McBrides and none of them the baking sort. McBrides who left Junebug with a lot of pots to wash, a lot of laundry to scrub, and a lot of damn cooking to do. And she hated cooking.

"I thought for a while about catching a train to Butte to go find a wife," Beau sighed as he pored over the ads. "I figured I'd be more saleable in person. A nice face goes a long way in winning a wife."

He wasn't wrong. He did have a nice face. And girls liked it. All of her brothers were decent looking, but Beau stood out like a peacock in a flock of hawks. Not that hawks flocked, but if they did, Beau would peacock their flock right up. He was the elegant sort. Not thick and hulking like Morgan and Kit, but willowy and graceful. He relied on slyness rather than brawn; the only time he won a wrestling match against either of them was when he got crafty. He was tall like the rest of them, but leaner and more refined of face. His jaw was almost heart-shaped, and he had a dent in his chin and a perky cupid's bow to his fat mouth. It was only the fact that he had the same heavy brows as Morgan that saved him from being *too* pretty, Junebug thought in disgust. They afforded him some of the irascible family spirit. He had dark eyes like Kit, only they were more glistery, like he was always on the verge of some high emotion. He had the same wild dark hair as the rest of the family, although he snipped at it constantly with Ma's old silver scissors, so it curled around his neck, licking at his jaw. He was also prone to shaving more than was usual for a backwoodsman and had even been known to be bare faced in the depths of winter, which was just plain insanity. There were more than a few weeks in January when even Junebug wished she could grow a beard to keep out the chill. Beau liked his duds too. He pored over catalogs and ordered up the most ridiculous things, like that rolled brim derby hat with the tall crown that he wore rain or shine. He'd probably step off a train into a town like Butte and be hitched before lunchtime.

Personally, when the time came for Junebug to hunt for a man for herself, she'd prefer less looks and more gumption. She didn't really get the point of peacocks.

"But *then*," Beau drawled, pulling her out of her thoughts, "I got to thinking about how you already had these papers full of women looking for a husband and I figured it'd be plum easier to just pick one of them."

See? Lazy.

"You don't want to answer those ads," she told him scornfully. "They ain't no good. You'd have to hunt for ages to find a decent one. You're much better off writing your own specifications so you can get exactly what you want." Junebug scooted down the raw timber ladder and headed for the trading post's counter for a pencil and paper. She stole a glance out the window, towards the big house; from across the meadow she could hear the ringing strike of Kit's hammer in the smithy, so she assumed she wasn't likely to get caught. It was worth the risk. Junebug couldn't trust Beau to do this right without her. Besides, she'd never said she wouldn't *help* order a wife; she wasn't actually doing the ordering herself. Junebug snatched paper and pencil from the counter and raced back up before Beau could make a bad decision.

"Here, write down what you want, and I'll show you how to get it in the paper."

Junebug peered over his shoulder as he put pencil to paper.

Good looking guy seeks gal for fun, Beau wrote.

"That ain't an ad for a wife," Junebug said, disgusted. "That's for a whole different kind of relationship."

"I'm open to it."

"You can't go inviting just anyone into the family," Junebug protested. Jeez. If he wanted a whore, there were plenty down in Bitterroot.

"Sure, I can. Who I marry ain't no one's business but my own."

"I could find you a better woman than you could find yourself," Junebug insisted. "You'll pick someone for short-term fun. That's no way to go about it. When I do it, I make sure they know what they're getting into, with a view to long-term happiness."

Beau didn't buy it, she could tell. But that was only because her first two wives hadn't quite worked out as she'd planned. You couldn't expect a girl to get it right without some practice. And Kit and Morgan were happily married now, weren't they? So, she had a perfect record, even if the process had been messy.

"There ain't no way you could find a better woman than I can," Beau disagreed. "You don't have a clue what a man wants in a woman."

Well, that was flat-out untrue. She'd married off two brothers already, and they were sickeningly happy. And Thunderhead Bill and Sour Eagle, her trapper friends, had explained all the ways a man could get himself kicked-in-the-head lovestruck by a woman. Junebug had attended closely to their tales of bare feminine shoulders and sideways smiles and the like, and it had paid off, because both Kit and Morgan were about as in love as men could be without being totally witless. Junebug's sisters-in-law should thank her too, because neither of them had been the naturally wily sort. It had taken some elbow grease on Junebug's part to provide their happy endings. But did anyone thank her? No. They just carped on about how she needed to keep her nose out of other people's business. But what they didn't understand was that it *was* her business. The wives were as much for her as for her stupid brothers, weren't they?

"Here, what about this?" Beau held out the paper with his draft advertisement.

Junebug thought his ad was stomach-turning in the extreme. *Charming gentleman seeks beguiling woman to warm the long Montana winters.*

"That makes it sound like you want a whore," Junebug protested.

Beau didn't look displeased at the notion.

Junebug had a suggestion. "What about: *Good looking layabout seeks frontier bride.*"

"No decent woman is answering that ad." Beau was offensively dismissive.

"Wanna bet?" Junebug said mutinously.

Beau's eyes narrowed. "A bet?" He glittered with that piratical look he got when he leapt headlong into trouble. Beau got into more trouble than anyone Junebug knew. Save herself. "You want to make this a bet?" he asked. "What kind?"

Oh, this was getting good. Junebug was beginning to see how this could work to her advantage, on multiple fronts. "It's simple. We both advertise, and we see who hooks the best wife." Junebug knew she'd win. It wasn't even in question.

"And what are the stakes?" Beau's dark eyes were gleaming.

"If I win," Junebug said, "you take me to a circus."

"A circus?" Beau looked at her like she'd grown a second head.

"I've always wanted to see a circus. We might have to go to Iowa or somewhere, though. From what I can tell there ain't no circuses in these parts."

"You get the daftest ideas." He shook his head. "Fine. What about if I win?"

"I'll buy you a mirror?"

"Get off it." He swatted her with the paper. "How about you take over mucking out the stables from me? For a year."

"A year!"

"Well, you want me to take you to Iowa—that ain't cheap," he sniped.

Junebug thought on it. "Deal." She held out her hand for him to shake. "May the best McBride win."

"I plan to." He gathered up as many *Matrimonial News*es as he could and tucked them under his arm before he headed down the ladder of the loft. "I'd best read up on these ads, so I can write the perfect one." He disappeared. And then his head popped back up. "And, Junebug, not a word of this to the others."

Junebug snorted. What did he think she was, stupid?

She grinned as she considered the kind of wife she'd need. Soon, there'd be another wife to help around the house, and she'd have beaten the pants off Beau and be on her way to the circus.

Life was looking good.

WANTED

Charming gentleman seeks beguiling woman to warm the long Montana winters. Said gentleman is attentive, of landed family, and more than ready for the love of a good woman. Although not judgmental and open to all feminine charms, the gentleman would prefer copious and symmetrical attractions.

WANTED

Good-looking layabout seeks frontier bride. Be warned: he's well aware of his own charms and would just as soon kiss a mirror as a wife. The ideal woman would fill his empty head with some book learning and take him down a peg or two. But he does come with a nice patch of Montana land and a good singing voice.

One

"Junebug!" Kit's disembodied voice rolled through the mountain pass like thunder, echoing off the slopes. "Git back here!"

It was a gusty, blustery, downright temperamental October in Buck's Creek. Morgan was still off honeymooning with his bride Pip, his postcards tacked up in the trading post until they just about filled the wall next to the counter. Jonah had absconded for the month, prospecting with his friend Purdy Joe deep in the mountains. Even the old trappers had abandoned Junebug for the down-mountain town of Bitterroot, where they now sat around people's porches all day, gossiping about the going-ons of the miners and passers-through. Junebug, meanwhile, was still stranded up the hill in Buck's Creek, with a bunch of burned pots and a list of chores as long as her arm. And her arm was plenty long after her summer growth spurt.

"Junebug, you lazy cat, git your ass back down here this minute!"

Well, let Kit thunder. Junebug wasn't going back to scrub those darn pots. She'd cooked the breakfast, she didn't see why she had to clean up after it too, no matter what Kit said. Let him wash the dishes.

She tightened her grip on the old flour sack she was carrying and slid deeper into the fall woods. It had been a sodden week; the ground was mulchy underfoot and everything had a mushroomy smell that made Junebug think of the root cellar. Which she was also expected to reorganize, she thought grumpily. Hell. Not for the first time, she wished her eldest brother Morgan was back with his bride. Morgan was the one who cared about stocking the cellar, not Junebug. So let him do it. Or Beau. She wasn't their maid. Or their goddamn wife.

She was a lone wolf, she thought fiercely as she climbed higher, determined to get as far from her bossy brothers as she could. She wasn't made for domesticity; she was made for greater things. Like getting to that circus Beau had promised her if she won their bet.

It was her keenest desire in life to see a circus, one with gals in spangles standing on the backs of fancy high-stepping horses, aerialists flipping about like bull trout pulled fresh from the stream, and tigers and elephants from places where it was hot and jungly. Hell, she could imagine the circus so vivid she could just about smell the sawdust.

But to get to that circus she had to pick Beau that wife she'd promised him at the end of summer. A *better* wife than he could pick for himself. The contrary peacock.

It was a bet Junebug planned to win. Although . . . Beau had been collecting an awful lot of mail down at the Bitterroot post office lately. And he refused to share any of his correspondence with her. Junebug scowled at the soggy ground underfoot, kicking at the mulchy fallen leaves. How was she supposed to beat him if she didn't know what she was up against?

Did he have a genuine contender yet? It was a wonder that he had any correspondence at all, given how terrible his advertisement was. *The gentleman would prefer copious and symmetrical attractions.* Junebug snorted. He made it sound like he was looking for a whore. But it was entirely possible he *had* found a few symmetrical attractions, given how he kept sneaking off and returning with his fingers all stained black and blue with ink. That rat was writing letters. And Junebug wanted to know who to.

At least Beau wasn't a first-rate letter writer, not the way Junebug was. His correspondence was bound to be lacking. He didn't have a knack for conversation either—Junebug thought sourly of the long winter nights in the cabin, when he abjectly refused to entertain her. Spit, he could write all the substandard letters he wanted, it would do no good—Junebug would out-write him and out-wife him. Not least of all because she didn't fancy mucking out the stables while Beau lazed about fishing. Probably with Junebug's good hickory fishing rod. She still hadn't forgiven him for snapping her last one and she couldn't stomach him using this one.

The fact that it hadn't happened yet didn't stop Junebug from getting riled about it. She imagined all the ways she'd give Beau a piece of her mind when she discovered him with her hickory rod. Envisioning the fury of the confrontation got Junebug's blood up. It was good for the constitution; at least so she told her trapper friend Sour Eagle whenever he scolded her for raging about things that had yet to happen.

She'd show Beau. That no-good, jumped-up fishing rod stealer. Junebug had her own stash of letters, hidden in a flour sack. They'd been arriving in flurries over the past weeks; she was bound to find a woman who could out-dazzle one of those damn fool symmetrical attractions her brother was writing to. She struggled with the bulging sack of mail as she navigated her way through a tight stand of aspens. It was flat-out astonishing to Junebug how many women were keen for a good-looking layabout; her ad in the *Matrimonial News* caused a flurry among the conjugally inclined, despite the fact Junebug had stressed that Beau's good looks were balanced by vanity of outrageous proportions. These women didn't seem to care. In fact, she'd had more responses than she'd got for Kit and Morgan combined. Maybe because pretty men didn't usually resort to advertising for a mate? Like the way an eight-pointed buck barely had to compete for a doe. They just tossed their antlers about and the lady deer came running.

Most of the men in the *Matrimonial News* were too busy listing everything they wanted in a woman to bother talking about themselves. And if they did talk about themselves, it was in terms of their jobs: *Rancher looking for a pretty little lady; Ostler seeking brown-haired sweetheart; Widower with kids wanting firm-handed woman, not older than twenty-five.* Men seemed to put a lot of stock in what they did all day.

But the women didn't seem to care particularly what Beau did. They were plenty interested in his attractions, though. Junebug supposed that if you had to live with a man and let him kiss you all over the place, you might want to pick one who didn't turn your stomach. It was a stroke of luck, in that case, that looks were Beau's strongest selling point. She reckoned most girls would want a kiss or two from Beau. Her brother was too pretty by half. The women down in Bitterroot (what few there were) got downright stupid around him. Even old Mrs. Langer at the post office got fluttery, and she wasn't the fluttery type. She was more the slap-your-hand-if-you-touched-anything-on-her-desk type. And Mrs. Champion at the hotel gave Beau extra cookies when he visited, which burned Junebug up no end, as *she* was the one who loved cookies. She was also the one who put in all the work listening to Mrs. Champion's stories. It was sickening the way Beau could just swan in and get cookies without suffering through so much as an aside. Ellen, the hotel's housemaid, giggled and blushed and generally embarrassed herself trying to get Beau's attention while he ate those cookies too, and all the whores at the cathouse over the road (the ones that Junebug wasn't supposed to know about) managed to find their way out onto the porch wearing not much at all when Beau was in town for the day. They fanned at their half-exposed chests and batted their eyelashes, and made a bunch of remarks Junebug didn't understand and couldn't find in any book when she tried to look them up.

Sick of wrestling the overstuffed flour sack uphill, Junebug rested a spell. She shook out the muscles in her arm. She was headed for her secret clearing at the top of the rise, where she could find some privacy to sort through her prospective brides. Up here the quaking aspens were splashes of gold amid the dripping conifers and there was a constant rustle of critters gathering stocks for the winter. October was settling in with its fogs and drizzle and darkening days, and Junebug was running out of time. She didn't fancy waiting until next February's thaw to get a wife and win the bet.

As she leaned against the aspen, fuming about the injustice of it all, Junebug caught an odd scrap of sound on the wind. She frowned. It wasn't the crackling of fall leaves, or the scurrying of squirrels. It was *humming*.

Junebug wasn't alone up here, damn it. And after she'd slogged her flour sack of letters all this way for some privacy. She scowled. Well, whoever it was could just get the hell out of her woods. Junebug had things to do. Tucking her sack of letters out of sight under the droop of a serviceberry bush, she slipped through the woods towards the sound of humming. Maybe it was a trapper? Only it wasn't trapping season yet, since the animals hadn't grown in their thick winter coats.

Junebug cocked her head and listened harder. It wasn't just humming. It was *tuneful* humming. Not only tuneful, goddamn *delightful*.

Which meant only one thing.

Beau.

That wily rat! He was supposed to be pickling cucumbers for the root cellar. Kit and Maddy had refused to let Junebug do it anymore after the lids had popped off the jars one by one, at velocity, shattering one of their new kitchen windows. Maddy was mighty displeased about not having any glass in the window to keep out the fall chill.

Still, at least it meant no more pickling for Junebug.

Beau was supposed to be spending the day sweetening Junebug's batch of sour cucumbers and stuffing them into jars, so what was he doing here, skiving off his chores? That lazy rodent.

And what was he so cheerful about that he was bursting into song all over the place?

Junebug crept closer, glad the sodden ground muffled her steps.

Beau was right out in the open in the little grassy clearing, singing to himself like he didn't have a care in the world. Or any cucumbers to pickle. He really did have a lovely voice—her advertisement hadn't lied about that. Far be it from Junebug not to give praise when praise was due: the man could sing. His singing might even be the thing Junebug liked best about him.

But what in the *hell* was he doing?

Beau was standing oddly in the middle of the clearing, with his arms held out rigid like a scarecrow. Like he was holding onto an invisible something. Or someone, she realized in startlement, as she saw him take an awkward step back and to the side.

Was he . . . *dancing?*

There was a book open on the damp grass in front of him and he was peering at it and muttering between verses. Now and then he'd squat down and examine the book closely with a furrowed brow. Junebug rose on tiptoe as she peered around the conifer. She wished she'd thought to bring the spyglass up with her from the trading post. She glanced around, wondering if she could get a better vantage point.

Stealthy like a bobcat stalking a deer, Junebug crept between the soppy trees, trying to get closer. Beau seemed powerfully absorbed in his book and didn't notice her. Eventually she came to the trunk of a fallen sapling and managed to furtively gain higher ground. From here she could see that his book had diagrams and everything—little feet and dotted lines spackling the page in arcane loops.

Beau stood again and his arms wrapped around an imaginary dance partner.

Goddamn, he *was* dancing. And he didn't look half bad. This wasn't the usual McBride kind of dancing, which they did in the summer meadow to Jonah's fiddle; this was actual proper civilized dancing, like they did at fancy cotillions and such. At least so she'd read. Junebug had never actually been to any cotillions. Nor even to a barn dance. But that was the kind of dancing Beau looked like he was educating himself for, the cotillion kind, where ladies in fancy dresses had dance cards looped to their wrists and wielded little bitty pencils at gentlemen to make them dance. And they drank champagne and ate fancy sandwiches, like those cucumber sandwiches without the crusts Junebug had got Pip to make once. Junebug didn't think those sandwiches would do a thing to satisfy an appetite got up by dancing. But that was cotillions for you, she supposed. A lot of dainty nibbling.

Beau had started singing proper as he swung his invisible partner around the clearing. It was that sappy 'Eileen Alannah' song that Maddy was always asking him to sing. He was crooning it to the empty air with his whole heart.

Which meant only one thing . . . the blockhead had found himself a wife. Because who the hell else was he going to dance with around here? Thunderhead Bill? Purdy Joe? He certainly wasn't dancing with Junebug.

"I know you're there, you little sneak."

Junebug jerked in surprise at the sound of his voice, and almost fell off the log.

Beau gave his imaginary partner a spin. "If you're so keen to see what I'm doing, why don't you just come look?"

"Sneak!" Junebug was outraged. "If anyone's sneaking in this circumstance, it's you." She was annoyed at being caught, but even more annoyed at Beau singing and dancing and generally being all Beau-ish all over the place. How dare he find a wife before she did. Junebug jumped off the log and stalked over to his dumb dancing book. She looked down at the pattering of black steps on the page. "What the hell are you learning to dance for?"

"My wedding," he said smugly. And then he gave the most irritating twirl.

Junebug scowled. "Now hold your damn horses. You ain't allowed to go getting married without considering *all* the options. We had a deal!"

"I'll stick to the deal. But consider this bet won, Bug."

Junebug had an urge to stick out her foot and trip him as he danced by with some offensively ostentatious footwork. "This bet has barely got going," she said hotly. Hell, she hadn't even begun sorting her mail. "You ain't even seen my wife yet. I've got some mighty fine candidates." She hoped.

"I'll take a look," he said, giving her a grin that made her want to scream. "But I've got to tell you, I think I've found the perfect woman." He spun to a halt and offered his phantom dance partner a flirty bow. And then the blockhead reached into his pocket and pulled out an envelope. Carefully, almost reverently, he opened it and withdrew a card. He held it out for Junebug to see, grinning like he was already kicked in the head, and he hadn't even met anyone in person yet. At least as far as she knew.

Junebug reached for the card, but he snatched it back. "Uh-uh, no touching, Bug."

Oh, this was *bad*. He was looking down at that card with an expression that could only be described as amative.

Junebug made an irritable show of tucking her hands behind her back and then bent so close to the card her nose was just about touching it.

"It's a photograph!" Junebug pulled her head back so she could see it properly. "Like that cabinet card Morgan and Pip sent from Nebraska." That one had been a sepia photograph of the two of them, flanked by Pip's whole wealth of unsmiling relatives. Morgan had looked like a startled hare; Pip had been grinning ear to ear. Junebug hadn't seen many photographs in her life, and it was kind of a thrill to see Beau's, even if it was a threat to her circus ambitions.

The girl in Beau's picture had a queenly look. She stood posed beside a velvety looking chair, holding onto its curved back and giving the camera a sideways glance. She was glowing like moonshine, but that could be the vagaries of photography—if she glowed like that in real life Junebug didn't stand a chance of winning the bet. The girl had silvery pale hair, all swept up in an elegant hairstyle. Her nose was straight, and her figure was willowy and graceful. Her clothes weren't too fancy, though. Junebug could tell because the first wife she'd (misguidedly) picked for Kit had been plenty fancy. Willabelle's clothes had looked like a box of ribbons had exploded everywhere, and the fabrics were all shiny and exotic. This woman, on the other hand, was in modest calico cotton, all buttoned up to the chin, with a hint of lace at the collar. But she was a hell of a lot prettier than Willabelle, who had been . . . well, *obvious*. This woman was—

"A natural beauty," Beau declared, sounding satisfied as all hell.

"You like 'em natural, huh?" Junebug couldn't keep the sourness out of her voice.

"When they look like this I do." He was grinning fit to bust.

It was true that the moonglow girl was better looking than was normal. Again, it was probably the vagaries of photography, but she sure looked like something that belonged in a book. Like one of those illustrations of goddesses wrapped in sheets. She was the kind of girl poets got wordy about. Roses in June and all that junk. Junebug guessed it made sense that Beau's instinct was to find someone as pretty as he was, but she thought his instinct was impaired. He had looks enough for two people. What he needed was someone sensible, someone who could steer him straight. She had to be appealing, sure, but appealing didn't have to mean glowing all over the place at innocent people.

How was Junebug supposed to find a woman to compete with this?

"Did she write you at all, or did she just send the photograph? Have you picked based *just* on looks?" Junebug demanded. "Because that would be powerfully stupid."

Beau was magnanimous in his assumed victory. "Oh, she wrote. I've got a stack of letters."

"She know how to spell?" Junebug asked, frowning at the way he slid the photograph back in its envelope like he was wrapping up a treasure.

His eyes were actually *twinkling* at her he was so happy. Goddamn it.

"She spells better than me," he said.

"That wouldn't be hard."

"She's a delightful correspondent."

"I'm sure. Can I read her letters?"

"No." He had the gall to laugh, still twinkling. Since when did Beau twinkle? He wasn't the twinkling type. He was the flat-out irritating type.

"They're private," he told her firmly, and there was a tenderness in him that made her blood run cold.

Junebug's mind raced. "How long have you been writing to each other?"

"A few weeks."

"A few weeks!"

"She was the first one to answer my advertisement."

Junebug swore. She couldn't help it. This was irksome in the extreme. She hadn't even finished reading her mail yet and here he was, through the choosing already. "You ain't supposed to pick the *first* one who answers, you sap. You're supposed to survey the field."

"I didn't need to. I liked this one. And now that she's sent me this"—he patted his pocket, where the photograph was resting against his heart—"I know I picked the right one."

"Don't get ahead of yourself. She might have a voice like screeching cats."

"You wish."

Junebug did wish, very much.

"She's smart," he said smugly, "and funny, and—"

"You know all this from a few letters?"

"More than a dozen letters."

"How often have you been writing? And stop that."

"Stop what?"

"Twinkling." His fat lips twitched in response. "I hate seeing you this happy."

"I thought the whole point of finding me a wife was to make me happy?"

"Maybe so—but I ain't found her yet!"

Beau laughed. "You ain't, huh? I thought you had some fine candidates?"

"I do. I just haven't narrowed the field." Junebug harrumphed. "And now I might have to get photographs out of them before I narrow it down." What were the chances of finding a second moonshine woman? Maybe she could find out what kind of camera made a woman glow like that . . .

"Or you can just concede defeat now?" Beau put his hands on his narrow hips and gave her an understanding look.

"I'd rather die."

He laughed again. "Well, while you're contemplating the afterlife, how about you put yourself to use. I need a partner."

"I ain't helping you."

"C'mon," he coaxed. "Who knows, maybe I'll end up dancing with the woman you pick. Then you'll wish I danced nice, won't you?" He grabbed her hands and tugged her forward. Junebug just about hissed at him. "Now, now, is that any way to treat a Beau at your first dance?" He laughed at his own pun.

"What's her name?" Junebug asked as Beau started humming a merry tune and skipping her around the clearing. She let him, because it was actually quite fun. Not that she was telling him that.

"Her name is Miss Diana Newchurch." He said it like he was speaking poetry. "And she's from Fall River, Massachusetts."

"That sounds like a long way away." Junebug's brain whirred, wondering if she could nab a closer bride and beat this Diana Newchurch to the finish line.

Beau burst into song and kicked up the pace a notch.

Junebug brightened as a thought occurred to her. "How do you know that's actually a photograph of her? I mean, she could have sent a photograph of anyone, couldn't she? How are you to know?" Junebug gave him a sly smile.

Beau missed a step.

"She could look like me for all you know." Junebug pressed the point.

He gave her a pained look.

"I'd recommend not promising anything in your letter," Junebug advised. "I mean, remember Willabelle—she weren't what she seemed in her letters."

"Willabelle is a damn fine-looking woman."

Now it was Junebug's turn to look pained. "Looks ain't everything. Remember her personality?"

"Well, Miss Diana Newchurch's personality is just as pretty as her picture."

Junebug doubted that. Surely it was impossible for a woman who looked like moonshine to have a moonshiny personality too. "Can she cook? Launder? Do the things a wife needs to do?"

"Junebug, there's only one thing my wife needs to do . . ."

"Oh, ick. No."

He spun her around gleefully and she tried not to enjoy it.

"I just need a woman who likes me, Bug. I want her to make me happy. And *I* want to make *her* happy."

"Well, a dirty house and an empty stomach ain't likely to make you happy."

"Given I already have those things, I'm sure I'll cope."

"Hey!" Junebug stomped on his foot as they spun. "I cooked you a whole panful of eggs this morning!"

"Well, there you go. I don't need her to do it—I've got you."

Junebug swore at him.

"Admit it, Bug. I've got this bet won. You'll not find a single woman as good as the one I've got."

It was that bold claim that smacked the genius into her. *You'll not find a single woman . . .*

Maybe not. But what about *more* than one . . .

Beau had been raised on this mountain and had known only a dozen or so women in his life, and half of those he was related to. He was *starved* for lady company. Junebug considered that maybe he was looking for courtship more than an actual marriage. Look how happy he was about this dancing business. Maybe what he really wanted was dancing and flirting and a whole lot of goddamn attention.

So why not give it to him?

Junebug felt herself get her own twinkle. What if she ordered up more than one? Two or three girls might give Miss Moonglow a run for her money—they'd certainly improve the odds in Junebug's favor. Hell, why stop at three? She could order up four. Or five. Or, spit, even a dozen. Although she probably didn't have enough money to cover a dozen train tickets or accommodation for all those women. How many could she afford? Five girls? Maybe six? So long as Beau didn't take too long to pick one, she could probably afford a couple of weeks' worth of room and board for six girls. She had her poker winnings saved up, and she really wanted to win this damn bet.

She could haul six pretty girls up this hill and make her brother lose his damn mind. And there was no reason one of her six couldn't end up the new Mrs. McBride. Especially if Junebug chose them well. She could easily pick six versions of happiness for him.

Looking at Beau spinning around the clearing, giddy at the thought of dancing with his moonglowy girl, Junebug knew that she was right. Imagine him having a whole passel of girls to dance around! He'd be happier than a pig in mud. And while he danced them about, she'd work her ass off to make sure he got kicked in the head over one of *her* wives, and not over his. Because she wasn't losing. Junebug McBride didn't lose at anything.

Two

Fall River, Massachusetts

Eleanor Neale tore off her apron the moment the factory bell rang, signaling the end of another long day at the looms of Chattaway Mills. The start bell had sounded at seven that morning, and it was now seven in the evening, full dark outside. Ellie had been itching to leave all day; she was expecting a letter and needed to get back to the boardinghouse to see if it had arrived. Snatching up her coat and hat, she jammed her way through the crush.

Today she was going to get an offer of marriage, and she was going to *accept it*. That is, if the letter had arrived. The thought of it filled Ellie with a turbulent feeling, like a rushing river. She couldn't quite believe she was going to be a mail-order bride. *Her!* Plain old Ellie Neale! Like some kind of heroine in a book.

The aisles were full of loud, tired girls, complaining and joking as they flooded out of the mill and into the sharp Fall River night. Ellie elbowed through them impatiently, pulling on her calico bonnet as she searched for her friend Diana. Diana wasn't hard to spot; she was taller than most of the other girls, and prettier than all of them. *She* was just like a heroine in a book. She could be the lost child of a duke or a marquis, the result of a deliciously tragic affair, abandoned to the gutter after her unwed mother was swept aside by the misfortunes of circumstance. It gave Ellie a thrill just to think about it.

Ellie herself could never be mistaken for an aristocratic love child. Unfortunately, she looked every inch the mill girl that she was. She was pale from hours indoors at the looms, and thin from the frugal serves at the boardinghouse table. Sometimes she liked to imagine that she had the romantic pallor of a heroine recovering from a wasting disease, but most of the time she had to accept that she was just ordinarily pale. Just like she had ordinary brown hair and ordinary brown eyes and a face that was pleasant, but nothing to set a man's heart on fire. She was average height, average build and average everything. She was like wallpaper. Attractive enough, and useful, but not something people particularly paid attention to.

Not like Diana. Diana was the kind of girl who turned people's heads. And she had charm by the bucketful; everyone loved her. Even Mrs. Tasker at their boardinghouse liked her, and as a rule Mrs. Tasker didn't like anyone.

Despite Ellie's daydreams about Diana's ancestry, in actuality Diana was just another mill girl like herself, sent off to work because her parents couldn't afford to keep her. And there were no dukes or marquises around here, that was for sure—just a steady stream of cheeky mill boys who flocked to Diana like a moth to a flame, ignoring old Wallpaper Ellie. But Diana had grander plans than marrying a Fall River man and settling into a tenement house; Diana was escaping this town and its myriad mills, headed for the mountains of Montana as a mail-order bride, so desperate to get away from the mills that she was prepared to marry a stranger.

And now so was Ellie . . .

She certainly had no intention of being left behind. Ellie wasn't about to let Diana marry herself off to a wild man without her there. Diana was the one person in the world who mattered to Ellie, and she planned to be there for her, no matter what.

After all of Ellie's years at the mill, Diana was the only real family she could count on. She thought of her mother, crammed into a tenement with a pack of kids, not to mention with Ellie's violent stepfather, who drank away most of the money he earned at Sagamore Mill and was prone to roughing her mother up when he was out of coin. Sometimes he'd roughed Ellie up too. Ellie's real father had died in the fire of '74, after which things had been hard and hungry, and then Mama had married Hank, who had been a nightmare from the first, and they'd had kid after kid after kid. So many kids there wasn't enough space, or enough food. And Hank drank more, and Mama cried more, and there was always another mouth to feed. Eventually Ellie had been sent off to work at Chattaway Mills. She'd been twelve. That was nearly ten years ago.

Working at the mill meant living in one of the orderly brick row boardinghouses owned by the company. It had changed Ellie's life immeasurably, for the better. The boardinghouses were directly around the corner from the mills—so the girls could hear the bells and get to work fast—and room and board was deducted from their pay in advance. Mrs. Tasker was as inflexible as iron, but also sober, predictable and fair; she ran the house like clockwork to the timing of the bells. None of Mrs. Tasker's girls were ever late to work. If a girl overslept, Mrs. Tasker was prone to chasing them out of bed with her broom. Ellie never needed to be chased out of bed, not even when she'd been up most of the night reading.

The girls boarded four to a room, sharing beds, and their employment depended on their temperance, attendance at church on Sundays, and their chastity. It was a cloistered existence, and the others generally hated it. But for Ellie it was a revelation. No one was ever drunk and angry, there were no days without food, and there was fresh linen on the bed that smelled of Mrs. Tasker's vinegary laundry soap—not the bodily odors of small children. At the boardinghouse Ellie only shared a bed with one other person, not a whole tangle of hungry little kids, and it felt like sheer luxury. Mrs. Tasker served a pleasant if slightly stingy table, with a dollop of hot oats in the morning and a two-course supper with soup and soda bread to start followed by a main meal that mostly featured meat. It was far better than Ellie had ever had at home. Best of all, there was quiet time after supper, where the girls gathered in the parlor with their books and mending and whispered gossip to one another. That was Ellie's absolute favorite time of day. There were no screaming children, no staggering stepfather, no threadbare weepy mother, no neighbors hollering through the thin walls. She was safe, and she felt like she could breathe.

Diana had come to Fall River in Ellie's second year at Chattaway Mills. She was a year younger than Ellie and had been so homesick for the first week that she couldn't sleep at all. They'd been assigned to the same bed because both their surnames started with N and Ellie's previous bedmate was moved on to the next room, where the rest of the Os were. Ellie had been glad to replace dour Marian Osborn with the sweetly pretty Diana, and she'd taken to whispering stories to the homesick girl, mostly scraps of things that she remembered from her books. It gave Ellie a warm feeling, like holding cold hands to a homely fire, to comfort Diana. After the company docked room and board, Ellie sent half her income to her mother to help feed all those kids, but the other half she used to indulge her reading habit, subscribing to Beadle & Adams and Street & Smith for the latest dime novels. Ellie's whispered retellings of those dime novels got Diana through the worst of her homesickness, and after that they were fast friends. More than friends. Sisters, really.

And Ellie absolutely couldn't miss her best friend's wedding. Nor could she abandon Diana to an unknown fate.

No. Ellie had to get herself to Montana too.

And given she had no money and no prospects of getting herself west, she'd resorted to answering an advertisement in the *Matrimonial News*, just like Diana had. If it was good enough for Diana, it was good enough for her. Her only requirement had been that the man had to live in Montana, specifically in the Elkhorn mountains, where Diana was headed.

Now, as her shift ended on this chilly fall night, Ellie was eager to get home to see if she'd finally received a proposal. She caught up with Diana in the after-work surge toward the train station and grabbed Diana's arm, dragging her along. "Come on," she urged.

"Calm down," Diana said, refusing to hurry. "My feet are sore. The mail may not even have come today. You know how patchy it can be from Montana."

Ellie did. Which is why she'd rushed home every day this week, sure that this was the day, only to find the letter hadn't come. But *today* was surely the day. She *needed* that proposal.

The whole mess of Diana's impending flight west was Ellie's fault in the first place. She was entirely culpable if Diana was led to ruin by this hare-brained adventure. It had never occurred to her that bringing home the *Matrimonial News* would lead to such a catastrophe. Ellie had only brought the paper home for voyeuristic entertainment, not to actually *answer* any of the ads. It was fodder for daydreams, that was all.

Ellie liked reading the advertisements and imagining the people on the other end of them. It was like reading a novel, but better, because the people were real. There were advertisements for industrious shopkeepers in towns with names like Hatchett Springs and Mule Hill; from lonely miners in California and Colorado; from a bereaved minister in Belle Plaine, Kansas; and from farmers from every territory on the Great Plains. The brief advertisements inspired flights of fancy in Ellie. She imagined the grieving minister meeting his blushing bride at the Belle Plaine station, his hat clenched in his nervously sweating hands. What kind of bride had he chosen? One who reminded him of his saintly lost wife? Or someone brightly, shockingly different? Whoever she was, she'd make his heart skip a beat for certain. For the miners, Ellie imagined a row of pretty brides like colored buttons, and for the farmers she dreamed up apple-cheeked girls in sprigged calico, their smiles fresher than April clouds.

But she certainly hadn't imagined *Diana* stepping off a train to marry a total stranger!

Diana had initially scoffed at the ads. She'd been impatient with Ellie sighing romantically over the brave brides.

"They're not brave." Diana had rolled her eyes at Ellie's relentless romanticism. "They're desperate."

They'd been sitting in the airless parlor of their boardinghouse after supper, passing the brief hour before the bedtime bell rang over at the mill, shrilling through the sleepy streets of Fall River.

"This one's not," Ellie had replied, reading aloud a delicious advertisement placed by a *woman of substantial means*. "Imagine being of means at all, let alone substantial ones. I bet she could have her pick of any man—and yet here she is advertising for one. Wouldn't you love to know why?"

"Maybe she's sour as a lemon." Diana was unmoved. She'd been in one of her dour moods, moods which had rolled in more frequently this year. "What do you think Montana is like?" Diana had asked her abruptly. She'd been staring at a landscape painting on the wall. It was a picture of a brooding mountain scene, complete with an eagle circling a dreary sky. Mrs. Tasker liked a stern landscape. She said it was due to her Northern English blood. Ellie personally would have preferred something sunnier, with a flower or two; maybe a daffodil, or better, a host of them, like in the poem.

"They have a lot of cows, don't they?" Diana mused. "In Montana."

Ellie was perplexed by the sudden talk of Montana and cows. The picture on the wall was of the White Mountains in New Hampshire—it said so on the little brass plaque on the frame. What did Montana have to do with anything?

"You just read that ad a moment ago, from the man in Montana," Diana reminded Ellie impatiently, as if reading her mind. That was the kind of bond they had. Even though Diana was a touch cross, it still warmed Ellie to have someone read her mind like that. She was eternally grateful that Diana had joined Chattaway Mills and not another company. Imagine if she'd gone her whole life and never met Diana. It would have been a tragedy of substantial proportions.

"Ellie." Diana was more than a touch cross now. She tended to get worn out by Ellie's woolgathering.

"*Did* I read an ad from Montana?" Ellie scanned the folded newspaper in her hand. Yes, she had. *Charming gentleman seeks beguiling woman to warm the long Montana winters.* "Well, judging by this, Montana is cold." Her nose wrinkled as she re-read the ad. Copious and symmetrical attractions indeed. This "gentleman" sounded no better than the men at the mill, who were prone to whispering indecencies to girls as they walked past them at the end of the day.

"I wager there are no mills in Montana," Diana sighed wistfully.

"Probably not," Ellie conceded. "I think it's still a frontier, isn't it?"

"Wasn't that dime novel you read me yesterday set in Montana?"

"No. That was New Mexico." The book had been about a woman abducted by rustlers and the lone cowboy who'd rescued her. It had ended with a kiss and a delectable bit of swooning. Ellie wondered how it would feel to swoon. Good, she imagined, judging by the ways her toes tingled when she read about it.

"Montana, New Mexico." Diana waved a dismissive hand. "Either would be better than here." Then Diana had snatched the newspaper from Ellie to see the ad for herself.

"What's got into you?" Ellie asked, perplexed. "Since when do you care about Montana or New Mexico?"

"Since today, when I decided I couldn't stomach the mill for another minute." Diana wasn't alone in hating the mill. Most of the girls dreaded the sound of the wake-up bell, followed by the start work bell. Their whole lives were regulated by the company. Where they lived, what they ate, how they behaved. Their ears rang at night from twelve hours of the cacophony of the looms and their hands were calloused and stiff; they had sore feet and sore backs, and their eyes were irritated from the cotton fluff which thickened the air.

So when Diana had snatched that copy of the *Matrimonial News* out of Ellie's hand, she'd known her friend well enough to feel a frisson of unease. "Diana, you're not thinking . . ."

"I *am* thinking." Diana had shot Ellie a fierce look. "I'm twenty years old next month," she'd said shortly, "and I don't intend to be in that mill when I turn twenty-one."

"But you don't mean to answer an ad for a mail-order bride!" Ellie had given a horrified laugh. "I only bought that thing for a laugh."

"It could be a way out of here, El." Diana was serious, flipping the pages with sharp snaps as she scanned the advertisements.

Ellie had grown prickly with dread. She couldn't imagine her life without Diana. "There are other jobs, if you hate the mill so much," Ellie said weakly. Although if Diana got another job, she'd have to move out of the company boardinghouse. Away from Ellie.

Diana had issued a bitter laugh. "Sure, I'll go into service and scrub out chamber pots."

Ellie tried to think of another job that didn't involve mills or chamber pots.

"We work six days a week, El," Diana complained. "Twelve hours a day. We get up when they tell us to, eat when they tell us to, sleep when they tell us to."

Ellie hadn't known what to say to that. It was all true.

"Doesn't it bother you that we're trapped here?"

Trapped was a strong word. Ellie's mind went back to the tenement—*that* was being trapped. With a boorish husband, who kept you pregnant and poor.

"Don't you ever want to spend an afternoon in the sun?" Diana demanded.

"I do spend afternoons in the sun. On Sundays." The pun made her smile weakly. But Diana didn't smile back.

Diana made a noise like she was suffocating. "When my parents had their farm, I spent every day in the sun."

But Diana's parents didn't have the farm anymore. Now her father worked in the boiler room of a mill, and her mother worked in a laundry, and they could barely keep their heads above water, even with most of their kids put out to work.

"Diana . . ." Ellie sighed gently. "We should be thankful for what we have."

Diana gave her a disbelieving look. "Thankful! For *this*? Don't you want something better?"

"This *is* better." Ellie rubbed her sweating palms against the twill of her dark skirt. Here, she could sleep. Here, she had enough to eat. Safety counted for a lot. Food counted for a lot. Being able to read books in a quiet corner counted for a lot. And having someone like Diana, who actually cared for her, counted for everything.

"What about all those books you read?" Diana demanded. "What about the things they promise? Open trails, mountains, *freedom*. Don't you want those things?" Her blue eyes were shining. "What about a man who knows how to make you swoon? What about *that*? What about love and romance and tingling from your head to your toe?"

Ellie was stunned. "Those are *stories*, Diana. They're not real." Having a job and a roof over her head, a full belly—that was real.

"Well, what about this?" Diana shook the *Matrimonial News* at Ellie. "These aren't stories. These are real."

Ellie laughed. "You think one of *those* men could make you tingle from your head to your toe?"

"Why not?" Diana was obstinate. "It's a chance anyway. I'd rather take the chance on a rancher or a cowboy or *anything* other than a mill boy and a lifetime here."

Ellie shifted uneasily. "What are you saying? You'd answer a mail-order bride ad?"

"Why not?" Diana smoothed out the paper on her lap. "I could move somewhere without mills and factories, without bells ringing at me to eat, like I'm a cow being brought into the byre. Look, this says 'gentleman is attentive, of landed family, and more than ready for the love of a good woman'. Landed means wealth, right? And he sounds nice enough."

"He sounds lecherous! He's the copious attractions one, isn't he?"

"Oh, Ellie. Honestly. As if lechery isn't *everywhere*. Just look at our overseer at the mill!" Diana pulled a face. "At least this one is looking for a consenting wife and not just molesting innocent girls."

"How do you know? You don't know him! He could be the worst kind of molester, for all you know."

"Well, I'll get to know him, then." Diana had a rebellious set to her. "I'll write to him."

Ellie saw the fatal flaw in that plan but bit her tongue. Diana was hot enough under the collar as it was—Ellie didn't need to go pointing out her shortcomings, which included the fact Diana hadn't had much schooling. While she could read, her penmanship was illegible—which was perhaps a blessing, given her spelling.

Diana read her mind again and looked even more rebellious. "Fine, so I can't write well. *You* write to him for me, then. I'll tell you what to write and you can put it down nice."

"But I don't want you to go," Ellie had said, appalled. "I'd be miserable without you! And I couldn't live with myself, imaging the horrors you might encounter in the wilds!" Ellie's imagination was in full flight. She imagined a leaking cabin in bear-infested woods; a beast of a woodsman with unchecked lusts; hunger and threats galore. And poor Diana, wilting like a stomped rose . . .

Diana's ink-blue eyes stared deep into Ellie's, knowing very well Ellie's propensity to flights of fancy. Diana flapped the newspaper to get her attention. "These advertisements are offering lives away from the mill. *Freedom,* Ellie. Imagine living in Montana!"

"I *am* imagining it." Ellie's heart was thudding, she was imagining it so vividly. "You could end up living in a swamp, Diana!"

"Does Montana have swamps?"

"See, you don't even know! It could have swamps in deserts on glaciers for all you know! With bears and bugs and bobcats!"

"So, write to him for me and ask him to describe where he lives. You can get him to describe it in detail, swampy glaciers and all." Matter-of-factly, Diana folded the paper around the advertisement and handed it back to Ellie. "I'll get the writing paper."

"This is ludicrous."

"No. Staying here until we're as old as Mrs. Tasker is ludicrous!" Diana was half buried in the writing desk in the corner, digging through it for paper.

"Is she that old? I know she looks old, but someone told me she wasn't even forty yet." Ellie felt ill at the thought of Diana leaving her.

Diana gave a cross shriek, dropping the lid of the desk with a bang. "I don't want to look old before my time because I let Chattaway Mills suck the blood out of me! I want romance and adventure before I shrivel up and die. Don't you?"

Ellie supposed so . . . but Diana was talking about taking a terrible risk. And the only kinds of risks Ellie liked were the imaginary kind.

Diana changed tack. She put the writing paper down and took Ellie's hands. "They're only letters, El. What can it hurt to write a letter or two?" Her voice was softly cajoling, like she was talking to a child. "Won't it at least pass some time, exchanging letters with some lonely man out on the frontier? We don't have to promise anything."

And because Ellie hated to see Diana unhappy, and would do anything in the world for her, she gave in and let Diana push her down in the chair at the writing desk and press a pen into her hand. She let herself be coaxed into writing that letter, all the while imagining the worst that could happen.

She had told herself that Diana would soon come to her senses. That this was just a diversion to get her through her latest mood.

But that had been months ago. Summer had long since curled on the bough; it was now a fitful fall with erratic showers and scudding clouds, and Ellie had done more than merely write to Diana's Mr. Copious Symmetrical Attractions for her—she had *secured him*.

Because she was an idiot.

The thing was, Diana dictated the most boring letters, and Ellie hadn't been able to resist, well, *helping her*. So, she'd embellished a little here and there. And then maybe she'd been a little seduced by the whole adventure and embellished, well, *a lot*.

And the man on the other end had been smitten.

It was possible her letters had been a little *too* good.

Was it her fault that writing to Mr. Copious Attractions had turned out to be fun? The man was just as charming as his ad promised. Funny too. And the way he described his home was so vivid that Ellie felt like she'd been there.

We live close to the top of a mountain, he wrote, *in a meadow that is an ocean of seedy grassheads in summer. They wave about in the wind in little flicks and it's the prettiest sight in the world. When I was a kid, I used to lay down in it, so I could look up at the big sky, all painted with clouds, and watch the bugs jumping and the butterflies flitting. Lying there I could hear the creek chattering by and the sound of the wind in the woods, whispering secret messages, which I liked to imagine were from Ma and my sweet sister Maybud, who we lost long ago. I don't know if Massachusetts is anything like Montana, but here the air is always in perfume. You got the spice of the pine and the sharpness of the mustard leaves, the sweet jumping of the flowers in your nose, and the sun-smell, which I don't quite know how to describe except that as it warms everything it lets loose an eddy that just about knocks me senseless. My older brother was always itching to leave Buck's Creek, but I couldn't ever understand it. There ain't nowhere that could be as beautiful as here.*

"See, El? Afternoons in the sun!" Diana had wriggled gleefully as they read his letter, side by side. Her eyes had been shining like summer lakes. "No looms, no bells, no wretched cotton! Imagine, I could lay about in a meadow half the day."

It did sound idyllic, Ellie had to admit. She'd never been in a mountain meadow, or smelled a creek, or lain flat on her back and looked at the sky. Reading his letters, Ellie felt like she had a sense of this Beau McBride. His epistolary efforts were so good she even forgave his fixation on symmetry in women. He was poetic and sensitive, and when he spoke about his family, Ellie felt like she'd met them.

I got a little sister who dresses like a boy, swears like a sailor, and is crafty as a fox. I figure about half of what she tells me is falsehood, but she's a good kid for all that. You'll like her. Everybody does, although mostly against their better judgment. My brother Jonah is the absolute opposite (except he too dresses like a boy and swears like a sailor). Jonah is as honest as the day is long. He's kinda puzzled by people a lot of the time and prone to wandering off by himself a lot. Although that might be because our town ain't nothing but McBrides and we're a fractious lot.

Although he'd stressed looking for "copious attractions" in his ad, he was solicitous and hungry to get to know Diana beyond how she looked.

Tell me about your day. What do you do when you get up in the morning—I'm keen to know all the machinations of your schedule. I ain't never left these mountains and got no clue what factory work might be like. What do you do? What do you think about when you're at your work? What's your favorite flower? Song? I like music a great deal and I hope you do too.

Ellie may have taken artistic license with the answers. Diana wasn't much of an orator and tended to give answers like, "Tell him I like roses, and while I'm working I think about putting my feet up."

Ellie didn't lie exactly, but she did give some life to Diana's responses, life that may have been drawn from her own experiences, rather than Diana's . . .

I don't know if you have many roses in Montana, she wrote to him, her nib swirling across the page in enthusiastic loops, *but here in Fall River the mill owners have gardens bursting with them. The bosses mostly live on the Hill, in houses that look like something out of a storybook. There's one icing sugar-white house on a corner that's positively exploding with roses from early June to the first frosts in fall. On our Sunday afternoons off I walk up to the Hill and soak in the scent, all powdery sweet. That sugar-white house has roses winding and twining around its porch posts and up the siding, just a waterfall of fat pink and yellow flowers. When I'm at work sometimes I think about that house and imagine that one day I'll live there, and when I open my windows, I'll be swimming in their perfume. Don't you think that would be a thrill? Nothing bad could ever happen to you in a house like that.*

We have wild roses up here, he wrote back, *they grow in tangles and are flat-faced pink flowers with only four petals. But they're very pretty and they smell of magic. We could plant some around our house.*

She'd been so caught up in her imagining that it had taken Ellie a moment to realize *our house* meant his and Diana's. Not hers. But for one shimmery moment she'd envisioned it—*their house*—decked with wild roses, and her heart had skipped a beat. She'd pictured a modest little cottage by his creek, whitewashed the shining white of icing sugar, surrounded by meadow grass and flitting butterflies. The windows would be flung open to the scent of roses and they'd . . .

That's when she'd caught herself. There was no *they*. It would be Diana inhaling all those wild roses, not her.

She was happy for her friend, she really was. But she might also have been a little bit sorry for herself, she admitted, when she saw Diana twirling around the room with the letter. And not just because Diana was leaving her.

Perhaps Diana had been onto something answering one of these ads. Because Beau McBride was just the kind of man who might make you swoon, with all his talk of planting roses. Sometimes, while Diana slept, Ellie surreptitiously re-read his letters, and in her secret heart she pretended he was writing to her.

For all I got a lot of family living in my pockets, sometimes I get lonely. It's a nighttime kind of feeling, silent like. It feels like midwinter nights, when the snow is thick and the light is blue and everything is muffled and spring seems like something you dreamed. Lonely is a winter feeling, don't you think? Even though in winter you're cooped up with everyone. Somehow, being surrounded can make you realize there's no one to know the inner workings of you. Does that sound silly? I guess it does.

No, it wasn't silly. Sitting there in bed, reading someone else's mail, surrounded by sleeping mill girls, Ellie knew exactly how he felt. She'd been surrounded her whole life, and yet she'd always felt alone until Diana came along.

Loneliness is a working feeling for me, she wrote back while Diana slept, wondering if she'd have the nerve to send the letter without telling her friend. *I feel it worst at the mill, when I'm hemmed in by people and noise. The looms crash and the shuttles click and it's too loud to speak and it's hard to even think. I think loneliness would be a nighttime feeling too, if I didn't have my friend.*

She'd glanced down at Diana and felt a stab of guilt. Diana always handed Ellie Beau's letters after skimming them, but she had no idea how closely Ellie read and re-read them. Diana no longer bothered dictating letters back to Beau, trusting Ellie wholeheartedly to write the right thing for her. Which made Ellie feel even guiltier, as she stayed up late into the night writing page after page, cramming them into tightly folded packets, hoping Diana wouldn't notice their bulk and wonder why on earth Ellie needed so many words.

When I first came to the mill, before my dear friend was here, I used to read all night long, and then I wasn't lonely at all. Do you think it's strange that people who aren't even real can make you feel less alone than people who are?

No, he wrote back. *When we were kids, in the bad times after Pa ran off, Kit used to read to us. To Junebug, really, but we all listened in, and there was one hungry winter where he read us an epic—it must have been a thousand pages long, and it took him all winter to get through. It was a French book about a criminal, and a revolution, and all kinds of upset, but somehow all that imaginary upset made ours easier to bear.*

"How odd to start with just the word 'No.'" Diana had frowned when she'd read his response. She'd been doing her usual skim, but this time had snagged on the opening. "Like he was answering a question. Did I ask him a question? What was it?"

"It's probably a rhetorical flourish," Ellie had told her hurriedly. "But it's nice he likes books, don't you think?"

"I suppose so." Diana had shrugged.

I ain't never told anyone half these things, he wrote in *the* letter, the one where he finally proposed. *And I don't reckon I quite understand what's got into me. Except I feel like I could tell you anything. I wonder how it would feel to tell you all these things in person, rather than spilling them out in ink and sending them off. I'd like to watch your face, to see your thoughts happening, to know how you feel. I was walking the woods the other day, not for any purpose, other than thinking about you away from people, where I could give it my full attention. And the fall color was in full riot, the leaves falling slow and spiraling, like gold and orange snowflakes, and I wanted with all my body for you to be here with me. It seemed I wished so hard I almost made it happen. I know this is rash and hasty, and my brothers will never understand it, but it's what I placed the ad for in the first place . . . Would you do me the honor . . .*

"Go on, you can say it," Diana had said gleefully as she spun on the spot, the pages of his letter make a whooshing noise in her outstretched hand. *This* letter she'd done more than skim. *This* letter she'd read with painstaking care.

"Say what?" Ellie's mind was stuck on the vision of Beau McBride walking the fall woods. In her imaginings he was a mysterious figure outlined against the spiraling autumn color, a dashing silhouette, pining for a woman he wrote secret letters to like a hero from the most swoon-worthy novel. Ellie's heart was missing beats like it had forgotten its task. She'd only been half listening to Diana.

"Say that I was right." Diana was bright with triumph.

"You were right," Ellie sighed, feeling overwhelmed by the romance of it. "Ish," she amended. "You were right-*ish*. You still haven't met him yet. He might not be as good in person." Her gaze followed the pages of his letter as Diana held it close. No one who wrote like that could be anything but perfect . . .

Diana gave a sly giggle. "Oh, he is."

And that was when Ellie learned she wasn't the only one who'd been keeping secrets. It turned out Diana hadn't shared *every* letter she'd received from Beau. And she hadn't let Ellie see every letter she'd sent to Beau either.

"I might have sent him a photograph of me," Diana confessed, her blue eyes shining.

Ellie felt an odd twisting in her belly. She felt queerly jealous.

"I went down to the photography studio last month and got one of those little cabinet cards made of me." Diana was pink with pleasure. "I got the man at the studio to address the mail for me."

If Diana had sent Beau a photograph, then no wonder he was proposing. It was her beauty, more than Ellie's letters, that had won him. Ellie tried to ignore the dark stab of feeling the thought caused.

"And look what he sent back!" Diana fished in her pocket and withdrew a folded scrap of paper. She unfurled it and handed it to Ellie.

It was a portrait done in charcoal on a ragged bit of paper; the energetic lines were smudgy at the edges, but the artist was talented. And the subject was . . . too good to be true.

"That can't be him," Ellie protested. Her heart had forgotten to beat again. The man in the portrait looked like a Bourbon prince. He belonged in one of the etchings in the history book on the parlor shelf. He had a high forehead, strong cheekbones, and a heart-shaped jaw; there was a dashing dent in his chin and his plump upper lip had a strong cupid's bow. The artist had directed the man's sultry gaze straight out at Ellie, and she felt oddly unsettled. "There's no way *this* man is a backwoodsman!" Although he did look like a man who could write about roses and meadowgrass and walking autumnal woods dreaming of his bride. "Who even drew this, out there in the middle of nowhere?" Ellie said in disbelief.

"He said there was an artist at one of the mining towns nearby." Diana was smug, removing the portrait from Ellie's grasp. "He rode a whole day to go get this done for me."

"But why would an artist be in a mining town?" Ellie couldn't accept the portrait. She couldn't have been writing to *that*. Mercy, if she met a man that beautiful in real life she probably wouldn't even be able to squeak hello.

"Honestly, Ellie! Who cares! Focus on the important things—*look at him*."

Ellie *had* looked at him. She had the racing heart to prove it. "That could be a picture of anyone," she'd said limply.

Diana pinched her playfully. "Listen to you. 'He might not be writing the letters; this might not be a picture of him.' You cynic. I thought you were supposed to be the romantic one!"

"So did I." Ellie felt numb at the thought of Diana marrying Beau McBride. For many reasons. "Are you really going to say yes?"

But that was a ridiculous question. Who wouldn't say yes to that face, and those letters?

"Yes!" Diana was giddy. "Yes, yes, yes, yes, yes!"

From the moment Diana had said that first yes, Ellie had known she'd have to find a way to follow her, and by the time Diana had said the last yes, she'd decided how.

"I *knew* you weren't a cynic!" Diana squealed the next day when she caught Ellie scouring the advertisements, circling any that mentioned Montana. "Oh, this will be perfect! We can have a double wedding!"

Yes. Only Ellie had trouble finding a suitable husband. She wrote to a few, but they were all crude, and many were borderline illiterate, if not totally illiterate. Some hired public letter writers to respond, and those letters were stiffly formal. Not one of them wrote with so much as a sprinkle of poetry. And as much as Ellie wanted to follow Diana, she didn't want to lock herself into a life with someone she had nothing in common with. Her needs were modest(ish): someone kind, who wasn't a drunk, or violent; someone who cared about more than finding just a brood mare or a housekeeper.

And he had to live near Diana's new home in Buck's Creek. That proved to be the sticking point. Ellie and Diana ordered a map from a catalog and pored over the sketchy width of Montana, trying to calculate distances. "There's really no point if I can't be within half a day's ride of you," Ellie fretted, ripping the latest letter in two when she realized Grasshopper Creek was more than a hundred miles away from Diana's new home. "Who knew Montana was so big?"

She'd really begun to despair. But then one day she'd received a response and, miracles of miracles, it came from Buck's Creek, Montana. The exact same town Beau McBride was from. It was like finding a needle in a haystack.

"I thought Beau said there were only McBrides in Buck's Creek," Ellie said disbelievingly as she read the letter, which contained no name, only the identifying number of the advertisement: 262.

"Maybe they're related! Oh my, we could be actual sisters!" Diana lit up. "Imagine that, El!"

Ellie flushed with pleasure at Diana wanting her for a sister. But she was nonplussed by the letter itself. She'd only answered advertisement 262 out of desperation. It had been a very strange ad. *Good-looking layabout seeks frontier bride.* What kind of man advertised himself as a layabout?

An exceedingly honest one, Ellie learned. Mr. 262's letter was brutally forthright.

I've got no desire to peddle you fantasies, he wrote. *So don't be expecting no model husband. I'm not the diligent sort and I'm not one for listening to advice, nor orders neither. I'm more likely to go dancing than to pickle cucumbers, that's for sure.*

Dancing? In the middle of the wilderness? Ellie blinked, disconcerted at the image.

I can be insufferably rude to those I love but I've got no violence in me and my vices are mostly vainglorious in nature. I'm not a drinker or a coward. I know how to argue well enough but you can be assured I'll be nice to you and that I'm capable of charm when I can be bothered. I'm not unkind. That counts for a lot in this world, don't you think?

Ellie thought a lack of violence and being kind to your wife should be the bare minimum. She'd written back nervously, asking Mr. 262 the same questions she and Diana had asked Beau McBride. The answers came back, plainer than Beau's, but not displeasing.

We're mountain people but we ain't uncivilized. We read a lot of books, so we know a lot more than your regular backwoods folks might. And we know more big words than anyone in Montana, I'd bet my hat on that. Like amplitude. That's a good word, ain't it? I learned it last week.

The fact that he read books heartened Ellie. That was at least one thing they had in common. She made a mental note to ask him what he read. Could he possibly be the brother who'd read the French epic to Beau?

We run a trading post, so we see a notable variety of people. Just last week a couple of Gros Ventre traders came through and they had some mighty satisfying war stories about when they joined forces with the Crow back in the '60s to fight the Blackfoot. My buddy Sour Eagle is Crow and he was enthused to join the reminiscing, but Thunderhead Bill is Bitterroot Salish and was none too pleased about the slandering of the Blackfoot Confederacy. It was the liveliest debate I can remember, and one of the many reasons you'll find that living on an Indian trading path is a hoot. You never know what story you'll hear next.

That was the first Ellie had heard about Buck's Creek being on a trading path—Beau McBride certainly hadn't mentioned it.

Do you know of another gentleman looking for a wife in your town? Ellie couldn't resist writing. *There was one other advertisement from Buck's Creek, and yet I was led to believe it was a very small place.*

You've been writing to Beau, I suppose, he wrote back, sounding snappish. *I can only imagine the damn fool things he told you. It is a small place but we ain't far from the town of Bitterroot, and that's a growing concern what with the mining. There's plenty of men looking for women in these parts.*

Ellie hadn't thought any of Beau's correspondence was foolish, but she supposed she could see how a hard-bitten mountain man might be leery of Beau's poetic nature. Beau McBride seemed like he might be a square peg in a round hole, surrounded by backwoodsmen and miners.

Well, I guess you should know that Beau McBride is what some might call a ladies' man, Mr. 262 wrote, still snappish. *So I ain't surprised you got a letter.*

A ladies' man? Ellie darted a glance across the room at Diana, who was sewing a snippet of lace onto a new nightgown—one she planned to wear on her wedding night. She hoped Mr. 262 was wrong about Beau being a ladies' man, for Diana's sake. But she remembered the charcoal sketch, that face like a Bourbon prince, and she had a twinge of unease.

But if you liked the sound of him, you'll like me just fine too, I reckon, Mr. 262 continued.

Ellie was dubious.

I'm just as pretty as he is.

Oh, my goodness. *Were* they brothers? Or cousins? Ellie added that to her list of questions for him. Not that he was one for answering all her questions. He'd not given his name, no matter how many times she asked for it. Ellie's mouth had gone dry at the thought of his looks. She wasn't sure she could measure up as a bride for a man who looked like a Bourbon prince.

You answered the ad, Mr. 262 wrote, *so I guess you're on the hunt for a comely man. I won't let you down on that front. It should make up for my other shortcomings. Can you send me a picture of yourself?*

Ellie guessed by now he'd seen Beau's photograph of Diana and was hoping for someone equally pretty. *I'll send you one of me, if you send me one of you,* she scrawled hastily back to him.

"Well, that's over, then," she'd said sourly, folding the letter with a sharp crease.

"Oh no, why? Is it a different Buck's Creek? Is it a million miles away?" Diana had paused in her needlework, looking stricken.

"No, he wants a photograph." Ellie scowled.

Diana was perplexed. "So? The studio wasn't that expensive."

"It's not about the money, Diana, it's about *me*." How could she ever explain to Diana, who had no idea what it was like to be ordinary?

"There's nothing wrong with you." Diana frowned.

Ellie made a disgusted noise. "I'm *wallpaper*."

"You're what?"

"Banal. Boring. Forgettable. *Ordinary*."

Diana had no patience with that. "Poppycock. You're pretty enough."

"Pretty enough. Like *wallpaper*."

"You're being ridiculous."

"Fine for you to say, you're beautiful. And so's *he*."

Diana was struck when Ellie explained the latest letter. "Are you telling me they *are* brothers?"

"They must be," Ellie said glumly. "Or cousins. A couple of stupidly good-looking McBrides."

"But that's perfect, El!" Diana dropped her sewing and darted over to Ellie, smothering her with a full-body hug. "We'll be sisters! Or cousins! In the same town! What are the chances!"

"Not good if I have to send a photograph."

Diana eyed her good naturedly and smoothed Ellie's hair back off her forehead. "You goose. We'll pretty you up, and you'll take a photograph that will knock him senseless."

A couple of days later Diana had trussed Ellie up in her own best dress, curling her hair and rubbing forbidden rouge on her cheeks. Ellie thought she looked ridiculous as she posed in the studio in Diana's dress, composing her face according to the photographer's instructions and feeling like a fool. But she'd sent off the photograph.

And now, this very evening, after a long day at the looms, she was hurrying home to check the mail, hoping against hope that Mr. 262 approved of her wallpapery self enough to propose.

And include a photograph of himself. *And* finally give her his name. Because Diana was leaving soon, and Ellie was out of time.

Ellie had driven herself half mad all day at work, sometimes sure the letter would be there on the sideboard, sometimes sure it wouldn't be.

"I can't bear it," she moaned to Diana as they turned the corner, and the row of boardinghouses loomed against the brooding night sky. She needed that proposal. She couldn't, *wouldn't*, stay here without Diana.

Ellie couldn't swallow or breathe. She pushed Diana ahead of her as they reached the front door. "You go in first. I can't look."

Diana squeezed her hand and then opened the door. The smell of boiled cabbage and corned beef rolled out at them, a damp and vinegary assault on the senses. It only added to Ellie's nausea. She hid her face in her hands as Diana as reached for the mail on the sideboard. There was the sound of envelopes being shuffled, then a sharply indrawn breath. "El! It's here!" Diana thrust it at her.

Ellie's hands were trembling as she tore open the letter. She was aware of the other girls coming in now, filing past, too tired from their shifts to bother with Ellie's drama.

"What does it say?" Diana whispered sharply.

Don't be expecting no proposal. Those were the very first words. There wasn't even a salutation.

Ellie's heart shot to her toes and her face turned red. Oh no. Had the photograph been *that* bad?

I'm looking for a kicked-in-the-head kinda feeling and that's hard to gauge in written form. Although I like your letters fine enough and you ain't bad looking. But looks ain't that important in the long run, given we all lose them eventually. Your nature will do more to kick my head in that your looks, even if I'm sometimes too much of an idiot to realize it.

Ellie didn't know how to take that.

I don't believe in marrying people I ain't met. I reckon it's best you come out here and we get to know each other, proper like. Enclosed is a money order for a train ticket. I'll cover a room at the hotel in Bitterroot, all proper and above board. I've learned a thing or two about ladies and I know they like things proper. Don't worry about the cost, I turned a good hand of cards with some of the Ella Jean miners last time they were in Bitterroot. Don't tell my brothers when you meet 'em, though. They're censorious of me gambling, even though I'm flat-out good at it. And don't be fretting that I'll expect anything in return—I ain't the type to take advantage of a woman. Not that I've ever had the opportunity before, but I reckon even with the opportunity I'll prove trustworthy.

Oh. Oh my! The import of his words hit her solidly. *Of course* they should meet and see if they were compatible before they promised anything—how entirely sensible. Ellie was flooded with relief.

"So? Did he ask you to marry him?" Diana demanded.

"Not exactly." Ellie grinned. "But this might be even better." She held up the money order. "I'm coming with you!"

Diana snatched the letter out of her hands and scanned it. "This is as good as a proposal! You're going to be Mrs.—" She broke off. "McBride? *Is* he a McBride?" Diana frowned. "Did he tell you his name?"

Ellie reappraised the letter and laughed. "Sort of." There was a smudgy scrawl across the bottom. She couldn't make out the first name, but the second was most definitely *McBride*. She showed Diana, who squealed.

"We'll be together!" Diana threw her arms around Ellie and squeezed the life out of her.

"Watch out McBrides," Ellie gasped, "here we come!"

Three

Buck's Creek, Montana

Beau McBride had never been so nervous in his life. He was queasy, like he'd woken up from a night of moonshine and whiskey. His stomach was churning, his hands were sweating, and his heart was skittering about like a rabbit on the run. He'd shut himself in his bedroom in the old cabin, which had been Morgan and Kit's room before they'd up and married, and fussed with his new shirt, trying to get the collar straight. He'd shaved and given his hair a trim, and he'd scrubbed his teeth and shined his boots. But he still felt rumpled and in disarray—mostly because his emotions were rumpled and in disarray.

Was he really about to collect a bride from the railway station down in Bitterroot? A woman who was for all intents and purposes a complete stranger to him—a woman who might be any kind of person at all? Beau met his own dark gaze in the shaving mirror and winced at the nerves he saw reflected there. He knocked the mirror flat. Goddamn. It wouldn't do to look like a lamb going to slaughter when he met his bride.

His *prospective* bride.

Because now he was having doubts.

It was Junebug's fault—she'd gone and wormed into his head. *What if she gets off that train and she's mean as a sack of snakes? What if she has breath like raw onions? What if she's about as much fun as Morgan when the root cellar runs dry? What if that ain't a rightful photograph of her?*

His annoying little sister had a point, much as he hated to admit it. Beau had no idea if Miss Diana Newchurch was truthful or not. It *could* very well be a misleading picture of her. His gaze flicked to where it was tacked onto the wall next to his bed. She *did* look too good to be true. What if she was the deceptive sort? She could be itinerant, immoral, debauched; this whole thing could be a con. How was he to know? Hell. And he'd as good as hitched himself to her. Maybe he'd been too hasty . . .

Beau's hands were shaking as he shrugged into his new coat. It was midnight blue broadcloth and hugged his shoulders like it had been painted on. He'd ordered it up from a catalog and it had come all the way from New York. He fumbled the buttons, his hands too unsteady to do his bidding. Sweet damn, he was a wreck. He glanced back over at Miss Diana Newchurch's photograph. She was more than he could have dreamed of . . .

His stomach turned over as a new thought occurred to him.

What if she was *exactly* what she said she was? What if she was as smart as she seemed in her letters? As sensitive, as soulful, as amusing? Why would a woman like that want a man like him? A woman that beautiful, with that much character, could have any man on earth. And Beau was the runt of the litter. He knew it. He wasn't as strong as Kit, or as powerful as Morgan, he wasn't even as independent as Jonah, or as crafty as Junebug. He had a nice face, and that was about it. His brothers teased him mercilessly about his looks and Junebug had the nerve to call him *pulchritudinous,* in a tone that made it clear she wasn't using it as a compliment. The butcher Hicks called him "Princess" behind his back and the miners over at the Ella Jean called him "Pretty Boy" to his face.

People laughed at him. They called him vain and mocked him when he used big words. Which was annoying in the extreme, since *all* McBrides used big words, but no one laughed when Kit or Morgan did it.

Beau tried to take it on the chin and laugh along but it still itched at him. He hadn't *chosen* this face. And his face didn't say anything about the man behind it. He had *depths*, damn it. And so what if he liked nice clothes?

Beau had spent most of his life feeling plain wrong. Like he was a pony in a field of cows. Now he was worried that Miss Diana Newchurch might prefer a nice solid cow. He fussed with his collar to ensure it was sitting right. Morgan and Beau would never be able to carry off a coat like this. But then, they didn't seem to need one. When Beau's older brothers rode down the street, people's heads turned. Womenfolk might be drawn to Beau's pretty face, but they didn't go silently breathless, the way they did around Kit and Morgan. They giggled and flirted and teased Beau, but they weren't awed.

Beau didn't intimidate anyone.

In his mind, Beau pictured bringing Miss Diana Newchurch up to Buck's Creek and introducing her to his brothers. He could only imagine the comparisons she'd draw . . .

Maybe it would be better if her breath did stink of onions. Maybe then she'd be content to settle with someone like him. Someone who could pickle a cucumber, but not work a forge; someone who could sing, but not mine for silver; someone who didn't intimidate a single blessed person. Not even Junebug.

Although not much in this world intimidated Junebug. Not even Morgan.

Enough of these thoughts. He wasn't *useless*. He could hunt and trap better than any of his brothers, and he ran the trading post better than any of them too. Hell, he was the one who'd set up trade with the Gros Ventre and the Blackfeet, and he was the one who'd organized to sell Kit's cookware at the mercantile down in Bitterroot. Not that his overbearing brothers ever gave him credit for it. Nor had they credited his brokering with that catalog company out east, which provided fur for ladies' hats. He was goddamn *enterprising*. Enterprising enough to make any bride proud.

Beau carefully untacked Miss Diana Newchurch's photograph from the wall and tucked it in his pocket. This was a *happy day*, damn it, and he was going to enjoy it. And Miss Diana Newchurch was well aware of what she was getting into—the lord knew he'd written her a mountain of letters. He'd spilled his insides out in those letters. He felt a touch embarrassed about it, really, writing about meadow grass and memories and all kinds of secretive feelings.

"Wowee, you sure look fancy."

Beau jumped at Jonah's voice. He snapped around to find his little brother in the doorway, the weight of his saddlebags making him list to the left. Only Jonah wasn't so little anymore; he'd bulked up while he was off prospecting with Purdy Joe. Shoveling all that dirt had given him some serious shoulders, although he was still only nineteen and struggled to grow a full beard.

"When did you get back?" Beau didn't mean to sound surly about it. He was just surprised. And Jonah's new shoulders underlined his fears about his own runtiness.

"Nice to see you too," Jonah said mildly. He dumped his bags on the closest bed.

"Git that off there, that's my bed."

"Since when?"

"Since you and Morgan lit out and left me the cabin. You can have the old bunk in the main room to yourself." Beau went to lift the saddlebags off his bed but recoiled from their sweat and grime. He didn't want to ruin his new coat.

"I didn't leave you the cabin," Jonah protested. "I only went for a month. Besides, Junebug's still here—unless she finally agreed to move into her bedroom up at Kit's place?"

"I wish," Beau grunted. Junebug was still very much lodged in the loft of their cabin, like a racoon.

"What happened to make you so sour while I was gone?" Jonah removed his hat, revealing a dirty tumble of dark curls that needed washing and cutting. He hung his hat on a hook over Morgan's old bed.

"I ain't sour." Beau snatched the hat back off the hook. This was *his* room now, damn it.

"Fine. What happened to make you so flat-out peevish, then?" Jonah took the hat off Beau and hung it back on the hook. "What's Junebug done now?"

"Nothing. That I know of," he said grudgingly. "And I *am* glad you're back, it ain't the same around here without you. It's just that you caught me heading out."

"Out where?" Jonah looked Beau up and down, his gray eyes narrowing. "You know Morgan don't like you hanging around the whorehouse. Especially not in broad daylight."

"Morgan ain't here. Besides, I'm full grown and can do what I like. But I ain't going to the whorehouse." Beau didn't particularly like the whorehouse neither, not that he was telling his brothers that. He knew he was supposed to like it, but he didn't. It wasn't that he didn't *want* to enjoy it—hell, the sight of those girls in their skimpy underthings made his blood run hot. He stayed awake nights thinking about it. But thinking about it and acting on it were two different things. It was plain awkward to have a stranger get so intimate and his few fumbling experiences had been excruciatingly embarrassing. It had just been so, well, *pragmatic*. There wasn't a lick of romance in it, or any real feeling at all. Although the girls at the cathouse were nice enough and they all tried to coax him back, Beau would rather flirt with them from the safety of the porch than join them inside. And he honestly thought they were kinda glad too—he didn't imagine all that groping was a picnic for them neither.

"So you're not visiting the whores." Jonah got an amused look on his face. Which was rich, because as far as Beau knew, his little brother had only stepped inside the whorehouse once, and he'd stepped straight back out again. Jonah didn't seem interested in the women in the slightest, and he liked to joke that Beau had taken all the interest for himself.

"Huh," Jonah drawled, "I guess you already found out about the girls, then."

Beau frowned. "What girls?"

"There's a plague of girls happening." Jonah sat down on Kit's old bed and bent over to pull off his muddy boots. "It was all anyone was talking about when Purdy and I came back through Bitterroot."

Beau was poleaxed. "What in hell are you talking about? There ain't no girls in Bitterroot. Have you and Purdy been at the moonshine again?"

"Nope. There's definitely girls. We saw a few of them out taking a stroll, three or four of them in flowery dresses, with their hair in fat curls, and ribbons on their bonnets. Old Abner even laid some boards along the main street so they don't muddy their boots and skirts up."

"*Abner*? From the saloon?" Abner was a scarred civil war veteran who tended bar in a rickety one-room cabin in a clearing, which he had the temerity to call a saloon. He was an old coot who spat tobacco in the street, tossed his chamber pot out his back window, and cussed like it was a competition. Beau couldn't imagine him knowing what manners were, let alone employing them.

Jonah grinned. "You wait till you see him. He's shaved that face mop off and styled himself some sideburns. Judging by the smell, he's invested in some cologne too. And he's brushed off some very old-fashioned courtesies. Bowing and the like every time he sees one of those pretty girls."

Beau's thoughts were racing. "But where'd the girls come from? There certainly weren't any last time I was in town. Not besides the usual, anyway." Hell, if there'd been girls, he wouldn't have had to resort to ordering up a wife.

"Fritz Langer says they've been arriving on the last few trains. A girl here and a girl there." Jonah yanked his socks off and the odor of his unwashed feet filled the small room.

Beau swore at him. "You're stinking up my room."

"Maybe I should borrow some of Abner's cologne." Jonah sniffed at his socks and then at his feet. He grimaced. "Guess my first order of business is to take a bath in the creek."

"These girls." Beau clicked his fingers in front of Jonah's face, to return him to the topic at hand. "Are they for the whorehouse?" There were a lot of new silver mines springing up and miners sure were prone to an excess of whoring.

"I doubt it. They don't look like whores. They're over at the Bellevue hotel and Mrs. Champion is acting the mother hen instead of housekeeper. I heard the preacher had tea with them, which I don't reckon he's ever done with the whores." Jonah shrugged out of his jacket and dropped it on the floor.

Beau snatched it up and threw it out into the main room. He took Jonah's hat off the hook and tossed it out too. "This is *my* room," he reminded his little brother.

"I know." Jonah stretched out with a pleased groan. "But now it's mine too. These beds are far more comfortable than our old bunks."

"You didn't move yourself in here when it was just Morgan's room," Beau complained.

"Well, neither did you. No one wants to be trapped alone in a room with Morgan." Jonah grinned. "Except maybe that wife of his. Poor Pip."

"Maybe I don't want to be trapped alone in a room with *you* either." Beau felt like dragging the bed out of the room, Jonah and all. He certainly wasn't bringing Miss Diana Newchurch up here to share a room with his goddamn brother.

"Feel free to go back to the bunk in the main room, then," Jonah suggested. "Or if you're headed down to Bitterroot to get acquainted with those girls, why don't you take a room at the hotel and stay there for a while?"

"Why don't *you*?" Beau growled. His nerves had turned to straight out agitation. "Why would a bunch of girls come to Bitterroot anyway?" Beau glared down at his brother. "And why now?"

"Hell if I know. Maybe they've gone and answered ads like Maddy and Pip did? Wasn't old Roy still advertising for a yellow-haired wife? A lot of the miners seem lonely too, maybe they're ordering up wives for themselves." Jonah eyed Beau. "But if you didn't know about the girls, how come you're all dressed up?"

"None of your business. And you better be out of my room by the time I get back."

"That'll give me time for a nap, at least."

Beau headed for the door. "Junebug!" he bellowed as he stepped out into the bright fall day. He bet she knew something about these girls; Junebug was the biggest gossip on the mountain.

Junebug was nowhere to be found. Not in the stables, not in the henhouse, and not in her vegetable patch, which was overrun with unpicked pumpkins. She wasn't in the forge with Kit, nor in the big house with Kit's wife, Maddy.

"The cow hasn't even been milked," Maddy fretted, her Irish accent making even her displeasure sound like music. "The poor thing is complaining fit to die." She rolled up her sleeves. "I guess I'll be doing it again." Then she'd narrowed her blue eyes. "What are you all dressed up for?"

"Just going into town," Beau said evasively, backing away from the kitchen door and out into the meadow.

"Why are you going into town?"

"No special reason." He turned and headed for the stable, trying to act normal, and wishing he'd thought up a suitable lie. He hadn't planned on talking to anyone before he left.

"Why are you looking for Junebug?" Maddy called after him suspiciously. "What's she done now?"

"Nothing." Beau headed for the stable, swearing under his breath.

He *hoped* Junebug wasn't up to no good anyway, he thought grimly as he saddled Dutch, his spirited Appaloosa. But where the hell was she?

Damn his family. It was supposed to be a *good* day. *His* day. Why did Jonah have to come in with all this talk of girls? Why did Junebug have to go and run off, on today of all days? And now he just bet Maddy was going to stir up Kit about Junebug's absence and the day would go completely to hell, with Kit raging and storming down to Bitterroot, causing a fuss. There was nothing romantic about your bride seeing your family in full tempest before you'd even properly introduced yourself.

Beau's mood darkened even further when he mounted up and registered that Junebug's pony was gone from the stable. And her ridiculous dog was nowhere to be seen either. Usually Beast was bouncing around the meadow, chasing critters and yapping his little head off. Junebug had been too quiet lately, he realized. She'd been slipping about her business each day without a ripple of trouble, which wasn't like her at all. Why hadn't she been shoving mail in front of his face and arguing for her choice of bride?

A realization hit Beau like a blow to the head. Today his bride was arriving. And Junebug was missing . . .

He wouldn't put it past that little sneak to have read his mail. He swore. And he thought he'd hid it so well, down in the root cellar, which she avoided like the plague. He tried to think back to when Junebug had last mentioned the bet. He couldn't remember.

In fact, she'd been quiet ever since that day in the clearing, when he'd told her about Diana . . . Shoot. He'd been so busy making plans with Miss Diana Newchurch that he'd lost track of Junebug—which was always dangerous. Damn that kid. She had a dose of the devil in her. She got that from their father, Beau thought sourly, as he rode out. His ma certainly hadn't been devilish, and neither had his other sisters, God rest their souls.

That fool kid wasn't allowed to ride off on her own and yet her pony was missing. Beau felt like kicking something. He'd bet his hat she was trying to horn in on his first meeting with Diana. She probably had some half-assed plan to snarl it up and ruin it for him. She was goddamn infuriating. And bloody stupid to go haring down the mountain on her own. She had no idea the risks she faced, especially now the mountains were crawling with prospectors. Beau glanced over at the forge as he pointed Dutch down the meadow. He could see Maddy at the forge door, holding a milking pail, and knew she was alerting Kit. Damn it. He didn't want Kit coming down to Bitterroot today. But he also didn't want to go over there and head him off, because Kit would take note of his fancy get up and he wasn't one to let things lie, the way Jonah and Maddy had. Kit would give Beau bloody hell once he found out Beau intended to marry a stranger.

Beau would rather put off talking to Kit until the deed was done. That way his brother couldn't snarl it up for him either. He'd sort Junebug on his own, meet his bride, enjoy this happy damn day, and handle his brother later.

Dutch felt Beau's tension and turned skittish as they headed down the mountain for the four-hour ride to Bitterroot. Beau tried to soothe him, but it was near impossible, given Beau was just about as skittish as the horse was. His mind conjured up nightmares, all of them featuring Junebug, and he knew that whatever he imagined, the reality was bound to be worse. That little brat better be in town. She better not have been thrown from her horse in the woods somewhere or molested by prospectors. If anything happened to her out there alone, he'd damn well kill her. At least he would after he'd killed whoever, or whatever, had hurt her. And then he'd kill her again for whatever she was up to down in Bitterroot. Because he knew she was up to no good.

Maybe she didn't know about Diana, a hopeful little voice whispered. Maybe she'd heard about all those girls and was heading down to get a look at them. That would be just like her. She was curiouser than a cat. Not that he wasn't curious himself . . .

The thought of a flock of women in town made Beau's blood run fast in ways that were confusing. Hell, he had a wife coming in on today's train. It wasn't a good time to have a passel of girls arrive. Even if his imaginings were suddenly full of skirts and smiles, curves and giggles, silky skin and . . . God*damn*.

By the time he reached Bitterroot, Beau was in a conflagration of feeling. His hands were unsteady on the reins, and he was jumpy as a squirrel. He took a deep breath as he slowed Dutch to a trot. It was a bright fall day, and the sun streamed through the blazing woods, gilding the leaves brassy gold. Bitterroot itself was a raw little place, still mostly uncleared land, and the buildings were nestled among the fir and larches like mushrooms sprung up from the mulch. The trickle of a creek running right through main street was shining and babbling and Beau could hear the erratic tapping of woodpeckers echoing through the woods proper. It should be the perfect day to meet the woman you were going to marry. But instead, he was absorbed in thoughts of his bratty little sister. And the girls she might be off introducing herself to . . .

Beau's gaze flicked around, looking for dresses and curls and hats with ribbons. But Bitterroot looked as empty as always. No sign of Junebug, and no sign of any girls.

Beau slowed as he neared the new little white church with its colored glass windows. The same church he'd planned to get married in. *Still* planned to get married in. He saw the preacher out front, caught up in conversation with Thunderhead Bill, who seemed to have built up a head of steam. Bill was waving his old stovepipe hat about as he spoke, emphasizing each point with a thrust of the battered old thing. Bill's usual companions, Sour Eagle and the scruffy trapper Roy, were further down the street, out on the porch of the mercantile. They were sprawled lazily on the top step, oblivious to old Mrs. Langer, who was trying to sweep around them in peevish strokes. Those trappers were thick as thieves with Junebug. If anyone knew where she was, it would be them.

"Bill," Beau called, annoyed by the conversation before it even started. Talking to Bill was like wrestling a fish. He was a slippery, thrashing kind of a conversationalist.

Thunderhead Bill gave Beau a sideways look and then dismissed him, continuing on at the preacher as though Beau hadn't even spoken.

"I'm looking for Junebug." Beau's hands tightened on the pommel of his saddle. "Bill!" he snapped. "Tell me where she is. *Now.*"

"Junebug? Here? In Bitterroot?" The old trapper affected surprise, as though Junebug had never been to Bitterroot in her life.

"Bill." Beau had no patience for these games. He leaned forward and glared at him. "You don't want to try me. Not today."

The pastor stepped in. "She came through a couple of hours ago," he told Beau quickly, trying to keep the peace. "I imagine she's at the hotel talking to—"

Thunderhead Bill erupted into an explosive coughing fit. He bent double and set up a ridiculous display, covering up the pastor's words. He grabbed the pastor and spluttered something about needing water, rheumatism of the lungs, and a torrent of other nonsense. It was clear as day to everyone involved that he was covering for Junebug.

At least she wasn't dead in the woods somewhere, Beau thought darkly, glancing in the direction of the hotel, where his sister was apparently holed up with a bunch of girls. Wait till he got his hands on her.

Still, she wasn't here to interfere with his plans.

"Feel better, Bill," he said sourly, flicking his reins.

Thunderhead Bill's coughing fit died suddenly as Beau rode off, then he heard the old windbag start up again at the pastor, who gave a full-bodied sigh.

Beau noted Sour Eagle and Roy had disappeared from the porch of the mercantile while he was talking to Thunderhead Bill. They were probably off warning his sister he'd arrived. Those rodents.

"Good morning," Beau said tightly, tipping his hat to Mrs. Langer, whose son Fritz owned the store.

Mrs. Langer paused in her sweeping. She was a keen-eyed, sharp-faced old woman, who undoubtedly had some idea of the shenanigans Junebug had going on today. She nodded towards the clock at the train station. "I've heard enough of that wretched thing chiming today, Beau McBride, to know it's no longer morning." Her thick German accent accentuated her sharpness.

Beau caught a glimpse of Roy slipping between the firs in the direction of the hotel. "Good afternoon, then."

"I suppose you've come to court the young ladies," Mrs. Langer said slyly, noticing the direction of his gaze. "I knew you were up to something with all those letters." Mrs. Langer was also the town's part-time postmistress and had been witness to Beau's recent flurries of mail.

"I hate to disappoint, but I'm afraid not." Beau kept his voice even. "I don't know anything about no girls." Much as he'd like to understand where they came from and what Junebug had to do with it. "I'm here to meet the afternoon train."

Mrs. Langer's sharp gaze grew even sharper. "Ah. I suppose you're meeting the same person your sister is?"

Beau's blood ran cold. Goddamn it. His smile faltered, and he knew Mrs. Langer noticed it, because she noticed everything. "She's at the train station already?" He tried to keep his voice mild but couldn't quite keep the edge out of it.

"Bright and early so she wouldn't miss it."

"Of course she wouldn't want to miss it," Beau said tightly, turning his horse, his smile evaporating as soon as his back was turned.

"What in hell are you doing here?" Junebug exploded.

She wasn't pleased to see him. Which suited him, as he was none too pleased to see her either.

"What in hell are *you* doing here?" He threw her question back at her. "And what are you wearing?" He'd clearly caught her red-handed. At something.

As Beau had hitched his horse, Junebug had come barreling out of the train station, Sour Eagle in her wake and her yappy dog bouncing along behind. Only she didn't look like her normal self. She was in a dress he'd never seen before, a long one, and she looked like a *girl*.

"So I'm wearing a dress," Junebug said bullishly, propping her hands on her hips and looking for all the world like she might charge him. "You've seen me in a dress before."

"Not often." He wasn't about to be stared down. He glowered back at her.

The only dresses he'd ever seen Junebug wear before were the childish yellow thing Maddy had made for her, which she'd hated with a passion, and one of Willabelle's overly adult gowns. *That* was a sight he was trying hard to forget. Willabelle's dress had been entirely too revealing, and his little sister had been entirely too . . . well, grown up. Morgan had just about hit the roof over it.

Today's dress was also grown up, but not in a Willabelle way. There were no bared shoulders or excess display of skin. It was harebell blue, high necked, with gently puffed sleeves and a hint of a bustle. The blue dress made Junebug look like a lady, which was disconcerting. Her wild hair was growing out of its short summer chop and was a mess of dark curls; she'd tied her white satin ribbon over the top and the whole effect was oddly charming. Cleaned up like this, she looked the image of a sweet young thing and nothing like the demon spawn she actually was. Even her silly little dog was freshly washed and brushed, his tail streaming like a pennant as he wagged it.

"I *am* a girl, you know," Junebug said sourly, noticing his astonishment. "Girls wear dresses." She seemed to wrestle with herself. "Sometimes." Another pause. "When they feel like it."

"And what's got you feeling like it today?" Beau folded his arms and fixed her with a dark look. Let her worm her way out of this.

Typically, Junebug went on the offensive. "Well, what are *you* all dressed up for? I ain't seen that coat before. It looks plenty fancy; that ain't a coat from these parts, which means you've been clandestinely catalog-shopping again." Her eyes narrowed. "You trying to impress someone?"

There was no point in dissembling. Not anymore. "I'm dressed up, as you might have guessed, to meet my bride."

"Your *bride*?" Junebug gave an outraged gasp and then she let out a stream of the foulest curse words he'd ever heard. Some were even new to him. "You cain't be meeting no bride!"

"Well, I am." He checked the clock. "And by my reckoning, she'll be here soon."

"Is this that moonshiny gal?"

"I don't see what you're in a pique about, I told you I was marrying her." He frowned. "Wait. What do you mean I cain't be meeting no bride? Ain't *you* here to meet her too? Ain't that what you're up to?"

"Your bride!" She all but stomped her foot. "You chiseler, Beau McBride! We had a goddamn bet. You ain't even let me show you mine yet! You can't go marrying anyone or you're violating the terms of our agreement. Which would mean, by default, I win."

Her dog barked sharply. It dashed in front of Junebug, baring its teeth at Beau.

Beau was blindsided. What in hell was she doing here, if she wasn't here to snarl up his wedding? "The bet was to find the best wife," he said sharply. "And I have. So according to my reckoning, *I* win."

"Screw you. This bet ain't over, but only because I ain't got the stomach to win by default. I want to win that circus fair and square. Besides, I've gone to all this trouble!"

"All what trouble?" Beau had a very bad feeling. Worse than the normal Junebug kind of feeling. And that was plenty bad enough . . .

But Junebug wasn't in any mood to answer his questions. "Just because a woman glows at you is no reason to marry her! Spit, this is just like my hickory fishing rod all over again! You skunk-weasel!"

Beau frowned, disconcerted by her nonsense. "What in hell are you talking about?" What did fishing rods have to do with anything?

"Ah, excuse me." The station master, Bascom, came sidling up in his spotless uniform, the shiny buttons glinting in the afternoon sun. He glanced up at the clock, which had set up a cheerful chiming. "The train is due to arrive in ten minutes, so I'd be appreciative if you can speed up your disagreement and get to the resolution. It ain't seemly to have passengers disembarking into a kerfuffle."

"This ain't no kerfuffle," Junebug snarled. "This is goddamn cold-blooded *treachery*!"

Her dog set up a frenzied barking, as though agreeing with her.

"Right." Bascom blinked. He glanced back and forth between the siblings and then over at Sour Eagle, who gave a helpless shrug. "Can you resolve this goddamn cold-blooded *treachery*, then?" He looked back up at the clock. "In less than nine and a half minutes?"

"This crooked dodger lied to me, Bascom. That takes more than nine and a half minutes to explain, let alone forgive." Junebug was ireful.

Bascom had never been one to accept Junebug's nonsense. Beau watched as he straightened his jacket and fixed Junebug with his best officious stare. "Well, then, I'd be happy to settle it for you in my official capacity," Bascom announced. "Put forward your case—succinctly, mind—and I'll judge it."

Beau rolled his eyes. Bascom might not accept Junebug's nonsense, but he certainly could *add* to it. "You ain't a goddamn judge, Bascom. The railway don't give you no official capacities beyond blowing that shiny whistle."

Bascom held up a warning hand. "No speaking out of turn when court is in session."

For the love of . . . This town was full of lunatics, he thought as he watched Bascom listening soberly to Junebug's comprehensive account of their bet.

"Well, from that testimony, it does seem as if Beau has violated the agreement," Bascom decided.

"Exactly!" Junebug was fervent. "That's why I had to up my game—because he was saying he'd marry this Miss Moonglow before I even got a shot! I needed an ace in the hole!"

Bascom was nodding with increasing understanding. "Oh, so *that's* why you've been meeting all those girls when they arrive. They're yours."

Beau flinched like he'd grabbed a hot pan. *What?*

What the hell was Bascom talking about?

Junebug's eyes flared and for a moment she looked like a cornered rabbit. But only for a moment. "I can't believe you,

Beau McBride!" she spat, backing away from him and glancing to see if there was somewhere she could run to. "You got some nerve, double crossing me."

"Whoa! No, you don't, you little schemer." Beau was ready to wring her neck. "What does Bascom mean *all those girls*?" he growled, taking a step towards her. He noted with satisfaction that she took a step back.

"Don't go changing the subject." Junebug shook her fist at him. "You slippery eel."

"Bascom," Beau growled. "Explain what you mean by *all those girls*. I want to know if I'm justified in committing sororicide."

"What's sororicide?" Junebug demanded.

"Killing your sister."

"Good word," Junebug conceded. Then she kicked a puff of dirt at him.

"Shut up and let Bascom answer the question. What the hell do you mean by *all those girls*, Bascom?" Although Beau had a fair bloody idea.

As he listened to Bascom describe Junebug greeting a flurry of females, girl after blessed girl, Beau wasn't sure whether to laugh or scream.

"They're from all over," Bascom marveled, his chest puffing up in his shiny-buttoned vest, as proud as if he'd ordered them up himself. "The first one that came in was the schoolteacher from Grand Rapids. She's a forthright little thing."

"She ain't so little," Junebug interrupted, scowling at him. She didn't seem to enjoy Bascom stealing her thunder, but she was too wary of Beau to say much more. She made sure to keep well out of arm's reach, bouncing on her toes like she might scamper if Beau so much as twitched in her direction.

"She's plump but she sure ain't tall," Bascom clarified. "And she's plump in all the right places, if you know what I mean. I bet the boys sure couldn't concentrate in class, with her instructing them."

"What makes you think you can talk about my wives like that?" Junebug growled at the station master.

Wives! Beau's fists clenched at the thought. "Keep going, Bascom. It ain't just the schoolteacher from Grand Rapids, is it now?"

"Miss Katherine Burrell is her name," Bascom told him brightly, "although she mostly goes by Kate."

"Not to you, she don't."

"Junebug," Beau warned. "Shut the hell up and let him talk."

"The next one was the sweet one from Florida, Miss Flora." Bascom actually started blushing like a smitten youth. "She's Spanish."

"Puerto Rican," Junebug snapped. "If you're going to tell it, tell it right."

"Wherever she's from, she's pretty as a picture and a perfect sweetheart. And then the next three arrived in a row: Miss Mabel from Wisconsin, Miss Frances from Maryland, and Miss Nancy all the way from Ireland, just like your brother Kit's wife." Bascom shook his head again. "They're all right pretty too, although some of them are spicier than others. I prefer the sweethearts myself." He was about the color of a hot coal now. "They were all rather confounded that you weren't here to meet them, I must say." He gave Beau a reproving look. "Although your sister here did an admirable job of explaining your absence."

"I didn't know they were coming!" Beau was losing his battle with his temper.

"Well, now I know about the bet, it sure does make more sense. I mean, it seemed awful rude of you. Miss Flora just about cried she was so upset."

Beau felt like kicking Junebug all the way to the Dakotas. "How many are there?" he asked eventually, when he'd caught his temper by the tail.

Junebug was unrepentant. "Including the one on today's train?" she asked.

Beau didn't trust himself to speak. He barely managed to nod.

She lifted her chin and gave him an imperious stare. "Six."

He closed his eyes. *Six*. His insane little sister had ordered up *six* mail-order brides.

"I *had* to," Junebug sniffed. "Because you're such an ornery blockhead. You need to see you've got choices and not go marrying the first woman who sends you a glowy picture. Which is probably a trick of photography, by the way. Abner says they smear Vaseline on the lens, and it lends a moonglow to the plainest girl. *My* girls ain't plain, that's for sure. At least, not most of them. And the ones that are got other assets to make up for it." She gave Bascom a sour look. "Sweet *and* spicy."

"And is one of these plain girls with other assets on the train today?" Beau was grinding his teeth.

"You'll like this one, she's got a way with a letter."

"I've got a damn wife, Junebug! I don't need another."

There was an echoing whistle from down the hill and the faint chug of steam above the trees.

Oh God. Miss Diana Newchurch was on that approaching train. With one of Junebug's surplus girls. And Diana Newchurch was about to get off that train and find a town *full* of brides.

His brides.

Screw holding his temper. He was going to kill her.

Junebug caught the look in his eye, and before he could lunge, she ran.

Four

There was a commotion on the platform. Ellie was plastered to the window as they chugged into Bitterroot, and so witnessed it firsthand. Some poor girl was being chased around the station by a man more than twice her size. Good lord, what kind of lawlessness were they walking in to?

As she and Diana had changed trains and continued west, the stations had grown smaller and rougher, the towns barely worthy of the name. It was exciting, but also nerve-wracking. Ellie's imagination took flight as they sped through sprawling plains, past homesteads and ranches, through cow towns and vast stretches of wilderness. She felt like she'd been dropped into one of her books. She saw actual cowboys eating at the half dime lunchrooms, their spurs jingling as they kicked their heels waiting for their coffee; she saw vast herds of cattle driven across the plains, raising clouds of dust the height of thunderheads; and she saw clusters of women in skimpy bright clothes calling to the open windows of the train, offering services that made Ellie blush to the roots of her hair. Everything westward grew steadily wilder. And now she was witnessing a poor young woman getting molested, possibly even assaulted, right before her eyes, and no one was doing anything to help her. No one even seemed to bat an eye.

It was appalling.

Although the girl seemed to be helping herself just fine. She was *fast*. She had the guy running circles around the little clapboard station; her blue dress was a blur through the dirty train window, she moved so quick.

"Diana, I don't know about this. Look . . ." Ellie tugged at Diana's arm, trying to get her to focus on the scene outside. "I think we might be witness to a murder!"

But Diana was busy pulling their carpetbags down from the racks above their heads, oblivious to what was unfolding on the platform. "Oh, I'm sure it's nothing. This place looks sweet enough. It's not as rough as the last stop, at least. How cute is that little station with its clock?"

Diana was determinedly delusional. This place wasn't even a town. The woods were as thick as a fairytale forest, the kind of place where children were abandoned to their fate. It was deep fall and everything had a mulchy look, discarded leaves littering the ground like the remnants of a forgotten celebration. Here and there roughhewn log buildings peeked between the vast boles of the trees.

Ellie swallowed. Was she really going to strand herself here?

"Welcome to Bitterroot, folks!" There was a rooster of a man in a tidy uniform striding across the platform, acting for all the world like a girl wasn't being molested right behind him. He traversed the hard-packed strip of dirt, smiling jauntily at the disembarking miners, not one of whom seemed to care a whit about the beastly man chasing the girl around and around the station house. Now and then the station master gave a blast of his shiny whistle and beamed proudly at the train as it settled on the tracks, billowing steam. "Right on time, at ten past two." He gestured upwards to the oversized clock.

Ellie didn't move from her seat. She craned her neck to see if there was an actual town further down the road where she could find help for the girl—but there wasn't even a road. Ellie doubted they had any police. Maybe there was a sheriff somewhere? But where . . . ? There was *nothing here*. Only a little run of a creek with some raw cabins scattered around. No help in sight for a woman alone . . .

"I hate you!" The girl in blue screeched as she careened around the corner of the station, her voice carrying like one of the mill bells back home. The man pursuing her snatched at the back of her dress, and she gave an outraged shriek as she streaked past. The station master barely acknowledged the disruption, smiling brightly and continuing to welcome the disembarking passengers. Although he did stick his leg out as the girl's attacker ran past, and the man went sprawling into the dirt.

"Goddamn, Bascom, you've ruined my new coat!"

"Really, Diana," Ellie gulped. "It's not too late to go back . . ." Ellie turned away from the window. Her heart was skittering at the raised voices. For a moment she was back in the tenement, with her stepfather yelling in her face.

"Don't be such a goose." Diana gave her a puzzled look. "This place is perfect! There's not a factory in sight."

Oh my, Diana was getting off the train. Ellie scrambled to follow. She didn't fancy being left alone. There was a knot of miners still in the back of the carriage, and they made Ellie nervous with all their staring. She could feel their eyes on her as she stumbled down the aisle after Diana.

"Hold on." Diana paused two rows back from the door. "How do I look?"

Ellie blinked. "What does it matter how you look?" Hadn't she seen the state of this place? No one here was going to care if she had a hair out of place; everyone was walking around with ten inches of dirt on their hems.

"What does it matter? Ellie! We're meeting our *husbands*."

Oh yes. Ellie nodded. Yes. Husbands. She'd been trying not to think about that. Whenever she did, her mind flew to dark places. Like isolated houses with locked attics, where wives were imprisoned by brooding husbands.

"Ellie!" Diana snapped. "Focus. Now is not the time for woolgathering."

But it *was*. Now was exactly the time. Because what they were doing was unadulterated madness! They could be selling themselves into fates worse than death! How could she escape the threat if she didn't imagine it first?

"How do I look?" Diana repeated firmly. "First impressions count." She twirled on the spot.

"You look perfect," Ellie admitted, clutching her carpetbag tightly and glancing over her shoulder at the miners as they watched Diana twirl. They looked like starving men at a banquet. Ellie's palms were sweating terribly, and she imagined she felt a bit lightheaded. She'd never fainted in her life, but there was a first time for everything.

"The dress looks good?" Diana was oblivious. "Ellie?"

Diana was in a new dress of printed calico the exact pink of fresh watermelon. She'd taken great pains with it, and it had sweet little buttons, and lace at the wrists and collar. Diana had a tenderness for lace and would have stitched it even to her bedsheets if she could. The lush pink of the dress made her cheeks and lips bright, and her eyes seem even bluer than normal. Her silvery blonde hair was swept up in a neat roll and she didn't look at all like she'd just dragged herself thousands of miles across the country. Whereas Ellie assumed she looked exactly as she felt, like someone who'd slept sitting up and hadn't seen a bar of soap for days.

"Um . . . yes. The dress is lovely." Why hadn't she invested in smelling salts? Just because she'd never fainted, didn't mean she never would.

Diana exhaled, relieved. "Good. I'd hate for him to regret it now." She pinched her cheeks, even though they didn't need it.

"Don't you dare put that bonnet on. You want your man to get a good look at you first."

Your man. Ellie's heart skidded unpleasantly. *Her* man. Mr. McBride. Beau's brother. Or cousin. Or kinsman of some kind . . .

She had to pull herself together. She wasn't a heroine in a book, able to faint into the arms of a dashing hero whenever she had the urge. She was in the wilds, with a bunch of woman-starved men, and she needed her wits about her. No fainting allowed.

"How do *I* look?" Ellie asked gingerly, glancing back out the window. Beau McBride was going to be mighty pleased when Diana stepped off this train looking like a romantic heroine, but how was Ellie's prospective husband going to feel when he saw his?

She couldn't see any soon-to-be husbands on the platform; there was only the girl and her attacker, who had erupted into a loud argument in the lee of the station. There didn't seem to be anyone else waiting.

"You look just fine." Diana's voice yanked Ellie back to attention. Her friend took stock of Ellie, reaching out to fuss with her hair. "It was a good idea to braid it," she said gently, as she tried to tuck stray strands away. "It's kept it much neater than usual, even with all the traveling."

It had been Diana's idea to braid Ellie's hair. It had also been Diana's idea to refashion Ellie's ugly old brown Sunday dress, slicing away the high neck and revealing more skin than Mrs. Tasker would ever have allowed. "You have very pretty collarbones," Diana had said, when Ellie protested. Now, as they stood on the train, Diana untied Ellie's shawl, which she'd pulled tight, to make those collarbones visible again. Ellie was painfully aware that the miners were watching every move and, as soon as Diana turned her back, she planned to re-tie the shawl.

Diana gave Ellie's arm an excited squeeze. "Oh my, El, are we really doing this?"

"We don't have to." Ellie couldn't keep the note of hope from her voice.

Diana rolled her eyes. "Come on, scaredy-cat."

Ellie swallowed hard, re-tied her shawl, and followed her friend off the train. At least she didn't have to marry anyone straight away, she reassured herself. She and Mr. McBride were just getting acquainted—if she didn't like him, she could see Diana married to the Bourbon prince and then take a train back to Fall River. Where she could sleep alone, and walk alone to the mill, and live every single day without Diana . . .

Oh, *why* had she brought that copy of the *Matrimonial News* back to the boardinghouse?

Ellie stepped off the train and into Diana's shadow. She was unprepared for the perfume of the place. It quite knocked her senseless. Pine and woodsmoke, the peppery bright scent of fallen autumn leaves and the loamy scent of earth; even the warmth of the sunshine seemed to carry an aroma—a linen fresh smell, like sheets pulled from the press. There wasn't a lick of wind, and the woods were somnolent and lazy in the sunny fall afternoon.

Diana seemed unstruck by the scents and was scanning the platform for her groom. "I can't see him," Diana murmured.

"Well, good morning, miss," the station master greeted Diana, tipping his cap. He was beaming from ear to ear. "Welcome to the fine town of Bitterroot. Population somewhere north of thirty as of yesterday."

"Thank you." Diana beamed back at him. The station master didn't so much as glance at Ellie, he was so dazzled by Diana.

"Miss Newchurch!"

They both turned in the direction of the voice.

Diana seemed composed. Ellie was not.

Because the man greeting Diana was same man who'd attacked the poor girl in blue. He strode away from his victim, abandoning her mid-fight. And when the girl stepped out of the shadows Ellie could see that she couldn't be more than sixteen. What kind of man threatened a *child*?

As the man approached, Ellie saw he was most definitely the man from Diana's portrait. Only the portrait hadn't done him justice. Which seemed absurd. How could he be even better looking than a Bourbon prince?

No bit of charcoal could capture the depth of his lush sensuality. He doffed an expensive hat, his dark curls tumbling whimsically across his high forehead, a charming smile curving that sharp cupid's bow, his thickly lashed eyes shining like liquid as he took Diana in. He was tall, broad shouldered and lean hipped, and he moved with lazy grace.

This was Beau McBride.

Ellie watched, appalled, as he smiled at her friend.

No. It couldn't be him. Not the child-abuser.

And yet, there they were, he and Diana, sizing each other up. *Good lord*. They made a stupidly good-looking couple, Ellie thought dumbly. Diana was silvery as moonlight against Beau McBride's velvet night. And, judging by the way they were staring at each other, they both liked what they saw. Diana even gave a soft breathless sigh, which Ellie had never heard before.

But Diana could only sigh like that because she hadn't seen him tearing after that poor child, screaming bloody murder. He still had the dirt on his coat from when the station master had sent him sprawling.

"Miss Newchurch," Beau McBride said softly. His voice was as pretty as his face, a low warm husk, deeper than Ellie expected. He exhaled as he regarded Diana, and his smile broadened. He had perfectly straight, white, beautiful teeth. "I'm Beau."

"Delighted to meet you . . . Beau." Diana lifted her hand for him to take, and he stared at it briefly, a little starry-eyed. Dazed, he bent over it in a ducking little bow.

"Oh, for Pete's sake," the poor abused girl in blue declared, kicking a puff of dust in their direction. "You make me sick." And she stalked off down the length of the platform, peering up at the windows of the train.

"Excuse her, she's out of sorts," Beau McBride apologized, without even looking at the girl in blue as she strode off.

"I can't imagine why," Ellie said sharply. He'd harassed that girl in broad daylight and now he was completely without shame about it!

Beau McBride finally noticed her, there in Diana's shadow. He had to peer around Diana to get a clear look at her, his gaze sweeping over her ugly brown dress and figure-hiding shawl, lingering briefly on her messy braids before he met her gaze.

Ellie stared back. She didn't like bullies. She'd met a lot of them in her life, starting with her stepfather and continuing with all the overseers at the mill. Her stepfather had raged at her and manhandled her, and she'd been too young and cowardly to fight back. But she hadn't made the same mistake at the mill. She'd refused to give those browbeaters the satisfaction of seeing her fear. Because if there was one thing Ellie had learned, it was that if you let a bully take an inch, they'd take a mile. And she'd seen enough of Beau McBride chasing that poor child to know that he was a bully, through and through. Even if he did have beautiful liquid dark eyes.

Beau blinked, startled by her bold and frankly disdainful stare.

"Oh." Diana was smiling prettily, ignoring Ellie's sharpness. "Beau. This is my friend Ellie. Eleanor. I mean, Miss Eleanor Neale."

"Pleased to make your acquaintance." But he didn't sound pleased, he sounded disconcerted. With a face like that he was probably used to women melting at his feet, no matter how appalling his behavior.

Honestly, Ellie had a hard time reconciling this man with the letters she'd read. She couldn't in her wildest dreams imagine this man lying in a field watching the bugs and butterflies. He'd mess up his fancy clothes. She'd imagined the Beau McBride from the letters in working clothes, not this fancy blue coat and rolled brim hat. Even now, he was brushing the dirt off himself with brisk strokes. She couldn't imagine him wandering through autumnal woods. She glanced down at his boots. They might be dusty, but they were new, and they looked expensive.

"You brought your friend with you?" Beau McBride turned back to Diana, effectively dismissing Ellie. His gaze had softened again now it was back on Diana, but he looked puzzled.

"Oh, no. I mean, yes. But she's also here to get married." Diana threaded her arm through Ellie's. "Ellie is my oldest, dearest friend. We're practically sisters. She also answered an advertisement, so we could be together. I think one of your brothers might be expecting her?"

"Or cousin," Ellie reminded Diana. After all, no matter how they tried they couldn't decipher the first name on that letter.

"My . . . ?" Beau McBride blanched, as though someone had stomped on his foot. "She answered an advertisement too . . ." He seemed at a loss. "*She* answered an advertisement? *Your* friend? *She* did? To be a wife?"

Ellie flushed. She didn't like his tone. She might not be a beauty like Diana, but she wasn't *nothing*. She was wallpaper, not a *ruin*, for heaven's sake. Was it so impossible to believe that someone would want to marry her? Did he think she wasn't good enough for his brother?

His gaze was back on Ellie now. "*You* answered an advertisement?"

"Yes," she said shortly, feeling more and more insulted. If anything, she was *too good* for anyone related to this child-assaulter.

Beau McBride was looking pinched. "And what's his name, this man you're marrying?"

Ellie flushed. Her ears burned hot as coals. Where *was* his brother or cousin or whatever he was, anyway?

"Junebug!" Beau's abrupt yell made Ellie just about jump out of her skin. "Git your ass here now!"

The girl in blue had reached the caboose at the back of the train and had climbed up to peer inside. "I ain't talking to you!" she yelled back. Her hand jabbed the air in a rude gesture.

A muscle jumped in Beau's heart-shaped jaw. "I think you'll find what you're looking for over here," he bellowed at the girl. "Sorry for her crudeness," he apologized to Diana. "She has the manners of an untrained dog."

"Are you just going to stand there and let him yell at the poor child?" Ellie demanded of the station master, who was watching the exchange with bewildering amiability.

"Oh, he ain't really yelling," the man said affably, "he's just getting her attention."

"She deserves to be yelled at." Beau McBride was terse. "Trust me, any yelling I do at her is righteous."

"Excuse me," Diana's cool voice slid into the heated exchange, "may I ask who she is? The girl you may or may not be yelling at?"

Ellie jumped in. Diana had to know. "She's the girl who was being assaulted when we arrived! And this is the man who was assaulting her." Ellie pulled on Diana's arm. "We need to leave here, Diana, you can't possibly marry a man who assaults children!"

"Assaults children?" Beau McBride was astonished. "I ain't never assaulted a child in my life! And you should know that she ain't a child, she's a demon."

Ellie glared at him. "I saw you with my own eyes!"

"Well, he ain't exactly lying," the station master said, a touch reluctantly, "she can be a bit of a handful."

"I ain't no handful!" The girl in blue had joined them and was sizing them all up with snapping grey eyes. "I'm at least an armful, possibly two. More'n he can handle anyway." She shot Beau McBride a disdainful look.

Now that she was up close, Ellie could see her striking resemblance to Beau McBride. The same heart-shaped face, the same wild dark curls, the same expressive brows. The same scowl. Both of them were beautiful, in a profane kind of way. They were also both the worse for wear, dusty and rumpled from their fight.

"May I introduce my sister," Beau said tightly, not bothering to hide his exasperation. "Miss Junebug McBride, the biggest pain in the ass this side of the Great Plains."

Junebug. The sister from the letters. *You'll like her. Everybody does, although mostly against their better judgment.*

Beau made a sweeping gesture, drawing Junebug's attention to Ellie. "And Junebug, may I introduce . . . ?"

He'd forgotten her name already. Ellie lifted her chin and tried to channel Diana's icy poise. "Miss Eleanor Neale."

"She's Miss Newchurch's friend," he told his sister pointedly. "They arrived *together*."

The girl ignored her brother. She examined Ellie from braids to toe. "You wore a nicer dress in the photograph," she said eventually, a touch disgruntled. "This thing is hideous."

Ellie went hot and cold. She scanned the platform for her prospective groom, but there was only a knot of miners fetching their luggage, and a solemn Indian resting in the shade of the station. Well, Ellie would have to tell her McBride that this wasn't going to work. In their letters Beau had been the more sensitive of the two, and he was clearly *awful*, so his brother, or cousin, or whatever he was, was bound to be even worse.

"Her dress is less hideous without the shawl," Diana interjected hurriedly. And then she reached over and pulled at the knot on Ellie's shawl, whipping it off her.

Ellie felt like a pastry on a plate as the McBrides considered her anew. She pinched Diana warningly on the arm, not appreciating her "help".

"Is your brother here too?" Diana asked, tucking Ellie's shawl under her arm where she couldn't get at it. "Ellie would love to meet her husband-to-be."

"Yes, Junebug," Beau chimed, "where *is* this woman's husband? My . . . brother."

"*Prospective* husband," Ellie corrected sharply, "I haven't agreed to anything yet." And nor would she after this.

"Probably for the best," Beau said dryly.

Ellie smarted at the insult. "Your brother didn't seem to mind me," she found herself snapping. "He sent for me, after all."

"It was a much nicer dress in the photograph, though," Junebug said. She sighed. "I ain't never understood the color brown. It ain't the color of anything worthwhile."

"Chocolate cake," the solemn Indian interjected from where he sat on the bench by the station. He had a long serious face and was slowly cutting off a chunk of chewing tobacco.

"Huh." Junebug seemed taken aback. "Well, you got me there, Sour Eagle. I might need to rethink some things."

"This here chewing tobacco is also brown," he added.

"I ain't partial to the stuff so you're only proving my point."

"Even if you were partial to it, you ain't allowed it," Beau interrupted.

Ellie and Diana exchanged a bewildered look. Talking to these people was like walking into a windstorm; it was hard to keep your feet.

"I really think brown is best for chocolate cake, not dresses, though," Junebug was saying.

"Chocolate cake and chewing tobacco." The man called Sour Eagle popped his chunk of tobacco in his mouth and commenced chewing slowly.

Beau McBride sighed. "The dress ain't the problem here, no how."

"It ain't? So you don't mind her looks?" Junebug McBride nodded. "Well, that's something."

Diana cleared her throat. "Ellie and I are exhausted after our long travels, and this isn't quite the greeting we expected."

That was putting it mildly, Ellie thought.

"It seems like there's been some kind of misunderstanding," Diana said.

"Why don't we ask Junebug if there's a misunderstanding," Beau suggested. And then he stared at his sister, waiting for her to explain.

Junebug let out an irritable exhale. "I can explain, but I didn't expect to be giving my speech with *you* here," she told her brother. "And I didn't expect Miss Moonglow to be here either."

"Miss Moonglow? Do you mean me?" Diana asked her icily.

Ellie admired Diana's regal poise. She herself felt far from poised.

"Right. Fine. I get it. Everyone's testy after a long journey." Junebug reached into the pocket of her dress. "I'll just give my speech."

"You were serious?" Beau wasn't pleased. "It's an actual speech?"

"It's a good one too," Bascom the station master said approvingly. "I've heard it a few times already and it's a corker."

"It sure is," Sour Eagle agreed, spitting a stream of tobacco juice into the dirt. "Leaves no stone unturned."

"How long is that thing?" Beau snatched the sheaf of paper out of Junebug's hand. He flicked through the pages. "Don't you dare tell me you read this whole thing to all those girls."

"Hold on," Ellie interrupted. "All *what* girls?"

But no one was listening to her.

"Give me that. It works best orated, not read silently like a damn book." Junebug snatched the pages back off Beau.

"It's the size of a damn book."

"All *what* girls?" Ellie refused to be ignored. Something was very wrong here. Her imagination kicked into action, conjuring up all kinds of horrible scenes. Had they been trafficked west into a life of iniquity? She'd once read a lurid serial about a girl who'd been trafficked; an unworldly innocent's spiral into sin on the streets of London. The wholesome country girl had been tricked into taking a mail coach to the city, and had ended up working the streets, drowning her sorrows in gin sinks and longing for the pure love of her village sweetheart, forever lost to her now that she was a soiled dove . . .

"You're not listening." Junebug clicked her fingers in front of Ellie's face, snapping her out of her reverie. "I went to all the trouble to write this just for you and you ain't even listening."

Ellie blinked, startled to be on the dusty platform and not in the dankness of a London gin sink, drowning her sorrows. Sometimes her imagination was a little too good.

"You wrote it just for her?" Beau McBride was sour. "Her and five others, you mean."

"What?" Startled, Ellie met his gaze. His midnight eyes were turbulent with displeasure. "What do you mean *five others*?"

Junebug stomped her foot. "You ain't got a lick of circumspection in you, Beau!" She took Ellie by the arm and yanked her over to the station house. "Sit here." She pushed Ellie down onto the bench next to the Indian, who spat a stream of tobacco juice into the dust. "We'll do it over here, where he cain't ruin it."

Ellie shot Diana a helpless look. They had to get straight back on that train.

Junebug held her papers grandly in front of her. "Felicitations, Miss Eleanor Neale, and welcome to the congenial town of Bitterroot, the jewel in the territory of Montana." Junebug McBride read with impressive gravitas, although she seemed to digress abruptly, looking up from the pages with a flare of irritation. "Although it should be admitted to goddamn statehood by now and if I could get my hands on those foot draggers in Washington—"

"Junebug," Beau warned. He'd stepped up behind her and was reading over her shoulder. "Stick to your darn speech."

Junebug shot him a look but went back to her script. "Where was I? Jewel in the territory . . . I hope you had as comfortable a journey as possible, given we could only spring for a third-class ticket, and that you enjoyed your time on our fine Montana rail, which I hear is the best in all the United States." Junebug paused. "Although we should also be one of those states," she muttered under her breath. "I'd like to sincerely apologize for my brother's absence here today."

"You can cut that bit this time," the solemn Indian observed. He gave Ellie a kind smile. "Given he's here today."

At the Indian's words Ellie's gaze flew around the platform. Her own Mr. McBride was here? *Where?* Was he lurking surreptitiously, trying to get the measure of her before he stepped forward? Because that seemed ungentlemanly in the extreme, not to mention unfair and unjust and downright rude. Especially given his family's insanity.

"Can everyone stop interrupting? And can *you* stop drifting off and pay attention?" Junebug clicked her fingers in front of Ellie's face again.

"Do we really need this whole carry on?" Diana's cool voice cut through the chaos. "Why don't you just give us the gist of that speech of yours and then we can get on with things."

Ellie rose from the bench and slid past the McBrides to join Diana. They were getting out of here *right now*. She was going to sit on that train until it pulled away.

"What did you mean, five girls?" Diana pressed Junebug.

"I'm getting to that." Junebug went back to her pages. "My brother is a flighty man," she read.

"I ain't." Beau glared at her.

"She's not talking about you," Ellie told him sharply, "she's talking about *my* Mr. McBride."

"They're both flighty," Junebug said, stepping out of Beau's reach.

"They would be, given they're the same person," the station master said sagely.

"They *what*?" Ellie and Diana turned shocked faces on the McBrides.

"I ain't at that bit yet!" Junebug raged. "You men ruin everything! And you're upsetting my bride."

"*Your* bride?" Ellie couldn't understand what was happening. But she had an idea of how to find out. She snatched the speech out of Junebug's hands.

"The meat of things is on page three," Beau advised her, "the rest is a lot of palaver."

"Palaver!" Junebug let loose a salty string of curses at her brother. "I worked hard on that and you better believe me every other girl liked it!"

As Beau advised, page three offered up the answers.

"You ordered more than one woman?" Ellie said, appalled. "Wait. Hold on . . ." Her stomach curdled lemon-sour as she turned the page. "There's *no* other brother . . . ?"

"There's too many brothers," Junebug said in disgust. "That's my whole problem."

"But . . . all these women . . . and *me* . . . are for *you*?" Ellie thought she really might swoon as she met Beau's gaze again. There was no other Mr. McBride. There was only him. She'd come all this way to marry *him*. Her interiors didn't know if they should be floating or sinking.

"You've extirpated this whole thing." Junebug threw up her hands. "I didn't have any of this upheaval with my other brides. If you'd just let me read that thing in full, you'd calm right down."

"I don't *want* to be calm!" Ellie scrunched the speech up.

"Ellie." Diana was sounding less cool now. "What is going on? What's this about other women?"

Ellie turned a fierce glare on Beau McBride. He flinched. "Well?" she demanded. "Tell her. Go on. Tell your intended that you have a whole town full of brides! You flimflammer!"

Beau flushed. "Now, wait a hot minute—"

"These people have lured us here under false pretenses." Ellie was gathering steam. "Who knows what their real motives are. It's a scam. A con! We've been grievously deceived, Diana. They're probably going to sell us to woman-starved mountain men!"

"Hey!" Junebug protested. "None of that's in the speech."

"No," the station master agreed. "The speech is about how it's wise to get to know someone before hitching yourself to them for life. And how Beau here hasn't had the opportunity to know many women and how, as his loving sister, Junebug here has taken it upon herself to see he chooses wisely."

"She also wants to make sure you women choose wisely too," the solemn Indian added, around his mouthful of tobacco. "You may decide he's not the man for you."

But Ellie wasn't listening. Wild pictures had filled her head, of a backroom operation where women were hooked by romantic letters and brought all the way to these dark woods to be sold to snaggle-toothed men who carted them off to the mountains in order to have their way with them . . . Oh, who knew what horrors had befallen the five women who'd arrived before Ellie . . .

She was so deep in her imaginings that she was barely aware of Diana prizing the speech out of her hand. And while she imagined gaunt and misused brides pale as wilting moths in the greenwood, subject to the whims of men who held them against their will, she missed the terse conversation Diana had with the McBrides. It was only when Diana started leading her away from the train that she came to her senses.

"I don't want to hear your nonsense," Diana said firmly when Ellie exploded with descriptions of what she'd imagined. "There's enough nonsense here as it is without you adding to it. Give Beau your bag to carry and we'll go sort this mess out."

"There's nothing to sort!" Ellie wasn't about to give her bag to that entrapper of innocents, and she certainly wasn't going anywhere with these people. But, as Diana set off into the raw town with the McBrides, Ellie realized she had no choice. Because she had to protect Diana. "Stop!" she shouted as she chased them down. But none of them listened, and none of them stopped.

Five

This was an unholy nightmare. Beau regarded the room full of women in silent consternation. They were crammed in the front parlor of the Bellevue hotel, an overwhelm of pretty dresses and bright eyes and loud chatter. One by one they fell silent as they noticed him standing there in the doorway, his derby hat in his hands. The air was full of scent: roses and lavender and orange water and musk.

Was it hot in here? He was sweating like a pig on a spit.

"Well, what did I tell you, ladies? Ain't he pretty as a picture?" Junebug was crowing like a damn rooster. She even had the nerve to clap him on the back.

"You can't be serious," he heard Ellie Neale, Junebug's sixth and final calamity, mutter at his elbow. "How many women does one man need?"

On the way to the hotel, Beau had stopped by Martha Colfax's house, which was a new pine cabin smack bang in the middle of town. He'd left Diana there, drinking coffee with Martha, his sister-in-law Pip's grandmother. Diana didn't deserve to be dragged further into Junebug's insanity. He'd much rather she was welcomed into Martha's cozy two-room cabin than have her walk into a nest of Junebug's brides. The last thing he wanted was his striking new bride witnessing his humiliation as he explained Junebug's deception to all those poor women.

It had taken Beau a solid hour of talking to convince Diana that he'd had no part in Junebug's scheme. In the end, it was Martha's support that swung her.

"Junebug has a history of causing matrimonial havoc," Martha had assured Diana and her friend as she poured them tea. They'd all turned to look at the window, where Junebug was glaring in at them from the porch. Beau had locked her out there, like a badly behaved puppy, not wanting her to snarl up his explanations.

"I promise there's no trafficking going on," Martha told Diana's discombobulated friend. She put extra sugar in the girl's tea. "For the shock," she said dryly, as she passed her the cup.

"Don't worry," Beau assured Diana fervently. "I'll sort this out and be back to collect you and we can continue as planned."

Diana hadn't lost her icy composure once; she seemed unflappable, which was a novelty around here. His own family did nothing but flap. He didn't know a woman could be so beautiful, either. She was flawless. Better even than her photograph, if such a thing was possible. She had a kind of elegance that was out of place in Bitterroot; she'd sunk into a chair at Martha's table, like a dandelion seed settling, and regarded him with cool blue eyes. "It's all rather confusing," she said diplomatically.

"I'll be back," he kept repeating idiotically, his thoughts quite scrambled by both her beauty and her poise.

He wished her friend Ellie had stayed behind too, as she was unpleasantly hot under the collar, but she flat-out refused. "You don't know if you can trust him," she'd told Diana, giving Beau a lethal stare. "I'll go and listen firsthand and let you know what he says to them. If I don't come back, alert the sheriff."

"We don't have a sheriff," Martha told her, amused.

"Then send for the National Guard."

"I don't think they trade in lost women," Martha said mildly.

"You're not going missing." Diana was calm. "You're only going down the road to the hotel. I can see it from the front window there."

Beau watched as Ellie drained her tea and straightened her shoulders, adopting a mien of quiet, brittle bravery. Like she was going to the guillotine.

"It's only right you come with us," Junebug told Ellie when she found out the plan. She'd been on them like a tick on a dog the minute they stepped foot outside. "Given you're with me."

"I most certainly am not *with you*. I never would have crossed the country for a meddlesome girl like you." The quiet bravery fell away the moment Ellie saw Junebug, transforming to spiky irritation. She had been incensed by Junebug's scheme. While Beau couldn't blame her, he didn't appreciate sharing the brunt of her displeasure. She kept giving him lethal looks, like she wanted to thwack him with her carpetbag. He hadn't done anything wrong. If she had to be glaring at people, she should keep the glaring to Junebug.

Ellie looked significantly worse for wear from her travels. Unlike her poised and polished friend, she was a scrappy mess. Her hair was escaping from her looped braids in a tangle of loose strands, which made her look like a spaniel, and her ugly brown dress was creased and travel worn. She was far more of a pain in the ass than her friend too. She might be tired from her journey, but it certainly didn't stop her talking the whole way to the hotel. She rivalled Junebug for loquaciousness.

"How far is this hotel? Is it deep in the woods? Is it a long walk? Don't you worry there might be bears?" She pranced nervously over the little creek that ran through town, eyeing the bronzed fall woods.

"Stop fussing, or he'll think you don't want to marry him," Junebug scolded her. The ridiculous little dog was trotting along beside her, occasionally letting out a harsh yap of agreement.

It splashed through the creek, ruining its fluffy clean fur. Now it was mud-splashed it was more the Beast Junebug had named it after. "Besides, I ain't never seen a bear yet and I've lived here all my life. It's one of my primary disappointments."

"I *don't* want to marry him," Ellie Neale insisted. "He's Diana's. And there's always a first time, even for bears. You've really never seen one? I read in a book once that some bears can live more than thirty years. That, coupled with the fact Montana supposedly has lots of them, should mean the woods are crawling with the things. Although crawling doesn't seem the right word, does it? Hulking with them? Lumbering with them? Oh, I know, *bearing* them."

Beau sincerely wished there *was* a bear, to put him out of his misery. He took a deep breath of the woodsmoke spiced air, which carried the chill edge of the season, and told himself everything would be okay. But he wished for a bear even harder once he got inside the hotel and came face to face with all of Junebug's brides. How was he going to let these women down? Look at them all. He felt a bit queasy as he stood in the parlor doorway. They stared at him with frank and unsettling curiosity. "Uh . . ." he stuttered, "hi."

There were so many of them. He couldn't take it in. It was like staring directly into the sun. They were all shapes and sizes—and all of them appealing. He cleared his throat. "Ladies . . ." His voice cracked a little. He cleared it and took care to speak in a deeper register. "Uh . . . Junebug says she's explained . . . what . . . I mean, how . . . I mean . . ."

"She gave a very thorough speech," the woman sitting closest to him said, a touch dryly. She was a plump brunette in a dress the color of wild violets; she had unsettling eyes the bright pale blue of a winter sky. She also had copious and symmetrical attractions . . .

"It was kind of a relief," said another girl in spring green, her accent twangy. She had expressive hazel eyes and a playfulness that made Beau feel . . . overwhelmed. "I was a bit worried about marrying someone I'd never met. It *will* be good to see if we're suited first."

"There are a lot of us, though," another brunette chipped in. She looked more spirited than the rest. She was tall, in sprigged orange cotton with a flounced hem. "How's he going to spend enough time with us, to decide who to choose? And I can't say I would have come all this way if I'd known I was going to be part of a cattle auction." She put her hands on her hips. Beau wished she wouldn't, as it drew attention to the lines of her body. Which was also impressively symmetrical.

"I think it was very clever inviting so many girls." A more mature girl with sloe eyes and shining dark hair gave Beau a provoking smile. She was in a blue-green dress that cut low across her shoulders, showing a distracting amount of skin. "When you live in a town without women, I suppose you want to meet a few before you settle down."

There were a lot of brunettes, Beau noted, fiddling with his collar, which felt very tight. Junebug clearly had a type . . .

"I assume you'll take your time to get to know us," the sloe-eyed girl purred.

Good God. He was in trouble here.

"Now," Beau cautioned. "I don't plan to—ow!"

Junebug had pinched him, hard.

The girls kept staring at him. He tried to continue, turning his hat in his sweaty hands. "Ah . . . I don't plan to—"

"He don't plan to rush things," Junebug jumped in.

"Now that's not it, exactly . . ." Beau trailed off as he realized they were hanging on his every word. Damn there were a lot of them. And they were so darn pretty . . .

He felt a sharp finger poke him in the back. This time it wasn't Junebug. It was Ellie Neale jabbing at him. "Diana," she hissed quietly, so only he could hear.

Yes. Diana. He conjured up the image of her silvery blonde beauty. She was waiting for him back at Martha's. He had to get this, ah, unpleasant task over and get back to her.

But somehow, as he stared at all these women, the words dried up in his throat. He felt like a spooked stallion.

"I can't," he blurted.

There was a flutter, like a flock of birds had taken wing. Beau flinched.

"He can't wait to spend time with you all," Junebug said, stepping in front of him. "You've got to forgive his inability to string two words together—he's lived in the mountains his whole life and he ain't sure how to behave with ladies. You seem to have discombobulated him."

More fluttering, and now some sighing, and a host of shining eyes radiating anger, bewilderment, amusement, understanding and . . . something else that made Beau feel a bit light in the head.

"Excuse me, ladies, I'll just take him off for a minute and let him collect himself," Junebug said cheerfully. "Maybe open the window—your perfumes might be a touch too intoxicating." Junebug grabbed Beau and yanked him out of the parlor.

Normally Beau would have kicked up at being manhandled, but he was painfully aware that he had an audience. And he *was* a little lightheaded, probably from all the perfume, like Junebug said.

Rigby had clearly lifted his game as a hotelier now that the Bellevue was playing host to all these pretty girls, because the dining room was looking *fancy,* Beau thought dumbly, as he fanned himself with his hat. He was vaguely aware that Ellie Neale had followed them through to the quieter room, closing the door behind her. She opened the window a fraction and the freshness of pine and creek water rushed in on the breeze. Beau's head cleared a little. Rigby had also cleaned his windows, Beau realized, which gave a disturbingly clear view of the whorehouse over the road. Beau wondered what Junebug's brides thought of that.

Ellie Neale was certainly staring. "Is that . . . ?" she asked, scandalized.

"Yes," Junebug said shortly. Her dog barked and jumped up on one of Rigby's chairs.

"You'd think they'd at least throw a shawl over their . . . um, shoulders." She cleared her throat. "They must be cold." It was a sunny bright day but November nonetheless, the shadows cold as a cellar.

"Go back to the parlor," Junebug instructed Ellie. "Git in there with the others where you belong."

"I'm not marrying him, so I don't need to join the harem." Ellie pushed Junebug's dog off the chair and sat herself down at the table by the window, tucking her ugly brown dress under her neatly. "Do you think I could have another cup of tea while I wait? It's been a long day. I might even faint," she said, in an oddly hopeful voice.

Junebug ignored her.

"I might faint right in the middle of that harem in there. Wouldn't that be a horrid thing to happen."

"Go ask Mrs. Champion for tea, Bug," Beau ordered. His head was getting clearer by the minute. Sweet damn, being around those gals had acted on him like a shot of moonshine. "And get her to send some tea into the . . ."—he resisted the word *harem*—"parlor. Tell her to send some cake or something. I'll pay."

"I'm not a waiter," Junebug protested. "But if you're paying, you can get me some cake too. I ain't had no lunch. It's possible I could faint too."

"You don't seem the type," Ellie said dismissively. "You're far too robust."

"Not without cake I ain't."

"Go, Bug, or I'm walking out that front door right now, your brides be damned."

"Make sure he doesn't go anywhere," Junebug told Ellie, jabbing a threatening finger at her. "He's a treacherous sort. You don't look strong enough to stop him by force, but you're wily enough, I'm sure you'll figure something out."

"I've never considered myself wily," Ellie mused as Junebug slipped out. "It seems like a quality that belongs to the great beauties of the world. Like Cleopatra."

Beau sighed and sank unsteadily into the chair opposite her. "I'm sorry about my sister. It's worse than having a rabid dog."

"I suppose I'm more sympathetic to you chasing her around the station," Ellie said warily. "Now that I've met her."

"I told you. She's a demon." Beau rubbed his face tiredly. "I wish Morgan was back—he always could handle her better."

Now that she wasn't glaring at him and accusing him of child abuse, Ellie Neale was oddly calming. She had a sensitive face, with big dreamy brown eyes. She wasn't beautiful, the way Diana was, or even disturbingly pretty, like all those girls in the parlor, but something about her unruly braids and distracted air was appealing. She looked like a girl who would gladly go on a ramble in the woods, probably asking questions the whole time. She had an oval face with a pointy chin, an upturned nose, and lips that were thin but perfectly formed. Junebug was right, though, her brown dress was hideous. And given Ellie had brown hair and brown eyes, it gave her a pervasive brownness. Like gravy.

"My brother Morgan's in Nebraska," Beau told her, and even in this mess of a situation he smiled at the thought. He might not like Junebug ordering up brides for *him*, but watching her order one up for Morgan had been amusing in the extreme. The idea of Morgan trapped in Nebraska with his wife's family tickled Beau. His brother didn't like people at the best of times and imagining him trying to behave himself with that strait-laced bunch made Beau grin from ear to ear. From what Pip said, her folks were rectitudinous in the extreme. And Morgan sure as hell wasn't.

"Oh. You didn't mention that in your letters . . . I mean . . ." Ellie blushed. She turned red more often than anyone he'd ever met. When she was mad, when she was confused, when she was thinking about bears, when she was staring out the window at whorehouses. Right now her whole face blazed pink and her ears were red as ripe strawberries. "I mean . . . Junebug," she corrected herself. "In Junebug's letters . . ."

"Yeah, he got himself hitched." Beau shook his head. "I could have died when he wrote and told us." But he remembered the way Morgan acted around Pip and grinned. His brother had looked like he'd taken a solid blow to the head, he'd been so struck by the buxom redhead. It had been one of the things that had got Beau thinking about ordering up his own wife—being struck looked like one hell of a fun time. Morgan had fought it, but that was Morgan for you. He never knew how to embrace a fun time. "Morgan seemed as likely to get married as a beaver is to fly," he said affectionately.

Beau was taken aback when Ellie laughed at his beaver line. Her whole face changed. It was like dawn breaking or something. She just lit up. She had small white teeth, and they caught on her lower lip as she smiled at him. It really was a very nice lower lip . . .

Beau mentally pinched himself. He needed serious help if even this waif in brown was pricking his interest. Clearly this was what happened when there were too many girls—it overwhelmed the system.

Junebug burst back into the room carrying a tray. "Mrs. Champion's getting cake for everyone else, but I said no way in hell was I eating a cake made of carrots." She put the tray down with a clatter on their table, knocking over the jar of dried flowers. Beau and Ellie reached for it at the same time and their fingers tangled. Beau snatched his hand back, feeling callow.

"Pip started all this carrot nonsense and it's a crying shame Mrs. Champion has seen fit to continue it." Junebug unloaded the teacups and teapot, and a plate teetering with cookies. "These are only sugar cookies, but they beat carrot cake, hands down."

"I like carrot cake," Beau said, rescuing the teapot as Junebug almost sent it flying. "Ellie might too." He smiled at her again, hoping despite himself to see her shine back. She didn't.

"I've never had it," Ellie confessed. "We didn't get much cake back home."

"You ain't missing anything, not with carrot cake." Junebug splashed tea into the cups and ladled in sugar and cream. "Chocolate cake is a whole other situation, though."

"Bug! She might not want sugar."

"Stop fussing. The girl's been travelling for days—she needs sugar." Junebug pulled up a chair and grabbed a cookie. "Now, let's sort this mess out before you scare off my girls."

"There's nothing to sort." Beau felt his irritation rising.

"No. Because he's marrying Diana," Ellie told Junebug firmly.

"Ignore her," Junebug told Beau. "She won't be making sense until she's got some sugar in her."

"I'm making perfect sense. He proposed and Diana accepted. There's nothing more to discuss."

Beau felt a wave of gratitude. It was nice to have support when facing Junebug. And it was especially gracious of Ellie, given she'd come all this way to marry . . . him.

Hell. How must that feel, to travel halfway across the country to find yourself promised to the exact same man as your best friend . . . He felt a spurt of sympathy.

Beau glared at Junebug. His amoral little sister had gone way too far this time.

"If anyone should be glaring, it should be me," Junebug said blithely, before cramming a cookie in her mouth.

"No," Ellie told her sharply. "It should be *me*."

"Agreed," Beau said.

Junebug rolled her eyes. "Well, we can sit here and argue about who's more aggrieved or we can get on with the task at hand."

From the parlor, Beau could hear the rising chatter of female voices as Junebug's brides were delivered their carrot cake. The sound made Beau feel like an animal in a trap. He had to tell them he was marrying Diana, and he had to get it over with as soon as possible.

"No!" Junebug slammed her hand on the table when he made to stand. The teacups rattled in their saucers and the pile of cookies went tumbling. "Sit back down. You made that bet fair and square and you're going to see it through."

"Bet?" Ellie frowned. "What bet?"

Beau winced.

"What bet?" Ellie turned on Junebug.

Junebug placated her. "I can explain."

Beau wished she wouldn't. The more Junebug explained, the redder Ellie grew. And he knew it would all get back to Diana . . .

"This is because of a *bet*?" Ellie gasped. "Your speech back at the train station didn't say anything about a bet!"

"Well of course it didn't. I wanted everyone to stay."

"You lied to me!"

"No, I told the truth. That ad was unvarnished!"

Beau decided he'd let them fight it out between them. This was Junebug's mess to deal with. Although he did feel powerfully sorry for Ellie right now.

"You hauled *seven women* across the country, to the middle of *nowhere*, for a *bet*?"

"Don't get all tangled up in your corset strings," Junebug protested. "And I only invited six."

Beau sighed. Junebug was just making things worse, as usual. As calmly as possible, he stepped in and explained the bet to Ellie, who was raspberry colored and looking like she might assault someone with her teaspoon. "Now, it ain't as bad as it sounds."

Only as he began to explain he realized it sounded plenty bad. "The idea was to find the best wife . . ." he said, trailing off.

"The *best* wife?" Ellie's voice went up an octave. "And what are the criteria for the best wife? *Copious and symmetrical attractions?* Is that how you rank women?"

"Now, it ain't like that," he protested weakly. But, uh, it was exactly like that.

"It certainly ain't," Junebug scoffed. "My prize woman is the book smart sort. Someone with a brain in her head and enough steel to keep this idiot in his place."

Beau ignored her. "You're making it sound bad," he sighed. "But there ain't nothing wrong with wanting to meet a pretty gal, is there? Surely it's the most natural thing in the world . . ."

"Betting who can trick the prettiest girl into marriage is *natural*?" Ellie Neale had worked herself into a right dudgeon now.

"I didn't trick anyone! Junebug did. And she's the one who made it a bet—I was just looking for a nice gal to settle down with."

"And what's to happen to the *six of us* who aren't chosen at the end of this wretched bet?" Ellie turned on Junebug. "What happens to us? We're real, living people, you know, and you've stranded us in the wilderness, alone. Do you think we're made of money? Do you know how expensive it will be to get home?"

Beau felt about an inch tall. She was right. Even though he'd never expected to strand one woman, let alone six.

"You're not *alone*," Junebug told Ellie impatiently. "That's the whole point, isn't it? There's a heap of you. And I'll cover a train ticket home. I ain't a monster. Third-class, mind. I ain't made of money neither."

"I gave up my *job* for this." Ellie's voice cracked. "A job that came with room and board. Now I get here to find that I gave up solid employment for an illusion! And I'm homeless and without a situation—and there certainly aren't any mills around here for me to work in."

Beau blanched. He wondered if the other women were in such dire straits too. Mentally he calculated his savings. He could help, at least a little . . . because she was right. This was partly his fault.

"There's no need to carry on—you might win Beau yet." Junebug spoke through a mouthful of cookie. "We've only just started."

Beau thought Ellie might actually push Junebug off her chair at that. He wouldn't have stopped her.

"Your brother is marrying Diana," Ellie told her fiercely. "I don't want him."

"You heard her. She doesn't want me." Beau backed her up.

Junebug harrumphed. "Well, that greatly reduces my chances, doesn't it?"

"Your chances are nil," Beau assured her. "I pick Diana. You lose. We're going to break it to those gals and then you can get the shovel and start mucking out that stable."

"I'll muck that stable right out onto your grave, Beau McBride, if you don't see this bet through."

"JUNEBUG!" A familiar voice roared from the street, loud enough to rattle the windows in their frames.

Oh hell, it was Kit.

Beau had known Kit wouldn't take it well. It was only the five ladies in the parlor that kept him from exploding. Five ladies who had melted at the sight of him—which seemed to horrify Kit no end. He beat a swift retreat to the dining room, away from all those shining eyes and heaving bosoms.

"You!" He pointed a furious finger at Beau, who withdrew all the way to the back wall. "You should damn well know better than to encourage Junebug."

"Encourage *me*? It was *his* idea," Junebug told Kit.

"Don't you dare," Beau warned. "You're the one who ordered wives up in bulk!" He pointed his own finger. "I wanted *one* wife—I ordered up *one* wife. It's Junebug who made this a circus!"

"Only because you cheated! And don't you mention circuses to me, you double-crosser."

Ellie Neale refilled her teacup and was eating cookies as she watched him take a scolding from his older brother and Junebug. Beau didn't appreciate the fact that her shining smile was back as Kit lit into him. No one had any right to have a smile that distracting, especially at his expense.

"Those poor girls!" Kit barked. "They came here in good faith, and now they're stranded."

Ellie Neale nodded along at that. More than a touch smugly, Beau thought.

"They ain't stranded," Junebug scoffed. "I'll get them home."

Kit towered over her. "On that note, where'd you get the money for all those train tickets? Six brides don't come cheap. You better not have had them waste their hard-earned money, given all but one are going home disappointed."

"*All* of Junebug's are going home disappointed," Beau reminded them.

Ellie nodded vehemently and he felt stupidly pleased that she was agreeing with him.

"This ain't the time for details," Junebug said, shifty as a weasel. "We can talk about train tickets later. We don't want to keep those gals waiting, it's rude."

"Junebug paid for my train ticket," Ellie said calmly from her table, wiping cookie crumbs from that first-rate lower lip. "And she's paying for my hotel room for two weeks too. I assume she's paying for the harem's as well."

"How the hell can you afford to pay for all that?" Beau asked Junebug, horrified.

Junebug eyed the exits, which Kit and Beau had blocked. "I have some savings. And Rigby gave me a deal for booking rooms in bulk. I had to argue him down but he came through in the end."

"She won the money at cards." Ellie tapped her teaspoon against the teacup, and it gave a silvery chime.

"Why, you snitch!" Junebug turned on Ellie, outraged. "I told you that in private correspondence!"

"No. My imaginary husband-to-be told me that in private correspondence. Given that he was a complete fabrication, I don't feel it's a confidence I need to keep."

"He's not a fabrication—he's standing right there!"

"Junebug. Who have you been playing cards with?" Kit seemed to be directing his ire at Beau as he asked.

"Not me!" Beau said defensively. "I mean, we play in the cabin sometimes, but not for money."

"She's playing with the miners." Another silvery chime of spoon on cup.

"You were a *terrible* choice of bride," Junebug raged at Ellie. "And that's a terrible brown dress."

Kit ran his hands through his hair and counted to ten under his breath. He didn't even make it to four. "Are you *insane*? Junebug, what do you think would happen if you lost?"

Junebug shrugged. "It don't really signify, as I don't lose."

Beau stepped between Junebug and his brother, worried Kit might lunge. He was looking mad enough. "Try counting *backwards* from ten. Morgan says it works better."

"Morgan!" Kit froze. "What's Morgan going to say when he hears about this?"

They went silent at the thought. Except for Ellie, who hadn't met him yet. She calmly finished her second cup of tea. Beau envied her equilibrium.

"You send those women home this instant," Kit ordered Junebug.

"No."

There was sharp, shocked silence. Beau couldn't believe the nerve of the kid.

"No?" Kit repeated flatly.

"No." Junebug crossed her arms. "I got a lot of money in the hole on this one and I ain't throwing in. So I call your bluff."

"You call my . . . why you little . . . I'll . . ." Kit looked fit to burst.

"You'll what? Beat me? You ain't never laid a hand on me in your life. Besides, Morgan would kill you if you did."

"I'll lock you in the cabin till you're of age."

"No, you won't. The fact is, Kit, you're all bluster."

Beau felt sorry for his brother. Kit had turned a dark angry red. But Junebug was right. He was nothing but a gentle giant. Not like Morgan, who might actually lock her in the cabin. For a night or two anyway.

"This is easily fixed," Beau soothed Kit. "We'll tell those gals what's what and put them on the train home and it'll be like Junebug never did any of this."

"Will it?" Ellie Neale was acerbic.

"No you don't, Beau McBride," Junebug blazed. "Because if you interfere with my brides, I'm going to telegram Morgan about your wife hunting scheme. He'll be here on the next train. And I doubt he'll be happy."

That little witch. Threatening him with Morgan like that. Who did she think she was? Besides, she'd be in more trouble than he would . . .

But Junebug was crazy like a fox. She'd likely take the tongue lashing from Morgan, just to enjoy seeing Beau suffer his turn. She'd always been like that. "There ain't no telegram in Bitterroot," Beau reminded her.

"No, but there's one downhill in Snakehead, and I got old Roy standing ready to ride there and send it. You think this is my first rodeo? I know how high-handed you and Kit are, always stomping on my plans."

"Fine. Tell him," Beau dared her. "Tell Morgan. I'll be married by the time he gets here. What's he going to do?"

"You think? You think Miss Moonglow is still going to marry you once I tell her you made a *bet*? And you think Morgan will let you off easy for gambling with me? Your sweet innocent little sister."

"You're as innocent as that snake in the garden of Eden."

"That snake was just being a snake. I don't get why everyone blames it for that."

Kit swore. "Shut your yapping, Junebug, and let me think." He ran his hands through his dark mane.

"You know the easiest thing would be to just let this play out," Junebug told him smoothly. "We can give those gals in the parlor the option of whether to stay or not—and I know they'll stay because they all took my speech in stride. You saw 'em. They're happy enough. They see the sense in taking the time to get to know Beau before marrying him."

"But they're not all marrying him!" Ellie Neale burst in. "Six of them are *not* marrying him!"

"Shame, because I could put them to good use up at Buck's Creek." Junebug seemed genuinely regretful. "Anyway, stop interrupting. This is between me and my brothers."

"Thanks to you, I'm part of this too!"

"I've only got enough money to keep 'em for two weeks, so this won't take long," Junebug continued, her gaze fixed on Kit. "We can have this done and dusted before you know it. And Morgan doesn't have to be told, so long as you let me finish this bet. Beau shook on it. It's a binding contract. The gals who consent can stay, the ones who don't can leave, just like I promised in my letters. And Beau will end up hitched at the end, to the woman of his choosing, just like he wanted." Junebug cocked her head. "So, I don't get what all the fuss is about."

Ellie gave a sarcastic laugh. "You don't get what all the *fuss* is about? Didn't you listen to a word I said? What are we going home to?"

Junebug shrugged. "Whatever you want." She fixed Ellie with a sympathetic but firm look. "You knew the deal when you agreed to come. We were just getting to know each other, not getting hitched straight up."

"*We* weren't doing anything. You weren't part of the equation."

"Fair. But he was. And he still is. You like him, don't you? Most everyone does. Look at that face!"

"This is the worst thing you've ever done, Junebug," Beau told her grimly.

"No, the worst thing I've ever done was breaking my arm. That hurt like blazes."

"Beau," Kit barked, straightening his spine like he was about to head into battle. "You really made this stupid bet? You shook on it?"

Beau scowled. "Yeah. But I didn't know she'd lure *six women* out here."

"He didn't say I *couldn't* lure six women—"

"Shut up, Bug." Kit kept his focus on Beau. "And you didn't tell Junebug you'd chosen a bride and sent for her?"

"Well, no, but—"

"So you broke your word?"

Beau flushed. "No, I—"

"He did!"

"Shut *up*, Bug."

For once she shut up. Something about Kit's seething look seemed to convince her he was coming over all Morgan-ish.

Kit shook his head at Beau. His disappointment was palpable. "Junebug's right."

Beau felt like he'd been knocked flat. "What?"

"What!" Ellie Neale stood, and her teaspoon fell to the table with a soft thud. "What do you mean, Junebug's right?"

"Morgan warned me to keep an eye on you," Kit said in disgust.

"Don't beat yourself up, she's impossible," Beau told him.

"Not on her. On *you*." Kit glared at him. "He had a notion you'd get yourself in woman trouble. I laughed. But he was goddamn right. And he'll enjoy telling me so. After whomping me first." His dark gaze was furious. "This is your fault and you're going to fix it. I ain't getting whomped for the likes of you." He looked like he'd swallowed something sour. "It sticks in the gullet to agree with Junebug . . ."

"Hey!" Junebug took umbrage at that.

"So *don't* agree with her," Beau said hotly.

"But she's right. You're a goddamn McBride and we don't break our word. I cain't believe you shook on this. What kind of damn fool makes a bet with a kid like Junebug? It's your fault all these poor gals are stranded out here, without the husband they were promised."

"Stop saying that! They *have* the husband I promised. He's right there. They're going to get to know him, just like I said in the letters."

"Yes, they are," Kit agreed flatly. "Beau. You got yourself in this mess; you can get yourself out. Two weeks, you said?" Kit looked to Junebug for confirmation, and she nodded her head, a touch of glee entering her expression. "You got two weeks, the both of you. Morgan ain't back before winter. You get this done and settle your bet like an honest man and we can get out of this without having to suffer Morgan's temper."

Beau gaped at him. "Have you caught a case of Junebug's stupid?"

"Probably. But you made the damn bet. And with *Junebug*. You really think you're getting out of this easy?" Kit sounded angrier than Beau had ever heard him. "You made your bed, Beau. Now you'll have to lie in it. It ain't just about Morgan. It's a matter of family honor. You make a promise, you see it through. And you sure as hell ain't leaving these girls high and dry. Think of *them*."

Junebug's triumphant grin made Beau want to punch something.

"They ain't my responsibility!" But Beau sure felt responsible. He kept hearing the echo of Ellie's words in his head: *I gave up my job for this.* All those women had given up something to be here. For him. Beau wilted. He knew defeat when he saw it.

"And are you planning to tell those ladies in the parlor that this is a *bet*?" Ellie demanded. "And Diana. She deserves to know too."

"No way in hell." Beau would rather die. "What's the need?" he said wretchedly. "It will just cause upset, and surely there's enough upset already."

"There ain't upset at all," Junebug protested. "The only time I had any upset was today, when you got involved. The rest of them were perfectly fine with my speech. I explained that you're a fussy sort and feel like marriage should involve love and sparks and that whole kicked-in-the-head feeling. I said it in their letters too, so they knew they weren't getting hitched immediately, and that you'd need to take stock of each other." She gave Ellie a look. "You knew this was a try and see deal. The only thing you didn't know until you got here was that you weren't the only one. The others were fine about that, once I explained."

"Well, *I'm* not fine about it," Ellie snapped.

Junebug rolled her eyes. "Only because Beau screwed everything up. If you'd been alone with me, it would have been fine."

"But I wouldn't have been alone with you, would I?"

Beau didn't envy Junebug, fixed with Ellie's burning stare. Ellie Neale might be a wisp of a thing, but she had a fierceness to her that was singularly daunting. Particularly when her fierceness was about protecting her friend.

"I came with *Diana*. Who is the only one of us who *has* been corresponding with Beau directly. She likes Beau, Beau likes her. The harem and I, on the other hand, never corresponded with him—we corresponded with *you*."

"You're splitting hairs."

Now Beau had to step between Ellie and Junebug. "Try counting to ten," he counselled Ellie, "backwards. Twice over if you have to."

She looked up at him and there was such a mute mixture of anger and frustration in her big brown eyes that he instinctively put his hands on her shoulders to reassure her.

"I promise I'll work this out," he told Ellie quietly, as Kit and Junebug continued to argue hotly. He was aware it was the same promise he'd made to Diana.

"If you hurt Diana . . ." Ellie's eyes grew suspiciously shiny.

Was she about to *cry*? Beau shook his head at her. Honestly, here the woman was, left high and dry, and she was worried for her friend rather than for herself.

Brown sure was an under-rated color, he thought as he stared into her eyes. There were so many shades in those enormous eyes—a dark, dark rim around her iris, and swirly browns the color of rich spices in the center . . .

"Beau," Kit snapped, cutting Junebug off mid-oration, "you're going to fulfill your side of the bet and give each of these ladies a chance, and then you pick one. End of discussion."

"I don't care how much time he spends with the others, Beau will be picking Diana." Ellie Neale's spicy gaze shot sparks at Beau. He felt them right down to his bones.

He tore his eyes away from hers. "Yes. Diana." He cleared his throat. "I'm picking Diana."

"Fine." Kit didn't care. "Pick Diana. But at least fulfill your end of the damn bet first and get to know the others—play fair."

Beau would do it. But not because of his darn bet with Junebug—he'd do it because these poor girls had dragged themselves across the country, in the earnest belief they might be Mrs. Beau McBride. At the very least he owed them the courtesy of getting to know them. Diana was the woman for him, he was near sure of it, but it wouldn't hurt to at least say howdy to these poor girls.

"How's he fulfilling the bet if he's already decided," Junebug raged. "How's that fair?"

"Don't push your luck, Bug," Kit told her. "Be glad if he does it at all. And I'm sure you'll stack the deck against him and get your way."

"How's *that* fair?" Beau said bitterly.

"You get to control how you choose," Kit reminded him. "If Junebug wins, it's because you picked one of hers. That's entirely up to you, as far as I can see."

"He'll have to stay here in town if he wants to get to know those gals," Junebug insisted. "So that he can spend time with them."

"What?" Beau didn't like the sound of that. Goddamn it, today had gone straight to hell and back. He'd planned to be taking Diana home to Buck's Creek . . .

"I'm not leaving the fox in the henhouse," Kit growled. "He ain't staying here at the hotel with all these women. Beau, you can stay with Martha."

"I ain't staying in town at all!" Beau sat back down at the table, feeling petulant. He slouched in the chair. His family always went and ruined everything. Why couldn't he just marry the woman he'd chosen and have done with it?

"Martha only has the one bedroom," Junebug reminded Kit. "And she, uh . . . entertains . . ."

"You ain't supposed to know about such things," Kit said sourly.

Ellie had resumed her seat opposite Beau.

"Is it my fault if I'm perceptive in the ways of human nature?" Junebug said tartly.

"There ain't enough numbers to count in order to cope with you."

"You aren't seriously finishing this awful bet?" Ellie asked Beau, staring at him in shock.

Beau was resigned. "Yeah. I have to." But it wasn't about the bet; it was about doing right by that roomful of women in there.

"Well, you don't. You could just go marry Diana right now in that little white church."

Beau shook his head tiredly. "When I marry Diana, it'll be proper, with everyone happy in attendance. Including my sister." He caught her look of disbelief.

Junebug was still going head-to-head with Kit in a way Beau never did. "If Martha's place ain't appropriate I guess he'll be staying at the hotel after all," Junebug argued.

"Over my dead body." Kit was immovable.

"Well, he's got to stay *somewhere*. Where's left, the whorehouse?"

"Junebug!" Kit was thunderous.

"Beau can stay at my house," a muffled voice called through the closed kitchen door.

Beau groaned. "Ain't there any privacy in this town?"

Gingerly the door opened, revealing Mrs. Champion's rosy face. She looked sheepish. "I wasn't eavesdropping," she said hurriedly, "it's just that your voices carry . . ."

Beau shot the parlor an anxious glance. Hell. What if all those pretty girls had heard his family carrying on?

"Oh, I'm sure not that far, honey," Mrs. Champion clucked. "It's just that the kitchen is right here . . ." She was blushing in earnest now, as it was obvious she'd been listening in. "But if you need somewhere to stay in town, you're very welcome to stay at my house. I have a couple of extra rooms. And it's right next door, so you wouldn't be far from your . . . from the . . . ladies."

"If he's staying in town, I'm staying too," Junebug informed them stolidly. "I'll stay here at the hotel, though. I want to be where the action is."

"No way in hell. You're coming back to Buck's Creek," Kit told her.

"Absolutely not," Junebug raged. "This is my bet and I don't trust him."

"God grant me strength."

"You get any more strength you'll be too muscly to walk," Junebug said acidly.

"You're going to have to explain all this to Diana," Ellie told Beau. "And if you don't tell her . . ." Ellie paused for effect. " I will."

Diana. Beau's stomach sank to his toes. He'd have to look into Diana's cool blue eyes and tell her that he'd be spending time with a passel of pretty girls before they got married.

And then he'd actually have to spend time with all those pretty girls . . .

Six

"What the hell have you got in here?" Beau McBride grunted as he struggled with Ellie's trunk. "Rail spikes? An anvil?"

Ellie ignored him, not appreciating the complaints after he'd taken so long to deliver her luggage. He'd gone back to collect it from the station, but only after he'd settled Diana into the hotel, hauling her trunk first. He'd also taken the time to deliver Diana a bunch of "flowers", which weren't flowers at all, given nothing much flowered in November. It was a bouquet of fall branches he'd snapped off. Ellie had been hypnotized by the way the autumn leaves shone like captured firelight. It was *such* a romantic gesture. Diana had accepted them gingerly, not quite as taken with them as Ellie had been.

Ellie had left them to talk, climbing the narrow flight of stairs to her attic room at the Bellevue, imagining Beau McBride out in the shadowy woods, selecting the most vibrant branches he could find. She hoped Diana didn't give him too much of a hard time after he went to all that effort.

They must have found enough to talk about, because Ellie had waited and waited upstairs for her belongings. She wondered if he'd forgotten her. She was grimy from travel and wished she could change her clothes. Or at least have her books to pass the time. As twilight gathered its lavender folds, Ellie stood at the casement window and tried to pretend she wasn't as exhausted as she really was. There was a little cottage next door, and she had a view of the back porch and a yard of vegetables and cooped chickens. A paling fence separated the yard from the woods proper, which reared beyond it in a wall of dense foliage. That must be the cottage where the housekeeper lived—where Beau would be staying.

Ellie was all mixed up with feeling. She'd come here to be with Diana, but the man she'd come to meet was a mirage. So where did that leave her?

Nowhere.

She fell into sad daydreams about having to say farewell forever to Diana. Ellie could picture her friend standing on the dirt platform at the train station, weeping, waving a lace-edged handkerchief as Ellie's train pulled away, taking her out of Diana's life forever . . .

As night spilled from the shadows of the woods, Ellie started wondering if she should just haul her belongings from the station herself. But her trunk was frightfully heavy, and she was so very tired. And to be honest, she was a little frightened at the thought of venturing out into the darkness alone. This town wasn't just *in* the woods, it was part of them.

She lit the lantern, and the room hugged in around her, a haven of golden light. Her stomach rumbled; she supposed she'd just have to go down to supper dirty, and in the dress that she'd been wearing for days.

Sighing, Ellie decided to scrub the dirt from her face and hands in preparation for supper. She poured the pitcher of water into the wash basin and set to work on the travel grime. After unbuttoning the top few buttons of her bodice, she rolled up her sleeves and gave herself a soapy scrub while she waited for Beau McBride to bring her luggage. The hotel's homemade soap smelled of lost summer flowers and Ellie lathered enthusiastically, filling the room with the scent of sunny blooms.

Beau McBride finally came grunting up to her room just as she was toweling her face dry. Thank goodness, because she'd had a few stray imaginings about highwaymen holding up the station and running off with her belongings. She didn't know if they had highwaymen in Montana, but she assumed there was at least an equivalent. Anyway, it was good to know her trunk had survived the trip. And also that Beau had survived his talk with Diana. Watching him wrestle with her trunk, Ellie was glad she hadn't tried to do it herself. She would have done herself an injury.

"You packed everything you own, huh," he grumbled.

Ellie held the door wide for him, wincing as he knocked his elbow on the doorframe. "It's only a few books . . ." she assured him.

"How many books? Three hundred? Four?" His face was red and shiny from the effort.

She ignored that. "You can put it over there in the corner, thank you."

Beau was in his shirtsleeves and there was a damp patch of sweat in the middle of his back. The cotton clung to his skin as he lowered the trunk to the floor. "You brought five hundred of your favorite books with you to Montana, when you weren't even sure you wanted to stay?"

"Of course," Ellie said primly, tearing her gaze away from his well-shaped back. "What else would I do with them?" She quickly rolled down the sleeves of her dress and checked she'd buttoned her bodice properly. It felt very intimate up here in this little room, without adding bare skin to the mix.

"They really put you up in the attic, didn't they," he moaned, stretching. "That was a lot of stairs."

"I suppose I'm lucky they had a room for me at all, given your—"

"Don't say it." He gave her a dark look.

"—harem." Ellie didn't mind being up in the attic; she liked the romance of its sloping roof and casement window. Imagine having a bed all to herself and being able to read all night without worrying about waking someone else up.

"It ain't *my* harem," Beau said gruffly. "If it's anyone's, it's Junebug's."

"Well, so long as it doesn't *remain* your harem, it doesn't really matter. I don't imagine Diana will hold with being one of many."

A shadow chased his face. "Yeah, she wasn't too pleased."

Ah. So that was why he'd taken so long to come back with her trunk.

"You told her everything?" She felt rather sorry for him, all boyish there in his shirtsleeves, rumpled, stained, his hair disheveled. Today certainly hadn't gone the way he'd planned it. But then it hadn't gone the way she and Diana had planned it either.

"Yeah. I told her about the bet and all." He ran a hand through his curls. "I explained my part in it—and Junebug . . . well, I explained best I could about Junebug. She ain't a bad kid, you know. She's just . . ." He shrugged. "We did the best we could with her, but what do any of us know about raising a girl? Especially a girl like Junebug . . ."

"How did Diana take it?" Ellie's mind was racing. She should probably rush straight to Diana's side to offer succor. Diana had been dreaming about her wedding to Beau McBride and her new start in this wilderness. She would be devastated by the day's events.

Ellie would be a mess if this had happened to her.

Although it *had* kind of happened to her . . .

How odd to think that she'd been intended to be Beau's bride too. Or one of them. Ellie stared into space. Imagine. All that time she thought she was coming here for his brother, when she was actually coming here for *him*.

She remembered all those poetic letters he'd written Diana and his promise of the cottage with its wild roses . . .

"I thought Diana might go straight back to the station and buy the first ticket out of here," Beau said miserably, breaking Ellie's reverie. "But I swore to her that she was the one. The *only* one." His dark eyes met Ellie's. "This is more of a Junebug problem than a me problem . . ."

"You made that bet," Ellie reminded him tartly. "So I think it's definitely a you problem too."

He frowned at her. "That's what Diana said."

Ellie nodded. Of course. She and Diana were utterly simpatico. "Because it's true."

"Fine. It's a me problem too. But it's *more* of a Junebug problem. Without Junebug in the mix, I'd be married to Diana by now and we'd be home in Buck's Creek."

Ellie was shocked. "Surely you weren't going to marry her straight off the train?"

"Of course I was." He gave her an odd look. "When we were downstairs, you suggested I take her straight to church and marry her, so I don't see what's so shocking about it."

"But I said that because of your harem," she told him. "You didn't know about the harem before today. Yet you planned to meet her at the train and just *marry her*?"

"What else would I do?"

Ellie had plenty of ideas. And she was happy to share them with him. "A wedding takes planning," she told him. She'd had a lot of time to think about Diana's wedding, to make it perfect in her mind: a ceremony outdoors in his mountain meadow with the evening light hazy like a veil around them. She described it to Beau McBride. Vividly. And then she explained that Diana would need time to make up her gown, that she would require a bouquet of roses—

"The wild roses finished flowering months ago," Beau interrupted.

Ellie waved him away. "I can imagine roses if I want to. And none of your flat-faced wild roses, these are proper roses, fat as cabbages, in all shades of pink, from the palest pearly dawn pink to the lushest, darkest sunset pink. Diana is in white lace—"

"Her hem will get awful muddy out there in the meadow." But he was sounding interested, like he was catching a glimpse of how enchanting it could be.

Encouraged, Ellie persisted. "And she'll be as beautiful as the first spring day after winter, her hair falling loose around her shoulders—brides should wear their hair loose, don't you think?"

He nodded, looking quite struck by the idea.

"And you'll be in that blue coat you wore today, but with all the dirt cleaned off, and you'll have a lovely white rosebud in your lapel—"

"No fat pink rose for me?" He sounded faintly amused.

"Oh no, it would be too much."

"Right. Of course."

"Sometimes I think Diana should also have a veil with scalloped lace edges, and as she walks down the aisle—"

"There ain't no aisles in a meadow."

"Of course there are, for a wedding. There are people in two blocks of seats, with an aisle down the middle. You must have an aisle for a wedding, or where's a bride to walk?"

"Fair point, I suppose."

"And as she walks down the aisle," Ellie spoke over him, the vision so entrancing she had to capture it immediately before it evaporated, "you'll pull a handkerchief from your breast pocket, to stem the tide of your tears."

"Of my *what*?"

"You're overcome, of course, by both her beauty and the flood of your affections."

"But I ain't *crying* about it. I'd just smile at her."

"You're smiling through your tears."

"I ain't. I'm just smiling."

"Fine. We'll hold the tears until after you lift her veil. That's after the vows, when the minister—"

"You imagined a minister but not a church?"

She ignored him. "—says 'you may kiss the bride'. Holding your breath with expectation, you'll take the scalloped lace between your trembling fingertips."

"I'm trembling?"

"Of course. You're *quivering* with anticipation."

"I am?"

"You are," she said firmly. "You lift the veil . . ."

"And I like what I see," he guessed, satisfied.

"You're *awed*," she instructed. "As you behold your bride—"

"Wife," he corrected. "The minister just hitched us."

"A wife is still a bride for the honeymoon period."

"Do I kiss her now?"

"Stop rushing. This is the best bit."

"The kissing? I know." His lips twitched, amused.

"No. The moment before . . ."

"*Before* the kissing is better than the kissing?"

"Anticipation is always the best bit, don't you think?" She regarded him earnestly. "Which is why you were misguided to plan for an immediate wedding. You're wasting the chance to look forward to it."

"I've looked forward to it enough. I'm ready for it."

"At least Junebug suggested a period of getting acquainted first, before rushing down the aisle," she said, exasperated.

"That's only because she had six of you to get acquainted with," he reminded her.

"I think you're too rash."

"Or impressively decisive."

Ellie sized him up. "No. Definitely rash. You practically had the minister ready to say the blessing and consign you to all eternity, and you weren't even going to take a day to find out if you liked her?"

"I'd seen her picture. I liked the look of her a lot." He waved away her pessimism.

"What if you didn't like *her*? What if she got off the train and you didn't like her personality?"

"Trust me, I like her personality. More than I even like her looks, if I'm honest." His dark eyes softened. It did odd things to Ellie's stomach. "I must have read her letters a dozen times over, each. You ever feel like you knew someone, all their secret corners, just from a letter?"

Yes, she thought as she watched his gaze grow dreamy. Ellie felt like she was caught in a rising tide, and it was lifting her feet from the floor. It was a confusing, warm, flooding, floating feeling. She felt like she knew him from *his* letters and right now, listening to the husk of his voice and seeing the dreaminess of his expression, Ellie could picture him lying in a meadow, staring at the clouds, dreaming half the day away. For just a bright little moment, Ellie saw the poetry in him.

But then he shook his head and snapped back to the present. "She's the one for me and I got no doubts," he said firmly. "I'll do the right thing by Junebug's brides, but I plan to marry Diana. And I told her so."

Ellie imagined standing in Diana's shoes, listening to that— *You're the one for me*, said so fervently, with such passion—and she just about floated away from the romance of it. Him holding that bouquet of autumnal wildness, his dark eyes shining like moonlit lakes, telling her that he wanted only her, that he'd loved her since her letters . . .

Oh my. The letters. The letters that *Ellie* had written.

Color flooded Ellie's face as she came back to reality. He was smacked in the heart by *Ellie's letters*. Ellie felt her own heart stop, then lurch, then stop again. She was in a welter of feelings she couldn't name. Surging, completely inappropriate joy, and spiraling, sisterly despair. *She* was partly the cause of Beau McBride's dreamy expression. Well, her letters and Diana's photograph.

Oh no. What if Diana didn't have the same kinds of secret corners that Ellie did? She bit her lip, hoping she hadn't set Diana up for disaster. Well. Hopefully he'd love Diana's secret thoughts just as much as he'd liked Ellie's . . . He just needed time to find them out.

Ellie must have drifted away into her imagination, as she was wont to do, because when she returned to the present Beau McBride seemed to have moved on from the topic of marriage. "You don't even have a fireplace up here—you'll freeze." He was exploring her attic room and frowning.

Startled from her thoughts, Ellie looked around. He was right. There was no fireplace up here. She moved to the window and pulled the gingham curtains closed. They wouldn't do much to keep out the chill, but they were better than nothing.

"Rigby can't leave you up here." Beau shook his head in disgust. "It ain't right."

"I volunteered to take it. There weren't enough rooms downstairs. Diana said I could share with her, but I couldn't deprive her of the opportunity to sleep in a room of her very own," Ellie said, feeling the thrill of it, all fresh again. "I've never had my own room either, so this is a delight. Do you know what that's like, to have the opportunity of your very own room, even just for a night or two?"

"Yeah," he said, with an unexpected dash of irony, "I do. But this ain't a room. It's an attic."

Ellie ran her hand over the bedding on the narrow cast iron bed, which consisted of a patchwork quilt over a cotton sheet. "I'll be fine. I've certainly had worse." She tried to ignore the fluttery feeling in her belly as his gaze followed the movement of her hand on the bed. It didn't mean anything, of course. It wasn't like she was having feelings for her friend's fiancé. Not really. Heavens, a block of *wood* would probably feel a flutter when it came to this man.

"Ellie."

Oh goodness, now she was feeling odd all over. It was his voice saying her name. There was a tone to it, an uncertain hitching quality that made her insides shiver.

"I really am sorry," he said slowly. "That you got dragged out here, I mean, like this, under false pretenses. I feel real bad about it."

What was it about those eyes? She just fell headlong into them, like she was drowning in dark water. They swallowed her up whole. As she drowned, she felt a hot loosening in the center of her, like something mysterious and wonderful was uncoiling.

Was this how a swoon felt?

"I hope we can be friends," he said awkwardly, and she realized she'd been staring like a fool. "Given I'm planning to marry Diana, and she says you're practically her sister, I think we should be friends, don't you?"

Yes. Diana. Friends.

"Oh yes," she babbled. "Of course. Friends. Family really, because, yes, sisters . . ." She took a step back. She was blushing again. "Yes, we can be friends."

"I hope the other gals are as understanding as you are." He pulled an anxious face.

"Doubtful," she laughed nervously, "as they don't have a Diana to think of." Oh, my goodness, she'd just been swooning over *Diana's fiancé*. What had got into her? How could she be so disloyal?

Ellie heard clomping and skittering on the stairs and then Junebug stuck her head in, her little fluffy dog following with a clatter of nails on the floorboards. Ellie had never been so glad to see anyone in her life. She couldn't be trusted alone with this man.

"We're all eating together in the dining room tonight," Junebug announced. "That means you too, Beaumont."

"Your name is Beaumont?" Ellie was startled. He hadn't mentioned that in his letters.

"No, she's just being a pain in the ass. My name's Beau. Just Beau."

"Sure, it is, Beauregard. You go over to Mrs. Champion's cottage and freshen up. You look like hell. Be back here for supper in an hour. Mrs. Champion says she's cleaned the dirt off your coat and you can collect it from the kitchen on the way out." Junebug turned to Ellie. "That's what happens when you flirt with people: they spoil you rotten, cleaning your coat when you don't even deserve it. She's probably got cookies waiting for him too."

"I don't flirt." Beau sounded sour.

"Why are you still here, Beaufort? Go."

"I *don't* flirt," Beau muttered to Ellie as he passed her. "I'm just nice to people."

"You can watch him flirt tonight," Junebug promised Ellie. "It's a thing to see. So far, I think he's been off his game."

"I'm sitting next to Diana tonight," Beau snapped at Junebug, "and she's the only one I'm flirting with, so make sure you save her a seat next to me."

Junebug shook her head. "You've already *met* her—there ain't no point in you sitting next to her. Or flirting with her. She's already softened up. You haven't met any of my other ones yet, only Ellie here."

"I'm *not* one of yours," Ellie told Junebug sharply. "I'm on Beau and Diana's side." Ellie ignored the warm glow she felt when Beau gave her a thankful smile.

"You're good at this," Junebug told Ellie approvingly after Beau left. "You've managed to spend more time with him than anyone else, and I think he kinda likes you."

The little pest was impossible, Ellie thought. She put her hands on her hips and fixed Junebug with a stern look. "I'm not doing anything except looking out for my friend."

"Sure." Junebug tapped the side of her nose and winked.

She was worse than impossible.

"What other dresses have you got?" Junebug demanded. "That one smells bad as well as being ugly."

Ellie would have closed the door on her but Junebug had already slid into the room and was unlatching Ellie's trunk. Her dog jumped up on its hind legs, resting its front feet on the lip of the trunk to peer in.

"Get out of there, that's my private business."

"Me or Beast?"

"Both of you."

"Fine," Junebug said, scooting back. "*You* find a dress." She sat herself down on Ellie's bed. "Your other ones ain't brown, are they?"

"Out," Ellie ordered.

"In a minute. I just wanted to get to know you first, and maybe apologize."

"*Maybe* apologize?"

"Sure. I can apologize when I need to."

"You definitely need to."

The kid wasn't going anywhere. She leaned back on her elbows, kicking her heels so her blue skirts swirled. Ellie shrugged and knelt by her trunk, pushing the little dog out of the way. What did she care if the little monster watched her unpack? She considered her options for dressing for supper. She was already wearing her best dress, and it was worse for wear. She had the two blouses and the skirt she wore to work at the mill, and her second-best dress, which was a cheap calico in a dusty yellow, sprigged with tiny flowers the color of rust. The dress was without bustle or frill. She'd made it herself years ago and she wasn't good with a needle, but it was clean, and it wasn't brown.

"Spit, you've got some ugly clothes," Junebug said from the bed. She reached down and lifted her dog up onto her lap.

"Some of us don't have the luxury of winning money at cards," Ellie replied sharply. "We have to make do."

"I'll have to teach you how to play cards, then. You can't go around wearing those awful things, or no one will ever want to marry you."

Ellie flushed. She knew her clothes were awful. Diana had begged her to get at least one new dress before she came to Montana, but when Ellie had gone to say goodbye to her mother and had seen the hunger on the children's faces, and the hollows in her mother's cheeks, she just couldn't bring herself to waste money on a dress. Her clothes were perfectly serviceable, and her family needed food. She'd given what little cash she had to her mother and packed her ugly old clothes.

"Well, it has to be either this dress, or the skirt." Ellie held them up.

"At least the skirt ain't brown." Junebug's nose wrinkled in distaste at the sight of the dress.

"This isn't brown." Ellie shook the yellow-ish dress at her.

"As good as. It's just a brown so pale it's lost its liveliness."

Junebug's dog barked in agreement.

"The skirt then," Ellie sighed, as she plucked cotton fluff off the hem of the dark twill. There was so much cotton floating about at the mill that it attached itself to clothing and was near impossible to remove. She picked at it listlessly, remembering the lovely dresses the girls in the parlor had been wearing. Cheerful bright colors with ribbons and flounces, puffs and frills. Ellie would look like a little brown sparrow amid that host of beautiful birds.

"Where's the dress from the photograph you sent?" Junebug demanded. "That was flattering."

"It was Diana's. I borrowed it." Ellie stood, holding the skirt up in front of her. It would be fine. No one was looking at her anyway.

"What have you got there?" Junebug sat up ramrod straight, staring into the trunk now that the dress had been removed.

"My blouses?" Ellie lifted the blouses too. One was white and one was washed out blue. They'd both been laundered to within an inch of their lives.

"Not the blouses." Junebug was off the bed and hovering over the trunk, like it held treasure.

"Oh. My books?"

"There's more books in there than Kit has in his entire collection!" She shot Ellie a wide-eyed entreaty. "Can I borrow one?"

Ellie saw the hunger on Junebug's face and the germ of an idea took root. "I'll tell you what. If you forget about your bet and let your brother marry Diana without a fuss, you can borrow as many as you like."

Junebug snorted. "When hell freezes over."

Ellie closed the trunk. "Well, you know where to find me if you change your mind."

Junebug pulled at her dog's furry bat ears and eyed the closed trunk. "What if I drop the idea of *you* marrying my brother, is that worth borrowing a book or two?"

Ellie laughed. "No, because I'm already not marrying your brother."

"Why not? Don't you think he's pretty?"

"Very pretty," Ellie said before she could stop herself. "But he's also very much engaged to my best friend, who I love more than anyone in the world."

"I don't suppose *she* has a trunk full of books?" Junebug asked hopefully.

"No, but she does have some very beautiful dresses."

"Maybe you could borrow one of hers. That one from the photograph."

"I don't have any reason to—I'm not the one trying to get Beau's attention."

Junebug gave her a sour look. "You were a complete waste of money. What's the point of you, if you ain't here to kick him in the head with a wile or two?"

Ellie knocked on Diana's door on her way down to dinner. Her friend was in her dark blue dress and had loosened her hair into a more relaxed chignon. She was as beautiful as ever, but in a mood. She wasn't at all pleased about the harem, and Ellie couldn't blame her.

"So, you're part of the bet too," Diana said coolly. She let Ellie into her room and took a moment to check her appearance in the looking glass and dab on some scent from the tiny little bottle that was her most beloved treasure.

"*Was* part of the bet." Ellie was vehement. She wrinkled her nose at the pungent scent of narcissus. "I *was* part of the bet. But not anymore. Except to help you win. I'll do all I can on that front," Ellie said hurriedly. "And don't worry, he hasn't wavered about you." Ellie sat on the big brass bed and watched Diana finish her toilette. She bounced appreciatively. Oh, this bed was comfortable. There was a thick whole cloth quilt stuffed with a puffy eiderdown. It was like sitting on a cloud. Ellie couldn't imagine ever being unhappy in a bed this comfortable. She was so glad Diana could have the pleasure of it. She hoped it gave Diana as much joy as Ellie's charming little attic gave her.

"Entertaining six other women counts as wavering," Diana disagreed.

"Five," Ellie corrected. "Not me. And he doesn't *want* to. You should hear how he speaks of you, Diana." Ellie's eyes shone, remembering Beau up in her little attic room, swearing fidelity to Diana. "I think I'd *die* of delight if someone spoke of me that way."

"Well, speaking and doing are two different things."

"No one else got a harvest of autumnal glory." Ellie admired the bouquet of branches on the dresser.

"Yet," Diana amended tersely. "No one else got one *yet*."

"Nor will they. Not one of those girls can hold a candle to you. And none of them exchanged all those letters with him." Ellie firmly believed Diana was the most beautiful girl in the world.

Diana turned. She took a shaky breath and nodded, and Ellie was horrified to see the shine of tears in her dark blue eyes.

"Oh Diana." Ellie rushed to hug her.

"I'm probably just tired from the journey." Diana's voice was muffled, her face buried in Ellie's shoulder. She had to bend a fair way down to bury it. Ellie rose on tiptoe to help her out.

"Of course," Ellie soothed, patting her on the back. "It was a *trial* of a journey. But after some supper and a sleep in that big cloud of a bed, you'll be full of zest again."

"You seem to be much more zesty, yourself," Diana said, pulling back and dabbing at her eyes with a lace-edged handkerchief.

"Well, I did eat a whole plate of sugar cookies before. And," she grinned, "secretly I'm frightfully glad I'm not marrying a man from an advertisement. That was one part of coming to Montana with you that I wasn't at all keen on. I'm so happy I get to be here with you, with no distractions. I'll be at your wedding—"

"If there *is* a wedding," Diana interrupted, her eyes going all swimmy again.

"Of course there'll be a wedding. And you'll be the most beautiful bride there ever was, and he'll be the most besotted groom there ever was." Ellie pushed away thoughts of what would happen after the wedding. When she'd be alone and jobless and facing some hard decisions about her future . . .

Diana pressed her lips together. When she nodded, a tear cascaded down her pale cheek. "Yes." She gave a watery smile. "And you'll be my maid of honor."

Ellie beamed. She'd known she would be, but hearing it lit her up. She imagined herself in that meadow, walking down the aisle before Diana—because there would most definitely be an aisle—in her new gown of . . . Ellie paused, not sure what kind of gown to imagine herself in. Her gaze flew to the looking glass. Her reflection showed an ordinary working girl in a twill skirt and a white blouse without even a puff of sleeve to cheer it. She couldn't quite imagine these old clothes away.

Diana had followed her gaze to the looking glass and Ellie could tell she was doing her mind reading trick again. "Your hair looks so lovely down," she said, smiling at Ellie in the mirror.

Ellie lifted a hand to her dark hair. The braids had been unsalvageable, so she'd taken them out. After days plaited, her hair had exploded into a mass of kinks. Usually her hair was mostly straight, but today it was a wild bush. She'd tried to comb it out, but that had just bushed it more. She'd tied a couple of strands back with a bit of white ribbon, to hold it out of her face, but she wondered if she should just give up and cram it all up into a knot.

"It suits you," Diana reassured her.

Ellie bit her lip. Well, either way there wasn't much to do about it. This was her, like it or not. "I should probably have taken your advice and got a new dress," she said miserably. "Everyone's going to look as wonderful as you do, and I look like I should be at a loom."

"Would you like a spray of my perfume?" Diana asked, and Ellie recognized it for the extreme generosity it was, because Diana rationed that narcissus perfume tightly.

Ellie shook her head. She'd never take Diana's special scent from her. But also, she much preferred the ghostly summer flowers of the hotel soap on her skin.

Arm in arm they went downstairs, bolstered by one another's presence.

"Remember," Ellie whispered as they reached the door to the dining room, "it's you he wants."

They stepped through the doorway and Ellie felt Diana's fingernails digging into her arm. The room had been rearranged; now there was a single long table stretching the length of it. A cheerful fire crackled in the grate and candles danced in their sconces. The sound of high-pitched chatter greeted them, and the room was bright with gowns in violets and blues and pinks and greens. It was so enchanting that Ellie had to stop for a moment to take it in.

"I feel like I'm in a book," she breathed.

"Well, your book better not be a tragedy," Diana whispered fiercely.

Ellie followed Diana's gaze to where Beau was backed against the wall. He was wearing his midnight blue coat again, only now it was spotless. His hair had been tamed, and it licked against his neck and jaw in delightful dark curls.

"Look at them all," Diana hissed.

A semi-circle had formed around him, and the ladies looked so beautiful Ellie's heart gave a squeeze. "Aren't they lovely," she breathed before she knew what she was saying.

Diana made a horrified, hurt noise.

"Not as lovely as you, of course," Ellie said hurriedly. "I only meant, it's like something from an illustration. Their dresses are so enchanting."

But the damage was done. Diana's eyes were shimmering again.

Ellie wasn't used to being the steady one. Usually Diana was practical and cool, and she was the one weeping, usually over some delicious imagining. But of course Diana was fighting tears. Her soon-to-be-husband was like a bee in a bed of flowers right now. And bees loved flowers!

Ellie tried to catch Beau's eye to no avail. He was tangled up in conversation.

"I won't go over there, El, I just won't."

Ellie thought that was a mistake, but she knew Diana well enough to know she could be immovable. She certainly had her immovable face on right now.

"Junebug," Ellie grabbed Beau's sister as she flittered past, holding a basket of bread rolls. "Should we find our seats? Beau said Diana is sitting next to him."

"Not according to the seating plan."

That little witch. Ellie glared at her. "I'm sure you'll find it *is* according to *Beau's* seating plan."

"No, Miss Newchurch is at the head of the table down there," Junebug pointed to the far end of the table, "while Beau is all the way in the middle here." She gave Ellie a look of angelic innocence.

"Excuse me," Ellie apologized to Diana, "I just need a minute." Ellie took Junebug by the arm and pulled her further away. "You move Diana next to Beau or I'll . . ." Ellie struggled to think of an effective threat.

"You'll what?"

Oh, the kid was smug. It was too irritating for words.

"Fine," Ellie said, deciding abruptly on another course of action. "If you sit Diana next to Beau, you can borrow one of my books."

That got her attention.

"Just one," Ellie stressed. She might need more bargaining chips up her sleeve in future.

"Any one I want?" Junebug cocked her head and considered it.

"Any one you want. For one week," Ellie added. "And then I want it back."

"I do know what borrowing means," Junebug said tartly. "Fine. I'll sit her near him."

"*Next* to him."

Junebug rolled her eyes. "Next to him." Then she grinned. "For another book, I'll sit you on his other side."

"I don't need to be near him. This isn't my circus."

The kid got a sparkly look at that. "What do you know of circuses? Have you ever been to one?"

Ellie blinked, startled. "Once. Two summers ago, we went on our day off."

"Well, I reckon you can sit near me, then, and tell me about circuses." Junebug lifted one of the rolls from her basket and tore off a mouthful with her teeth. "I've got an interest in circuses," she said through her bread, and then she was off, dropping bread rolls onto side plates with her hands.

"I need your help."

Ellie jumped a mile at the voice in her ear. "Oh my goodness, you startled me half to death. You're as silent as a cat." She turned to find Beau McBride looming over her.

"No, you were just a million miles away."

"I wasn't," she lied. Although she might have been thinking about Junebug's manners and that might have led her to thinking about Beau's letters, which had led her to his stories about losing their mother, and their sisters, and thinking about Junebug as a poor motherless child, with no one to teach her manners . . .

"You're doing it again," Beau sighed.

"Doing what again?"

"Staring into space."

"I'm not." She fixed him with her full attention. "See?"

He pulled nervously at the cuffs of his coat and glanced over at Diana. "I need your help."

Diana was standing miserably by herself, caught in a shivering net of candlelight. Ellie thought she looked *exactly* like a heroine on the cusp of a grand romance, the moment someone spied her across the room at a society supper and fell ravenously in love with her . . .

"I've already done it," Ellie told him absently, caught up in her fancy.

"Done what?" He frowned, bemused.

"Helped you. Junebug's going to sit Diana next to you."

"I'd already sorted that. I said I'd talk to all these girls tonight if she sat Diana with me. We shook hands on it and everything."

Ellie gaped. "Why that little . . ."

"Why? What did she get out of you?"

"A book," Ellie sighed. "I said she could borrow a book."

Beau looked impressed. "Very clever. She loves books."

"But it's a waste of cleverness, if you've already arranged things."

"Yeah, well, I've arranged myself into a nightmare."

Ellie didn't understand.

"If I sit next to her, I have to *talk* to her." Beau shot Diana a vaguely panicked look.

"And?"

"And I realized earlier that I don't know *how* to talk to her. You should have heard me; I was a stammering idiot."

Ellie doubted it. Maybe he *felt* like a stammering idiot, but he'd probably been . . . But then Ellie remembered Diana's uncertainty. She hadn't seemed impressed by his ardor or his fidelity at all. Maybe he *had* been a stammering idiot. Sometimes Diana's beauty did that to men. Ellie bit her lip.

"Anyway, you have to sit next to me, so you can help me." He took her by the wrist. "Come on, before Junebug hitches someone else to me."

"Wait. You need to take Diana too." Ellie pulled him towards Diana, who had been watching them surreptitiously. She heard Beau swallow hard. "Don't worry," she soothed. "I'll be here the whole time."

Honestly. How did he expect to marry the woman if he couldn't even talk to her?

"Beau wants to escort us to the table," she told her friend brightly. Discreetly, she pried Beau's fingers off her wrist.

Somehow she herded them both to the table, and then everything was a whirl of color and noise as the ladies flocked to their chairs. Ellie shyly introduced herself to Flora, who was beside her, and Frances who was opposite; they extended the introductions to Kate and Nancy. Ellie almost felt like she was back at the boardinghouse.

"Everyone's been just delightful," Flora confided. "I initially thought we might end up at each other's throats, but I think everyone's so glad that he's not a complete beast that they're willing to be friendly."

"And none of us chose to be in competition with each other," Frances added.

"I'm quite relieved not to be the only one," Nancy chipped in. "I spent the whole train journey imagining the worst. Like I'd arrive to find a burly monster of a man who'd beat me as soon as look at me."

"Me too!" Ellie was relieved to hear she wasn't the only one prone to imaginings. All her own awful daydreams surged up: the lonely cabin, the scary husband with big fists and unquenchable lusts.

"And I thought for certain I'd be all alone in the middle of nowhere with him, with no protection," Nancy said, as though she'd plucked Ellie's thoughts from the air.

Judging by the nodding and sighing, they'd all felt the same.

Ellie felt Beau's elbow jabbing at her.

"I'm busy," she whispered. He was interrupting Frances, who was describing her darkest fears, which were better than any gothic novel.

"*Help*," he whispered fiercely.

Ellie plastered a smile on her face and passed Beau her bread roll. "Of course you can have it," she said, as though he'd asked for it.

He frowned at it. "I've got my own."

"I'm trying to be discreet," she whispered, dropping the roll on his plate. "This way they'll think you only wanted to ask me for my bread."

"Why do we need to be discreet? You're supposed to be helping me. That's why you're here. And I've got my own bread."

Yes, but she was painfully aware that everyone was casting curious glances and eavesdropping madly. She didn't want anyone to think she was after Beau for herself. She tried to use her eyes to convey that fact to Beau.

He looked exasperated. "You look like you're having some kind of attack. I just want help. Tell me what I should say."

She rolled her eyes and stole her bread back. "Start by giving her a compliment," she suggested as she reached for the butter.

He had that panicked look again.

"You do know what a compliment is?"

"Of course I know what a damn compliment is."

Rigby and Mrs. Champion chose that moment to start serving the table. The chatter rose as the girls exclaimed over the platters of roast beef and potatoes. Ellie's stomach rumbled as her gaze followed the food.

"*Why* do I have to compliment her?"

Ellie reluctantly tore her gaze from the food. "You just do. It's called courting." Ellie was painfully aware that Diana was sitting there on his other side, being ignored. "Go on." She elbowed him.

"I don't know what to say," he said through gritted teeth. "That's why I asked you in the first place," he reminded her.

Honestly. "Well, practice complimenting me first," Ellie suggested. "It will get the nerves out of your system."

Beau looked her up and down. He seemed at a loss.

"Hurry up or I'll be offended." Ellie bit into her bread. Oh, it was good. Much better than anything on Mrs. Tasker's table.

"I helped make these," Junebug told the table proudly. "If there's one thing brothers have given me practice at, it's baking bread."

The roll was fresh baked and fluffy and the creamy butter just melted in Ellie's mouth.

"Stop that," Beau told her.

"Stop what?"

"That face. It ain't decent."

"Is that your idea of a compliment?" Ellie eyed his plate. "Do you want your bread?"

He dropped his roll on her plate. "Have it. I've had a pained lifetime of Junebug's bread; although she's a sight better since Pip taught her a thing or two. Now, come on, help me."

"You seriously can't think of a compliment to give me?"

"You look a lot cleaner."

"That's not a compliment," she said dryly as she buttered her second roll.

"What? You'd rather I said you were still dirty?"

"Compliment a woman on her hair. Her ribbons."

"Diana ain't wearing any ribbons."

Honestly. She could see flashes of Junebug in him sometimes. "Compliment her eyes then."

"How do you compliment eyes? They're eyes."

"I thought Junebug said you knew how to be charming?"

"What would she know, she grew up on a mountain with a bunch of backwoodsmen."

Fair point.

"Try complimenting *my* eyes," she suggested. "Go on. Take a look. I'm sure you can think of something."

"Right." He examined her eyes.

Ellie tingled as he stared deep into her eyes. Oh. It was like her stomach was falling slowly through the center of her. He was being a little too thorough, though, she thought as he kept staring. People were noticing. She cleared her throat, and he jerked, remembering where he was.

"You have the eyes of a confused badger," he blurted, sounding surly.

Ellie pressed her lips together, refusing to give him the satisfaction of laughing. "How romantic."

He made a despairing noise.

"You'll win her in no time with compliments like that," Ellie said sarcastically, turning her back on him.

She heard him curse under his breath as he turned to Diana. Ellie piled her plate with beef, potatoes, pumpkin and green beans and poured gravy over the mountain of food. Her stomach was pinching violently, and her mouth was watering. She'd never seen so much food in her life—and it smelled so good. Mrs. Tasker never had generous portions—she said she had budgets to keep—and Ellie felt like she'd been hungry for *years*.

Vaguely, as she ate, she heard Beau telling Diana that her hair was *nice*.

Ellie grinned. It was no confused badger, but it would do.

Seven

Beau had to give it to his sister. She'd found some disconcertingly high-quality women. In any other circumstance he would have enjoyed getting to know them. A lot. But with Diana watching, it was torturous.

As he drank coffee in the kitchen while Miss Mabel from Wisconsin demonstrated her apple pie recipe, he was painfully aware of Diana sitting at the table behind him with her needlework. She was pretending to be absorbed, but he knew she was eavesdropping madly. Ellie was with her, as always, only she didn't hide the fact she was watching him like a hawk. Her book wasn't even open in front of her.

"Usually I use green apples," Mabel said brightly, dragging his attention back to the bench. "But there don't seem to be any in the whole of Bitterroot." Her accent was cheerfully hickish. *Dere don't seem to be any-uh.* She had sparkling hazel eyes and a dimpling smile. And she was enthusiastic in the kitchen, her knife making quick work of peeling a basket of mottled red apples. "But Mrs. Langer at the shop says these are Montana-grown and superior to any green apples from elsewhere," Mabel assured them with a laugh.

"Our brother's wife just planted a whole mess of apple trees around their house," Junebug said with satisfaction, watching hungrily as the apples were chopped. "So there'll plenty for you to be turning into pies."

Mabel gave Beau a shy look and he flushed.

"You ever baked an apple pie?" Junebug turned to ask Diana pointedly. She was annoyed they were intruding on his time with Mabel. Junebug had been militant about Beau spending equal time with each girl.

"Of course she's baked a pie," Ellie said swiftly. She also had an accent. *Of cawse she has.* He was noticing accents all the time now that he was surrounded by such a mix of pretty girls with pretty voices.

Diana gave Ellie a sharp look. "No, I can't say I have." *No I cahn't.*

"She could if she wanted to," Ellie insisted.

"But does she want to?" Junebug asked dryly.

"The only time I ever cooked a pie the bottom fell out it was so wet," Beau laughed, jumping in to rescue Diana from Ellie's bristling and Junebug's poking.

"Just as well, as it was so sour it near about made my face collapse," Junebug said. "You got more pie recipes, Mabel, other than apple?"

Mabel happily started listing her pie recipes and Beau could tell Junebug was already smitten with her. Ellie, meanwhile, looked like she might throw her book at her.

"I think I need better light to see my needlework by," Diana said cooly, rising to her feet and gliding from the room.

"Ain't you going with her?" Junebug asked Ellie. "She might stick herself with a needle or something if you ain't there to protect her."

Beau could see Ellie was torn between following her friend and staying in the kitchen to spy for her. He rolled his eyes. He'd told her a million times that he was marrying Diana and that they had nothing to worry about. But Ellie Neale was like a hound on the scent.

"Come join us," Mabel invited her. She was the friendly sort. Beau appreciated that in a woman. "There's plenty more coffee in the pot."

"Have *you* ever baked a pie?" Beau asked Ellie, snagging a mug and pouring her a coffee.

"I've read about it," she said stiffly, unable to resist joining them, the little spy.

"Well, I'd be happy to teach you," Mabel offered.

"Ain't that nice of Mabel, Beau?" Junebug said pointedly.

"It sure is."

Ellie glowered. Beau grinned at her.

Ellie was still glowering later that afternoon when Beau escorted Flora to the post office, to post a letter home to her folks. Ellie insisted on coming along and dragging Diana along too, saying it would be good to pick up stamps. Just in case.

"I'd be happy to buy stamps for you," Flora had offered. She was sweetness itself. Old Bascom hadn't been wrong about that.

"Oh no. We need to stretch our legs anyway." Ellie had hooked her arm through Diana's and kept hot on Beau's heels as he and Flora ambled the short distance to the post office.

"You got a big family, Miss Flora?" Beau felt like he had a target on his back and Ellie was steadying her weapon. He sure felt hunted. He wished she'd stop, as she was only making Diana more miserable. The poor girl didn't want to watch him serving his time with all Junebug's brides.

"I do," Flora said. Her accent was southern, with a Spanish twist. "But my sisters are all married now. My mother lives with my older sister, Maria, and I was living with my next oldest sister Ana. I helped with the children and the housework, but I got tired of being a third wheel, you know?"

Beau nodded. He did know.

"Your family seems . . . close," Flora said carefully. She glanced over her shoulder at Ellie and Diana and forced a smile. "Don't you both think?"

"Your sister is certainly getting closer by the minute," Ellie observed, pointing.

Junebug was cantering up on her fat little pony. "I wondered where you got to!"

"My family's more than just close," Beau said dryly. "They're the eye of the storm."

"Diana and Ellie, you're needed back at the hotel," Junebug ordered, inserting her pony between them and Beau.

"What on earth for?" Ellie snapped.

"Pie eating." Junebug started herding them, using the animal to force them back. "I need opinions on Mabel's baking."

"Don't you want Beau's opinion?"

"Not particularly."

"But isn't he the one . . ."

"He's busy. He can eat pie later."

"She's bossy, your sister," Flora said as they watched Junebug herd Ellie and Diana to the hotel. "But I am glad to have a moment alone with you." Diana pulled her arm away from Ellie, shot Beau a haughty, embarrassed look and strode ahead.

Beau felt guilt crash into him as he watched Diana disappear into the hotel. She didn't deserve this. He'd tried to explain, he really had. He didn't blame her for thinking less of him and he resolved to make it up to her. He'd be charming and find a way to romance himself back into her good graces . . .

Only . . .

The thing was, he couldn't relax around Diana. She was too . . . perfect. When he was around her his palms sweated, his mouth went dry, and his head emptied out of thoughts. He didn't have that problem with Mabel, or with Flora. Or with Frances, who joined him in the yard as he chopped wood for Mrs. Champion's stove. Frances kept a conversation moving at such a pace that he never had to scrabble for a thought.

"I honestly thought fall couldn't be prettier than it is in Maryland," she said, as she gathered the kindling into a stack by the door for him. *Merrilin,* she said, her accent blurring the word. She was industrious, he noted approvingly. Not like his sister, who was supposed to be gathering eggs in Mrs. Champion's chicken coop, but who was actually yawing away to Thunderhead Bill while he stuffed his pipe on the back porch and filled Junebug's head with nonsense about gunslingers and high noon shootouts.

"But Montana gives home a run for its money. This place is beautiful," Frances chattered. "I love fall, don't you?"

She kind of looked like fall embodied, Beau thought as he paused in his chopping to wipe the sweat from his brow. She had earth brown hair and lively reddish brown eyes and was in an autumnal sprigged orange dress. Against the backdrop of the fall woods at the end of the yard, she made a charming picture.

"I don't know that many people would wax so lyrical about old Bitterroot," Beau laughed. "I've heard it called a mudhole and a wild nowhere, but never beautiful before."

"Oh, I like things wild." And then she gave him a look that made his toes just about curl.

She wasn't the only one to give his toes a curl neither. Nancy also just about curled them into knots when he helped her haul water for her bath. It was the silky robe she slung over the back of the chair in the washroom that started it. It was a shiny slip of a thing, in bright springtime colors. It didn't look big enough to cover a body, which got his mind whirling. And then she'd gone and poured a heady fragrance into the tub as he emptied a pail of hot water into it and the steaming perfume of musky flowers made him lightheaded in the extreme.

"Whoops," she'd giggled. "I might have added a bit much." Her Irish lilt was as heady as the fragrance. Nancy was a lush blonde with a rosebud mouth and a captivating laugh in her voice. The thought of her sitting in that bath, in all those perfumed bubbles, made Beau a little unsteady. He'd beat a quick retreat, her laughter following him.

The problem was that there was nowhere to go to restore his equilibrium. Even when he headed for the stable, he ran smack bang into a discombobulating woman. Kate Burrell was reclining on a hay bale in a shaft of dusty sunlight, reading a book. Worst of all, she'd pulled her boots and stockings off and her bare feet and ankles were stretched out into the sunshine that fell through the open door, the first thing he saw when he blundered in.

"Oh, I'm sorry," he blurted, halting. He averted his eyes. For a moment anyway. But she didn't seem bothered by his fluster.

She sat up and closed her book, keeping her place with her finger. "That's okay, I was slogging through a boring bit. I'm quite glad to be interrupted." Gracefully, she pulled her feet beneath her skirts and crossed her legs. She did it calmly and subtly and he appreciated it. Kate had a knack for managing situations to keep people comfortable, he'd noticed. She'd steered conversations at dinner the night before, keeping everything genial and smooth.

And yet she was forthright too.

Beau was also appreciative of her, uh, symmetry.

"I know I'm supposed to like Virgil, but really I find him tedious. One must keep up one's Latin, though."

"Must one?" Beau smiled at her heavy resignation.

"If one expects to teach in a decent school, yes, one does," she told him. Then she smiled too. "Although I was hoping those days were behind me when I answered your ad. I mean, Junebug's ad."

Beau blanched. "Sorry about that."

"Your sister does strike me as a girl who needs some schooling herself," Kate said, reaching for her stockings.

Hurriedly, Beau busied himself feeding his horse, pulling his gaze away from the flash of bare skin as her feet emerged from under her skirts. "No, we ain't got any schools in these parts."

"But there are all those Langer kids. And more over at the mining settlements, I'm told?"

"We only just got a butcher and a preacher. Give us time and we might get a schoolteacher too."

"We? You have a butcher and a preacher up in Buck's Creek?"

"No," Beau admitted. "I meant Bitterroot. We only got a trading post and a smithy up there. And no kids anymore except Junebug." He could hear the rustle of her skirts as she pulled her stockings on. It made him antsy. "I guess I say 'we' because Buck's Creek is kinda remote, and this is our nearest town, even though we're four hours uphill."

"Remote sounds good to me. You can turn around now. I've got my boots on." She sounded amused. "I've spent years in the midst of people, mostly children. The idea of some peace and quiet is mighty appealing."

Beau could picture Kate in Buck's Creek. She'd fit right in with her practicality and her forthrightness. And her diplomacy would sure come in handy. She was a distracting looking woman too. Copiously so.

"So, which one do you like?" Junebug asked, bailing him up when he went into Mrs. Champion's cottage to wash up. She followed him into his room.

"Diana," he said shortly. But he did wonder how he'd feel if he'd met them all before he'd written to Diana.

But he *had* written to Diana. He had the stack of letters in his bag to prove it. Letters that were so well-read they were smudgy. And those letters had turned his head something fierce. If it was possible to fall in love via correspondence, then that's what he'd done. And the woman in the flesh was prettier than a dream.

He made sure to seek her out as soon as he'd washed up for dinner, feeling uneasy and queasy with guilt. Beau was determined to make sure they could have some alone time. So they could talk the way they had in all those letters.

"You seem to have had a busy day," Diana said flatly, when he knocked on her door to escort her down to dinner. He'd stolen one of the dried flower arrangements from the dining room to offer her.

"Well, this is the highlight of it," he told her, holding out the flowers.

She stared at him but said nothing.

He sighed. "Diana, I'm sorry. I know this is a right horrible situation for you. But please know it ain't no picnic for me neither. If it were up to me . . ."

"It *is* up to you." Her blue eyes met his. His palms started sweating and the words dried up. One of her elegant eyebrows rose archly. He wished he could think of a single thing to say to that.

Luckily Ellie came along before the silence could suffocate him.

"Flowers!" she exclaimed, sounding relieved. "He brought you flowers. Isn't that wonderful, Diana?"

"Wonderful." But Diana didn't sound half as pleased as Ellie did, and Beau couldn't blame her.

"I was hoping you might do me the pleasure of sitting with me at dinner again," he blurted. He gave Diana a nervous smile. "I asked Rigby to set us a table of our own. Just the two of us. So, we can, uh, get to know each other a little better." Although, oh God, it meant he'd have to talk to her. And he was proving bad at it.

She loosened at mention of a private dinner. He saw it happen. The eyebrow lowered and her jaw unclenched. There was even a ghost of a smile as she took the dried flowers from him. "That sounds lovely."

Beau shot Ellie a panicked look. She gave him an encouraging smile and shooed them downstairs. As he escorted Diana into the dining room, which had been reconfigured tonight into smaller tables, he tried to remember how to converse. The sight of all those pretty girls in their finery, watching him closely as he pulled out Diana's chair for her, made him feel like a rabbit in a fox den.

Ellie mouthed the word *compliments* at him.

He swallowed hard and sat down.

"I have to confess something," Diana told him softly as she unfurled her napkin across her lap. "I'm not the pie baking sort."

Beau exhaled. Thank goodness she was starting things off. "That's okay. It's not high on my list of priorities in a wife."

That pleased her. Her blue eyes gave a little twinkle. "It seems important to your sister."

"It does. But Morgan's wife bakes just fine, so there's no need to worry yourself about Junebug's stomach." He could do this. He could talk to her.

"Copious and symmetrical attractions *were* high on your list, though," Diana said slowly. "And there are plenty of those in this room."

Over Diana's shoulder, Ellie leaned sideways to catch his attention. She was sitting alone. *Comp-li-ment her,* she mouthed dramatically.

"Uh, not that compare to yours. You've got more attractions than all the rest combined," he told Diana baldly. He winced and glanced at Ellie, but she was no help at all. Rigby had delivered her food, and she was staring at it exultantly. She liked eating as much as Junebug liked pies.

Diana followed his gaze, turning to find Ellie alone at her table. "Oh, El," she sighed. "Do you mind if she joins us?" she asked Beau. She seemed pained. "I hate to see her alone. I feel bad enough that she'll be alone after we . . . I mean . . . if . . ." She cleared her throat.

"I don't mind." Beau jumped to his feet, a gush of relief washing over him. He tried not to think about why that was.

It was unsettling to be averse to being alone with your own bride-to-be. It was just nerves, he reassured himself. And nerves meant you had feelings for a girl, didn't they? Which was a *good sign*.

He couldn't deny he relaxed as soon as they settled Ellie between them. And he thought Diana did too.

But maybe that was just his imagination.

Eight

"It's the brother, the big one!" Frances was leaning over the porch rail, staring down the muddy street. There was a commotion as the others joined her. "And there's someone else with him."

"His wife, probably," Ellie said absently. "They're supposed to bring Beau's things down today." She hadn't moved from the rocking chair, where she was absorbed in her copy of *Daisy Miller*. She was just up to the part where Daisy and Winterbourne meet unexpectedly in Rome and her chest was tight with anticipation. She'd read the novel three times and every time it gave her a giddy feeling.

"No, the wife's in the wagon with him. There's another one, on a horse."

"Ah, stop your fussing, it's only Jonah." Junebug stuck her head out of the open parlor window. She was holding one of Ellie's books, which she'd half devoured already. She'd chosen a scandalous gothic novel called *Carmilla*. Ellie could tell when Junebug was reaching the juicy bits because she'd inhale sharply. And then she'd demand Ellie tell her more about vampires and their "unnatural lusts".

Ellie was glad Kate wasn't around. She'd been very vocal when she'd spied Junebug with the book—*As a schoolteacher, I hardly think it's appropriate to her age*—but Ellie didn't really think Junebug qualified as your usual child. After all, she was sitting right here, in full view of a whorehouse.

"Ellie, go tell Beau the whole family have come to see him," Junebug ordered, going back to her book.

"You do it." Ellie had her own book to read.

"I would have thought you'd relish an opportunity to interrupt him and Kate." Junebug slid backwards through the open window and reclined on her chaise. "But if you're okay with him falling in love with someone other than Diana . . ."

"You really are a trial." Ellie got to her feet, without looking up from the book.

"Can I have that one when you're done? It looks good, judging by the fact you cain't stop. Are there more vampires in it?"

"No," Ellie said shortly. She shuffled down the porch, past the front door, heading for the dining room window.

"No, I cain't borrow it? Or no, there ain't vampires?"

"Both." Ellie paused in front of the dining room window, her hand outstretched to knock on the glass, but she was so engrossed in Daisy and Winterbourne's walk through the streets of Rome that she forgot to knock. She stood there until Daisy had met her Italian friend, her heart squeezing in her chest at Daisy's innocence and Winterbourne's deep and secret knowledge of her.

The sound of the sash window being thrown up made her jump and she blinked, startled to be on a porch in Bitterroot, Montana, and not in wintery Rome.

"What in blazes are you doing?" Beau asked her. "You've been standing there like a portent of doom for a good ten minutes."

Ellie took a moment to come back to herself. "Sorry. I was in Rome."

He shook his head. "Well, go be in Rome somewhere else. You're blocking my light."

Ellie peered in and saw Kate sitting at the table by the window, razor focused on the battered wooden chess set. Ellie's shadow fell entirely over Beau's side of the board. "Who's winning?" She didn't know anything about chess, but there did seem to be an awful lot more white pieces than black pieces.

"He's in check," Kate said.

"Good for him."

"Check ain't a good thing," Beau informed her sourly.

"Oh. Well, sympathies then."

"He's a decent opponent," Kate said, "but more interested in talking than playing. If he played more and talked less, he'd put up more of a fight."

"Yeah, well you didn't tell me you were some kind of chess sharp," Beau complained.

Kate gave him a sly smile. "You didn't ask."

Beau shook his head, but he was smiling. "What were you looming for, anyway?" he asked Ellie.

"Oh." She remembered. "Your family's in town." She turned. "It looks like they've hitched up at the mercantile store."

"All of them?" Beau asked. He leaned all the way out of the window.

"Shall we just call it check mate and let you go say hello?" Kate asked smoothly. "I'll have you in another move or two anyway."

"No way." Beau jerked back to attention. "If you're going to beat me, you have to earn it."

Ellie gave him a suspicious look. Was he *flirting*?

"Is that right?" Kate's crystal blue eyes glittered. "Challenge accepted."

"Who's in check now?" he drawled, moving a piece.

He was! He was flirting with Kate. Who was *not* the woman he was going to marry. Ellie glared at him.

"You're looming again," he said, sighing at Ellie, not looking up from the board.

"Have you seen Diana?" she asked him pointedly.

"She went for a walk with Nancy," Kate told her as she made her move. "Check mate."

"Goddamn, woman, you're brutal." Beau sat back in his chair and hooted. "I cain't wait to see you play Junebug."

Ellie scowled. Kate wasn't supposed to be the one to make him happy. Look at him, all relaxed and enjoying himself. Yet every time he was near Diana he clenched up.

As soon as Kate had packed up the chess set and headed off, Ellie reached through the open window and pinched him on the arm.

"Ow! What was that for?"

"You're flirting with her!"

"Who?"

"Kate!"

"No I ain't." He shook his head, giving Ellie a disgusted look. "I'm just being friendly."

"Well, stop it."

He gestured to the empty chair opposite him. "If it escaped your notice, it's stopped already. You went and chased her off."

"Why didn't you go for a walk with Diana?" Ellie asked, disgruntled. She braced her hands against the window frame and leaned into the room.

"Because I was playing chess with Kate." He rose from the table. "And because she didn't invite me. And now, if you'll excuse me, I'm going to say howdy to my family and check they brought my things."

Ellie dashed along the porch and into the hotel. She knew he'd be heading out the back door, to avoid the cluster of women on the porch. Sure enough, she caught him as he slipped out the kitchen and into the yard.

Ellie broke into a trot to catch up to him. "Where on earth are you going?" she asked, frustrated as he climbed over the low paling fence between the hotel and Mrs. Champion's cottage next door. She looked for a gate. There wasn't one.

"I'm going out this way, down the side, so I don't get caught by any more of you wives," he called over his shoulder.

"But I haven't finished talking to you."

"Well, talk while I walk." He was disappearing around the cottage.

Ellie felt like throwing her book at him again. But she lifted her skirts instead and climbed over the paling. She squealed as her underskirts caught. For the love of . . . She was snagged. She yanked at her skirts and was horrified to hear a tearing sound.

"Ellie?"

Oh no, he'd come back at the sound of her squeal. And here she was, with her underwear caught on the fence.

"Don't tell me it's a bear," he said dryly as he came back into view.

Ellie dropped her skirts like they were hot coals. Her old yellow-ish dress settled, hopefully hiding her predicament. "No. Go away." Oh God, this was mortifying. She was caught on the palings, and now she was blushing again, so hard she felt like she had severe sunburn. She surreptitiously yanked at the back of her dress, trying to free herself, and was rewarded with another tearing sound. She froze, alarmed. Oh God. What if she ripped herself indecent? She had no desire to be left unclothed in front of Beau McBride.

"You want me to go away?" Beau stood by the vegetable garden, giving her an odd look.

"Yes." She cringed as he examined her. "Now, please." She saw the exact moment that he registered her problem. His thick dark brows rose and his lips twitched.

"You know," he drawled, "it occurs to me that I should probably be *here* when my family come."

"No. You should definitely go meet them—they're bound to be expecting you."

The wretched man was *sitting down*. He grinned at her as he settled himself on the back porch of Mrs. Champion's cottage, which didn't have a railing. He leaned back on his hands, giving her his full attention. As he kicked his heels, he reminded Ellie unpleasantly of Junebug. "You wanted to talk to me anyway, didn't you?" he prompted her.

Oh, he was an ass. Look at how much he was enjoying this. Ellie's hand clenched on the book she was still carrying. She could feel the palings digging into the backs of her thighs. She wouldn't give him the satisfaction of asking for his help. She couldn't ask him to rummage around her underskirts—imagine! She lifted her chin and looked down her nose at him. "Yes. I did. I wanted to talk about you and Diana." She crossed her arms and tried to ignore the fact she was caught on the fence.

"Well, by all means, talk away," he said lazily.

Aside from her burning ears and face, Ellie thought she kept her composure admirably. "You aren't spending any time with her," she told him bluntly. She lifted her hand to shield her eyes from the sun. It was a shiny bright coin of a day, the golden fall light casting long shadows. The sky was a bluebird blue and the yellows and golds of the aspens and maples hung like bunting through the woods.

"I sat next to her at dinner last night and breakfast this morning." He wasn't kicking his heels now, at least. And his lips had stopped that infuriating twitching.

"But you don't *talk* to her."

"Sure, I do. This morning I asked her to pass the butter." He was disgruntled now. "And I told her she had clean hands."

"You what?" Ellie was appalled. "Clean *hands*?"

He shrugged. "It's true, she does. I ain't never seen hands that clean. Her nails are like those smooth little stones you find on the bottom of the creek."

"You said *that* to her?"

"Yeah," he said, bristling. "*You* were the one who told me to compliment her," he reminded her.

"'That's a lovely dress, Miss Newchurch' is a compliment. 'You have fingernails like rocks' *is not*." Ellie could see she had her work cut out with Beau McBride. He might write a lovely letter, but in person he was hopeless at courting.

"It *is* a compliment." He was stubborn about it. "Those little river stones are pretty. You just ain't seen them to know."

"Well, neither has Diana!" Oh, he was impossible.

"Well, she said thank you, so I think she understood me. She seemed happy enough when she went off for her walk."

"But she didn't go for a walk with *you*."

He went sullenly quiet.

Ellie took pity on him. She'd read that men were often humbled by great beauties—it wasn't his fault that Diana was intimidatingly beautiful. "If it will help, I can give you topics of conversation I know she enjoys?"

Beau gazed off into the vegetable patch and grunted.

Ellie supposed it was a blow to a man's pride to realize he was humbled. She'd be kind to him. "She likes being read to," she ventured. "And she very much likes afternoons out in the sun. We worked so hard back in Fall River, we hardly had any time to ourselves, let alone time outdoors. I know she'd love some lazy time in the sun—with you."

He took that on board. "She did say that in her letters."

"A picnic, perhaps?" She considered the autumnal woods. They positively sang with romance.

"Alone with her?" His dark gaze flew back to Ellie and she didn't miss the barely disguised panic.

"Of course not. That wouldn't be seemly. You'd need to be chaperoned."

He made a thoughtful noise. "We often go mushrooming at this time of year. Morgan makes us, so we've got a stockpile for winter. Maybe we could do that—all of us, I mean," he said swiftly. "A day out, with a picnic."

Ellie's head filled with visions. Oh yes, this could work. "You could carry Diana's basket and look for mushrooms together," she said. "It would be so romantic. And an excellent excuse for talking to a girl." Ellie could picture it in her mind's eye. The brassy tones of the autumnal woods, the intimacy of bending to pick mushrooms in secluded thickets . . . "You'd have to take her hand, to help her," Ellie said, growing dreamy. "And perhaps, by chance, you'd forget to let it go, and hand in hand you'd wander into a private dell . . ."

"Where I wouldn't have to do any talking," Beau said, with no small measure of satisfaction.

"Of course you would!" Ellie frowned at him.

"No, I'd just kiss her. That seems easier."

"You can't just *kiss* her."

"Why not? I might get overcome with passion. Women like passion in a man, don't they?"

Was he teasing her? There was definitely some kind of twinkle about him.

"But you're throwing away the best bits," she told him, irritated.

"Ah right, this is your anticipation thing again."

"It's not *my* anticipation thing. It's a *fact of life*. Haste is the enemy of romance, Beau, everyone knows that. You need to *savor* things. Every little catching breath, each skipping beat of your heart. Feel the thrill of walking by her side, the swirling delight of even the most incidental touch. Imagine the first time you hold her hand . . ." Ellie imagined being Diana, walking in the woods through shafts of arboreal sunlight. In her imagination Beau reached out and captured her hand. She could *feel* his long fingers tangling with hers, his warm skin against her palm. She shivered.

"What's to linger over? It's a hand." Beau's pragmatism stopped her shivers in their tracks.

Oh no, that wouldn't do. "You'll never get a wife with that attitude," she told him, feeling a surge of pity. How much the man was missing!

"If you hadn't noticed," Beau said wryly, "getting wives ain't my problem. I got more'n a man needs."

He'd never win Diana if he didn't understand this basic lesson.

"Come here," Ellie ordered. She would have gone to him, only she was stuck on this silly fence. At least until he left and she could hike her skirts up and un-snag herself.

"Why?" he asked suspiciously.

"I want to show you something."

"You come *here* then."

He knew very well she was stuck, the ass.

"Fine," she sniffed. "Don't come here. Don't get my help with Diana. Don't learn how to use to anticipation to your advantage. I'm sure Junebug will be more than happy to win the bet."

Beau gave a long-suffering sigh and slid off the lip of the porch. He had very long legs, she noticed; their graceful strength was well flattered by the tightness of his black trousers. He slouched closer and hooked his thumbs in his belt. "Well, I'm here. What did you want to show me?"

She doubted she'd ever get over the effect of his beauty, especially when he was up close like this. His eyelashes were stupidly long, like thick black paintbrushes, and his lips were, well, *luscious* was the only word she could think of. And the scent of him . . . It was a warm, spicy smell, fresh and smoky all at once.

"Ellie, you're doing it again."

"Doing what?" She tore her thoughts away from his heady scent.

"Staring into space."

"I wasn't. I was staring at you."

He quirked an eyebrow and his dark eyes did that unsettling twinkly thing again.

"Don't get all big-headed," she warned. "I was only trying to work out what you smell like."

"What I smell like?" He seemed offended. "I washed this morning. I smell clean."

"Not that kind of smell. Not a bad smell. You just . . ." She cleared her throat. She'd been going to say *smell good* but caught herself. "Smell like something I can't name."

"It's probably just Mrs. Champion's soap." He leaned closer and tilted his head back, exposing his neck, inviting her to have a sniff. "She has these fancy bars from a catalog. They're supposed to smell like an English garden. Although," he teased, "you could just be noticing my alluring natural musk."

"English garden," she blurted, pulling back as far as she could without bending backwards over the paling. She wasn't about to sniff his neck. His effect was deadly enough without getting *that* close. "That's absolutely it. An English garden . . . right after it's been fertilized."

He laughed. "Come on, show me this thing you want to show me, before my family turn up."

Ellie tucked her book under her arm. "So, holding hands—"

He groaned. "We're still on that?"

"*Yes*. You have to understand anticipation, or you won't understand courting at all."

"You know a lot about courting, do you?" He seemed dubious.

"Yes," Ellie said. She'd certainly read enough books about it. "Now shush and let me show you."

"You had men flocking all over you back home, then? Courting you senseless?"

Ellie gave him a sour look. "Don't make fun." He looked startled. "I know I'm no beauty. You were very clear about me and my ugly dress." Ellie's hands clenched into fists.

Beau's midnight-dark eyes widened and he shook his head. "I never said *you* were ugly. Just the dress." He grinned. "I stand by it too. It's the ugliest dress I've ever seen. But you're fine. Confused badger eyes and all."

Ellie took a shaky breath and unclenched her fists. She shouldn't care so much about what he thought, she told herself firmly. "Lesson one of courting: don't insult a lady's dress."

"Oh. Am I courting you, now?"

Ellie turned bright red, and her heart tripped over itself. She went hot and cold—she wasn't sure if it was with shame, or something else. She wasn't pretty enough for a man like him. But sometimes, when he looked at her . . .

Ah, he knotted her all up. Ellie shook her head, trying to dislodge her thoughts. "Of course you're not courting me," she said stiffly. "Now will you please concentrate."

Obediently, he took his thumbs out of his belt and stood there, waiting.

"Pay attention," she instructed. Her heart was still all out of beat from that courting comment. It gave another lurch when he met her gaze, and then the silly thing started racing, like she was running up a flight of stairs. His midnight eyes were curious, but also soft with . . . something. Like his scent, it teased at her, just beyond her ability to define.

"Ellie," he sighed, "you've wandered off again."

"I haven't." She yanked herself back. How did he always know? "Stop breaking the moment."

"There's a moment?"

"There would be, if you'd just hush and pay attention." She forced herself to pay attention too. She shifted uncomfortably against the palings, which were digging into her something awful. Her underskirt was all bunched up where it had caught on the sharp point of the low wooden fence. Beau was standing heart skippingly close and there was nothing she could do about it.

She had to stop being mesmerized by this man, she thought irritably, as she tried to feel behind her for where the skirt was caught. She was here to help Diana. Her dearest, beloved Diana. "Now," she told him firmly, "imagine you're in the woods."

He made a show of turning to look at the woods looming at the back of the little yard. "I'll do my best," he drawled.

She took advantage of him looking away to pull at her skirt, but it was no use. It was still caught fast. "It's a mellow fall day," she invented, putting her hand on his chest and trying to push him back a step, "with the ghost of warmth in the buttery sunlight, but the shadows are crisp with the coming chill of winter."

He seemed amused. She didn't know why, as it was a perfectly lovely description. But then he looked down at her hand on his chest and she realized he was amused by her struggle to get away from both him and the fence.

"Close your eyes," she said shortly, snapping her hand back. "It will help you imagine things better."

He sighed gustily and closed his eyes.

"You're hunting for mushrooms with Diana by your side." Ellie pictured him carrying Diana's basket for her. He'd be in these same tight black trousers and crisp shirt, with that herbal, smoky smell about him. But he'd have a better attitude. "The loamy earth is uneven beneath your feet. She stumbles. You reach for her hand . . ." As she spoke, Ellie reached for Beau's hand with her own, moving slowly, so as not to startle him. He still jumped when her fingers touched his. His eyes flew open.

She frowned at him.

He cleared his throat. "Sorry, you took me by surprise is all."

"Hush," she scolded. Then she waited pointedly until he closed his eyes again. She felt his fingers twitch under the barest touch of her own. "As you take her hand, you feel the slide of her warm skin against yours." Ellie slipped her palm against his, caressing his fingers as she intertwined their hands. She thought she heard his breath catch. She glanced up but his expression was unreadable. "All your attention is on that one small patch of skin," she whispered.

His lips parted. Ellie was hypnotized by that full lower lip, by the point of his cupid's bow. She felt like her hand was on fire.

This was better than any book.

"You feel like a leaf tumbling from the tree," she whispered, "a slow drifting spiraling through your entire body." Ellie ran her thumb across the back of his hand. She felt him tremble against her as she gave his hand a long, slow squeeze.

His eyelashes shivered against his cheeks, then his eyes slid open. Ellie felt like someone was squeezing the breath from her as he stared into her eyes. He looked drugged. Languid. But also something else, something hungry.

"Anticipation," she heard herself whisper.

"Beau! Come get your trunk, you lazy bastard!"

Ellie felt Beau flinch. He yanked his hand away and stumbled back from her. His cheeks flushed.

For a timeless, breathless moment they stared at each other. Distantly, Ellie realized someone was hammering on Mrs. Champion's front door.

"I better go before Jonah yells the house down," Beau said huskily. And then he fled.

Ellie pressed her palms to her burning cheeks. The book dropped from under her arm, thudding to the ground. Lord. She might have taught that lesson a little *too* well.

Nine

The entire town of Bitterroot turned out for the mushrooming picnic. Beau watched from Mrs. Champion's porch, astonished as people filed along the little creek and up past the clearing where Abner's saloon crouched. Every place in town had closed up shop for the day, and even the girls from the cathouse were going along, dressed in sensible clothes and boots, carrying baskets to throw their mushrooms in. Beau didn't really get it. Mushrooms were fine and all, but were they really worth a whole town's attention? Even Kit and Maddy had come down the hill for it. And Junebug was in her element, bounding along in her old denim overalls, her dog splattering through the creek after her, looking less like a fancy lady's dog and more like its usual bedraggled self.

It wasn't even a nice day, Beau thought, as Purdy Joe and Jonah ambled past. What did Jonah and Purdy need with mushrooms, damn it? Had everyone lost their wits?

It was overcast and chilly, with the smell of rain on the brisk breeze. And they all wanted to slog about the woods pulling up fungus? The sullen weather wasn't the slightest bit romantic; it was nothing like the picture Ellie had painted, that day she'd gone and hooked herself on the fence.

Beau smiled despite himself, remembering the sight of her standing pressed hard up against the fence, her skirts hanging over the palings, pretending for all she was worth that she wasn't stuck. She was the oddest girl. He didn't know how long it had taken her to extricate herself after he'd left, but the next time he'd climbed over the fence to get to the hotel, there'd been a threadbare scrap of petticoat on one of the palings. He'd unsnagged it and tucked it in his pocket. The memory of her there, pretending everything was fine, tickled him no end.

His gaze drifted to the hotel next door, where Ellie stood on the porch waiting for Diana. She gave him a little wave. She sure wore the ugliest clothes. She was in a bulky old coat that looked like it belonged to someone twice her size. Underneath, she had on that ugly gravy brown dress. The only thing uglier was the limp calico bonnet she'd tied around her head. Its floppy bow sat under her pointed chin like a droopy spider. He wondered what she'd look like in something prettier, something more like what the other girls wore. Like Diana, he thought, his attention caught by his soon-to-be bride as she stepped out onto the porch next to Ellie. Diana's coat was blue. It wasn't expensive, or brand new, but it was in far better condition that Ellie's and tailored perfectly to Diana's willowy figure. You couldn't see Ellie's figure at all in that bulky black thing.

"I've packed you a hamper for the picnic," Mrs. Champion said, bustling out the door behind Beau. "It should have something for everyone. And I put in those little pastries that you like, the kind with the strawberry preserve in the middle." She handed him the hamper, which weighed as much as a calf.

"Thank you." He watched as she piled a stack of blankets on the hamper. Goddamn. Was he supposed to haul this thing all the way up to the rise behind Abner's? What did she have in there? More of Ellie's books?

"There's fried chicken and potato salad," Mrs. Champion chattered as she followed him off the porch. "And some of my fresh sourdough."

He suppressed the urge to pull a face. Mrs. Champion's bread was infamously bad. Her pastries weren't great either, as polite as he was about them. But her chicken was worthwhile. Maybe he could just sit on a blanket and eat chicken while the rest of them scrabbled around the leaf mold for mushrooms.

Not that Ellie would let him, he thought as he hefted the hamper and went to collect her and Diana. He had a feeling she'd rip the picnic blanket out from under him and snap it at his ass to chase him off into the woods after Diana.

"Isn't this nice?" Ellie said brightly as he staggered towards them under the weight of chicken and blankets. Her cheeks were apple pink in the brisk morning air and she was grinning from ear to ear. There was a tiny little dimple tucked into the corner of her mouth, he noticed. She took a deep, bracing breath. "Don't you love fall?" Ellie stepped right past him and left him to escort his bride. He watched her go, with an increasing feeling of anxiety. Diana smiled at him as she stepped down off the porch and his stomach twisted. What was he supposed to say to her?

"Don't you look a picture," Mrs. Champion clucked at her. "Doesn't she, Beau?"

"A picture," he agreed. His heart sank as Mrs. Champion bustled off too, leaving them alone. The older woman was swift as a mountain goat, overtaking Ellie and powering up the hill like she couldn't wait to start snapping off mushrooms.

"Do you, uh, like mushrooming?" Beau asked Diana. He felt painfully awkward around her. Maybe that was just what happened when you liked someone.

"I can't say I've ever been," she told him. He liked her accent. Ellie had the same one. They had a rounded, funny way of talking, with flat sounds mixed in. *I cahn't say I've evah been.* It was kind of charming.

"Shame it's not a nicer day," he said lamely.

Diana sure liked being quiet. She walked beside him, but didn't seem to feel the urge to chatter. As they followed Ellie uphill past Abner's clearing, Beau racked his brain for something to talk about. Why was it so hard to talk to her? It hadn't been hard to *write* to her. Maybe he should just pretend he was composing a letter?

"When Junebug was little," he blurted, jumping in feet first and instigating a conversation, which was really more of a monologue, "we had the devil of a time stopping her from eating the poisonous mushrooms. She thought the amanitas would be sweet because they were all red and white like candy. Morgan threatened to lock her in the cabin during mushroom season but, in the end, Kit told her pixies lived in them and if she ate them the pixies would die. That seemed to help." He cleared his throat. "Although we did catch her officiating a lot of pixie funerals, every time she found a smashed mushroom."

Diana laughed. It was a soft, breathy sound. "My father told me we had fairies living at the bottom of our farm," Diana told him. "When we lost the farm, I left flowers for them, so they'd remember me." She sounded sad. "There weren't any fairies in Fall River."

Okay. He could do this. Look. They were talking.

Ellie had advised him to ask Diana questions about herself. So, he asked her more about her family's farm, and then about Fall River, and by the time they'd deposited the picnic hamper in a clearing with all the other hampers and blankets, he'd moved on to asking her about Ellie.

"You met her in the boardinghouse?" he asked, glancing over to where Ellie was standing with Junebug, ostensibly listening to Thunderhead Bill orate on the qualities of poisonous mushrooms and how to recognize them. Ellie had gone off into one of her dazed states, staring into the woods with a quixotic half-smile. She was liable to pick every deadly mushroom in the woods, Beau thought, given she wasn't listening to a word Bill said.

"I met Ellie on my first day," Diana said fondly. She was gazing at Ellie too and shaking her head at the blatant daydreaming. "I hated that mill so much—I *still* hate it. You can't imagine. The long hours, the way your back aches, the noise, the suffocation, the homesickness. I never would have survived without Ellie."

As they headed into the woods, Diana told him about her early years at the mill, about the backbreaking work, about sharing a room with Ellie, about Ellie reading to her through long homesick nights. It was nothing he hadn't read in her letters, but it was nice to listen to it. As she told him about Ellie's propensity to get into trouble for daydreaming at work, Beau relaxed. The warmth radiating from Diana when she spoke about her friend loosened her up and made her easier to talk to.

"You really love her," he observed.

"I do. And she loves me. We're like sisters."

Beau snorted. "Not like my sister. She probably would have smothered me with a pillow if I'd kept her awake at night."

Diana did that little breathy laugh again. "Junebug does seem a little . . . wild."

"You have no idea. The last time she ordered up a bride—"

"The *last time*?" Diana gasped. "How many times has she done this?"

"Twice before. If you count now, I guess it's eight times, if you reckon with each individual bride. Morgan wanted to send her off to boarding school after the first time," Beau admitted. "I can't imagine what he'll do when he finds out about *this*." He took in the colorful herd of brides wandering the woods. "It's probably a good thing for Junebug that military schools don't take girls."

"Oh, you *can't* send her away!" Diana was vehement. "I think she'd be more homesick than I was." Diana paused and looked up at the canopy of pines. "I've only been here a little while, and *I* can't imagine leaving this place. It's even more beautiful than you described."

Beau followed her gaze. The stands of fir and pine were deeply green against the grey skies. Their clean perfume was sharp in the air. "Ah, you haven't even seen Buck's Creek yet," he said. "And I'd hope you can't imagine leaving, since you're supposed to be marrying me."

She gave him a searching and uncertain look. "You still want to marry me? Even with all these lovely girls here?"

Beau was astonished. She hadn't struck him as the insecure sort. "I told you I did—and I ain't changed my mind. Diana, I ain't written to, or wanted anyone but you, since you answered my advertisement. And as lovely as Junebug's girls are, not one of them is as lovely as you." It was the blunt truth. The others were pretty and all, but Diana's was a rare beauty.

Diana blushed. Not fiery red, like Ellie was wont to do; Diana's blush was a slow rosy flush that highlighted her creamy complexion. Beau's confidence grew as he realized that she was as nervous as he was.

He glanced at her hand.

Okay. He could do this. He remembered standing by that fence, startled by Ellie's touch. The slow tremor that rolled through him at the brush of her fingertips, the light summery smell of her, the *anticipation* . . .

Slowly, Beau reached for Diana's hand, his fingers brushing hers lightly, just as Ellie's had brushed his. Diana's skin was smooth and cool. She didn't jump at his touch, and time didn't slow down the way it had when Ellie had touched him. Her fingers simply closed around his and she smiled, pleased. He smiled back.

Oh. This was easy.

"There's some chanterelles over this way," he said, tugging on her hand, leading her to the little billow of mushrooms by the roots of a pine.

It was nice holding hands with her. Comfortable.

Beau relaxed, grinning. This courting business might not be so bad after all. This was nothing at all like the sweaty fluster he'd felt when Ellie had taken his hand. That had been unsettling. Discomforting. Whereas this was . . . nice.

"What do you mean, Ellie is missing?"

Beau pushed his wet hair off his face so he could glare at Junebug better. She'd come bursting into Mrs. Champion's cottage with Diana while he was squeezing the water from his hair with a towel.

The rainstorm had squalled in while they were finishing their picnic, and everyone had scrambled to pack up and scamper back to shelter. It had been chaos. All Beau's brides had flown squealing back to the hotel, and Beau and Diana had laughed as they slogged through the mud with Mrs. Champion's calf of a hamper. She hadn't been prissy about the mud or the rain at all.

"I'm a farm girl," she giggled, when he commented on it.

It was just another reason why she was exactly the right wife for him. He'd escorted her into the hotel kitchen, where all the girls were shrieking and laughing and slopping about in their wet skirts. It had been a melee.

It was far too public a place to try kissing Diana goodbye—which he'd been considering the whole way down the hill. Instead, he'd had to settle for a surreptitious squeeze of her damp hand. She'd squeezed his back.

"I mean what I said. She's missing!" Junebug was pinched and defensive as she confronted Beau in Mrs. Champion's cottage, not half an hour after he'd left the hotel. "You went and lost her, damn it!"

"Shut up and tell me what happened." Beau threw the towel down and reached for his boots. They squelched as he pulled them back on.

"I cain't shut up *and* tell you what happened, idiot. It's one or the other."

"She's not at the hotel," Diana interrupted. She was still soaked through, her silvery hair plastered flat to her head, her skin milky pale. Her lips were faintly blue and she was shivering.

Beau racked his brains. Ellie had been in the kitchen with the rest of them. Hadn't she? "She must be at the hotel." Surely he'd seen her bulky coat, or that ugly brown dress in the mix? "She's probably just getting changed into something dry."

"She ain't in her room!" Junebug stomped her foot, her boot squelching. "You think I'm so dumb I wouldn't look?"

"I looked for her after you left, Beau," Diana insisted. "I wanted to tell her . . . how well today went." Her teeth were chattering. Beau wrapped his towel around her shoulders.

"You'll catch your death," he said, rubbing her arms.

"Forget about me, what about El!" Diana wailed. "She's out there in this storm."

"It ain't a storm, it's just a bit of rain."

"What if she's lost in the woods? Ellie's a town girl—she'll have no idea what to do!"

"You're *sure* she ain't in the hotel? Staring into space somewhere?" Beau's thoughts were racing. When had he last seen her? She hadn't picnicked with him and Diana—but he'd assumed she was just giving them privacy, in that matchmaker way she had. And there'd been plenty of other blankets and plenty of other hampers. She'd probably been sitting with some of the other girls.

"No one saw her come back to town," Diana said desperately. "She's out there in the woods, alone." She gripped Beau. "You have to go find her."

"Maybe she's at Martha's . . . or the mercantile . . . or somewhere other than the hotel? Everyone ran back, higgledy-piggledy." Beau turned to Junebug. "She could very well be sitting by Martha's fire with Kit and Maddy right now."

"Do you think so?" Diana breathed. Her fingers were digging painfully into Beau's arm.

"Sure. She's probably talking their ears off."

But Junebug didn't look convinced. His sister was an annoying little cat, but she was canny. If she was this worried, then it was possible they *had* left Ellie behind in the woods. And Ellie *was* prone to inattention, damn it. The fool girl was probably so deep in a daydream she didn't even realize it was raining.

"Bug, have you counted all the other girls? There's no one else missing?"

"No, all five of them are stripping off their wet clothes in the washroom of the hotel, safe and sound."

There was an image. Beau cleared his throat, trying not to imagine five pretty girls dropping their petticoats just next door.

"Right, well. You grab Rigby and those old trappers—tell them to go door to door. We best make sure she's not in town first. While they do that, you go straight to Kit and let him know what's happened."

Junebug gave him a suspicious look. "And what are you doing? Staying here and rubbing Diana dry?"

Beau glowered at her. "I'm going back to the picnic spot to see if she's still there," he growled, not appreciating the implication.

"I'll come too," Diana said quickly.

"Over my dead body," he told her bluntly. "You're frozen half to death as it is. You go get warm and dry. We'll find her and bring her to you." He squeezed her arms. "Trust me, if she's out there, I'll find her."

Diana nodded reluctantly, her blue eyes pained. "I can't believe I left her behind," she moaned.

"If you've gone and killed one of my wives, there'll be hell to pay," Junebug told Beau ominously as she and Diana slipped out the front door.

Her words hit Beau right in the gut. Jesus. What if Ellie was hurt?

He hoped Junebug would find Ellie drinking tea at Martha's, chattering away about all the romantic nonsense that filled her head. He hoped that he was about to go thrashing through the mud for nothing and that he'd return irked and cold, but secretly glad she'd been safe all along. He had a sinking feeling, though.

He remembered the sight of Ellie daydreaming as Thunderhead Bill orated about poisonous mushrooms. If she hadn't listened about the mushrooms, she wouldn't have listened to anyone telling her to stay close to the picnic camp. He could just imagine her wandering off, inattentive to the path she was taking, losing herself deeper and deeper in the thick woods. What if she'd wandered too far from the picnic spot and couldn't find her way back? What if she'd fallen? Broken an ankle? Hit her head?

Hastily, Beau grabbed a lantern and a blanket. He threw on his oil slicked coat, tucked the blanket beneath it so it would keep dry, and yanked up the hood. Outside the rain was sheeting, squalls of wind sending water scudding sideways across the road. The creek was surging, a couple of feet wide now, and the trees were thrashing their branches. It was only late afternoon, but it was dark as dusk, a watery grey evening-ish light that was indistinct and grim.

Beau tucked his chin to his chest and bent into the wind. The temperature had dropped and the rain was icy. He slogged through the mud, past Abner's ramshackle saloon, and up the hill—which was fast turning into a quagmire, with gushes of water carving runnels into the sludgy earth. Damn the woman. Why hadn't she stayed with the group? Beau leaned into his anger—it felt better than the clenching fear that grabbed his gut whenever he thought about her lost out here in the sheeting rain.

"Ellie!" He yelled her name into the spreading darkness, the wind whipping his voice away as it left his throat. "Ellie Neale!" He reached the picnic ground, which had become a slick of sucking black mud. The rain was so heavy he could barely see a foot in front of him. If he found her up here, he was going to throttle her, he decided.

His stomach churned. *Please don't let her be stranded up here in this weather. Let her be back at the hotel now. Let her be in that washroom at the hotel, climbing into a warm tub of water. Don't let her be lost in the woods.*

Damn it, he should have kept an eye on her. Or Junebug should have. *Someone* should have. The damn woman couldn't even climb a paling fence without getting into trouble.

"Ellie! You answer me this minute or I'll send Diana back on the morning train and marry someone else!"

He stopped dead. Had he heard a noise? Or had it been the wind in the pines?

"Ellie?" He worried his voice couldn't compete with the rainstorm.

There it was again. A high noise.

Beau spun on the spot, trying to work out where it had come from. He slogged towards the far edge of the clearing. The woods were dark and the lantern didn't make much headway in the dense blackness; the night was full of moody gusts and the rush of water in the rivulets and creeks as they tumbled downhill.

"Ellie!" he bellowed. "That you?"

There it came again. A mewling kind of noise. He followed it, tripping over tree roots. At least in here the thick tree canopy protected him from the heavy rain. It became just a scattering of restless drops. He pushed his hood back. "Ellie!"

Again, the noise, only clearer now. It was a voice. A girl's voice.

"Ellie!"

It was definitely a voice.

"Keep yelling!"

Her voice came plaintively through the brooding forest.

"Beau!"

As he drew near, the sounds resolved into words.

"Beau, no, no, no, no, no!"

The voice was coming from *above*. He stopped, astonished, looking up.

Was she up a *tree*?

"Ellie?" He could just make out the pale smear of her oval face in the darkness.

"I said to stay away!" she yelled down at him.

"What?" He lifted the lantern higher so he could see the shape of her against the tree. She was hugging onto the bole of the pine for dear life.

Now that he could see she was alive, he was flooded with rage. She could have goddamn killed herself! People died of exposure in the woods at this time of year.

"I said *no*!" she yelled down at him. "I told you not to come closer!"

"Are you insane?" he yelled back, approaching the bole of her tree. "What in *hell* are you doing up there? Why didn't you go back with everyone else? If you got lost, why didn't you yell?"

"I did yell!" She was certainly yelling now. "No one heard me. Now get out of here!"

Had she hit her head? She was making no sense at all.

"Oh my God," she shrieked at him. "Don't just stand there. Get out of here, before it eats you!"

"Before . . ." Beau looked around. There was nothing but trees. "Before *what* eats me?"

"The bear!"

God save him from over-imaginative women. "What damn bear? There ain't no bears." There were never any bears, no matter how many times Junebug dreamed them up. And now here he had another infuriating girl screaming bears at him.

"There *is* a bear," she screeched down at him. "It's just over that way, and all your yelling is making it angry!"

"Honey, if anyone's yelling it's you!" Beau couldn't see where she was pointing, and he didn't care. "Git your ass down here," he barked. "You've got the whole town worried sick."

There was a deep rumbling sound behind him. Beau spun on his heel. Shit.

There was a *bear* over there.

He dropped the lantern and hightailed it up the tree as the bear opened its maw and gave a complaining bellow.

"I told you," she told him, sounding annoyingly smug as he reached her branch.

He looked down in time to see the bear lumbering up to the lantern. It nudged the glass. The heat burned the sensitive skin of its nose, and its enraged roar was so loud Beau felt his ears pop.

"That's a goddamn *grizzly*," he said, astonished. He'd never seen a grizzly bear in his life.

"It's certainly rather grumpy," she observed.

Beau shifted his weight and grabbed hold of the branch above him, to steady himself. The wind made the bough sway beneath them. Ellie was pressed hard against the trunk of the pine, her arms wrapped around it in a white-knuckled embrace.

"How long have you been up here?" He watched the bear anxiously, wondering how the hell they were going to get out of this.

"Oh, since about fifteen minutes into mushrooming . . ." She sounded rueful. "I didn't even find any mushrooms."

"I guess we should be glad it ain't a black bear," Beau sighed as he watched the bear circle their tree.

"Why? Are they bigger?"

"No, they climb better."

"*Better*? You mean he might climb up here?"

"I hope not."

Now that Beau was up close to her, he could see that Ellie was slick from the rain. They were marginally shielded by the trees, but the spattering was enough to wet her thoroughly. She'd lost her coat and bonnet and her ugly brown dress was a sodden heavy mass. He noticed she was trembling from cold and shock.

He did the math. "You've been up here for more than three hours."

"I think it's four. Maybe five."

"It ain't as late as you think. It's just the rainstorm making it seem dark."

"My legs say it's been four, maybe five hours," she disagreed.

"Don't you let go of that tree," he warned her, inching closer. She seemed peaky.

"I wasn't planning on it. Only, it's a bit slippery."

Beau inched closer until he was hard behind her. He wrapped his arms around her and the tree, his arms threading under her armpits. "I've got you," he told her. "You're okay."

"That's nice. But who's got *you*?" She looked up at him. Her face was ghostly pale in the gloom.

Beau winced at the bouncing of their bough. He hoped it could hold the weight of both of them. They were a good fifteen feet up. Beneath them, the bear made a low complaining noise.

"Do they eat people?" Ellie asked anxiously. "Because it really seems to be interested in me. And I assume not for my conversation. I kept thinking it would get bored and move on but it just sat over there under that tree. Do you think it's scared of the storm? Or is it just determined to eat me when I come down? I read once that bears catch fish right from the stream with their paws. Do you think it would toss me in the air if it caught me, like I was a fish? Oh, it looks like it's sharpening its claws on the bark. That can't be a good sign, can it? You don't think it's going to climb? How much do you think it weighs? I can't imagine something that big climbing."

Well, her ordeal certainly hadn't blunted her tongue. "What'd you do, pick the bear's personal tree to climb?" He sighed. The animal was definitely settling in.

"I was with Flora and Nancy and we were looking for mushrooms—red ones?"

"No," he said shortly. "Not red ones. They're poisonous."

"Hmmm. Maybe we *weren't* looking for red ones, then."

"Definitely not."

"Anyway, I started thinking about mushrooms and how odd they are and then I got to thinking about the mushroom in *Alice's Adventures in Wonderland*—"

"*Alice's Adventures in What-land?*"

"Oh, you haven't read it? It's delightful. It's about this little girl named Alice, and this white rabbit who's always running late—"

"Why don't you tell me the plot of the rabbit book when we're safely down and back at the hotel," he suggested. He tightened his grip on her as their bough dipped in the gusting wind. The rain was strengthening, bitter veils billowing around them, and his hands were stiffening from the cold.

There was another muffled growl. Beau glanced down.

"That wasn't the bear, that was my stomach," she admitted. "I missed the picnic. And I didn't eat breakfast because I was looking forward to the picnic so much. I've only ever been on one picnic before; the mill ran one for Easter after church once.

They made it compulsory to attend but the food wasn't very good. A lot of soggy sandwiches. I don't like sandwiches much at the best of times, do you? But that could be because I've never really had a good one."

"Who on earth did you talk to before I got here?" Beau rested his forehead against the back of her head, trying to work out how to get them down from the tree before the wind blew them all the way to Wyoming. Her braids were wet against his skin. Her hair smelled nice. Like rain on a flower bed.

There was a flicker of lightning and then the distant bass crack of thunder.

Beau groaned. That's all they needed.

"You didn't bring any food, did you?" Ellie asked him. She wriggled every time she looked up at him and the sensation of it was alarming. In many different ways.

"I cain't say packing food was top of my mind when I came belting into the woods to rescue you."

"Shame, because I'm hungry enough to eat a bear."

The bear growled.

"Sorry," Ellie called down to it.

"Stop annoying it."

"It's possible it *likes* my company. Maybe that's why it's still here."

"Stop talking to it, then."

Lightning chased the woods fulgid white. A few heartbeats later an ear-splitting crack rang out. Ellie moaned as fire blazed in the distance.

Beau swore. "We have to get out of this tree. Away from *all* the trees," he told her, striving to sound calmer than he felt. "That lightning means business."

The lightning was forking directly overhead now, and the bear was pacing and growling below. There was another earth-rumbling crack. Ellie screamed and jumped.

"Stop!" Beau gasped. "Or you'll send us both tumbling." He held her tighter. The feel of her in his arms gave him that flustery feeling again.

Crack.

The thunder was so loud it felt like it was *inside* of him.

It came hard and fast: *crack crack crack*.

Terrified, the bear bellowed and took off, crashing through the undergrowth in its panic.

"Do you think it's okay?" Ellie wailed.

"You're worried about *the bear*?"

"The poor thing."

Beau was more worried about them than the bear. "Come on," he said, gently extricating himself from her. "Now the bear's run off, let's get out of here before we get struck by lightning." He inched backwards, looking down. Hell, they were a long way up, and all the boughs were thrashing about in the storm. "How did you get up here anyway?" he asked, abruptly. He couldn't imagine her scaling the tree in those skirts.

"I don't know. The bear roared at me and the next thing I knew I was up here. Like my body had a mind of its own and knew just what to do."

"Do you think your mind-of-its-own body can find its way down again?"

She was still rigidly hugging the bole of the tree. "I'm not sure I can even let go of this trunk." She cleared her throat. "Maybe you should just leave me here to meet my fate. Do you think death by lightning is painless?"

She was impossible. "I doubt it," he snapped. Goddamn it. He considered his options for getting her down. They were all terrible.

"Do you think I'd survive jumping for it?"

"No. Don't you dare."

"I suppose it's kind of romantic to die trapped in the embrace of a tree in a lightning storm . . ."

"Suppose again. It's just pointless and stupid."

"You lack romance," she informed him.

"I'm perfectly romantic in the right situation. This ain't the right situation at all." He tugged at her. "Come on."

Ellie tried to inch herself back from the trunk, along the branch, but her feet got caught in the sodden hem of her gown and she almost sent them flying. She screeched and pressed back against the tree.

Beau clawed at her to keep her stable and tried to calm his heart, which had seized up at the sight of her stumbling. The woman was going to kill them both trying to climb down in that heavy gown.

Well, she wasn't staying up here. Skirts be damned.

Beau ran his fingers up her back, feeling for buttons.

"Hey!" she protested, when he began unbuttoning her. "This isn't romantic *or* the right situation, Beau!"

"I'm not keen to see you killed by your own dress."

"Well, I'm not keen to die in my underwear!"

"How about *not* dying in your underwear?" Once it was unbuttoned, Beau pulled the dress down over her shoulders. Her underwear was just as ugly as her dress, he noted, when the lightning flared the woods bright as day. It was homespun and yellowing, patched to within an inch of its life.

"Hey! Be careful. This is my best dress."

Beau struggled to keep his balance as he lowered the dress over her hips and it fell to her feet. "You can get a new one. But let's be clear, this isn't any kind of best dress. It's categorically the worst dress there ever was. Lift your foot. Now the other foot." The ugly dress went plummeting to the ground, where it landed with a wet slapping noise.

Beau put his hands on her hips, which were now clad only in pantaloons. "You have two choices. You can either follow me yourself, or you can get on my back, and I'll try and get us both down."

"Oh no. You couldn't. I'd end up killing us both. I'd much rather sacrifice myself and have you live. Tell everyone I died bravely." She looked down. "Lie if you have to."

"You really are the most—"

"—selfless person?"

"—infuriating woman."

"I'm not getting on your back." She straightened her shoulders but still didn't let go of the tree trunk. "I'll try and follow you." She was shivering hard now from the wet and the cold. Her undergarments were sticking to her like wet paper. Beau tried not to get distracted by it.

"You sure you can do it?" He tore his gaze away from her body. She had finely shaped limbs and small, perky breasts. Her legs were lithe and perfect.

"No, I'm not sure I can do it at all. But I'm really hungry and there's no food up here."

"Keep one hand on a branch at all times," he instructed her. "Watch me." He lowered himself slowly and reached with his feet for the branch below.

Beau was gratified to learn she was a quick study. She managed to get herself most of the way down, only giving him two or three heart attacks on the way. And when she finally slipped and fell, knocking him out of his branch on the way, they were close enough to the ground not to break anything. They went smacking into the mud, Beau first, and Ellie astride him.

"I did it!" Her relief was loud in his ear.

"Almost," he agreed, spitting out a mouthful of mud.

Good God, the way she slid against him in the slick mud was discombobulating. Those lithe and perfect legs had straddled him and she was pressing against him in places that were . . . waking up.

"Ah, you're not hurt?" He took her hips in his hands and tried to shift her away from his crotch. But she didn't shift. If anything, she pressed into him harder.

"No, I'm fine!" She beamed at him. "You saved me."

Saved wasn't the word for it, he thought dumbly, feeling a burst of pleasure as she rubbed against him. There was nothing of salvation about this situation.

Lightning speared and there was a crack of angry thunder.

"We better go," Beau said, pushing aside the spike of regret that stabbed him at the thought. He was enjoying the pressure of her against him entirely too much.

"Do you think we should see if the bear is okay?" Ellie asked, her arms wrapping around his neck as he jostled her when he tried to sit up.

Her breasts were pressing into his chest now. He could feel the firm spread of them and the jut of her cold nipples. It was untenable. But also kind of irresistible . . .

"Sure. We'll see if the bear is okay. Then we can eat all the red mushrooms we can find." Beau pushed her gently off him. She landed with a soft slap in the mud.

It should have helped, but it didn't. Because now he was looking at her exposed body through the mud-splattered transparent linen. She was filthy. And it was shockingly arousing. For a blazing second he imagined cleaning the mud off her, inch by inch . . .

"We have to go," he growled. *"Now."*

Ten

Fate was trying to kill her. It was because of her disloyal thoughts about Beau McBride. Ellie watched as a ferocious multi-pronged fork of lightning sparked overhead, sure it was going to spike her right through the head. The rain lashed at them like whips and the wind had reached gale force proportions. She clung to Beau as he half carried, half dragged her down the hill. Poisonous mushrooms, bears, storms—it was all because of those dreams she had about him, the ones where he was greeting her at the train station and there was no Diana, no Junebug, no anything but the two of them.

Just last night she'd had one where they'd been *on* the train, sprawled on one of those sprung benches. She'd been kissing his neck, which smelled of that summery soap and *him,* and she'd let her hands wander all over him, just like they itched to do. She'd all but climbed in to his lap, just like she'd done back there in the mud. Oh, the hardness of him between her legs, pressing into her . . . Her cheeks burned like coals. When she woke from dreams of Beau her whole body was one long ache. Just as it was now. It was a twisty writhing feeling that drove her mad.

Desire. She'd read about it before, but she'd never felt it. At least not like *this*.

An indecent train dream didn't warrant death by lightning. It was the dreams she had when he got her *home* from the train station, dreams that involved all kinds of kissing and touching and whispering and sliding and *oh my God* when she woke up from those dreams, tangled in her blankets, she was as high strung as a cat in a room full of dogs . . . *Those* dreams warranted divine punishment. They were *sinful*.

But even worse—much, much worse—was sitting astride Beau McBride in her underwear in *real life*. And *enjoying it*.

She was a horrible person. Beau McBride didn't belong to her, yet she was having fantasies about him that were indecent at best and downright carnal at worst. And now here she was in her underwear, which was so wet it was transparent. And was she covering her modesty? No, she had her arms wrapped around *him*!

Crack. Another tree went up like a roman candle.

Beau veered off the sloppy hill towards a cabin in a clearing. "We ain't going to make it to the hotel in this. We're liable to get fried. Abner's saloon will have to do." He threw open the cabin door without even knocking. "Abner!" he shouted.

But the cabin was dark, cold and completely empty.

"Where the hell is Abner?" Beau dropped her and scrabbled around in the dark.

Ellie stood there dripping.

"Goddamn it. He's probably cozying up with all the women at the hotel, playing the fool."

A sheet of lightning lit the cabin through the open door, just long enough for him to find a candle. He looked at it, as though wondering what to do with it. Then it went dark again. They couldn't die here, Ellie thought wildly. If they got struck by lightning, Diana would be all alone in the world. Widowed before she was even wed and deprived of her dearest friend. But at least she'd never know that dearest friend had carnal thoughts about her fiancé . . .

As Ellie listened to Beau scrabbling around in the dark, swearing under his breath as he looked for something to light the candle with, Ellie gave herself over to a sorrowful image of Diana, clad in mournful black, standing by their graves. They'd be buried in the picnic clearing, of course, and every year Diana would return, a heartbroken pilgrim, to lay flowers by their wooden crosses. She'd remain unwed until her dying day, her heart buried in the clearing with the love of her life, and her dearest friend. Ellie's imagination ran so wild that she almost brought herself to tears, but she was so cold, and shivering took precedence over weeping. It was a very affecting image, in any case.

The next crash of lightning gave Beau enough clarity to light the candle.

"You're half frozen," he told her impatiently. "We've got to warm you up."

Ellie could barely feel her hands, they were so cold. Oh lord. She was closed up in the cabin with him. Alone. In the dark. Worse than the dark, in intimate, barely-there candlelight. And she was practically naked.

But at least it wasn't a train?

Beau put the candle on the rickety-looking bar. Now that the cabin was lit by the soft glow of the single candle, his gaze snagged on Ellie. The air in the cabin seemed to get thick and hard to breathe as his eyes swept over her. She was covered in gooseflesh and her nipples were hard from the cold. Aware that her linens were sticking to her like a second skin, Ellie covered herself with her hands.

Beau ripped open his oilskin coat, sending droplets of water flying, and shook out a blanket. "Here." He held it out. He didn't seem to want to get closer. He tossed it to her. "I brought it for you."

Gratefully, Ellie wrapped it around herself.

"We need a fire." He made himself busy. "Go look behind the

bar and get us a couple of shots of whiskey—that should help warm you up."

Ellie shuffled behind the bar. His oilskin coat had done an admirable job of keeping him dry, she thought. His shirt didn't cling to him at all. Which was a shame.

See? She was doomed. She had the thoughts of a harlot.

The little cabin was redolent of tobacco, wet pine and stale booze. It was poorly built and the wind hissed and whistled through the uncaulked board walls. It was so cold Ellie could see her breath in the air. Now that she was out of the rain, she could feel how cold she really was. It was like she'd swallowed an iceberg; her core felt completely frozen.

Her fingers were clumsy and knocked the stack of little shot glasses over.

"You okay?" Beau asked, looking up from the fireplace.

She nodded, too cold to actually speak. Her teeth were chattering beyond her control.

"Jesus, you look blue." He hurried to build the fire and get it lit. "Get that whiskey into you, fast."

Ellie grabbed the first bottle she found and poured two shots. She spilled half of the glass she slid onto the bar for him. She had to use both hands to lift her own glass to her mouth, so she didn't send it cascading down the front of her dry blanket.

"Down the whole thing," he ordered. "Don't be taking any prissy lady sips."

She'd never had whiskey before. It was foul. She gasped and sputtered and bent double. Oh, that was disgusting. But it was warm. It lit a trail of fire right through her.

"Rough, huh? Abner ain't known for the quality of his liquor." The fire leapt to life under Beau's hands, aided by the hissing wind. Without rising from his crouch, he reached out and dragged a stool closer. "Git yourself in front of the fire." He pointed at the stool. "Now."

Ellie didn't need to be told twice. She came and sat down and leaned towards the snapping flames. She held her poor frozen hands out to defrost them.

"Your fingertips look pretty blue," Beau noted. He reached out and took her hands in his, rubbing them vigorously. It didn't warm her exactly, so much as knock the sense out of her. Between his hands, the fire and the whiskey, she wasn't sure she could be sensible.

She was only aware that she was staring at him when he cleared his throat and dropped his hands from hers.

"I'm going to find the good whiskey and get you some dry clothes. Hopefully Abner has something clean. Or at least clean*ish*."

Beau disappeared into a little room out the back and Ellie drew a shaky breath. Okay. She was just in shock from her ordeals, and now a little drunk on whiskey. For once, she had to keep her imagination at bay. He was *Diana's*. And she wasn't Diana.

"Well, it ain't much, but it'll keep you warm." Beau emerged holding a pair of long underwear and a red and black flannel shirt. "I'll stay back there while you change by the fire." He dropped the clothes on a stool nearby. It seemed odd to be so reticent, given he'd been rubbing her hands a minute ago.

He backed away and then she heard the exaggerated sound of him moving around the back room of the cabin, out of sight. He was trying to reassure her that she had privacy, she supposed, but it only heightened her awareness of him. Slowly, Ellie stood and unwrapped the blanket. She'd lived most of her life around other girls, changing in full view of other people, but she'd never felt as naked as she did now, peeling off her underwear all alone in this little room. She put her wet boots and stockings in front of the fire and unbuttoned her chemise, her fingers clumsy. She slid it off, enjoying the warmth of the fire on her bare skin. Her nipples were still hard, but now with more than just cold. It was delicious to be naked like this, with him in the other room.

She'd never known she had such wanton capabilities, she thought, as she divested herself of her bloomers. She took a moment to let the fire warm her and then she reached for the long underwear. It wasn't a full body suit, just a pair of oft-laundered red flannel leggings that hung soft and loose on her. She pulled the shirt on, glad to find it was clean and smelled of lye soap and river water. Luckily it was big, covering her hips and buttocks easily. She hung her wet underwear over a couple of stools, but she didn't have much hope of wearing any of it again, even if it dried. It was torn and covered in streaks of black mud.

By the time she'd wrapped herself back in the blanket, she was no longer shivering.

"I'm decent," she called out to Beau, wincing as her voice did a weird high cracking thing. She concentrated on squeezing the rainwater out of her braids, so she wouldn't have to look him in the eye.

"I found the good stuff," Beau announced, emerging from the back room with a bottle of whiskey, looking flushed and awkward. He snagged their shot glasses off the bar and joined her by the fire.

Outside the storm had intensified, if such a thing was possible. The wind screamed through the cracks and knotholes in the walls, sending the flames leaping and the shadows jumping. The rain sounded like an avalanche of stones on the roof and the thunder cracked overhead so hard the oilcloth shivered in the windows.

"I reckon we're stuck here for a while," he sighed. "I hope Kit and the others didn't head out into the woods looking for you too."

Ellie's mind swam with awful visions. "You don't think they'll hurt the bear, do you? I mean, it didn't hurt me. It was only being its bear self."

"I'd think you might be more worried the bear would hurt my brother. Especially since he's out there looking for *you*, in a storm."

"You don't know that," she protested, as she watched him fill their glasses. "Maybe he's smarter than you and knew to stay inside during a storm."

"I was *rescuing* you." He handed her a glass and their fingers brushed. Ellie felt it like she'd thrust her hand into the fire.

"A sane person would be thanking me right now," he complained, "not insulting me and my family, accusing us of imbecility and potential bear abuse."

Ellie sniffed suspiciously at the glass.

"It shouldn't taste like kerosene this time. It's better than the last one." He put the bottle and glass on the mantle and shrugged out of his coat. He hung it on a bar stool. Then he rolled up his damp sleeves and sat down to pull off his saturated boots. He groaned as they came off.

Ellie took an experimental sip of the new whiskey and wrinkled her nose. It was better, but it was still stronger than anything she was used to. The most she'd had before tonight was a snifter of Mrs. Tasker's sherry at Christmas and on her birthday.

Beau stripped off his sodden socks and rolled his pants up to the knee. His legs were muscular and furred with dark hair. He gave a blissful sigh as he wriggled his bluish toes in front of the fire. Ellie drank half the whiskey in her glass. She held her breath as it burned down her throat. Her stomach felt like she'd swallowed hot coals. But at least it had melted the iceberg lodged in there.

"Sorry if my feet smell," he apologized.

"I can't smell anything but this cabin right now. It's got its own perfume."

"At least its ventilated," he told her dryly, eyeing the flapping oilcloth in the window as he downed his shot. "Imagine how bad it would smell otherwise."

Ellie stretched her own feet out beside his. The fire toasted them nicely. She sipped at the whiskey and felt herself growing pleasantly warm. "I don't suppose Abner has any food lying around? I missed the whole picnic," she said regretfully. "Was it terribly fun? I imagined it must be, with all the blankets spread out like rafts on an ocean of grass."

"It's an ocean of mud right now." He refilled his glass.

"But it wasn't before it rained." She shook her head when he tried to offer her more drink. She was feeling quite lightheaded enough. "I kept imagining everyone stretched out, eating raspberry tarts and drinking cordial."

"I ate a lot of chicken," he told her, as though that should satisfy her imagination. He downed another shot.

"And did you do what I told you to—with Diana?" Ellie bit her lip. She'd spent a lot of time up that tree, listening to the bear grumble, thinking about Beau romancing Diana. "Did you take her hand?"

"Yeah," he grunted. "Only you talked it up too much. You got me nervy about it, like it was a big thing. In the end it was simple. I just reached out and took it. She smiled. That was it. We walked around, hand in hand, picking chanterelles." He shot her a dark look. "Which are *not* red and *not* poisonous."

Ellie stared at the fire, feeling an odd, unsettling sensation in her bones. She should be *happy* they'd held hands. She *was* happy. How perfectly lovely for Diana.

"I did what you said. I asked her a lot of questions about herself," he said. Then abruptly he changed the topic of conversation. "These stools are goddamn uncomfortable."

"Where are you going?" she asked as he stood up.

He just grunted.

"What kinds of questions did you ask?" she called after him as he disappeared into the back room. Her head was stuffed with visions of Beau and Diana holding hands, roaming through shafts of autumnal sunshine—even though she knew perfectly well there'd been no sunshine today. Sometimes that happened. She imagined a thing so hard it seemed more real than reality. That's what had been happening with all her dreams about Beau . . .

"I asked her *all* the questions. About the farm she lived on. About the mill. About you."

"About *me*?" Ellie squeaked. Her squeak turned into something a little more violent when she saw what he was dragging out of the back room.

It was a *bed*.

"If we're stuck here, we might as well be comfortable," he said, sounding pleased with himself. "Git out of the way."

She dragged herself and her stool out of his way as he lowered the very narrow iron bed sideways in front of the fire.

"You want me to share a *bed* with you?" She felt herself turning red.

He practically flinched. "No! Goddamn it, what do you take me for? We can use it as a sofa."

"Right. But it's a *bed*."

"Not if you sit on it like this, it ain't." He sat himself down on it, sideways. "See? It's a sofa." He was sitting at the head end. He pulled the pillow out from under him and tossed it in the middle of the bed, leaning sideways against the iron bedhead and stretching his feet back out.

It *did* look more comfortable than the stools. It had a puffy ticking mattress. Gingerly, Ellie crept over to join him. The minute she sat down at the other end of the bed, he leapt to his feet.

"You wanted food!" he blurted. "I forgot, with all your talk of hand holding."

Ellie settled in down her end of the bed . . . uh, sofa. She pulled the pillow closer and wriggled all the way up to the iron bars of the baseboard. She watched as he rummaged around the bar.

"There's peanuts?" he offered.

Her stomach rumbled so loud he laughed.

"Peanuts it is." He brought a burlap sack of them over to the bed. *Sofa*, not bed. He dropped the sack between them on the *sofa* and the peanuts rustled.

Some of the edgy tension left Ellie as she opened the sack. Lord, she was hungry. She threw the shells in the fire as she husked them.

"You make a lot of happy noises when you eat," he observed, also taking a handful.

"I love food," she admitted. "We had some hungry years when I was a kid, and then the boardinghouse was stingy with feeding us."

"We had some hungry years too," he sighed.

"You said in your letters you had a winter where you almost starved?" She prodded, desperate to learn more about him.

"Diana let you read my letters?" He sounded surprised. "You two really are close."

Yes. Yes, they were. And Beau was marrying *Diana*. Ellie was only having saucy dreams because she didn't know many men, she told herself firmly. Beau was handsome. And she had come to discover that he was also smart, and funny, and kind—it made sense she was having some teensy feelings for him. But they weren't *real* feelings. He and Diana were real. This was just . . . friendship. The kind you had with your best friend's fiancé.

"It's a bit embarrassing, you reading them," he said, rubbing his face.

"Oh no," she protested. "They were wonderful."

He winced. "They weren't. I sounded like an idiot, rambling on."

"No, they were poetic! I felt like I'd actually been to Buck's Creek," she said warmly. "And when you wrote about that winter where you ran out of food because you hadn't stocked the root cellar, I got so hungry I had to sneak into the pantry for some late-night bread and butter. Mrs. Tasker would have died if she'd known. Well, she would have denied me bread and butter for the rest of the week and *then* she'd have died."

"Your boardinghouse rationed your food?"

"Well, they gave us what we paid for, and no more." She explained how the system worked, how their pay was docked for room and board. When he poured her another glass of whiskey, she took it, even though she was aware it was loosening her already loose tongue. "I often wished I could pay more so I could eat more—but I didn't really have the money, because I had to send it to my mother and the kids."

He cocked his head. "Tell me about that."

She flushed. "Oh, you don't want to hear about that. It's depressing."

"You tell me about that, and I'll tell you about our winter of starvation."

His attention was heady. Ellie liked it entirely too much. As she told him about the tenement and her mother's curse of too many children to feed, he listened intently. Sometimes, he stared into the fire, as though seeing the pictures she painted, and sometimes he gave her a look of such compassion that her stomach twisted. When he began to tell her about the hard winter in Buck's Creek, she tried to be just as attentive in return, but sometimes when he was talking she tended to get a little distracted by watching him. She heard the sound of his husky, warm voice but didn't really register his words. The firelight edged him in shadow, cutting angles into his face. He looked more than ever like a Bourbon prince. Ellie kept picking at the peanuts and eventually she accepted another shot of whiskey. She curled up on the end of the bed—sofa—like a cat.

"So did you kiss Diana?" she asked eventually. She'd been dying to ask him all night. He'd held Diana's hand and asked her questions, but had he gone further?

"No," he said in disgust. "I was planning to, but then someone went and got herself chased up a tree by a bear and needed to be rescued."

"You didn't know that at the time," she protested.

He gave her a wry grin. "There were too many people at the hotel to go kissing her."

She gaped at him. "That's the most ridiculous thing I've ever heard."

"All Junebug's girls were there."

"You could have got her off alone if you'd wanted to."

"Hardly."

"Completely! If you really want to kiss a girl, you've got to make an effort." She shook her head at him.

"Oh, I like this. You're going to lecture me on kissing? How many times have you been kissed?"

"I've been kissed! Once. By Myron Bales, who worked as a doffer in my spinning room. He stuck his tongue in my mouth. It was quite revolting actually."

Beau almost spat out his mouthful of whiskey at that. "If you found it revolting, he wasn't doing it right."

"That's not how you kiss," she protested. "Kissing isn't about tongues, it's about lips."

He was giving her the oddest look.

"Trust me," she said, waving her empty shot glass. "I've read enough kissing books to know."

"Maybe not the right kind of kissing books."

She scoffed. "I'll show you, if you don't believe me."

"No, it's fine, I believe you." He inched away from her.

"No. You need to know. You can't be revolting Diana with your tongue!"

He snorted. "Trust me, I won't be revolting her."

"Look. Close your eyes." She put the shot glass down.

"No."

"Don't be like that," she coaxed. "It won't be revolting."

"That's not what I'm worried about."

She shuffled to the middle of the bed, rising onto her knees. "I promise you'll like it."

"Again, not what I'm worried about."

She took his stubbly cheeks between her palms, pushing his face so his lips looked like fish lips. She giggled.

"Remind me never to give you whiskey again," he managed to say through his fish lips.

"It's not the whiskey, it's my *helpful nature*. I want you to get it right."

He laughed and pushed her hands away from his face. "Honey. I don't need help on that front. Especially not from you."

Ellie felt like she'd been slapped. She went hot and cold. Oh.

She turned and stared at the fire, feeling like her stomach was full of acid. *Especially not from you*. She was making a fool of herself. Of course he didn't want her kissing him. Oh God. She *had* had too much whiskey.

"What?" Beau sounded nervous. "What did I say?"

"Nothing." Ellie pulled the rug back around herself and pulled it up over her head.

"Clearly not *nothing*."

She stayed silent. She was worried she was going to cry. Her eyes were hot and prickly.

"Ellie," he growled. "What did I say?"

"Nothing!" She rubbed at her eyes under the blanket. "Forget it. I'm sorry. I didn't mean to harass you." Her throat was all achy and she knew her voice sounded weird.

"Will you come out of there?" He pulled at the blanket.

She pulled back.

"Hey." He kept tugging.

"I get that I'm unkissable. I don't need you to tell me that."

The tugging stopped. There was a long silence. Ellie was going to cry. It was just the stress, and the drink, and the bear and all the rest of it, she told herself. She wasn't crying over *him*. Why would she? He wasn't even hers to cry over. She was just trying to *help*.

"Listen, you madwoman," he said, firmly yanking the blanket down from her head. "You're not unkissable. You are, if anything, *too* kissable." He sounded completely exasperated.

She scoffed. "Don't. I know exactly what I am." She was aware her hair was escaping from her braids as it dried, she was aware she was skinny, she was aware she didn't have plump lips or *symmetrical attractions*.

"You are goddamn *distracting* is what you are," he sighed. He rolled the blanket down, like he was unpeeling her. "You've got a way of talking me upside down and backwards." Now he took *her* face in *his* hands. "You ain't unkissable. You are entirely kissable. And if I weren't marrying Diana, I'd kiss you right this second."

For the first time in her life, Ellie was wordless. He wasn't lying. She could see it in his eyes. They were shining with all kinds of things that pulled at her like a tide.

"Since you're being helpful, though," he said, that familiar dark twinkle emerging, "I will take your kissing tutorial. I was only being cautious because of Diana."

"I want you to marry Diana," Ellie said in a small voice.

"I know." He gave her a rueful look. "But I'm a man, Ellie. Not a saint. You're a woman and you're *not* unkissable. I just thought it might be dangerous."

She nodded, dashing the tears away.

"But if we agree it doesn't mean anything . . ."

It didn't mean anything. It *couldn't*.

"Then . . . You can show me how to do it. Your way. Like they do in the books," he said kindly. He closed his eyes and leaned in.

Ellie was all messed up. She felt sober-ish, but not straight in the head. He found her kissable. *Too kissable.*

It didn't mean anything.

But he was waiting for her to kiss him.

Ellie started trembling. Oh, this *was* dangerous.

She shouldn't do this. But then, it didn't mean anything. It *didn't*. She was just a friend helping a friend.

"Am *I* unkissable now?" he asked, opening his eyes, and there was a mix of teasing and disappointment in his tone.

"I just . . . the mood went."

"What if you paint the scene for me first, and get us both in character, like you did with the hand holding?"

"Stop making fun."

"I'm not. You got me all worked up that time with your hand holding, your picture was so vivid."

Ellie bit her lip. She knew *that* was true. She'd been there.

"So go on, tell me how I went wrong. How would I get her alone and kiss her in a hotel full of people? Where are we, when she kisses me? I mean, I kiss her?"

Ellie tried to imagine the ramshackle, drafty saloon away, but she couldn't. She felt entirely, concretely present, on this narrow iron bed in this smoke and whiskey scented cabin. She was painfully aware of her body under the loose flannels, and his body, just inches away.

"Close your eyes," she begged.

He did.

"You're . . . on the stairs of the hotel," she invented. "Having a stolen moment."

"Yes," he said softly. "Go on."

"It's clandestine. Illicit."

He swayed infinitesimally towards her.

"You take her face in your hands." Softly, Ellie took his stubbly cheeks between her palms again. She wondered if he could feel how much she was trembling. His skin was warm against her palms. Scratchy, but in a pleasant way that made her stomach float and sink all at once. "And you move slowly."

"Because of *anticipation*," he agreed.

"Hush."

His lips twitched.

Ellie moved like she was underwater. She leaned closer, feeling the heat of his breath brush her mouth. He smelled so good. Like thunderstorms and peanuts and whiskey. Ellie touched his mouth with hers, in the lightest and slowest of kisses. She stayed there, barely moving for several slow heartbeats. His lips were soft. They quivered under hers.

Wait. Was he *laughing*?

"Don't be mad." The bastard followed her as she stormed to the door. "And where are you going? It's still torrential out there!"

"The thunder and lightning have stopped," she ground out. She hopped along, pulling on her boots as she went. "I can get back to the hotel now without being killed at least." Ellie had never been so furious, or so goddamn humiliated in her entire life. How *dare* he laugh at her!

"Ellie!" He blocked her way. "It's still blowing a gale."

"Get out of my way." She felt like punching him. Kicking him. Screaming in his face. "You *laughed at me*."

He was chagrined. "No. Well, yes. But not *at* you. I just laughed."

She drew herself up to her full height and gave him an imperious stare. "Get. Out. Of. My. Way."

"No."

"Fine." She glanced around. She'd go out a window then.

"Ellie!" He grabbed her by the arms and spun her around. "Stop. Let me explain."

"There's nothing to explain," she said stiffly. "I kissed you and you *laughed*."

"Well, it's just that you . . ." He cleared his throat, clearly trying not to laugh *again*. "You just sat there."

She tried to wrench herself away from his grip.

"Whoa," he soothed. "You . . . surprised me, that's all." He cleared his throat. "It was nice."

"It was *nice*?" She had to get out of here or she was going to commit violence. "Kisses aren't supposed to be *nice*," she hissed. "They're supposed to be *passionate*."

He cleared his throat again, looking suspiciously twinkly. "And that was, uh, passionate, was it?"

Oh, he was the *worst*.

Ellie headed for the window.

"Stop!" He stepped in front of her again. "Stop."

She crossed her arms and gave him the most evil stare she could muster.

"You can't leave until I have my turn," he said softly.

She narrowed her eyes.

"You showed me your book kissing, now it's my turn." He gave her a gentle look. "You can laugh at me after if it will make you feel better?"

"I'm not kissing you again."

"No. *I'll* kiss *you*."

Despite herself, Ellie felt a shiver run down her spine. "What was so funny?" she asked petulantly.

"I was just surprised," he said again. "You were so still. Like you'd drifted off mid-kiss."

"That's how you kiss," she said stubbornly.

"Well, no. That's not how *I* kiss." His hands cupped her shoulders. He drew her closer and lowered his head until their noses brushed. He stared into her eyes.

"This isn't kissing. It's staring."

"Hush. This time you close your eyes."

She sighed, but she obliged. She felt so embarrassed. So, she hadn't been kissed more than once. So, she'd learned it from books. She refused to believe she was wrong. What did he know about kissing anyway—he'd been raised in the woods.

Her eyes flew open at the first brush of his lips. He pulled her hard against his chest, and her head tilted back naturally to accommodate him. His mouth slanted across hers, firmly. His eyes were closed, his dark brows drawn together. He was intense.

Ellie got the giggles. She didn't mean to. He just looked so *serious*.

Beau pulled away, half frowning, half laughing. "What are *you* laughing at?"

She couldn't stop giggling enough to answer.

"Right. Now you're really going to get it." He was grinning as he hauled her up hard against him, lifting her feet off the floor. His mouth was on hers again, and she could feel him smiling against her lips. Ellie squealed as he spun her around; she wrapped her arms around his neck. She could feel her breasts flatten against the hard width of his chest. He backed her against the wall as the tip of his tongue flicked against her mouth.

"Ah!" She pulled away. "Not like Myron!" she giggled.

"Trust me," he said smugly. "This won't be anything like Myron."

Oh, God, his mouth was so insistent on hers. It made her toes curl inside her boots. She clung on for dear life as he moved against her, and then his tongue slid against her lips and she gasped. As her lips parted, his tongue slid into her mouth, and it was like nothing she'd ever experienced. It was certainly *nothing* like Myron. And it was far better than any of her wanton dreams.

"You can kiss me back," he whispered against her.

Ellie didn't need to be asked twice. She plunged her hands into his hair and tangled her tongue with his. She heard him groan and she felt a shiver in every secret part of herself. She felt herself losing grip on her ability to think. She was all sensation.

"Stop, stop."

His words brought her back to reality. She moaned as he pulled away. "Honey, stop." He was breathing hard.

Oh. Somehow, she'd wrapped around him, just like she'd wrapped around the tree earlier. Her legs were locked around his waist and he was cupping her buttocks with his hands.

"I'm not laughing now," he sighed, pressing his forehead to hers. "I knew this was dangerous."

Eleven

"When's it going to snow, Bill? You promised me snow." Junebug stood in the street in front of Martha's house, glowering at the sky, which was decidedly blue.

"I didn't say it was going to snow *today*." Thunderhead Bill was worse for wear after a night of drinking. He was hiding under his hat like a rodent hiding in its burrow. "I said the geese have flown and there's the sniff of snow in the air. Which is an entirely different thing from saying snow is imminent. Snow ain't a thing you can set your clock by, like old Bascom's trains."

"But I want snow for my party." Junebug stomped up the stairs of the porch and snatched his hat off his head. She wasn't interested in him sleeping through their confrontation. His grey hair sprung out like a lion's mane. "It's a *Christmas* party and Christmas ain't Christmas without snow."

"It's only November," Thunderhead Bill reminded her grumpily. "If you wanted snow you should have thrown your Christmas party at the proper time. At *Christmas*."

"You lied to me with all your talk of geese," Junebug snapped. "If you'd told me straight there'd be no snow I would have picked a different theme. Although I couldn't think of a better theme to inspire kissing."

"Now, Junebug," Roy warned her, "don't go bothering Bill when he's ill from the drink. It ain't a fair fight." Roy Duncan was sitting further down the porch, practicing his letters on a slate he'd borrowed from one of the Langer kids. Junebug wasn't partial to Roy, who tagged along with the other trappers like a stray who couldn't be shook. He was less amusing than Sour Eagle and Thunderhead Bill and he tended to be a sight more useless too. He was a scruffy, whining timewaster.

He was also currently in her bad books for teaching himself to write, because he said Junebug's public letter writing service was getting too expensive by half.

He didn't know a bargain when he saw one, because he was a cheapskate. Junebug prided herself on her reasonable rates. But she was grumpy enough today without thinking about Roy writing his own damn letters.

"What's Christmas got to do with kissing anyway? Surely there's better themes for kissing," Roy continued, too dumb to know when to shut up.

"Mistletoe," she said shortly.

"Oh. Smart."

"Ain't it! Only my dance is getting ruined by Bill's snow being tardy."

"This is the first I'm hearing of any dance," Roy said, squinting at her.

"That's because you ain't invited. Not after firing me as your letter writer."

"Well, now that ain't fair. Bill, tell her that ain't fair! I haven't been to a dance in forever."

"Dance? Who's having a dance?" Sour Eagle asked, emerging from Martha's front door with an old, much-read newspaper and a mug of hot coffee. Martha wasn't far behind, neatening her grey-streaked red hair.

"Junebug's throwing a party to distract her brother," Martha told him. She leaned against the porch rail and gave Junebug an evaluating look.

"I ain't trying to distract him. I'm trying to get him to *focus*," Junebug said in disgust. Beau was driving her insane. In the few days since the picnic, he'd been wandering about in a daze, and it certainly wasn't over one of her girls, because he was hardly spending any time with them. Or with his Miss Moonglow either. What was wrong with him?

"He should just propose and have done with it." Martha was pragmatic. "I know you want him to pick one of yours, but you can't argue with a man's . . ."—she gave a quiet cough—". . . heart."

"Oh, his heart ain't even in it," Junebug argued. "Not his heart nor any of the rest of his bits neither."

"I thought he'd be happier than a pig in mud with all these nubiles," Thunderhead Bill said gruffly.

"I know!" Junebug was seriously at her wit's end. Beau loved women. And he loved flirting. And he loved attention. So what in hell was wrong? "Do you think," she said slowly, "that it's all a bit too overwhelming? I mean, he loves women in theory . . . but he's never tested it in practice, has he?" She glanced down the street. "Except for the girls at the cathouse."

"Oh, he's not one for the cats," Thunderhead Bill said dismissively.

"What nonsense are you talking, Bill?" Junebug gave him an annoyed look. "Of course he is."

"Nope. You just think he is."

"He's always hanging about flirting with them. I've seen it."

"Exactly. You've seen it because it only happens out on the street. He don't go in. He just hangs about having a chat."

Junebug was gobsmacked. "But . . ." Her mind was whirring. Was her brother secretly *shy*? Junebug frowned. She couldn't believe it.

"He clearly doesn't want to marry Miss Diana, or he'd already be marrying her," Sour Eagle observed.

Martha gave a crackling laugh. "Is that so? Like Morgan with my granddaughter?"

"Ah, that ain't the same at all," Bill scolded her. "Beau ain't Morgan. Besides, Beau *wants* a wife. Morgan had to be convinced."

"*Does* Beau want a wife?" Sour Eagle asked mildly. He gestured down the street, to where Beau was riding off in the direction of Buck's Creek.

Junebug swore. "Where in hell is he going?"

"Home, by the looks of it."

"I swear, brothers are an unprofitable business." She smacked her hand against the porch post.

"Do you think he'll come back?" Roy scratched at his nose. "If he doesn't, can I have a crack at one of your brides?"

Junebug took the chalk out of his hand, snapped it in half, and handed it back to him.

"Don't fret, Roy," Thunderhead Bill rumbled, "Beau cain't marry all of them. Once he's chosen and these shenanigans are over, you'll have six women to practice your amative activities upon."

"You stay away from my women with your amative nonsense. I don't want no activities out of you, you old coot." Junebug loomed over him, glad to see he was heeding her. "You write your own damn letters and get your own damn women."

"How come other people can get—what was it, Bill?"

"Amative."

"How come other people can get amative with your women and I cain't?" Roy complained.

"Other people *cain't*," Junebug told him fiercely. "They're for Beau, and Beau only."

"Tell that to Purdy Joe and your brother," Roy sniffed, pointing at the mercantile store, where Purdy Joe and Jonah were leaning against the porch rail.

Junebug couldn't believe it.

The nerve of them. Jonah was flirting up a storm with *three* of her brides. Well, two and a half. Because Ellie Neale was still insisting that she wasn't in the running, on account of her friendship with Miss Moonglow. But Junebug saw how she followed Beau with her eyes and blushed whenever he was around, so she wasn't counting her out entirely. Junebug liked her more than most of the others too—she had a great collection of books and told some colorful stories about circuses. Her bear story could use some work though, Junebug thought sourly, as she jumped off Martha's porch and went to sort out Purdy Joe and her idiot youngest brother. Ellie had been skimpy on the detail about that bear, no matter how Junebug pestered her. In fact, she was skimpy about *all* the details of that night. She and Beau had come slopping in, wet from the pounding rain, both in peppery bad moods. Neither had been forthcoming about their adventures.

And now here she was, the close-mouthed bear-hogger, flirting with Jonah instead of Beau! Junebug took the mercantile steps two at a time. Mabel and Nancy were looking fresh in their pink and green dresses and bright shawls, giggling at something Purdy Joe had said. Their cheeks were rosy from the chilly winter air. Ellie, on the other hand, was in her ugly pale brownish dress with its even uglier rust-colored flowers. Even her shawl was ugly. It was amazing anyone even wanted to flirt with her, Junebug thought darkly. The woman made no effort at all. Well, Junebug wouldn't have it. Ellie would be making an effort for Junebug's Christmas dance or there'd be hell to pay.

"And you've found silver?" Ellie was asking Purdy Joe as Junebug barreled up to them.

Purdy fumbled for his pouch and Junebug rolled her eyes. She'd seen enough of Purdy Joe's little silver flakes to last a lifetime, but all three girls *oohed* and *aahed* as they bent over his open hand.

"Purdy! Jonah! Kit's looking for you," Junebug lied, elbowing her way in.

"Tell him we're busy," Jonah said, still leaning with faux nonchalance against the rail and grinning at Mabel and Nancy. Since when did he ever notice girls anyway? And why did he have to start *now*? Junebug frowned. The girls weren't here for Jonah, Purdy, Roy, or for any of these Bitterroot dolts. These women were here for Junebug's useless brother, Beau. She was paying a fortune putting them up at the hotel and she wanted her money's worth. Jonah could take his shot at the leftovers once the bet was settled.

"You don't look busy," she said, giving him a jab with her elbow. "Besides, the girls are coming with me. I need them to help me with the Christmas dance."

Jonah lit up at that. "*I'd* be happy to help."

"You're already helping. You're playing your fiddle. You'd better go practice. You don't want to embarrass yourself."

Jonah gave her a disgruntled look.

"Come on," Junebug tugged at Mabel and Nancy's arms, "we're going to see about decorations." She pulled them towards the door of the mercantile. "Ellie, you too."

"I can help with decorations," Jonah said stubbornly, and then he actually had the nerve to offer Ellie his arm to escort her inside. Purdy followed along, quieter. Like he'd taken note of Junebug's displeasure, she thought, with no small measure of satisfaction.

"I'm not sure we'll find much in here," Mabel said dubiously once Junebug had strong-armed them inside.

"Well, there ain't time to be ordering no decorations from a catalog," Junebug told them firmly. "So we'll have to make do." She considered the contents of Langer's shop. There were bags of flour and beans, and rows of pickaxes and shovels. "What do people usually decorate dances with?" she asked. "In books there's chandeliers and flowers, but that ain't really a potentiality here. Especially in late fall, when there's a dearth of flowers."

Junebug had big plans for her Christmas dance. She'd never been to a dance in her life, but she knew the kind of atmosphere it ought to have. There should be music, and golden light, and it'd be pretty and musical and romantical as all hell. She remembered Beau dancing himself around that clearing up past Buck's Creek. Her brother wanted dancing, so dancing is what he'd get.

But she needed snow. You couldn't have a Christmas dance without snow. And it would help if Beau was snowed in and couldn't get out. She'd prefer him trapped in with her girls and all the mistletoe. Junebug planned to rig the whole hotel with it. She wasn't leaving this romance business up to her idiot brother—she was taking matters into her own hands.

"Why don't you just get an excess of candles?" Nancy suggested. "If you can't have chandeliers, you can at least have a sea of candles."

"Oh, I know where the candles are." Now Purdy had come over infernally helpful. He led Jonah and Nancy and Mabel away to the candles.

Goddamn it. This was Beau's fault. He was neglecting these girls, and this was the result. They were falling for the charms of a hick like Purdy and a pup like Jonah.

"I saw Beau riding out," Ellie said with studied casualness. She was pretending to be absorbed in a row of cookpots.

It was clear Ellie Neale was dying to ask where he was off to.

"Maybe he's off looking for that bear you won't tell me about," Junebug said sourly.

Ellie flushed. "There's nothing to tell. It was just being a bear."

Junebug had been in the bride business long enough to recognize certain signs. Avoiding eye contact, blushing, evasiveness.

Actually, now that she thought about it, Beau had been downright evasive too. When she asked him about the bear he'd just said, "It was a goddamn bear, Junebug, what's to describe?" Even though he *knew* how she pined to see a bear.

Junebug examined Ellie. She'd been a total mess that night, and so had Beau. They'd both been wet and muddy and cold. Beau had said they'd taken shelter at Abner's and Ellie's dress had been ruined—which is why she was in Abner's flannels. Junebug thought it seemed odd that she'd somehow lost her underwear too, though.

"Well, I'd think if a bear ripped my dress to shreds, I'd have a story to tell," Junebug baited Ellie now. Beau had said her dress had been wrecked by mud . . .

"I'd rather not talk about it," Ellie said quickly. She was sunset red. "It was traumatic."

"Right." Junebug's mind raced. Her brother had been relaxed around Ellie before that night. And now he . . . wasn't. She examined Ellie, trying to imagine her in something other than ugly brown. She wasn't a beauty, but she was okay.

Maybe beautiful was intimidating, Junebug thought. Maybe Beau was daunted by the others? "What are you wearing to my Christmas dance?" Junebug asked abruptly.

Ellie looked startled. "What?"

"My dance. What are you wearing?" Junebug guessed the answer in advance and didn't like it.

"Um. This, I suppose." Ellie looked down at herself.

"No." Junebug exuberantly propelled Ellie to the back corner of the store.

"It's perfectly serviceable," Ellie insisted.

"It's perfectly hideous."

"It doesn't matter what I look like."

Junebug turned on her. "Of course it matters what you look like!" She'd never heard such nonsense in her life. Junebug shook her head. She'd thought Maddy and Pip had needed pep talks. *This* girl needed a pep parade. A circus even. "Hell, Ellie. Even if you ain't here to win someone, you can enjoy dressing up, cain't you?"

Ellie Neale blinked at her.

"Of course you can," Junebug answered for her. She yanked her into the corner where the rolls of fabric were stacked. "I reckon that bear did you a favor. You can replace that ugly brown thing with something nicer." Although all Junebug could see in the stacks at Langer's were denims and corduroys, twills and wools. All in dark shades. That's what happened when you lived in a town full of men, Junebug thought in disgust.

"I can't afford new fabric," Ellie told her firmly.

"Fritz!" Junebug ignored her and went looking for the shopkeeper. "Fritz! Where in hell are your dress fabrics?"

"Dress fabrics?" Fritz Langer emerged from the little office in back, his walrus moustache covered in cookie crumbs. "I don't stock dress fabrics." He pulled a catalog from a shelf. "But you can order some."

"I ain't got time for that." Junebug took Ellie in a firm grip and marched her out.

"How many candles, Junebug?" Nancy asked as they steamed past her.

"All of them." Junebug dragged Ellie out of the store.

"I'm not going in there!"

Junebug had expected this. "Neither of us are going *in* there," she soothed Ellie, as she approached the back door of the cathouse. "But we've exhausted all other possibilities."

Junebug had been to Martha, Ellen and Mrs. Champion and none of them had any fabric. There weren't many other options in Bitterroot. Except this one—because surely a house full of women would have a spare length of fabric or two?

"I'll borrow a dress off Diana."

"I don't reckon your friend likes lending her dresses, or you'd have been wearing one by now." Junebug noted Ellie's startlement.

"Of course she would," Ellie protested. "If I asked . . ."

Junebug grunted. As far as she could see, Diana was used to being the one taken care of. And Ellie was used to doing the caring. It was about time she started looking after herself instead of Diana. Especially if she had feelings for Beau.

"This is a bridge too far, Junebug!" Ellie snapped as they reached the cathouse. But Junebug noted that her gaze was riveted on the house. She was curious. Good. Because so was Junebug.

"Nah. It's just a bridge, like any other bridge." Junebug rapped sharply on the back door.

Junebug was endlessly fascinated by the whores in the cathouse. Morgan and Kit refused to let her speak to them, which she thought was dumb. What harm could *talking* do? She'd tried to get cathouse girls to sit with everyone else at the mushrooming picnic, but they sat at a discreet distance, off on their own.

"Good morning," she said brightly when the door opened, revealing a sleepy looking woman in a plain muslin dress. "Sorry to bother you. I'm Junebug McB—"

"I know who you are," the woman interrupted, slouching against the door. "And there'll be hell to pay if your brothers catch you here."

"Which is precisely why I came to the back door." Junebug tried to radiate amiability. She knew her brothers could intimidate people. "This is Ellie." She gestured to Ellie to come forward, but the stubborn woman refused.

"I know," the woman sighed. "Honestly, Junebug, there are barely more than two dozen people in this town. Everybody knows everybody."

"I don't know *your* name," Junebug pointed out.

The girl rolled her eyes. "Nor should you."

"Is it Mary?" Junebug guessed. "Jane? Sarah? Hortense?"

That got a vague smile out of her.

"I'm so sorry," Ellie abruptly interjected. "We really shouldn't be bothering you."

"We're not *bothering her*. We're just talking." Junebug pressed ahead. "Look, Whats-Your-Name, see Ellie here? Take a good look at her. How would you describe that dress she's wearing?"

The woman considered Ellie carefully. "Ghastly?"

"Ghastly! Exactly. And what color would you call it?"

"Brown?"

"It's *yellow*," Ellie protested. "Ish."

"This *ghastly* brown-*ish* thing is Ellie's best dress. Now, don't you think that's sad?"

The woman was attentively listening now.

"I don't know if you've heard, but I'm throwing a Christmas dance, and Ellie here is supposed to come. But *look at her*." Junebug increased the pathos.

The woman sighed. "Junebug. I don't really care."

"Fine. I've got money." Junebug dug out her cash. "I'm just looking for some dress fabric."

"What kind of dress fabric?" The woman eyed the cash.

"Nothing brown."

"Wait here." The door closed.

"I am not wearing a whore's dress." Ellie crossed her arms.

"Oh, get over yourself. They're just women like us."

"You're not a woman, you're a child."

"They have nice clothes—when they wear them. Anyway, we're not buying you a dress, we're just buying fabric. There ain't anything indecent in that." Junebug considered Ellie. "I wonder what kind of dress we should make you."

"We?"

"Well, *you*. I don't sew."

"Neither do I—at least not well."

"You think I *should* buy one of their dresses, then? So we don't have to do any sewing?"

"No!"

The door swung open and the whore was back, holding three bolts of material. "Which color do you like?"

There was a deep rose pink, a sherbet yellow and a screaming crimson. Junebug liked all of them. She reached out and stroked the fabric. "What are you charging?" she asked.

The woman named her price.

Junebug approved of her ambition but wasn't about to be exploited. "If I get two of them, can you give me a discount?"

"Don't waste your money. I don't *want* them," Ellie said stubbornly.

"Of course you don't. They're not brown enough." Junebug wasn't about to listen to her. "You should be thanking me, not being such a pain in the ass."

"It's good quality fabric," the woman assured Ellie.

"It's not the quality I'm worried about."

"Don't be rude," Junebug scolded her. "The lady's only trying to help."

"I don't need help."

"Trust me, you do."

"The kid's right," the woman chipped in. "You won't be winning Beau McBride looking like that."

"I'm not *trying* to win Beau McBride," Ellie said through her gritted teeth.

Junebug sighed. She'd really picked a dud with this one.

The woman took issue with Ellie's attitude. "Why on earth not? He's a stunner."

"He's not for the likes of me," Ellie said stiffly.

"She's got confidence problems," Junebug confided in the whore. "I mean, look at the state of her."

"You're not a bad looking girl," the woman told Ellie. "You just need a bit of fancying up."

"Thank you!" Junebug said. "I've been trying to tell her just that. So how much for the two bolts?" Junebug haggled hard but the woman stuck to her price.

"The pink and yellow would work on her. The red is too bold. She ain't the bold sort."

"Don't pay it," Ellie said tightly. "I don't want them."

"Yes, you do," the woman told her. "You can't go to a Christmas dance in that old thing. Go on, take them and make something nice. Go enjoy the dance for those of us who can't go."

Junebug was startled. It hadn't occurred to her that the girls at the cathouse would *want* to come to her dance. "What's your name?" she asked the woman as she paid her an exorbitant price for the fabric.

"Not Mary, Jane, Sarah or Hortense." The woman handed over the fabrics. "I'm Pearl."

"Nice doing business with you, Pearl." Junebug grinned at her. "I'd ask you to my dance, but I don't want to distract my idiot brother from my brides. But maybe I'll ask you to my next convivialities."

"Maybe I'll come."

"I'd hope so. My dances are legendary."

"Are they?"

"Well, they will be." Junebug unloaded the bolts of fabric on Ellie and gave Pearl a wave. Now that she'd made her acquaintance, Junebug figured she could pop by for a visit when she did her rounds in Bitterroot.

"Make it low cut," Junebug ordered. She circled Ellie, who was standing on a stool, draped in the rose-pink fabric.

"I was going to," Diana told her irritably through a mouthful of pins. "She's got wonderful collarbones."

"Forget her collarbones, men don't care about collarbones. It's shoulders they like. And the other bits."

Diana sat back on her heels and took the pins out of her mouth. She was frowning. "Why exactly are you so keen to show off Ellie's bits?"

"You know why. She's one of my brides."

"I'm *not*," Ellie exploded. "How many times do I have to *tell* you!"

"Look, I know it's strange," Junebug told Diana. "Getting you to help one of your competitors, but you're the only one she'd let me ask." Junebug threw up her hands.

"I'm not one of her competitors!" Ellie was red-faced and hot under the collar. She'd been increasingly edgy ever since they got back to the hotel.

"Well, you *should* be!"

"No, I shouldn't. Diana is my friend. And she's going to marry Beau."

"Well, Diana," Junebug said, turning to Miss Moonglow. "Ellie here is *your* friend as much as you're hers. Surely you want the best for her too? Because it seems to me Ellie bends over backwards to make you happy."

"Diana makes me happy too," Ellie insisted.

"Only because making Diana happy makes you happy."

Diana was very still and very quiet.

"Look, my idiot brother has been raised in the mountains and can count the number of women he knows on two hands. He went and proposed to the first woman who responded to his advertisement—you."

"I was the first?" Diana seemed surprised.

"The first, and the only one he wrote to. Which is why I asked all these girls here." Junebug figured this was a moment for the bald truth. "How's he going to know if he likes a specific girl, or just the fact it's a girl, any girl? I figured if he experiences a bunch of females, he won't be choosing an idea of a girl—he'll be picking an actual girl."

"That's absurd." Ellie was giving Junebug a dark look. "He likes *Diana*. They corresponded. He saw her photo. She is an *actual girl!*"

"But if he marries you," Junebug kept her attention fixed on Diana, "you'll be the only girl he ever wrote to. The only girl he ever kissed—"

Ellie made a strangled noise.

"The only girl he damn well courted. Is that what you want?" Junebug could see Diana's mind whirring behind her icy composure. "The least you can do is let Ellie compete," Junebug said smoothly. "What if Beau likes her more than he likes you? Wouldn't you want to know? And wouldn't you be happy for her, the way she's happy for you? Of course you would," Junebug continued. She often found if you kept the conversation moving, it gave people an increased opportunity to agree with you. "And I'm sure you don't want my brother by default. You want to know he chose you without a shadow of a doubt. If *I* were you—"

"Which you're not," Ellie snapped.

"If *I* were you," Junebug went on as though Ellie hadn't spoken, "I'd want to know he had zero interest in anyone but me."

"He *does* have zero interest in anyone but her!"

"Then you have nothing to worry about, do you?" Junebug gave Diana a blithe smile. "You can cut that dress low, and cinch that waist tight, and show off all Ellie's attractions without concern."

"My attractions are nothing compared to Diana's," Ellie said hotly.

"You've made your point, Junebug." Diana was as cool as Ellie was hot. "You can leave us now." She turned her back and fussed with the drape of pink fabric across Ellie's chest.

"Great." Junebug whistled loudly as she went down the hall to her own room.

Then she crept back to Diana's door, quiet as a hunter. She bent down to listen at the keyhole.

"I'm not interested in Beau McBride!" Ellie was saying. She sounded flustered.

"Are you sure?" Diana didn't sound so cool anymore. "You enjoyed writing my letters to him."

Junebug jumped like she'd been pinched. What did she mean, Ellie wrote her letters? The letters Beau had raved about? The ones he wouldn't let Junebug read? *Ellie* had written them?

Did Beau know?

"They were *your* letters," Ellie was speaking so fast all her words ran together. "I only helped get the ideas on the page. Diana, he wants to marry you—he's never said otherwise. And I have no interest in competing. I don't want him! Trust me."

"I *do* trust you. It's not that . . ." There was a brief silence. "It's just Junebug might be right . . ."

Junebug heard Ellie groan. "Don't let her in your head, Diana!"

"I want him to choose me without doubts."

Of course she did, Junebug thought. That was only smart.

"Maybe . . . maybe I *should* encourage him to spend more time with all those girls . . ."

"What?!"

Junebug bet Ellie was turning red.

"Well, he hasn't been doing it," Diana sighed. "Because he promised me he wouldn't."

Junebug rolled her eyes. Bloody Beau.

"But Junebug's right. I don't want to wonder for the rest of my life if he only married me because he had no real experience of women."

"Trust me, that man's had experience!"

"Not enough to know."

"Diana, that's plain wrong. When you know, you *know.*"

"Do you?"

"Yes!"

Junebug took note of Diana's doubt. And Ellie's vehemence. Well. This bet was still in play, as far as Junebug could see.

Twelve

Beau was in the hotel stable when Ellie ambushed him late that evening. Hurriedly, he closed the book of dance steps. He'd been trying to practice in advance of the Christmas party.

He'd been exasperated when Junebug had first announced her plans. Not least of all because it was nowhere near Christmas. He could only assume she was angling for all the cookies and puddings and treats Christmas usually brought. Not to mention creating an opportunity to throw all her brides into his arms. But once he'd gotten over his initial exasperation, Beau had felt a giddy thrill. He'd never been to a dance in his life, but he'd been practicing for one for months. His mind whirled with all the scenes from the books Kit had read them: royal balls and country dances, bunting and crystal and perfumed ladies in satin, the whisper of romance and kisses stolen in secret corners. *May I have this dance?* A warm hand slipping into his, another sliding up to rest on the back of his neck as brown eyes stared deep into his. The hair rose on the back of his neck at the thought of it.

He'd gone all the way up to Buck's Creek just to retrieve his book of dance steps and had taken to practicing again, whirling an imaginary dance partner around the barn. A partner who more often than not wore braids and nothing but a black and red flannel shirt.

"Diana said she spoke to you?" Ellie had a vinegary tone as she broke into his dance practice.

Beau had been avoiding Ellie since the night of the storm. It hadn't been difficult, as she'd been avoiding him too. He was aware of her avoidance because he was painfully aware of everything about her. His room at Mrs. Champion's looked onto her side of the hotel and he could see her little window from where he lay in bed. Her lantern burned late into the night—he assumed she was reading. She walked around with a book in her hand half the time. It was a wonder she didn't fall down the stairs or walk into a door.

Tonight was the first time she'd spoken to him directly since that night at Abner's.

That night that he couldn't get out of his goddamn mind. Even now, when he looked at her, he wasn't seeing her dark skirt and white shirt, he was seeing that soft red check flannel, hanging loose against her bare skin, or worse, the wet underwear, totally transparent as it clung to her. He was seeing the thrust of her small pointy breasts, with their large nipples, and the firm lines of her body. He could feel the way that body felt against his, the hungry press of her, the taste of her . . .

Jesus help him.

He was arousing himself just thinking of it. He turned away, so she wouldn't see. It had been a terrible mistake kissing her. He'd known it at the time. But she'd been so crestfallen when he'd rejected her offer of help. What was he supposed to do? Let her believe she was unkissable?

They'd been stuck at Abner's for a good couple of hours after he'd stopped kissing her and it had been sheer torture to sit there in guilty silence, not touching her. He'd been aware of every movement she made, of the uneven catching of her breath, of the rainy-warm scent of her. The only thing that had kept him from kissing her again was the knowledge that if he did he might not be able to stop. And she deserved better than being tumbled in a drafty cabin by her friend's fiancé. He might be a backwoodsman, but he was still a gentleman.

"Well?" Ellie prodded him, tearing him back from thoughts of the cabin. She didn't just sound vinegary, he realized. She sounded downright angry.

"Yes, Diana spoke to me." Beau played with the cover of his book, not brave enough to look at her again.

"And you told her she was being a fool?"

Beau sighed. First Diana, then Junebug, now Ellie. They were exhausting. "No, I cain't say that I did," he told Ellie softly. He was aware from her stony silence that she didn't like his answer. He leaned against Dutch's stall and rubbed the horse's nose. He had a feeling this wasn't going to be a short conversation.

Diana had come rapping at Mrs. Champion's cottage door that morning, catching him completely by surprise. Her breath had been misting in the cold morning air and she'd left footprints in the frost on the porch. The woods behind her had fewer coppery leaves and more bare branches.

"You can ask me in, even though it's not proper," she'd suggested in her usual poised way. "This place doesn't seem to put much stock in what's proper anyway." She'd given him a smile. "Don't worry, I won't take advantage of you."

He'd led her through to the kitchen and made her some tea, and then they'd sat at the table and had a very long talk. The longest they'd ever had. And Beau found that talking to her wasn't as difficult as he'd first thought. She was a very frank person, which he appreciated.

"There isn't a delicate way to say this," she'd sighed.

"Indelicate will do." He'd been feeling guilty. That's always how he felt when he saw her now. Lower than a bug.

"I'm concerned about your lack of experience with women."

He couldn't have been more surprised if she'd thrown her tea in his face.

She gave him a long moment to absorb her words.

"What's Junebug said to you now?" he groaned.

"Oh, it's not Junebug. Well, not only Junebug. It's everyone. Everything." Diana exhaled. "How do I say this? I practiced and it's still coming out wrong." Diana took a deep breath. "I've been thinking about how you were raised here—not even here, *more* remote than here—without access to women. Well, many women." She cleared her throat and blushed prettily. He was aware that she was probably thinking about the cathouse over the road. "I thought I understood it in theory when you wrote about it. But seeing it in practice is something else. It would be one thing if I'd arrived as planned and we'd wed and gone to your home, getting to know each other over time as a husband and wife ought." She blushed even more now. "I think then we'd have rather enjoyed getting to know each other. But this . . . trying to court, I suppose . . . with all these other girls competing for your attention . . ."

"It's a circus," Beau admitted glumly. His little sister had taken something that should have been simple and good and had tangled it right up. Only . . . he couldn't totally blame Junebug. He'd made that bet too. But back then, it had been conceptual—he hadn't been imaging the brides as real people. If he'd imagined Diana and Ellie and all the rest of them, he didn't think he would have made the bet at all. It seemed cruel. To everyone.

She nodded. "The fact is, I'm *not* the only girl. Now you have options."

"Diana—"

"No, let me finish. I've given this a lot of thought." She'd reached out and put her hand on his. "I didn't come to Bitterroot to compete for you."

Beau flinched. He should have offered to marry her right then and there. He could have walked her straight down to the church and had done with it. But he stayed quiet. Because he'd been doing a lot of thinking too. It wasn't right what he'd done that night at Abner's. It wasn't right that he'd flirted with Ellie, and . . .

He shouldn't be kissing other women if he was marrying Diana.

But also, what did it mean that he *wanted* to kiss other women? Or rather, *one* other woman. Was it just because he'd been put in that situation with Ellie? Would he have felt the same way if it had been another woman trapped at Abner's with him? If it had been Frances or Mabel or Kate? Would he be having intrusive fantasies about them now? He didn't know. And that bothered him.

"Beau." Diana had given his hand a squeeze. "It's okay to enjoy attention."

That hadn't been what he'd expected her to say.

She was proving to be nothing but surprises.

"It's nice to be admired, to be flirted with, to have some fun. I've spent the last few years surrounded by boys," she said shyly. "So I've had time to work out what I like and don't like."

Beau didn't know what to say to that.

"You need to work out what *you* like." She pulled a face. "I mean, I can't say I'm thrilled to come to this conclusion. But I'd be less thrilled to marry you and *then* find out I wasn't what you wanted."

"You're perfect," he told her, and he meant it.

"But am I perfect for *you*?" She held up a hand. "No. Don't answer that. Not yet."

Beau knew himself well enough to know that he didn't know the answer yet. Like she said, if she'd been the only one to show up, she probably *would* have been perfect. But all Junebug's girls had confused him. And one in particular had *really* confused him. Excessively.

"We don't have unlimited time," Diana continued, "as our two weeks are up in a few days. But I think we should use the time we have . . ."

"To do what?" He'd been uncertain, not sure what she wanted from him.

". . . to let you work things out."

Beau didn't even really know what he wanted to work out. That's how confused he was.

"I think you should open your mind," she told him. "To each and every one of Junebug's girls. You should get to know them, have some fun with them, enjoy yourself." She closed her eyes. "I can't believe I'm saying this."

He'd been shocked—but mostly because her words had caused a flare of anticipation. His mind had immediately gone to Ellie and that cabin, and the thought of kissing her again. Beau felt himself loosen. He hadn't realized how knotted up he'd been.

"You can have some fun with everyone," Diana suggested. "And then at the dance, you can choose—knowing you've given it some real thought. I know you've been trying to stay loyal to me, but I want you to really consider it. I give you *permission* to really consider it."

"You're more than I deserve," he told her fervently when she stood to leave.

"Well," she said, rising on tiptoe to press a butterfly-light kiss on his cheek, "you'll just have to earn me then, won't you?"

"You told her she was crazy, right?" Ellie demanded now, plowing into the stable, billowing dragon's breath as she spoke. It was a crystal clear, gelid night, so cold that frost sparkled in the air around the lanterns. "You told her that she's a moon-struck lunatic? And that you have no intention of romancing anyone but her?"

Beau regarded her, striving for calm. He felt tender tonight and wasn't in the mood for confrontations. "I didn't."

"What do you mean, you *didn't*?"

She hadn't brought her shawl out with her, and she was shivering.

"I didn't think her ideas were absurd, so I didn't tell her she was a moon-struck lunatic," he said patiently.

Her mouth fell open. "Has *everyone* lost their minds?"

Junebug had come to see him after Diana. She'd been less empathetic than Diana, but no less convincing. "The whole point of this activity is to enjoy yourself," she'd told him, watching as he chopped wood for Mrs. Champion's stove. She didn't offer to help. "Dance with some pretty girls, kick up your heels the way we never could at Buck's Creek. Hell, Beau, life don't have to be an endless chore. Didn't you set out to have a good time when you ordered up a wife?"

Their childhood hadn't been much fun, he thought, as he watched Junebug dash off, her dog scampering along behind. He remembered the long dark years when Pa had been around, half drowned in drink. He'd deposited the family in the wilderness without shelter, without stocks of food, without much hope for anything better. His one decent idea had been to establish a trading post—but even then he hadn't been much use. Ma and Morgan had pretty much run things. Only Ma was often sick, or pregnant, or nursing. And then there were the years after Morgan left, when Kit and Charlie had stepped in. Kit stoically, Charlie explosively. One by one they'd lost all the girls except Junebug. Beau remembered when Maybud had sickened. It still took the strength out of him to remember it. Maybud had been closest to him in age, and it had always been the two of them . . . until it wasn't. He'd dug her grave himself, under the chokecherry tree by the creek.

Morgan came back, Ma died, their father ran off, and then Charlie left and things had been bleaker than ever. As hot-headed as Morgan, Kit's twin Charlie had gone hunting after their father, alone, determined to drag the old man back to face his responsibilities. But they'd never had word of him again. Not Charlie, nor Pa. Charlie's absence was like an open wound, a pain that endured as the years rolled by; all of them felt their share of guilt for not being able to stop him, and for not being able to find him. The winter after Pa and Charlie had run off, the McBrides had almost starved—Pa never had been one for stocking the root cellar—but Beau thought the pain of Charlie's unknown fate was harder to bear than the hunger.

Beau's childhood read like a litany of grief and misfortune. No, there hadn't been much lightness and fun. Not until recently, when Junebug had started ordering up brides . . .

Beau had tangled himself up in thoughts of the past and wandered around in knots for the rest of the day. The only thing he knew was that he didn't want the rest of his life to be as cheerless as his childhood . . . Other than that, what *did* he want?

Who did he want?

Look at the disaster of Ma and Pa. He didn't want that. He much preferred the look of Maddy and Kit's marriage. They were calm, sweet and kind to each other. But then he didn't mind the spit and fire Morgan and Pip had either . . . That looked like its own kind of fun.

So no, he hadn't told Diana or Junebug that they were crazy. He actually thought they spoke a lot of sense. He *shouldn't* run into marriage headlong, without considering what he liked. Especially because liking on paper was different to liking in person. Diana in person certainly wasn't like she was in her letters . . .

"I don't see why you're so upset about it," Beau challenged Ellie now.

"I'm upset," she exploded, "because you're breaking Diana's heart!"

"She didn't seem so heartbroken." Beau was getting irritated now. Shouldn't the impossible woman be *glad*? Didn't she want more kissing? Because he bloody well did.

"She's pretending, you idiot." Ellie burst into tears.

Beau was astonished. Why on earth was she crying?

"She's so kind, and so brave, and so *selfless*," Ellie wailed.

Beau watched as she threw herself down on a hay bale and began crying in earnest.

"She just wants you to be happy, Beau!" Ellie convulsed on the hay bale.

"I don't see why that's something to cry about," he said, exasperated.

Ellie looked up from her sobbing for long enough to glare at him. "Don't you have a compassionate bone in your body?"

"Well, sure, but she seemed fine to me." Beau approached her like he was approaching a wild horse. He squatted down next to her hay bale. "She's only asking for us to take it slow—and to take it seriously. It ain't a game."

"No, she's asking for *you* to take it slow and seriously with *five other girls!*" Her brown eyes were sparkling with angry tears.

"Six," he corrected.

"Don't include me in this!" She leapt up again.

Beau sighed. She sure gave Junebug a run for her money when it came to melodrama.

"This doesn't really change anything, Ellie," he said, rising to his feet.

"It changes *everything*." Ellie seized him by the jacket. He could tell by the look in her eyes that her imagination was running rampant. "Now you're seriously courting six women, not just one. That's a change!"

"Seven women," he corrected.

"Imagine Junebug's Christmas dance," she instructed, not even listening to him. "The hotel's front rooms have been cleared of furniture. There are garlands of fir on the doorways and mantles, and paper snowflakes twirling on strings, and shimmering candlelight—"

"Have you told Junebug this, because she's struggling for decorations and that sounds pretty good."

"Hush." Ellie put her hand over his mouth. "It's a wonderland. The music fills the night and romance pulses."

She was shining again. Her eyes were glistening and her cheeks were flushed. She sure was pretty when she was being ridiculous.

"You're dancing with . . . Flora," Ellie sounded like she was choking on the name. "While Diana stands by herself, watching wistfully, her sensitive heart aching. She's smiling, because she's *kind*." Ellie's hand was pressing hard into his mouth now, like she was trying to smother him. Tears were sparkling in her eyes. "But then you whirl Frances—"

"Flora," he corrected, his voice muffled by her hand.

"Someone who is not *Diana*," she seethed. "You whirl her under the mistletoe. Are you imagining this?"

"Vividly," he promised, his voice still muffled.

"And then what do you do?" She was looking rather evil now. It was surprisingly attractive on her.

"Kiss her?" Beau guessed. He was a bit tired of being smothered, so he pulled her hand away from his mouth.

"That's right! You *kiss her*." She said it like he was murdering someone. "Right there, in front of Diana." The tears tumbled down her cheeks. "And Diana's heart *breaks*."

"She all but told me to kiss people," he said, reaching out to wipe the tears from her cheeks with the pads of his thumbs.

"But she didn't mean it," Ellie wailed.

"I think she did." He gave her a hug and a pat on the back. "You know you imagined this whole thing, right? None of this has actually happened."

"But it *will*."

"Not if I watch out for mistletoe."

"Do you have any idea what it will be like for her to watch you romance other people?" she wailed into his jacket, thumping his chest with her fist.

"I'll do it out of sight. Ow!" He caught her wrist before she could thump him again. "There, there. Maybe it will be Diana I'll twirl about under the mistletoe," he soothed her. "Maybe I'll kiss her and everyone else's hearts can break."

She reared back. "You shouldn't make light of it."

"I'm not," he promised, trying not to smile. "But I can't control what I do in your imaginings. Only in real life."

"And in real life, you're going along with Diana's stupid plan." She looked so betrayed.

"Aw honey, it's okay." He rubbed her back. "It really is."

She shook her head, tears tumbling. "It's not. It's all my fault."

"Yeah, that's usually how imaginings work. If you dream them up, you're responsible for them."

"Not that." She bit her wobbling lip. "It's because I kissed you. It made you weird after, and you being weird unsettled her."

"Well, now. It wasn't really a kiss, was it? I thought we established that. It was more of a touching of lips and holding still."

She glowered at him.

Somehow he managed not to smile. "It's not because you kissed me or because I kissed you," he soothed. "It's bigger than that. I'm weird for a lot of reasons."

She looked insulted.

"Not that it wasn't a significantly big kiss," he said quickly. "It was. Enormous. Gigantic. Seismic."

"Stop making fun."

"It's just about certainty, that's all. About not rushing headlong."

"You wrote to each other," she reminded him. "It wasn't headlong. You *know* each other."

"And they were great letters," he admitted, remembering his excitement every time one arrived at the post office. "But we only *started* getting to know each other. Diana's right—I need to be sure. And so does she."

What he was sure of right this minute was that she felt good in his arms as he comforted her. They stood behind the shelter of the half-closed barn door, in the frosty light of the lantern, which caught her eyes and made them shine. She smelled like a soft summer breeze, a surprising freshness on this cold fall night. He felt her exhale a shuddering breath.

"I love Diana," she said plaintively into his jacket.

"I know. And she knows it too."

"I shouldn't have kissed you. It was wrong."

"Well, now it ain't wrong," he said softly. "She's all but given permission."

Ellie reared back again. "What are you suggesting!"

He shrugged, his gaze dropping to her lips.

"No." She pushed him away.

He sighed. She was always so contrary.

"I'm fully committed to Diana's cause." She made it sound like she was entering an epic battle.

Beau couldn't deny that he was disappointed. He'd been thinking a lot about kissing her today. But if there was one thing he'd learned from Junebug, it was that there was more than one way to skin a cat. "Do I get to enlist your help, if it coincides with your cause?" he asked, reaching for his book. "How do you feel about helping me practice my dancing? I don't usually do it with a partner, which I reckon is a handicap."

"I don't dance."

"Perfect, me neither. We can learn together." He pointed to the page. "This here's a two-step. It says anyone can master it in minutes, so long as they know their right foot from their left." He took her by the hands. "Do you know your right foot from your left?" He felt a momentary resistance and then she let herself be pulled into him.

"I'm only helping so you can dance with Diana," she mumbled.

"I know." He slid his arm around her. "Alright, this is mostly walking. Quick-quick, slow-slow. Move your right foot back first and I'll move my left."

"Beau?"

"Yes?" For a moment, his heart pinched, thinking she was about to say something tender.

"There should be more space between us. The book shows more space."

"Well, the book is wrong."

"I thought you didn't know how to dance, which is why you needed the book."

"I know enough to know that close is always better. Now hush up and follow my lead."

She made a disgruntled noise. But she stayed close.

And that was enough for him.

Thirteen

Ellie had a wretched time of it, watching Beau take Diana's deluded advice to heart. It was bad enough that he was spending time with all these girls who weren't Diana, but it was infinitely worse how much he seemed to enjoy it. On Monday he'd sat at one of the dining room tables with Mabel and Frances, cutting paper snowflakes and stars to decorate the hotel for Junebug's party. The sound of his laughter raked Ellie like nails on a chalkboard. On Tuesday, he'd tied on an apron and let Nancy boss him around in the kitchen, icing cookies, also for the party. When Ellie had walked through he'd had the nerve to wink at her, the ass. On Wednesday, he'd sung Christmas carols with Flora, Kate and Frances, their voices bouncing exuberantly around the hotel. Of course he had an incredible singing voice. It sent shivers down Ellie's spine. On Thursday, Diana showed him how to make paper flowers and, one by one, the other girls had joined them, until they were filling the hotel with bunches of the stupid things. It ended up being a party before the party. Ellie had sat peevishly in the parlor, pointedly reading her book.

All of that was bad. But what was worse was imagining all the things she *couldn't* see. What happened when he was out of sight with them? Was there hand holding? Kissing? More? Her imagination ran riot.

"He hasn't kissed me yet," Diana confessed when Ellie could no longer contain herself and brought it up. Diana was making the final adjustments to Ellie's dress for the party. Ellie had overruled Junebug's nonsense about low cut dresses and had insisted the rose-pink dress be high necked and full sleeved. She wasn't here to seduce the stupid man.

She seemed to be the one person who wasn't.

"Do you think he's kissing *them*, though?" Ellie peered through Diana's bedroom window down at the street below. The creek had a crust of ice on it but there was still no snow. She couldn't see Beau anywhere, even though he and Flora had headed out for a walk.

"You'd have to ask them," Diana said stiffly. She gave Ellie an odd look.

"Oh Diana, I'm sorry." Ellie turned away from the window. "I'm being thoughtless."

"Has he kissed *you*?"

Ellie flinched. But then she realized Diana didn't mean it. She was just being sharp after Ellie's thoughtlessness. Ellie gave a nervous laugh. "Don't be silly. I'm not involved in this."

"He asked me to come with him to choose a Christmas tree this afternoon, so maybe he'll kiss me then," Diana mused, sitting back on her heels and straightening Ellie's hem. "Or maybe I'll kiss him."

"That's a great idea," Ellie said quickly, ignoring the hot spurt of acid in her belly.

"There, you're all done." Diana rose to her feet and turned Ellie towards the mirror.

Oh. Ellie blinked. Maybe they'd been right about her brown dress. Maybe its overwhelming ghastliness had infected her. And maybe they were right about her yellow-ish dress too. Because

Ellie looked like a different person in this pink dress. She didn't look like wallpaper at all; the dusky pink made her eyes shine and gave her a perfect roseleaf complexion. The simple cut of the dress flattered Ellie's figure, and the high neck framed her face; Diana had included a tiny frill in a square design around her chest, with little fabric buttons running down her neck and between her breasts, creating more of an illusion of curves than usual. The flare of the skirt low on her hips also accentuated their shape.

"Oh El, you look beautiful." Diana stood back and admired her, her sincerity evident.

No one had ever called her beautiful before. Ellie's eyes welled with tears.

"Don't cry all over it," Diana scolded. She handed Ellie a scrap of material to wipe her eyes with. "Now, we need to think about your hair." She took Ellie's single braid in her hand. "Do you want it down, or shall I make you a crown?" She wound the braid around the top of Ellie's head.

Ellie reminded herself she wasn't trying to catch anyone's eye. "It doesn't matter," she said.

"It does. If you wear it down, you'll have to wash it tomorrow. You don't want it to have been braided or it will go all bushy again. You need to plan for these things."

Ellie had trouble tearing her gaze from her reflection. She was plagued with imaginings: descending the stairs in this dress, Beau catching sight of her, his eyes widening and twinkling and growing hot, his lips parting. He'd be overcome by her beauty. And then when she paused at the foot of the stairs, he'd notice that she'd come to rest under the mistletoe . . .

"No," she said flatly. "It *doesn't* matter. No one will be looking at me."

Diana frowned.

Ellie knew how it would be in reality; a vivid new image swam to mind of Ellie descending the stairs in Diana's wake, like a shadow. Beau would catch sight, his eyes widening and twinkling and growing hot, his lips parting. He *would* be overcome by beauty. *Diana's*. Or Flora's. Or Mabel's. Or someone with *copious and symmetrical attractions*. Not a skinny plain girl like her, no matter whether her hair was bushy or not.

"Ellie." Diana snapped her fingers in front of Ellie's face, to bring her back to reality. "What on earth are you imagining, to get such a look on your face?"

"Nothing," Ellie said hastily.

Diana cupped Ellie's face in her hands. "Tell me."

"No," Ellie said, horrified, pulling away.

Diana gave her a look. "You've been like this ever since that night you got lost in the woods. Are you *sure* you don't want to tell me what's bothering you?"

Absolutely not. Never.

Diana sighed. "Fine. But I'll listen whenever you decide you want to talk. I hate it that we don't talk anymore."

"You know me. It's just woolgathering," Ellie said weakly. "And we *do* talk."

Diana's eyebrow lifted and Ellie winced.

"We *will* talk," she amended. "I guess the last couple of weeks have been . . . unexpected . . . and difficult."

"I think I forget that you came here to get married too," Diana said softly. "And that it must have been disappointing to find that your Mr. McBride was *my* Mr. McBride."

Ellie flinched. "No. It's fine. I only came here for you. I don't care."

But Diana was still staring at her with open sympathy.

"I really don't," Ellie insisted. "All I care about is your happiness!"

"I know." Diana sighed. "If you take the dress off I'll press it for you, and you can take it up to your room."

"Oh. Thank you."

"I should have the yellow ready in a couple of days. Then you'll have a new day dress too." Diana bit her lip. "And Ellie? It's okay to be disappointed. You can love me and care about my happiness and still want what you want . . ."

Diana was so good to her, Ellie thought miserably as she wriggled out of the beautiful pink dress. And how had she repaid such goodness? By kissing Diana's fiancé! She paused, dress in hand, as she caught sight of Beau and Flora wandering back towards the hotel. They were both carrying arms full of fir branches and talking animatedly. Flora looked very flushed. Was it a just-kissed flushed? Ellie couldn't tell.

"So have you kissed anyone yet?" Ellie winced as she heard the words exploding from her mouth later that night. She and Beau were in Mrs. Champion's little front room, practicing his dancing. It was too cold for the stable tonight. They'd pushed the furniture back and were twirling about by lamplight. Ellie knew she was flirting with trouble but she couldn't seem to resist when he invited her to help him. Besides, if *she* didn't do it someone else might, and the mere thought made her burn.

Everyone else was manically preparing for tomorrow's Christmas dance. The tree was being decorated, the paper snowflakes hung; Diana was weaving paper flowers into chains; Mrs. Champion, Mabel and Nancy were cooking up a storm; Junebug was bossing everyone around. And they all thought Ellie was up in her attic room, reading.

Beau missed a step. "Jesus, Ellie."

"What? I'm just asking."

"A nice boy doesn't kiss and tell."

"Did you kiss Diana while you were getting the tree this afternoon?" She just couldn't help herself. She'd been torturing herself all afternoon imagining it. She was seriously losing her mind.

She *wanted* him to be kissing Diana, and yet the very thought of it made her want to smash things.

"She didn't tell you?"

Ellie didn't dignify that with an answer.

Without music all they heard was their feet making muffled thudding noises on the rug. "Can't you hum like normal?" she complained.

"I'll do you one better," he said, amused by her temper. "I'll sing to you."

Now it was Ellie's turn to miss a step.

He gave her a wolfish grin. "I'll give you one of my sister-in-law's favorites. She likes the romantic ones."

Ellie shook her head. "There's no need for singing. Humming is fine."

He ignored her. Because he was an ass. Ellie felt herself break out in goosebumps as his voice curled around her like a silky ribbon. *I'll take you home again, Kathleen* . . . He had a smokiness to his voice that was like a shot of whiskey to her system.

He knew it too. Look at that smug grin. *To where your heart has ever been / Since you were first my bonnie bride.* Oh God, he smelled good. Like resin and pine from the Christmas tree, that garden soap, and then a unique Beau-smell that was warm and male and intoxicating. Against her best intentions, Ellie felt herself melting into him. He glided her in slow circles, crooning about his love for some woman named Kathleen. Like he needed another woman in his life.

"I think you've mastered dancing," Ellie said thickly.

"Just in time, given the dance is tomorrow."

She squealed as he dipped her.

"I didn't kiss Diana," he told her, once she was upright again. "Or Flora. Or Mabel. Or Nancy. Or Frances. Or Kate."

The bright dazzle of joy she felt was entirely inappropriate. Ellie pulled away from him. "You *should* be kissing Diana," she said stiffly. But then she remembered what Diana had said about kissing *him*. "Wait. You didn't kiss them, but did they kiss *you*?"

"What did I say about kissing and telling, Ellie?" he teased.

"Well, since Junebug has covered the hotel in mistletoe for tomorrow, you won't need to tell me soon, I can watch it for myself." Ellie reached for her shawl.

"What are you doing?"

"Leaving. You can dance now. You don't need me."

"Ah, don't be like that. I thought you liked dancing with me."

She did. Too much.

Beau cocked his head. "Fine. How about you help me with my next challenge, then?"

"I'm tired. I'm going to go to bed."

"I need help thinking up some compliments."

She paused in the middle of wrapping her shawl around herself. "You want *me* to think up compliments for you?"

"Yeah." He put his hands in his pockets and regarded her cheerfully. "I thought I'd take your advice and start complimenting people."

"Well, generally compliments should come from the heart," she said sourly. Her mind was conjuring up images of Beau showering all the girls at the hotel with praise. "They should also be true. For example, if I were to compliment you tonight, I'd let you know you dance like a drunk trapper."

His lips twitched. "Right. Okay, let me try." He gave it some thought. "You dance like a three-legged elk." He pursed his lips. "Maybe elk isn't the best choice. They're quite graceful aren't they . . . possibly even with three legs . . ."

"You dance like a hooked fish," she shot back immediately.

"You have the dainty hands of a squirrel," he said tenderly.

"You smell like sap."

"Your skin is as smooth as a bladderpod blossom."

"You sing like a mayfly."

"Your breath is as fresh as mustard greens."

"You're as charming as the pox."

"See, I knew you'd be helpful." He grinned. "As helpful as a frypan without a handle."

"You compliment as well as you dance, so my work here is done." Ellie headed for the back door.

"Wait! I still need help." He followed her through the kitchen. "Come on, Ellie. You said you were committed to the cause."

"*Diana's* cause, not yours." Ellie opened the back door and stepped outside onto the porch. It was so cold she almost forgot to breathe. The air smelled like the last gasp of fall, wet earth and sodden fallen leaves, with the cool breath of pine soughing through it. The wind was moaning low and intimately at the eaves.

"This *will* help Diana," he assured her, slipping in front of her and blocking her way. "And I know how helpful you are. Like a woodpecker in a lumber yard."

"That compliment doesn't even make sense." Her breath formed a white plume as she spoke.

"What can I say, I learned from the best." He tugged on her braid, which hung in a single fat plait over her shoulder.

It was infuriating how charming he was when he was being an ass. Even though it was dark on the porch, and she couldn't see his face, she knew he was smiling.

"What?" she demanded. "What do you want?"

He was still playing with her braid. She felt vibrations every time he twitched it. He leaned close. "I haven't kissed any of them, Ellie. And they haven't kissed me."

Oh, that stupid bright joy again. She wished she could stomp it out. It was making her life an unholy misery. She had to stop this.

He wound her braid around his hand. "I need to practice, though," he said softly.

She flinched. "Practice what?" But she knew.

"Kissing." He kept winding, reeling her in closer.

Her chest felt strange. Like it was full of storm clouds.

"Imagine it's tomorrow," he said, his voice low and intimate. "And we're at the dance."

"You don't need my help with kissing, you're fine," she interrupted. Her heart was falling over itself.

"But I do. I need your help badly. I only know one kind of kissing and it ain't appropriate for company." He'd reeled her in so close that she could feel the warmth of his breath on her face. "I need your kind of kissing more than my kind," he told her. "You know, polite kissing."

"*Polite* kissing?" Well, that was offensive.

"The kind you can do in public, under mistletoe. Because you're right, my sister has laid traps all over that hotel and kissing will be inevitable."

"You thought my kiss was polite?" She was still caught on that. "Odd. I was under the impression you thought it was hilarious."

"Polite ain't a bad thing. And neither is hilarity."

"It is when it comes to kissing," she said stiffly.

"Hush." He put his finger against her lips. His skin was cold against her mouth. "Imagine the Christmas dance is in full swing," he said, his breath clouding, "and we're dressed up and looking fine. Jonah's fiddling up a storm and the windows are steamed up from all the dancing. As the reel ends and we spin to a halt, we look up—"

"Who's the *we* in this situation?" she demanded.

"Would you like me to say Diana and me?"

"Will it *be* Diana and you?"

"For the sake of this imagining, sure."

Ellie scowled at him. Maybe she'd go take all that mistletoe down tonight while everyone was in bed.

"So, there we are, under the mistletoe, surrounded by people. This ain't the time for the type of kiss that leads to a woman wrapping her legs around you. Not with an audience like that."

He took his finger away from her mouth, caressing her cheek as he lowered his hand.

Ellie felt like someone had set her on fire. In a blazing instant she was back in that cabin, pressed up against the wall, her legs wrapped around Beau, his mouth on hers, his tongue slipping in.

"This seems like the time for a different kind of kiss." He was so close his lips were whispering against hers as he spoke. "A more polite kind of kiss."

"I'm not sure talking into her mouth counts as a kiss."

She felt him smile against her.

He pulled back. "Show me how I should do it, then?"

She should walk away right now.

Right. Now.

But she didn't. She couldn't. Her body refused to move.

"Do I touch her before I kiss her?" Beau prodded softly.

"No. Not for a polite kiss."

"So I keep my hands to myself?"

"Yes." *No.* In her imagination the scene flared to life. The two of them standing in a shimmering pool of candlelight, hypnotized by the mistletoe dangling above them, the white berries glowing against the dark leaves. In her imagination he took her face between his hands, the way he had in the cabin. And within less than a heartbeat she had her legs wrapped around him . . .

"Ellie, you've gone away again." Beau sounded amused.

"I haven't. I'm right here." Mentally, she pried her imaginary legs off his imaginary waist. Ellie cleared her throat. "We're in the middle of the room, in bright light, surrounded by people."

"That's right."

"I suppose you should lean in—politely." She demonstrated. "And then she'll probably lean in too."

"Like this?" He leaned.

"Can you do it more politely?"

He laughed softly. "Should I say 'please'?"

"Absolutely."

"Please, may I kiss you now?"

"Hold on," she sighed. "I've lost track, am I you in this scenario, or are you you?"

"I'm definitely me."

"Okay. Then yes you may kiss me."

"Wait, but you're supposed to be showing me?"

"Then I'm you?"

"Will you just shut up and kiss me? Please."

Ellie did. But only because he'd asked politely.

It was unlike either of their previous kisses, a slow unfolding that immediately fogged Ellie's senses. The moment her lips touched his, she turned to liquid. It was gentle, languid, tender—and hot as hell. The night was cold, but his mouth was searing. Ellie moaned and threaded her hands into his tumbled curls, pulling him as close as she possibly could. He moaned back, and then his tongue was in her mouth and his hands were at her waist, then slipping up her ribcage. She writhed, wishing she could get even closer.

"Wait, wait, wait." He disentangled himself, breathing heavily. "This is getting increasingly impolite."

Ellie nodded. Yes. Yes, it was. "Shall we try again?"

"Please," he breathed.

"Maybe put your hands behind your back?"

"Wise." He did as he was told.

This time when she kissed him it took at least two minutes before he had his hands on her. Maybe, she thought thickly, if they practiced enough they could get it up to four minutes . . .

"None of this seems suitable for a public parlor," Beau mumbled eventually.

"No. You're not a very good student." Ellie's skin was tingling from his stubble and her mouth felt swollen.

"I never was," he said ruefully.

"I think when you kiss someone tomorrow you should keep your lips clamped shut. And your hands in your pockets."

"Right." Obediently, he slid his hands in his pockets.

Ellie bit her lip.

"I think when *you* kiss someone tomorrow you shouldn't thread your hands through his hair. Or bite your lip like that," he moaned.

"I won't be kissing anyone," she said primly.

"That's a crying shame."

Ellie shook her head. "This is wrong." She tried to get herself neatened up. Somehow her shawl was in disarray and some of her buttons had come undone. "I've been terrible. Awful."

"Trust me, you haven't. You've been marvelous."

"Stop it. You're marrying my best friend."

"Maybe."

"Definitely. And *this* isn't happening." Now that she'd pried herself out of his embrace, Ellie felt the cold night air sharply. She shivered. "Goodnight, Mr. McBride."

"Mister? Since when am I not Beau?" he called after her as she headed down the porch steps and back towards the hotel. "Make sure you don't get caught on that fence again." He gave a husky laugh. "Or on second thought, do. Then I can come and rescue you."

Ellie's imagination took flight. His hands sliding under her skirts to free her from the fence, brushing against . . .

Oh God. She was *doomed*.

Faintly she heard him laugh as she careened back to the hotel. "Goodnight," he called. "Sweet dreams."

But she knew her dreams would be anything but sweet.

Fourteen

Beau woke up to the shimmery light and muffled quiet that could only mean snow. Sure enough, Bitterroot had a light icing-sugar dusting. Not the deep drifts of winter, but a sprinkling of cold-to-come. He heard barking and looked outside to see Junebug's dog Beast bouncing around in it, sending up sprays of powder. Junebug herself was standing in the yard of the hotel, sucking on a wickedly long icicle and looking self-satisfied. She was wearing her overalls and one of Morgan's thick flannel shirts.

"Now it's Christmassy," she called to him when he emerged from Mrs. Champion's. "It ain't Christmas-like without snow."

"It ain't Christmas-like until it's Christmas," he said. "November's too early for all this palaver." He crossed the little picket fence between the yards, holding a tin mug of coffee for each of them. She beamed at him as she took the coffee, her cheeks rosy and her eyes bright. It was nice to see her happy.

"You should be wearing a hat, Bug. You'll freeze." One handed, he pulled his own woolen hat off, trying not to spill his coffee, and yanked it down over her ears.

"I forgot to pick my pumpkins up at Buck's Creek," she confessed to him, as she sipped her coffee. "And now they'll be covered in snow. If it's a dusting down here, it'll be a proper blanket up there."

Beau rolled his eyes. "Maddy and Kit did it for you. Last time I was up there your vegetable patch was bedded down for winter. And what they managed to save of your rotten pumpkins are safely down in the root cellar."

She went queerly quiet at that. A light sprinkle of snow began to swirl around them; Beau held out a hand to catch some of the tiny evanescent flakes.

"This will be the first Christmas I won't be at Buck's Creek," she said in an odd voice. "Or with Kit, Morgan and Jonah."

"It ain't actually Christmas, Bug. I'm sure you'll be back by December," he said dryly.

In her usual overalls, instead of her pretty blue dress, she looked like a little kid again. Beau remembered the pinch-faced skinny girl who'd been half dead of fever when Morgan had returned that winter. That had been an awful season of death, when they'd lost Ma. He remembered Morgan trying his darndest to make Christmas nice, that year and all the years after Pa and Charlie had disappeared. Nice didn't come easy to Morgan, and he'd been gruff and grumpy that awfully sad Christmas, swearing when the tree he'd cut had been too big for the cabin, losing his temper at the chicken he'd tried to cook when it came out crispy and black. But Beau remembered Junebug beaming, sitting at their rickety little table, surrounded by the four of them, Morgan, Kit, Beau and Jonah, enchanted by their too-big tree and their incinerated chicken. He remembered Kit reading them *A Christmas Carol* by the stove after dinner, Junebug forcing him to repeat the bit about Marley and the chains, over and over again. He remembered her asking for a new fishing rod the year Beau had accidentally broken hers, and moaning every year after that no fishing rod was ever as good as the one he'd broken, even though Beau must have made her a hundred rods since.

"I never thought Morgan would leave me all alone for Christmas," Junebug said glumly.

Suddenly Beau felt keenly homesick for his brothers, and for their cabin and the snow-dusted landscapes of Buck's Creek. He wanted to look out his window and see the mountains and the frozen creek, to hear the echoing clang of Kit's forge, to see the smoke curling from the trading post chimney and the big house. Christmas just didn't seem like Christmas anywhere else.

Even though it wasn't actually Christmas yet, damn it.

He shook off the maudlin mood he'd caught from Junebug. "Ah, you ain't alone, Bug. I'm here, and Jonah's playing the fiddle for you tonight. Kit's liable to haul Maddy down that mountain for your Christmas dance too, even if it's blizzarding, just to see you."

"Us," she corrected. "To see us."

Us. It was a good, solid word. It made him feel firm on his feet.

"But even if Kit comes, there's still no Morgan," she fretted. "I thought he'd be back by now." She glanced over at the hotel. "When I imagined my party, he was always here too. I thought he'd dance with me."

Beau knew Morgan was Junebug's parent in every way that mattered. The two of them were so similar that they shot sparks every time they struck up against each other, but they loved each other fiercely. Morgan had been responsible for bringing Junebug up, as best he could. Junebug and Kit and Beau and Jonah. He'd been surrogate ma and pa to all of them.

"You want Morgan to pitch up *now,* and see all those women you ordered up?" Beau teased her. "Are you kidding? He'd go around ripping down all that mistletoe, yelling up a storm."

"What mistletoe?" Junebug asked innocently.

"Ha." He squeezed her. "And don't worry. *I'll* dance with you tonight. And I'll be at Christmas."

"I guess that's where it's nice having an excess of brothers," she sighed, leaning into him. "You've got backups in case of emergency."

"I ain't no back up, Bug. I'm the main attraction."

"You are today," she giggled.

"How much mistletoe *have* you strung up?"

"Enough to make life interesting." She pulled away and waved her icicle like a wand. "If you're lucky you might kiss someone and turn yourself into a frog."

"Frogs turn into princes, not the other way round." He followed her across the yard as she gamboled towards the hotel.

"They have to turn into frogs in the first place, don't they? Which means it's a two-way process."

"Fair point."

"Maybe some kisses turn you into a frog and some turn you into a prince."

"I'm already a prince," he was saying as he opened the back door of the hotel for her. He was met by a wave of women. A flurry of femininity poured out, the girls all rugged up and squealing at the sight of snow. He stepped back so he wouldn't get bowled over.

"Good morning," he greeted them, nodding at each one in turn as they came tripping out to see the snow, their coats buttoned up and their hats pulled firmly down. It was a delight to see such a passel of happy faces on a halcyon November morning. The clouds were being blown to shreds and a pretty eggshell blue sky was showing through.

"Oh look," Junebug said casually, "mistletoe."

Beau looked up. He heard Junebug laugh and the girls giggle. And then he saw who was under it.

"Ellie, looks like you're the one stuck under the mistletoe this time," Junebug crowed.

Ellie seemed appalled. She was the last one out the door and was frozen on the threshold, her gaze fixed upwards on the scrappy little bunch of mistletoe. Junebug had sure mangled it as she hooked it up there; the berries were all squished.

Ellie met Beau's gaze, looking vaguely panicked. "I'm not part of this anymore," she reminded everyone in a high voice. "I'm not one of Junebug's brides."

"That ain't how mistletoe works," Junebug told her. "It's only got one rule—you get caught under it, you get kissed."

Beau's heart did a slow tumble. "So," he drawled, aware of everyone's eyes on them. "If she's caught, does she kiss me, or do I kiss her?"

If looks could kill, Ellie's would have knocked him dead on the spot.

"Good question," Junebug mused. She was holding her icicle like a mace now. "Ladies, what do you think? We should sort this now, as we've got a long day ahead of us. We need one rule for everyone, to make the kissing equitable."

Beau heard Ellie make a soft hissing sound between her teeth.

Beau grinned. The woman really hated the idea of him kissing other people. Fair enough. He'd want to deck any man who thought about kissing her.

"I think Beau should do the kissing," Diana suggested.

Beau followed Ellie's gaze as it flicked to her friend. Diana didn't seem overly upset by the situation, but he knew Ellie agonized over her feelings.

"I'm not part of this!" Ellie insisted. "I'm not kissing anyone."

"Come on, El, it's just a bit of fun," Diana scolded her. "It's Christmas!"

"No, it's not! It's November!"

"Today is Christmas," Junebug told her firmly. "It's Christmas-dance Christmas, which is even better than the real one, which always involves me doing a lot of cooking and then washing a lot of pots."

"We never had mistletoe at Fall River," Ellie said stubbornly.

Diana laughed at that. She was as shiny as sun striking ice crystals this morning; she had a glitter to her. "We never had *anything* at Fall River!"

"We had each other," Ellie muttered under her breath.

Beau's heart squeezed for her. He remembered the stories of childhood she'd told him that night they were holed up at Abner's. The cheerless tenement building and worn-out mother. The drunken stepfather. The succor of the boardinghouse and Diana.

Diana meant everything to Ellie, the same way Morgan meant everything to Junebug. They were an *Us*.

"Beau should definitely do the kissing," Frances agreed with Diana.

"He can show us how it's done," Nancy giggled.

"Hands up who thinks Beau should take the lead on the kissing?" Junebug called out.

Every hand except Ellie's went up, even Beau's. He was up for some fun, but he wanted some control over events. If he had to kiss people, he was going to make sure the kissing stayed polite. His gaze drifted to Ellie's lips.

"Hear that, Beau? Whenever there's mistletoe, you're to do the kissing." Junebug waved her icicle.

Beau tossed Junebug his empty tin mug and rolled up his sleeves as the girls laughed and hooted. Ellie had turned red as tomato ketchup, her gaze still fixed on Diana. Diana was clapping and laughing with everyone else. "Come on, El!" she called. "It's Christmas!"

"Keep it polite," Ellie hissed at him, so no one else could hear.

He grinned at her. The poor girl was so tense she was like an overstrung fiddle. "This is supposed to be fun," he reminded her softly.

"Well, it's not."

"I'll make it quick and painless."

She clamped her lips together and stood rigid as a pole, her fists clenched, as he leaned in. He resisted the urge to laugh as she tried to radiate her lack of enjoyment to Diana.

"On the lips!" Junebug yelled when he made for Ellie's cheek.

"On the lips or it doesn't count!" the others squealed.

"You heard them," he told Ellie. "It's out of my hands."

Her face was frozen into a mask of dread. He could only imagine the melodrama playing out in that head of hers. Sweetly, he dropped the faintest of kisses on her expressive lips and a collective swooning sigh rose from their audience.

"You looked like you were kissing a toad," he heard Diana scold Ellie when it was over and they plunged off into the snow to build a snowman. "You could at least pretend to enjoy it."

Beau laughed. Enjoying it wasn't Ellie's problem. Enjoying it *too much*, on the other hand, most definitely was.

By the time the hotel was decorated and ready for the party, Beau had sweetly pecked every single woman in the place, including Mrs. Champion and Ellen, the hotel's maid. Spirits were high and there was cheering and applause and laughter every time someone was caught under the mistletoe. It was all in silly fun. Beau delighted in Junebug's glee every time. She honked like a goose as she laughed, and her infectious joy filled the whole hotel. The only person who wasn't infected was Ellie, who'd grown increasingly quiet and withdrawn. She'd made sure not to be trapped under anymore mistletoe. Which was a crying shame, as Beau was itching to kiss her again. Properly this time.

"Ain't it an enchantment?" Junebug sighed, once the decorations were complete and everyone had dashed away to make themselves pretty for the evening. Beau laughed as he watched his little sister twirl in the center of the parlor, her arms outstretched.

It most certainly was an enchantment. The paper snowflakes spun above her, and the room was perfumed with fir and pine, sugar and spice. "This is our first dance, Beau!"

"But not our last," he promised, offering her a courteous bow and holding out his hand to invite her to dance. "You were right about needing fun."

"I'm always right," she said smugly, taking his hand. She honked as he swept her off her feet and skipped her around the room, exactly the way Morgan did when they danced in the meadow in summer. Beau found himself wishing Morgan could be here too. And Kit. It really wasn't right without them.

"We should hold the next one in Buck's Creek," she suggested, throwing her head back as he twirled her. "Maybe we should have a real Christmas dance—in December."

"Or a spring dance, after the thaw, out in the meadow," he countered, remembering Ellie's wedding imaginings. In spring the buttercups and yellow bells would be flowering, and the air would be perfumed with the spicy sweet smell of phlox. The tender sky would spread like a cathedral dome over their high mountain meadow and the chokecherries would be in frothy bloom. "Spring's a good time for a wedding."

"Wedding!" Junebug's head snapped up. "Not just a dance?"

She looked like a groundhog popping up from its hole. Beau laughed. "Well, that's what we're here for, ain't it? Getting me hitched?"

"Oh!" The exclamation from the hall stopped Beau mid-twirl.

They turned, Junebug still dangling in Beau's arms, to find Ellie and Diana standing in the doorway. Both had towels wrapped around their heads.

"What's this about getting hitched?" Diana asked. "Don't tell me you've made a decision now that you've kissed every blessed woman in the house." She was more relaxed than Beau had ever seen her. The opposite to her friend.

Beau lowered Junebug. Ellie was staring at him like she'd seen a ghost.

"He's talking a springtime wedding," Junebug announced. "And another dance! Everyone's invited."

"Not everyone will want to come," Diana reminded Junebug. She still seemed sanguine. "I don't think the other girls will want to watch him say I do to someone else."

Ellie was very pale, her huge eyes reflecting a swirl of imaginings that Beau felt sure were nothing short of catastrophic.

Distantly they heard the muffled chiming of the train station clock. Junebug swore. "You've got to go get ready," she ordered Beau, giving him a shove. "And so do I!" She pushed him towards the door. "Go on, git."

As Beau passed Ellie, he brushed her hand with his. He felt her jump and smiled. Let her try and ignore him tonight.

Fifteen

Beau was singing. Ellie heard his voice all the way out in Mrs. Champion's muddy yard. The snow had all melted and Bitterroot had turned into a quagmire. *Oh! I'll take you back, Kathleen / To where your heart will feel no pain.* Ellie stood on the porch listening to him, lost in dark imaginings. She'd been standing there for at least three songs, tumbling down a dark well of thoughts, as night fell velvety dark. A heavy pearl of a moon rose over the inky frill of the treetops, and across the way the lights of the hotel blazed golden. *I know you love me, Kathleen, dear / Your heart was ever fond and true.*

His heart certainly wasn't true. His heart was like a distractable puppy, bounding after anyone who threw it a pat and a kind word. The sight of him today, sparkly-eyed, kissing all those girls . . .

This couldn't go on. She was tearing herself up inside.

Not an hour ago she'd heard him talk about his wedding. Because he was *getting married*. And she was flinging herself at him like a moth at a flame; eventually she'd burn herself alive on his light. And then he'd *get married*. While she'd be a crispy dead moth.

The golden hotel lights swam before her eyes as she wept.

Why did the sight of him have to flood her with this enormous shimmery feeling, electrical as the promise of lightning? Why did her skin sing in his presence, and her heart lose time? Why did she have no control over herself? As Ellie listened to the closing strains of his song, she enjoyed her weep in the snow, feeling every last shred of pathos.

But then he swung into a more upbeat—and honestly quite filthy—sea shanty, breaking the whole effect. She swiped away the tears and headed in to tackle him head on.

Oh my God. He was in the bath. She hadn't expected that. Why hadn't she heard splashing? What kind of man didn't splash in the bath! But maybe she'd been so deep in her thoughts she hadn't heard . . .

The tub was in the kitchen in front of the hot stove. A single lantern cast a soft glow over him as he soaped his face and hair. He was singing some obscene lyric about a mermaid as he scrubbed and hadn't heard her come in. The muscles in his arms flexed as he lathered up, and the lamplight chased his slick skin with golden light.

Tiny muscles Ellie didn't know she had clenched deep inside of her.

Then he reached for a tin cup on the table, his eyes scrunched closed against the soap as he began ladling water over his head. Ellie watched the rivulets run down his shoulders, across his sharp collarbones, over the contours of his chest.

And then he opened his eyes.

"Goddamn!"

"Don't stand up!" she shrieked. She'd scared the hell out of him, and he'd lurched up. "It's only me!"

"What in hell are you doing here?" He sat back down and scooped the white soap scum over his lap, to preserve his modesty. He pushed his wet hair off his face.

"I want to talk to you."

"*Now?* You're going to see me in an hour at the party."

"Alone," she clarified. "I want to talk to you alone."

"Well, this is about as alone as I get," he said dryly.

"I didn't know you'd be in the bath." She should turn away to give him his privacy. "Who has a bath in the kitchen?"

"It's the warmest place in the house."

"What about Mrs. Champion?"

"She's busy cooking over at the hotel." He swiped a stray soap bubble from his face. "Now, what couldn't wait?"

"I need you to answer a question."

His hands curled around the lip of the tub. "Is that what you're wearing tonight?"

Ellie looked down at herself. She was wearing her shawl over her twill skirt and blue shirt. She'd lost her warm coat running from the bear. "No."

"Oh, good."

She flushed. She was sick of everyone judging her clothes.

"Your hair looks nice down."

Her hand flew to her hair, which hung in a thick curtain down her back. Diana had washed it for her and then brushed it to a high shine. When it wasn't braided it fell in a silky waterfall, framing her face. She admitted to being vain about her hair. Not that she ever had much opportunity to wear it down like this.

Beau was lazing back in the tub now, giving her a smile that made her loosen in the most inappropriate ways.

No. She couldn't do this to herself. Or to Diana. This had to stop. She needed him to put her out of her misery.

"Are you going to ask your question?" he asked, his voice husky.

"Are you going to marry Diana?"

His eyebrows shot up. "Are we still on that?"

She lost her temper then. She snatched his towel off the kitchen chair, wound it, and snapped it at him.

"Ow!" He whipped his hand back off the lip of the tub.

"Yes, we're still on that, you lummox! You brought her here to marry her!" She snapped the towel again.

"Give me the towel, Ellie." The water splashed as he jerked out of its reach.

She shook her head. Not until he answered her question.

"If you don't hand me that towel, I'm going to come and get it."

"You wouldn't dare."

"Wouldn't I?"

The bathwater sloshed as he stood. Ellie couldn't help herself—she looked. Then she let out a soft gasp as her gaze lit on the entire stretch of him, and she scrunched her eyes closed. She thrust the towel out. "Fine. Take it. But you still have to answer my question."

She heard the water splashing as he climbed from the tub. She kept her eyes closed, but her imagination ran riot, building on what she'd seen. All that glistening skin, the dark trail of hair down his muscular stomach, his . . . oh his . . .

It was too shocking.

Who knew a man could look like *that*?

She felt the towel tugged from her grasp and she could imagine she felt the heat radiating from his damp body. Mere inches from hers.

"Ellie," he said, his voice a deep rasp. "Open your eyes."

She shook her head. *No*.

She could feel his breath on her face, he was standing so close. "I'm wearing the towel. I'm decent."

But he wasn't decent in the slightest. None of this was decent. Including her. The feelings shooting through her were the opposite of decent. They were *obscene*.

She felt the heat of his breath against her lips and she shivered.

"You didn't leave," he whispered against her lips. "You could have dropped the towel and run."

She swallowed hard. She should leave. She really should.

But she didn't want to.

"Open your eyes, Ellie."

Slowly, shivering with an onslaught of feeling, Ellie opened her eyes, and stared straight into his. They were dark pools. The kind you could drown in.

"Look all you want," he said in that uneven, rough voice that sent goosebumps down her body. "I don't mind." Those plump lips, with their sharp cupid's bow, curved into a wicked smile as he took a step back and held his arms out.

She looked. She couldn't have stopped herself if she tried. He had the towel around his waist, but it barely covered him. His body was pearly with water droplets, and she watched, hypnotized, as a droplet on his collarbone burst, rolling down the slope of his chest, over his dusky nipple. The drop rolled from nipple, to stomach, over his flexing muscles, to the sharp line of his hip, before hitting the towel. Ellie forgot to breathe.

He was *perfect*.

"You can touch too," he said, his voice slow and soft. "If you want to."

Oh *God*. She did want to. Ellie lost all ability to think; she was just a creature of wanting.

With trembling fingers, she reached out and touched his collarbone, in the exact spot where the droplet had burst. She felt his hot skin shiver under her touch.

"Ellie," he sighed, tilting his head back as she traced his collarbones. His thick eyelashes were quivering against his cheeks.

"Don't talk," she begged him, putting her hand over his mouth. If they talked, reality would crash in, and this would end. Because it *had* to end. This was impossible.

He put his hand over hers and pressed a kiss to her palm.

Ellie couldn't breathe. She was full of cascading liquid heat. She closed her eyes and enjoyed the sensation of his mouth against her palm. Then she felt the hot flick of his tongue and gave a soft moan. Her hand fell away and then she was kissing him. His damp arms enveloped her, hauling her tight and hard against him.

For once in her life, she didn't think. She was aware of every inch of her body in this moment. She wasn't daydreaming or ruminating or imagining, she was nothing but this body, in his arms.

His wet body was hard against her, soaking her shirt. His mouth was hot and insistent. Ellie ran her hands over his shoulders and down his arms as his tongue tangled with hers. He made low hungry noises, backing her into the wall. Ellie wanted more. As much as she could get.

"Say yes," he whispered between deep kisses.

She didn't know what she was saying yes to and she didn't care. She was just *yes*. To everything.

"Touch me," he begged. "Please."

Yes.

Ellie's hands slid over him as their kisses became one all consuming delight. Her fingertips ran down the hollow of his spine, up the ladder of his ribs, across his sharply erect nipples. The noises he made when she touched him made her ache. She was vaguely aware that he was pulling her away from the wall and that he'd lost his towel as he led her out of the kitchen. The air felt thicker, like water. Her movements were slow and clumsy as she stumbled with him, too hungry to keep kissing to look where they were going.

She gasped when they fell onto the bed. It was dark in his room, the only light distant spills from outside through the window. He didn't stop kissing her as he stretched out beside her. Her hand landed on his hip, spreading across his damp skin. Her thumb brushed wiry hair. And against her stomach was the firm, throbbing thrust of him. As she gasped, his tongue slipped against her lips. He tasted so good. Like sugar and salt. And the soapy scent of him overwhelmed her senses.

Abruptly, she was aware of cool air swirling against her skin. Somehow he'd unbuttoned her shirt. Ellie stretched, screaming with want, as his hand pushed her shirt open and found her breast.

Oh God. Her breasts were swollen and hurting, her nipples hard. The feel of his fingers circling her nipple made her slick and the ache was unbearable.

"I've been dreaming about this," he sighed, as he broke the kiss to stare down at her. In the barest light, his eyes were darker than night. They dropped to her chest. Her old chemise was threadbare and hid nothing. Her nipples pushed through the fragile cotton. "Beautiful," he breathed. His fingers ran circles around her pouting breasts, and she heard his breath become labored. She whimpered as he untied her chemise, peeling it back, to set her free. She arched her back.

She'd never imagined anything like this. She was beyond thought as his mouth lowered to her nipple, the hot suction lifting her off the bed and making her moan.

"Yes?" he asked, lifting his head.

"Oh God, don't stop!"

He laughed. "Your wish is my command."

Time was suspended. Ellie let herself sink into the magic of it. Her hands roamed his body as his mouth drove her wild. Her clothes peeled away, falling to the floor, and then there was the heaven of skin on skin. Ellie shivered as his hand ran up her inner thigh, all the way. She spread her legs and his fingers slipped across her, feather light, then deeper. The feelings that spread through her body were indescribable. There was a hot, melting, pulsating feeling that pushed outwards like a slow-moving wave right to the tips of her fingers and toes. And right in the center of her, where his fingers were, she felt a slippery molten ache, like she was turning into lava. It was a pleasant hurting feeling. And she wanted *more*.

"Ellie," he breathed.

"*Yes.*" Her hand found the length of him. He was hot and silky smooth. When she wrapped her hand around him, he groaned and his fingers dipped deeper into her. Her body had a mind of its own;

her hips rocked against his fingers, the pressure and slide setting off a catherine wheel of sensation in the core of her.

"Ellie."

"Hush!" She didn't want to think.

"Can I . . . ?"

"Yes! *Anything!*"

He kissed her again, as his fingers teased her. Then he pulled away. She groaned. And then, oh *God*, oh then she felt the hot smooth press of him between her legs. And then he was sliding into her.

"You feel so good," he breathed.

Ellie wrapped her legs around him as he slid deeper. She clenched. It was a stretching, pinching, full feeling that made her arch her back in sheer pleasure. His hands reached under her, cupping her buttocks and lifting her towards him. He went so deep. The friction was cataclysmic.

"Beau!"

"Yes, honey." His voice was rougher, huskier, warmer than she'd ever heard it. It made her shiver with its languid promise.

Yes. His slow thrusts gathered in tempo, his hands squeezing her ass as he took her. Ellie pulled him down to kiss her. His tongue slid into her as he thrust. Shivery sparkly feelings, like sparks swirling from a fire, gusted through her. *Yes.* She dug her fingernails into his back and locked her legs tighter around him. He was groaning into her kiss as his tempo increased. Ellie shuddered. Oh, oh, there was a delicious pressure building. Hot, sparkly, liquid. It was the sound of him that sent her flying in the end. The weak, hungry gasp of her name as he sank into her. She came, loudly, mindlessly, *completely*.

Afterwards, she lay stunned in his arms, unable to think, let alone speak. For once her imagination fell completely short. Nothing she could imagine could compare to this, being here in the darkness with him, after *that*.

Ellie didn't even know how to begin to think about what had just happened.

Beau wrapped them both in the quilt, cocooning her in his arms against the evening chill. "I should have brought some coals into the grate here and warmed the room," he apologized, pushing her hair off her face and pressing a kiss to her damp skin.

Ellie hadn't even noticed the cold. She'd been insensible to everything except him and the things he'd made her feel. But now she realized his room was frigid, the windowpanes frosty. His body was still warm from the bath, and from their exertions, and she was keenly aware of every single inch of him against her naked skin. His chest hair was silky-scratchy against her breasts, his thigh was between hers, pressing against her slick and aching center.

"I hope I didn't hurt you," he murmured. He'd lowered his cheek to the crown of her head and his fingers were lazily combing the tangles out of her tousled hair.

No. He hadn't hurt her.

Tears flooded Ellie's eyes. She'd done the hurting all herself.

Oh God. What had she *done*? She'd just lost her virginity to her best friend's *fiancé*.

Diana, she thought sickly. How on earth could she tell Diana? But how could she *not*?

Ellie felt a wild howling grief as she realized that Diana would never, ever forgive her for this. And she would never forgive herself.

Sixteen

Beau was whistling as he crossed the muddy yard to the hotel. He was carrying his dress shoes, so they wouldn't get ruined. After Ellie had left, almost inarticulate with bashfulness, wriggling out of his kisses, saying she had to get ready for the dance, he'd cleaned up after his bath and fancied himself up. It wasn't every night a man got engaged and he wanted to look good for it. He'd grinned as he poured the bathwater off the back porch, remembering the way she'd snapped the towel at him.

He was still grinning now, as he navigated the mud. He'd never felt so alive in his life. His body was singing. Memories of the feel of her, the taste of her, the sound of her moans kept flicking through his mind. Part of him wished there was no dance, and he could have kept her in bed. But another part was desperate to get inside and dance her around that romantic wonderland. If there was one woman who could appreciate romance, it was Ellie. There was no one he'd rather experience the dance with. She was fun, and lively, and open to throwing herself headfirst into things, whether it was surviving a bear or falling into bed.

Beau had never felt anything like he was feeling now. He didn't think there were words for it. It was a soaring kind of feeling.

"Oh love, don't you look fancy!" Mrs. Champion exclaimed when he waltzed into the kitchen. "Like a proper gentleman!" She clapped her hands. "Wait till the girls get a look at you!"

There was only one girl he cared about, and she'd already got a look at him, he thought, grinning as he shed his outdoor coat and changed into his good shoes.

"Beau!" Junebug came swinging into the kitchen, in her harebell blue dress, with her curls pinned up. She wore a paper flower crown and was itchy with excitement. "Kit's here!"

"I told you." He swung her about. He couldn't wait to tell her that she'd won their bet. But not yet. He had other people to talk to first.

"Can I take the sandwiches out now?" Junebug all but threw herself at the table of food as Beau headed for the back stairs. He could hear Jonah tuning up on his fiddle. It was going to be a night of nights.

Beau took the back stairs two at a time. When he reached the first floor, he ran into Flora and Frances. They looked like hothouse flowers in their bright dresses, with paper roses pinned in their hair. "Ladies, you look lovely!"

"Mistletoe!" Flora pointed up.

Beau laughed at the sight of the mangled stem and dropped a chaste kiss on each of their cheeks. "I have a feeling I'm going to be doing this all night."

"Hopefully!" Their giggles trailed after them as they glided downstairs.

Beau took a deep breath and knocked on Diana's door.

"Wow," he said when she appeared.

"You like it?" She turned on the spot. "I re-made it after I finished Ellie's." It was the watermelon pink dress she'd worn on the day she'd arrived in Bitterroot, but more formal. A cascade of lace fell from each sleeve at the elbow. She waved her arms, so he could appreciate the effect.

"You look lovely."

"So do you."

He scratched his nose and cleared his throat. "I was wondering if we could talk quickly."

Diana cocked her head and regarded him curiously. "Of course." She stepped back so he could enter.

"Best leave the door open," he advised. "For the sake of your reputation."

"I assume this is about Ellie?" Diana said, as she moved to the dresser and dabbed some perfume on her wrists. The thick scent of lilies filled the room. She gave Beau a knowing look.

"She told you?" He felt a wave of relief. That would make things easier.

"No. *She* hasn't told me anything. But I know my friend." Diana gave him a sly look. "And you're as easy to read as an open book."

Beau winced.

"Her blushes alone give her away." Diana laughed. "Not to mention the energy between the two of you. I'm sure you're both responsible for melting all the snow in Bitterroot today with the heat you generate."

Beau exhaled. "You don't mind?"

"Of course I mind. I came all this way for you!" But she didn't sound mad. "Still, I wanted out of Fall River, and I'm out of Fall River." She bit her lip. "And your sister said something the other day . . ."

Beau groaned. "Don't listen to her. Nothing good ever comes of it."

"Except Ellie," Diana said lightly.

Yes. There was that.

"What did Junebug say?" he asked warily.

"She asked me how I'd feel if you picked Ellie instead of me," Diana said bluntly. "'Wouldn't you be happy for her, the way she's happy for you?' she said. And to be honest, I had to think about it, and—I'm not proud of this—I didn't think I would be." Diana's ink-blue eyes grew suspiciously shiny. "Which is *horrible* of me. Because Ellie does everything for me. She's been there through every bad moment, holding me up, comforting me, rescuing me. Look at her with you! She's clearly head over heels in love with you, but she won't even consider it, because of *me*."

"You think she's . . . in love with me?" Beau's throat grew oddly tight at the thought.

"Of course she is. And you're clearly in love with her." Diana gave him an impatient smile. "I didn't even realize until after Junebug gave me that talking to. I didn't see it because I couldn't conceive of it." She cleared her throat, looking embarrassed. "I've always been the one men pay attention to, you see . . ."

He nodded. He did see.

"And Ellie's always been . . . well, my friend. It took me a moment to realize that maybe this time *she* was the one a man was paying attention to, and I was *her* friend."

"So when you came to talk to me . . ."

"I was telling you it was okay to be with Ellie." Diana smiled at him. "I figured it would take her a while to come around, given how loyal she is to me, but I also have enough experience to know it's hard to resist a man you have feelings for."

"She didn't resist me much," he admitted, feeling a bit smug.

Diana rolled her eyes.

"Sorry," Beau said sincerely. "I really did mean to marry you."

"I know." She shrugged. "But who am I to argue with love?"

Love. Beau felt a warm fizzing at the thought.

"There's something else I have to tell you," Diana said slowly. "And, again, I'm not proud of it . . ."

"The mistletoe was your idea?"

Diana shook her head. "No. The mistletoe is all Junebug." She took a shaky breath. "All those letters I wrote you?"

Beau felt a wave of bittersweet feeling at the thought of those letters. It seemed a long time ago that he was hurrying to the post office every week to collect her letters. He remembered how his heart used to pound as he opened them, how he used to re-read them, running his fingertips over the energetic scrawl of her writing, trying to imagine the woman at the other end.

"I didn't write them," she blurted. "Ellie did."

Beau felt like he'd been pushed from a ledge. "What?"

His mind spun as Diana explained. She was sheepish about the deception, but Beau had that soaring feeling back again. It was a big, winged feeling. Like he could fly off into the stars. Ellie had always been the woman for him. And on some level, he'd always known it.

"Ah, Diana, thank you!" He pulled her into a hug and spun her around. "You've made me the happiest man!" He pressed a kiss to her forehead. "You're an angel."

She laughed as she spun, her skirts billowing. "It's my pleasure."

"You're happier than a pig in mud," Jonah observed as he took a break from fiddling to grab a beer. The dance sprawled through the dining room, hall and parlor of the hotel. Rigby and Abner had set up a table with alcohol for the menfolk. Being Bitterroot, a lot of the womenfolk partook too. Mrs. Langer was three whiskeys in already and was teaching Thunderhead Bill and Roy an old German song, which seemed to involve a lot of maudlin eye rolling.

"Beau was built for this kind of life," Kit rumbled. After a long ride down the mountain from Buck's Creek, Kit had spent most of the night dancing with his merry wife, and his face was flushed and sweaty.

"I was," Beau agreed. He was also hot and happy from dancing with Junebug, and gleeful with anticipation. He'd expected Ellie to make him wait, especially after their tumble, and the longer she took the more he vibrated with expectation. She was right about this anticipation thing. It was a thrill.

The hotel was crammed to the rafters with people. Everyone in Bitterroot had come out, as well as a lot of the miners from nearby. Just about everyone from the Ella Jean mine was here, and Diana and Junebug's brides were the belles of the ball. They hadn't stopped dancing all night. Bascom was dominating Flora's dance card, courteous to a fault and clearly smitten. And the regular cries of "Mistletoe!" led to smacking kisses on cheeks and rounds of cheers.

Outside, the fall night was crisp and clear, while inside drifts of candles flickered. The paper snowflakes and stars twirled on their strings and the tables groaned with food. Junebug was the queen of the night and Beau, Kit and Jonah grinned as they watched her careen around, her honking laugh rising above the noise.

"Shame Morgan's not here," Kit said, nudging Beau's shoulder with his own. "It ain't the same when we're not all together."

Beau could tell by the look in his brother's eye that he was thinking about Charlie, his missing twin. "I'll wait to have the wedding till Morgan's back," he promised. There wasn't much he could do about Charlie, though. "It wouldn't be the same without him."

"I doubt he'll accept it as legal if he doesn't have a hand in it," Kit said dryly.

"And is this here the lucky lady?" Jonah teased Beau, gesturing with his beer.

Beau's heart leapt as he turned. But it wasn't Ellie, it was Diana. She was pushing through the crowd towards him, and he could tell by the distress on her face that something was wrong.

"She's gone," Diana gasped. She was flushed from the heat of the crowded room. She grabbed Beau and pulled him away from his brothers.

"What do you mean, she's gone?" Beau let her lead him out of the parlor.

"I went to look for her when she didn't come down . . ." Diana dashed up the stairs, Beau in her wake. "Come see!"

They wound all the way up to Ellie's attic room, which was dark and cold. And empty.

It was painfully neat. The little bed was made, but Ellie's trunk was closed in the corner. There was a hastily scrawled note on it: *The books are for Junebug.* Other than that, there was no sign anyone had been staying up here.

"She's taken her carpetbag and her clothes but left all her books," Diana told him. "Where could she go? We're in the middle of nowhere!" She was frantic. "And *why* would she go? Why now? Why tonight?"

Beau knew why now. Why tonight.

He sat down hard on the bed, trying to remember every second of the evening. Her expressions, her tone of voice. He remembered teasing her with bad compliments as he'd tried to kiss her as she dressed. He'd thought she'd been bashful and embarrassed—which was understandable. But what if it hadn't been embarrassment . . . What if it had been something else?

"Beau!" Diana was angry with him. "Get up. We have to find her! She could freeze to death. Or find another wretched bear!"

"Diana," he said sickly, "I have to tell you something." He needed help understanding Ellie right now. He didn't know what to think. She'd been nothing but passion in his bed . . . but now she was gone. "Tonight, before the dance . . . we . . ."

Diana's eyes widened. He closed his eyes and told her as baldly as he could manage.

"We, uh, were kissing. And things got, uh, *intimate* . . ." He cleared his throat. "But we didn't talk much. I mean, I didn't tell her . . . I was saving it for the dance." Beau felt a wild dread. "We . . . then she left . . . I thought she'd know . . ."

"What are you talking about?"

"I was going to propose," he blurted. "I mean, I thought she'd know that. I thought she'd know I wouldn't do those things with just anyone . . ."

There was a charged silence as his words sank in. Diana made a soft, shocked noise.

"I thought she'd be happy," he admitted in a small voice. "Like I was."

"Oh, you silly goose!" Diana wailed. "Now you really have to hurry." She dragged Beau off the bed and pushed him towards the stairs. "Before she does something stupid."

"Stupid . . ." he repeated numbly.

"Don't you see? She'll have gone off on one of her stupid imaginings, turning everything into an epic drama. She'll be thinking she betrayed me! Can't you imagine what that will do to her?"

Beau could. And his blood ran cold.

"Get your brothers!"

Beau was way ahead of her. He tumbled headlong down the stairs, yelling for Kit.

Seventeen

Snakehead, Montana
One week later

Zorić's lunchroom was a circus after the trains arrived. Ellie was run off her feet as the customers poured in, filling up the stools along her counter. She poured coffees and took orders for pork chops and frizzled ham, eggs and hot biscuits, sandwiches and fried potatoes. Her boss was a garrulous Serbian who was prone to cursing enthusiastically and forgetting to charge people for their lunch. Ellie had lost count of the number of times she had to go running down the street after a customer, waving the bill. But Big Z, as he was known by everyone in Snakehead, had been good to her, and she counted herself lucky to have a job.

Ellie had come dragging into the lunchroom the day after she'd run away from Bitterroot. She'd been in a state after leaving Beau's bed but she hadn't planned to run away.

That had only happened after she'd spied Beau and Diana through the open door of Diana's room. *You've made me the happiest man.* The sight of them twirling and laughing, Beau kissing Diana's forehead and calling her an angel, had been like a fatal blow to the heart.

Ellie had only seen them because she'd been slinking down from the attic to confess everything to her friend. She couldn't live with herself; Diana had to know the nature of the asp she held to her breast. An Ellie-shaped asp with sharp poisoned fangs. Who'd slept with her fiancé.

But then she'd seen them through the door and a noxious mix of feelings had fogged her. Diana had been so *happy*. And Beau . . .

Well, Ellie clearly hadn't meant anything to Beau.

She was filled with disgust for herself. She'd thrown her belongings into her carpetbag and run headlong into the night, without thinking about where she was headed or how on earth she'd get there. She'd only made it to Snakehead because Purdy Joe had taken pity on her. He'd found her weeping as she stumbled along the creek in Bitterroot that wretched night, carrying her luggage. The sound of jollity drifting from the hotel had only made her weep harder.

"What on earth are you doing, Miss Ellie?" he'd exclaimed, pulling his horse up at the sight of her. "Why ain't you at the dance?"

"Why aren't *you*?" she'd responded, wiping her tears away. But it was futile, because they just kept coming. She hadn't thought she'd ever stop crying.

"Ah, Jonah and I had a fight." Purdy Joe was equally miserable as he leaned on the pommel of his saddle. "A real doozy too. I don't reckon he'll talk to me again."

"What was it about?" Ellie asked, her lip wobbling.

"A girl," Purdy Joe sighed.

Ellie couldn't control herself. She let out a hiccough and dissolved. She was crying about a girl too.

"Ah, there, there," Purdy said awkwardly. "I'm sure it's not as bad as all that."

"It is. It really is," Ellie assured him. She'd lost Diana forever. She'd lost everything. Because she was a selfish, untrustworthy asp.

She couldn't think about it, or she wouldn't be able to go on. "Is Jonah upset because you both like the same girl?" she asked, trying to distract herself.

"No," he sighed. "Truth be told, I don't really like girls that much at all."

"Oh." It sank in. *"Oh."*

"Jonah ain't so upset about that," Purdy admitted. "Ah hell. You don't want to hear about my problems." He sighed, a deep and melancholy sound. "It's awful to lose a friend over something like love, ain't it?"

Ellie nodded, the tears strengthening again. Yes. Yes, it was. Maybe just as bad as losing love over a friend. Losing both, though, was absolutely unsurvivable.

And yet here she was, all these days later in Snakehead, surviving it.

Purdy had rescued her. He'd ridden her down the creek to a little mining settlement, and the following day further downhill to the town of Snakehead, where he'd given her enough money for coffee and some food.

"I can't take your money," she'd protested when he'd pressed it on her.

"Sure, you can. It ain't much. Just enough for a hot meal."

"Purdy, I can't . . ."

"Ah, stop your palavering." He'd given her a gap-toothed smile. "We sore-hearted folks need to stick together."

"Purdy, would you mind not telling anyone that I'm here? I mean, Beau . . . and Diana . . ." Her voice cracked on Diana's name.

He was understanding. "I don't reckon I'll be going back to Bitterroot or Buck's Creek any time soon," he confessed, "so your secret is safe with me. I reckon we all need some time for our hearts to heal."

She'd be forever grateful to him. His money had bought her to this very lunchroom, where Big Z had struck up a conversation with her, pouring her a coffee and trying to dig an interesting story out of her. Ellie had envisioned herself as a silently tragical figure, a wraith of heartbreak, who would drift through the rest of her days like a ghost. But it turned out she was more the talkative sort of heartbroken. She told Big Z the whole story and he'd wept with her, because he was the big-hearted sort. And then he'd offered her a job so she could save up for a train ticket home, and she'd spent the week working the counter, taking orders and pouring coffee and telling anyone who looked in need of a good story about the vagaries of love and friendship. And bears. She did tell the bear story too. Just not as much as she told stories about Beau and Diana.

"Diana gave him permission to sow his oats and sow he did," Ellie told the statuesque redhead at her lunch counter, "and I was just the stupid little fool who fell into bed with him. I was nothing more than a furrow. And an asp. I was both at once." She knew she was making a hash of her metaphors, but she was *destroyed* by love and betrayal and her own outright idiocy, so she forgave herself. "You can't judge me on metaphors," she told the redhead. "Heartbreak isn't compatible with elegant storytelling."

"I wouldn't dare criticize anyone's metaphors," the redhead said mildly, pushing her coffee cup forward for another refill.

"It's a tale as old as time," a middle-aged woman with half-moon glasses interjected. She was there with her husband, but he was buried behind his newspaper and wasn't listening to Ellie's stories at all. "Men pluck a cherry and then throw away the pit."

The redhead gave the older woman a distasteful look. "Are we really saying she's a *pit* now?"

"I don't feel like a pit," Ellie confessed. "I still feel full of juice. That's part of the problem."

"I don't think juice is ever a problem," Corina, one of the other waitresses, told Ellie sharply as she passed by with her arms loaded with empty plates. She'd heard Ellie's stories a thousand times over this past week.

"It does trouble my dreams, though, all this juice," Ellie sighed, leaning against the counter.

"You're dreaming about him?" The redhead was compassionate.

"Every night." Ellie flushed. They were intensely realistic dreams, where Beau ravished her, over and over and over again. Except for the times when she ravished him.

She woke up aching for him. "Which is a *sin*, given he's married to my best friend."

"You don't know that they're married," the redhead protested. "Anything could have happened. Maybe your disappearance woke him up. That happens sometimes. It happened with my husband. He didn't know a good thing till it was almost gone."

"I don't think Alistair would even notice if I was gone," the woman with the half-moon glasses said moodily, giving her husband a sideways glance.

"Oh, they're definitely getting married," Ellie said with certainty. "They have to be, or everything is far more tragic than I thought. At least if they get married, I can imagine them both happy."

"I can't believe he proposed to her the very same evening he . . ." The redhead lowered her voice. *"Bedded you."*

Ellie felt the familiar tears flood her eyes. She still felt the pain of it like a red-hot needle to the heart.

"Oh, don't." The redhead fumbled in her pocket for a handkerchief. "Here." She passed it to Ellie. "He's not worth it."

"Don't fret over her too much, she cries at the drop of a hat," Corina said, coming back past with a couple of serves of blueberry pie.

"To be honest, I don't think they are married yet," Ellie sighed heavily. "I think they'll probably wait until spring. But it's imminent. Don't you think a spring wedding is lovely?"

"I think all weddings are lovely," the half-moon glasses lady said. "Even mine was."

"Did you tell them about the mistletoe?" Corina asked, pausing on her way back to the kitchen. "About him kissing all the girls, right in front of you?"

"No, she most certainly did not." The woman with the half-moon glasses shook her head at her husband when he made to pay their bill. "What on earth do you think you're doing, Alistair. Go back to your paper. I'm in the middle of something. Come on, dear, tell us about the mistletoe."

Ellie was only too happy to. "Well, Junebug—"

The redhead spat her coffee, spluttering.

"Too hot?" Ellie guessed, swiping at the mess with a cloth. "Or too bitter? Sometimes the coffee here is terrible."

"Did you say *Junebug*?"

Ellie blinked. "Yes. Junebug McBride. She's the one who hung the mistletoe."

"Ah." The redhead's tawny eyes were wide. "And . . . I don't suppose this man who . . ." She cleared her throat. "He wasn't a McBride too by any chance?"

"Yes." Ellie was alarmed. "Oh no. You don't know them, do you? Because I don't want Beau to know where I am. Diana's happiness must be preserved at all costs!"

"Oh my God." The redhead grabbed her pocketbook and slid off the stool.

"She hasn't paid!" Corina reminded Ellie as the redhead made a dash for it.

Ellie groaned. Not again. She grabbed the redhead's bill and ran after her. Lucky the woman was tall and Ellie could see her straw hat bobbing above the crowd. She darted through the busy street, keeping the redhead in view.

"Miss! You forgot to pay!" Ellie was sure she could explain to the woman why no one could know where she was. She caught up to her just as she reached the Canada Hotel. Ellie followed her in. "Miss!" She tapped the woman on the arm. "Your bill," Ellie said breathlessly.

"Oh." She took it from Ellie. "I was coming back," she said. "I just . . ." She groaned. "I was just going to get my . . ." She trailed off.

"Purse?" Ellie guessed.

"Husband," the woman sighed. She took Ellie by the arm. "Steel yourself," she warned. "This might not be entirely pleasant."

Frowning, Ellie followed her gaze to see a tall, solid man crossing the foyer. There was something familiar about him, even though she'd never met him before. He had a square jaw and wild dark hair and an intense gray gaze. A very familiar intense gray gaze. For some reason it made Ellie think of mistletoe.

Then it clicked.

"Morgan," the redhead said nervously. "I'd like you to meet Ellie. Ellie, this is my husband. Morgan McBride. We were just on our way home . . ."

Eighteen

November had dropped its last leaves like a wilted bouquet, and Beau was mucking out the stables, doing his best to ignore Junebug, who was listing all the things that needed doing for her next dance. Which she was holding to welcome Morgan and Pip home. A postcard had arrived suggesting they'd be home in time for Christmas.

"Leave him be, Junebug," Jonah sighed. "He don't care about your next dance." He was busy clearing off shelves. Junebug was determined to throw her dance in the stable, which she felt was better looking than the barn. She kept saying no one wanted to smell cows while they danced, but horses were passable. She was hectoring her brothers to get things organized, so they could spring into action the moment their prodigal brother returned.

"Beau don't care about anything anymore," she complained. "And neither do you, Jonah. You're the most miserable bastards a girl's ever had the misfortune to live with." She jumped from the hayloft into a pile of hay.

"Junebug!" Beau roared. "You'll break your neck."

"Spit, you're turning into Morgan, Beau. Since when are you no fun?"

Since he'd had his heart smashed like pottery, he thought grimly, returning his attention to scraping out the stalls.

"Junebug!" Maddy's voice rang across the meadow from the big house. It fairly crackled with displeasure.

"That'll be about the menu I wrote out for her," Junebug said with satisfaction. "It was extensive. Oh, I need to go pick up those lanterns I ordered from the catalog. Sour Eagle said they've arrived. Can someone come with me? Kit says he'll cancel the dance if I sneak off alone again."

"I cain't. I'm at the trading post today," Jonah sighed. "You know this is a busy season, before the snows."

"Beau?"

"I'm busy." He did his best to pretend she wasn't there.

"Come on." She climbed over the stall and dropped in his path, blocking his shovel. "I'll buy you a soda at Diana's window."

Diana had opened a little soda fountain out of a side window at the train station, to earn some money now that Junebug was no longer paying her keep. It opened onto a nice little area under the firs and Bascom had set up some benches for folks to sit on. She did fair trade on days that the train came, and roaring business whenever the miners were in town, mostly because they liked coming to look at her. She said she'd chosen the train station so that she'd be the first to see Ellie if she came back. Also, Bascom had been glad of the company, especially when Flora came to chat to Diana. It gave him a chance to moon over her.

"Junebug!" Maddy was sounding increasingly impatient.

"I'll return once I've talked to Maddy," she threatened Beau. "And by then I hope you'll have improved your attitude and decided a ride and a soda with your sister is a perfect way to spend one of the last clear days before winter comes."

"You should go," Jonah told Beau as he stacked buckets in an empty stall. "It ain't doing you any good being stuck here."

"I'll mind the trading post. You take her."

"I cain't. I don't want to miss anyone if they come by. You know it gets busy."

"There's no point waiting for Purdy, Jonah. He ain't coming." Beau knew he was being cruel. He heard Jonah's sharp intake of breath.

"He's just been off prospecting," Jonah said tightly. Beau winced at the sound of Jonah kicking the buckets over.

"Jonah . . ." But his brother was gone. Beau swore and threw his shovel on the ground. He was growing crusty and mean.

Pain wasn't new to Beau, but this was pain of a whole different order. It was like someone had peeled the top layer of his skin off and now he was sensitive to the slightest little prick or scratch. He ran his hands through his hair and groaned. Goddamn that woman. He stared out the stable door at the meadow. He could see Jonah stumbling down to the trading post, shoulders slumped. His gaze drifted over the meadow to the big house, which sat contentedly in Maddy's little orchard. Damn it. Fine, he'd take Junebug down to Bitterroot for her lanterns, even though he hated going back there.

He finished the stable, saddled up Dutch and then collected his annoying sister.

"You wait till you see these lanterns," Junebug chattered as they rode out. "They're made of paper and you string 'em up and they look like little hot air balloons. I'm going to hang 'em all over the stable. Maybe some around the cookout area. You think anyone will actually come to our dance? We might be snowed in. In which case it'll just be us. But that's fine too. So long as you all dance with me."

Beau let her chatter, but his mind was elsewhere.

Junebug sighed. "You ain't no fun anymore, Beau."

He grunted.

"You know the girls can come. Jonah can play his fiddle and old Hicks the butcher says he'll bring his accordion, if the snows hold off and he can make it up to our place. Personally, I think his accordion sounds like someone's squeezing a cat, but people seem to like it. Thunderhead Bill says he'll call the dances. It'll be a time."

Beau grunted again.

Junebug muttered under her breath. Then she seemed to decide she was wasting good words. "She's not worth it!" she told him hotly. "She had awful clothes, and she was mean to you! Let it go."

"She wasn't mean to me." Beau wasn't letting that stand.

"She *left* you."

"She didn't leave me. She just left. It's different." The thought of her out there, somewhere, alone, ate him up. He'd torn the town apart looking for her—but there was no trace of her. He imagined all kinds of horrors. She could have frozen to death out in the woods. He'd walked every inch of the woodland around the hotel, his heart in his throat, terrified of what he might find. She could have fallen foul of miners or prospectors or trappers. She could be injured, captured, hungry, cold . . . And there was nothing he could do about it because he couldn't *find* her.

"When people leave, you got to let them go," Junebug said fiercely. "Pa, Charlie, Morgan, Ellie . . . There ain't nothing you can do about it."

Beau lost his ability to breathe for a moment. The loss of Charlie and Pa collapsed into his loss of Ellie. The pain was threefold, sharp as a knife. He hadn't connected it until now, that he was feeling all that pain at once.

"I know it tries the soul not knowing about people. Not knowing if they're alive or dead, not knowing if they're happy or sad, not knowing if you'll ever see them again." Junebug's voice cracked.

Beau pulled his horse up. "Bug. Morgan's coming back."

She turned her pony and glared at him. "I know. Because if he doesn't, I'll kill him."

He took in the hard glitter of tears in her eyes. He knew exactly how she felt.

For the first time since Ellie had disappeared Beau began to crawl out of himself. He wasn't the only one suffering, he realized. Jonah didn't know where Purdy was, Junebug didn't know where Morgan was, Kit didn't know where Charlie was, Diana didn't know where Ellie was . . . Beau's mind turned to other people too. Maddy didn't know what had happened to her siblings, Thunderhead Bill didn't know his family, Sour Eagle had lost all his wives and children . . .

Everyone had pain, he realized. Maybe everyone felt exactly the way he did, as though they were walking around without their top layer of skin.

It was possible Ellie would never return. It was possible he would never know what had become of her. He felt his own eyes prick sharp with tears. His throat was swollen and his stomach sore. It was possible he'd had all the time he would ever have with her. That those stolen kisses were all there would ever be. That their one magical hour in his bed was the last time he would ever see her.

"Beau . . ." Junebug looked panicked by his rising emotion.

He bit the inside of his cheek and let the tears fall.

"Beau, don't . . ."

"I love her, Bug."

Junebug's gray eyes were wide and horrified. "Don't *cry*," she said, appalled. "Get mad, but don't cry."

"But I ain't mad." His voice was tight. "I love her, and I'm scared and I'm sad and my heart hurts so much I don't know how it can go on beating."

"Stop it," Junebug wailed. Her own tears started falling. "Stop it!"

"I think I'll miss her till the day I die."

"I won't miss Morgan," Junebug railed. "I won't! I'll hunt him down and make him sorry he ever left me."

"You know what's worst of all, Bug?"

"You crying?"

He laughed. "No. Not crying is way worse than crying. Not crying is a flat-out misery. What's worst of all is I'd be okay if I just knew she was alive. I think I could breathe if I knew she was happy."

"I don't want Morgan to be happy without me," Junebug told him firmly. "And he better be alive, or I'll kill him."

"That don't make no sense."

"It's a different kind of sense. The kind you feel in your gut." She dashed her tears away with the back of her hand. "Now can we get these lanterns and plan a dance and actually enjoy our lives for once?"

Beau nodded. He followed her down the hill, his tears still dripping.

"If you love Ellie, that means I win the bet, don't you think? Which means you owe me a circus."

He didn't dignify that with a response.

"Well, hi, stranger." Diana lit up when she saw Beau. She leaned through her window and stretched out her hands to him.

"Hi." He took her hands and squeezed them. She was wearing blue mittens and they were fuzzy and soft in his hands. She was looking thin and pinched, but her smile was warm.

"You look terrible," she laughed.

"So do you."

"I looked worse yesterday. I hadn't slept at all. At least last night I got a couple of hours."

"Still having nightmares?"

She nodded. "You?"

"The worst kinds."

"Want to have a sarsaparilla with me?" She didn't wait for his answer. She closed her window and came around through the station to meet him, carrying two open bottles of fizzy drink. "There's not much custom till the train comes in anyway." She handed him a bottle and they ambled over to one of the benches under the firs. "Has Junebug come down for her lanterns?"

He nodded, taking a swig of the syrupy drink. "What was your dream about?" he asked her. He knew it helped her to talk.

"Oh, it was ridiculous. The bear again." She pulled a face. "This time it turned up at the Christmas dance and went on a rampage. It was coming at me, with long claws, and then I saw it had Ellie's face."

"Makes sense. She wore a lot of brown. A bear suit wouldn't be much of a stretch."

Diana smiled wanly. "I feel like she ripped my heart out, Beau."

"Me too." He toasted her with his sarsaparilla bottle.

"I walk around imagining what I'll say to her if I ever see her again."

"Me too." *I love you. I miss you. Don't you dare ever leave me again.*

"There's a lot of cursing," Diana told him. "And a lot of finger pointing. Sometimes I throw things at her." She let out a shaky breath. "Do you think she's okay?"

"I hope so." He felt Diana sag against him. He put his arm around her. "I really hope so."

Nineteen

"Let me do the talking," Morgan told Ellie.

She ignored him. For about a minute. Then she couldn't help herself. "I wasn't planning on talking. I wasn't even planning on being here. If you hadn't kidnapped me, I wouldn't *be* here."

"Here" was the train to Bitterroot. She was sitting opposite Morgan McBride and his wife Pip as the train chugged up the mountain. Morgan had paid for first class tickets and Ellie's imagination was caught by the velvety sprung benches and the chandeliers and curtains. She wished she could ride in first class in better circumstances, when she could actually enjoy it.

"I didn't *kidnap* you." Morgan was offended.

"No? How *would* you describe it? Forced abduction?"

"No brother of mine is taking advantage of a poor girl and not taking responsibility for her."

"He didn't take advantage of me," Ellie exclaimed, throwing up her hands. She didn't know how many times she had to say it. "If anything, I took advantage of *him*."

Once again, Morgan McBride didn't listen to her. "He has to do what's right."

"Listening isn't Morgan's strong suit," Pip sighed. "I find it's best to raise your voice. He seems to enjoy a fight." She stroked his arm.

Morgan's only redeeming quality, as far as Ellie could see, was how well he treated his wife. He clearly adored her. Sometimes Ellie caught him gazing at Pip as though he couldn't believe she was sitting right here next to him.

"I don't want him to 'do what's right,'" Ellie said, taking Pip's advice and raising her voice. "I want him and Diana to be happy."

Pip got a look.

"What?" Ellie demanded.

"You say that a lot," Pip observed.

"What? That I want them to be happy? Well, that's because I do!"

"You know you get to be happy too?" Pip said mildly.

Ellie blinked.

"All I hear from you is that you want Diana to be happy, and you want Beau to be happy, and you want Diana *and* Beau to be happy. But what about you?"

"I'm happy if they're happy." Ellie was unpleasantly reminded of something Junebug had once said, about Ellie's happiness being based on making Diana happy.

Morgan snorted.

"What?" Ellie demanded.

Pip pressed her lips together. "You cry a lot for someone who's happy."

"No. I cry the normal amount for someone who has happily sacrificed their happiness for the happiness of others."

"Definitely let me do the talking," Morgan grunted.

"I don't want to talk!" Ellie reminded him loudly. "At all! I don't even want to see them!" The mere thought of seeing them made Ellie feel lightheaded and queasy. Maybe even bad enough to faint dead away at the sight of them . . .

It would be her first swoon. Ellie tried to imagine it. But it was too difficult when Pip was poking at her.

"So long as you know that you get to be happy too," Pip told her. "It was a lesson that took me far too long to learn. You get to want things, just for the sake of wanting them."

"Well, I want to let them be happy together."

Pip rolled her eyes.

Oh God, they were approaching Bitterroot. Ellie pulled at the collar of her pink dress. Pip had made her wear it. In fact, she'd taken away all Ellie's other clothes, refusing to let her have them again. She'd ignored all Ellie's protests and had furnished her with two new skirts and two new blouses, ready made from a shop. In many ways, she was just as bossy as her husband.

Bossiness seemed to be a hard and fast McBride trait, whether by birth or marriage.

To Ellie's horror, as the train rolled into Bitterroot, to the silvery bright blast of Bascom's whistle, Beau and Diana were the very first thing she saw. They were sitting on a bench under the fir trees next to the station; Beau had his arm around her, and Diana was snuggled into his chest. They looked perfect together, moonshine and midnight.

"I can't do this," Ellie blurted. Her composure shattered the moment she saw them there, in each other's arms. A wild pain burst into flower behind her ribcage. She couldn't bear to watch them together. Not when she loved him so much that it felt like she couldn't exist without him.

Ellie felt like she'd been shot through the heart with an arrow. She loved him.

The truth was awful. She didn't want to love him. She *couldn't* love him. Because Diana loved him, and Ellie loved Diana.

At the same time that the awful, hurtful truth of loving him hit, a searing rage burned into being. She loved him and he'd cast her aside. He'd seduced her and then gone straight to Diana. Her hands clenched in her lap. He'd *hurt* her.

It was like she'd been in hibernation and now she'd woken up and all the feelings came crashing in. How could he have left her bed—well, his bed, that she'd been in—and gone to Diana?

Oh, that hurt. It hurt so much.

Oh my God. He'd gone straight from Ellie's bed to *Diana*. And Ellie had let him. She'd abandoned Diana to a serial seducer. Ellie had let him sleep with her, discard her, and then move on to Diana! He was nothing but a manipulative, corrupting reprobate. He'd *used* her. Played with her like a toy and then tossed her aside. And now he was playing with Diana.

"Don't worry. *I'll* do it," Morgan said grimly, following her gaze to where Beau was snuggling Diana.

"No," Ellie blurted. "I will."

"You just said you couldn't."

"I changed my mind."

"In the last two seconds?"

"Don't, Morgan," Pip scolded, "she's clearly upset."

"Clearly, as she's not making any sense."

"He used me!" Ellie said hotly.

"I thought you said *you* took advantage of *him*?" Pip challenged her.

"I did! But only because he made me."

"Talking to you is as bad as talking to Junebug," Morgan complained. He stood and pulled their carpetbags down from the rack.

"Are you ready for this?" Pip asked Ellie.

"No," she said honestly. Through the window she could see Beau stroking Diana's arm. Her silvery blonde head was tucked under his chin. Ellie didn't know what she was feeling. Too much for one human body to hold.

"You're alive!" Diana lurched forward, cannoning into Ellie. She burst into violent, hysterical tears. "Oh my God, you're *alive*!"

"You didn't tell them you were okay?" Pip was appalled. "You didn't even send a postcard, so they knew you were alive?"

Ellie stood frozen in Diana's embrace. "I didn't think they'd think I was *dead*," she said, defending herself.

"Oh, I could *shake you!*" Diana grabbed Ellie's face in her hands and then peppered her with aggressive kisses. "I didn't sleep for a whole week after you left! I have imagined you dead in every possible way." Diana was ugly crying now.

"Diana," Ellie said, trying to pull away, "I'm not dead. It's okay."

"Where have you been?"

"Snakehead."

"Snakehead!" Diana shook her. "Why did you leave me?"

Ellie was painfully aware of Beau, who was having a very intense conversation with his brother. "I'll tell you in private," she said cautiously.

"Morgan?" Junebug's clarion voice cut through the afternoon. She came striding down the platform in her denim overalls, her hair newly shorn. Ellie envied her aggressive elan. She wished she could be so sure of herself.

"Here we go," Pip murmured.

"Old Roy told me you were here, but I didn't believe him," Junebug growled, approaching her brother.

"Well, here I am."

As Morgan and Junebug stared each other down, Ellie succumbed to Beau's gravitational pull. He was staring at her.

Then there was a smacking sound and an angry yell, and everything devolved into chaos. Beau was pulling Junebug away from Morgan, who was holding his cheek and cursing; Bascom was angrily blowing his whistle at them; and Junebug's dog was savaging Morgan's ankles.

"I'm going to head to the hotel," Pip sighed, "McBride greetings can take a while. I doubt we'll be heading up to Buck's Creek today, given it's late." She took her carpetbag and Morgan's and set off, unperturbed by the bellowing she left behind in her wake. "Bascom, tell Morgan to bring our trunks when he's done."

"I'm not at the hotel anymore," Diana told Ellie. She couldn't seem to let go of her; she was holding on like Ellie might bolt. "I'm staying at Mrs. Champion's. I couldn't afford the hotel, and she kindly offered to let me board with her. She has two spare rooms, I'm sure she'd be happy to let you stay too." Diana wasn't brooking discussion. "Come on, we have a lot to talk about."

Ellie looked over her shoulder as Diana escorted her away. Beau had his arms full of Junebug, but his eyes were still on Ellie.

Diana led Ellie to Mrs. Champion's in sniffly silence, showing her to her room and promising to return for her as soon as Ellie had freshened up from her journey. Ellie had been put in Beau's old bedroom. She'd be sleeping in *that* bed. Ellie didn't appreciate the irony, and she didn't appreciate the way Beau came barging in without so much as knocking, like it was still his room. The door slammed on its hinges and there he was, filling the doorway like a vengeful god.

Her memory hadn't done him justice. He was seriously, heart-hurtingly beautiful. But he had deep bruised circles under his eyes.

"Who the hell runs off after . . . *that*?" He jabbed an angry finger at the bed.

She hated how glad she was to see him. And she hated how it *hurt*. She hated that Diana had cried herself into a puddle at the train station, leaving both of them worn out. She hated the anxiety and the guilt and the stinging pain. She wished Morgan McBride had left her back in Snakehead.

"I *saw* you," she exploded, retreating to the safer plains of anger. Anger felt better than pain. "I saw you and Diana, in her room. You were proposing to her! So yes, I ran off after *that*."

She gestured at the bed as well. The bed that she had no intention of sleeping in. She'd rather sleep on the floor.

Beau seemed genuinely bewildered. "I was *what*?"

"You said she'd made you the happiest man alive and you kissed her on the head." She grabbed a pillow off the bed and threw it at him. "Not an hour after you left my bed. *This* bed!"

He caught it. "I wasn't proposing to her, you annoying woman! I was telling her that I was going to propose to *you*!"

Ellie froze in the act of grabbing the second pillow. "That's not true."

"It is! I'm in love with you, you idiot. And everyone knows it, including Diana. She was happy for us. That's why I was thanking her. *That's* why I was spinning her around. I was going to goddamn well propose to you. But you ran away!" He threw the pillow at the wall. It made a loud smacking sound and then slid to the floor. "You put us through hell. I looked under every bush thinking you'd frozen to death; I walked through every last inch of the woods around Bitterroot, thinking you were lost; I looked up every tree in case you'd met another bear; I suspected every stranger of causing you harm. I interrogated Bascom but he swore black and blue you never got on any train. I went to every mine on this side of the mountain. And now I learn you were in *Snakehead*!"

"I was making you happy!" she told him hotly. "I was letting you be with Diana!"

"Well, you didn't make me happy! You ruined my goddamn life. Not to mention Diana's. Did she tell you about her nightmares? Have you seen how pale she is? Does she look *happy* to you?" He was wild eyed. "I mean, who the hell just runs off?"

"*I* do!" Ellie shouted. "I do, when the man I love is kissing other women every five minutes and going straight to my best friend's arms after I've *slept with him*."

Beau went silent at that. He was breathing hard. "I've wanted nothing more than to see you," he said, his voice tight with emotion. "I thought I just needed to know you were alive. That you were okay. That that would be enough." His roiling black gaze met Ellie's. "But it's not. Now that you're here, I want to wring your goddamn neck!"

And then he left her, slamming the door so hard the whole cottage seemed to shake.

Ellie didn't cry. She didn't swoon. She couldn't even think.

Which was a first.

Or rather a second. The last time she couldn't even think she'd been in this exact room. But in his arms.

Twenty

Ellie was a nervous wreck as they rode up the hill to Buck's Creek. She kept fiddling with her skirts, and smoothing her hair, which she wore loose. Diana had washed it for her.

"This is a terrible idea," she said. "I'm going to arrive and he's going to throw me headfirst into the creek." Ellie could imagine it clearly, the rushing waters sending her tumbling down the valley, closing over her head with frigid fatality.

"No, he won't." Diana was unperturbed. She held Ellie's hand in both of hers. "Well, he might," she amended. "But then he'll jump in straight after you, to rescue you."

They were in the middle of a whole train of wagons and horses picking their way through the mulchy mountain woods up to the McBrides'. Bascom was driving them. He was wearing his uniform, even though he wasn't on official train business. He said it was his best suit. He kept glancing sideways to make sure Flora was still safely beside him.

It was a silvery morning, in the early shivery days of December, and thin sunshine spilled through the trees, forming puddles and rills of light on the browning bracken.

"Besides, Junebug's been planning this to celebrate Morgan and Pip's return, and she'd kill Beau if he ruined it by being rude to a guest," Diana assured her. "She's been so happy they got back before the snows, so everyone in Bitterroot can make it up the hill."

Ellie took a shaky breath. She'd been back in town for a few days, and she hadn't seen Beau since he'd stormed out of the cottage. She hadn't seen any of the McBrides since then either. "Junebug's decided she likes giving parties then?"

"I'm glad she does," Nancy told Ellie brightly, from where she sat opposite them in the wagon. All Junebug's brides had stayed on. It turned out a town starved of women had plenty of uses for them. Mr. Langer had employed Nancy at the mercantile, where she'd increased sales merely by standing at the counter. It turned out miners bought a lot more when they were buying from a pretty girl. "Junebug's Christmas dance was the best dance I've ever been to."

Ellie listened to Nancy describe it with a heavy heart. While they'd been spinning around under the paper snowflakes, she'd been riding behind Purdy Joe, crying her eyes out. And now she'd discovered she'd tortured herself, not to mention Beau and Diana, for no good reason. It was possible that sometimes you could have a little *too much* imagination.

Behind them, she could see Mrs. Champion and Rigby bouncing along on the buckboard of Rigby's wagon, a picnic hamper hulking between them. Ellie felt oddly emotional about seeing them all again. It was a strange homecoming kind of feeling. Even though Bitterroot wasn't her home. Although she guessed maybe it could be now, given Diana had decided to stay. And if Diana was staying, Ellie supposed she was too.

"Do you think the Ella Jean boys will be coming?" Mabel asked with a giggle. She'd had more than a dozen offers of marriage and was trying to decide which to accept.

"Everyone's coming," Bascom said firmly. "No one in these parts would refuse an invitation from Junebug McBride."

Ellie had spent a lot of time imagining Buck's Creek, but her imagination hadn't done it justice. Not even close. They broke through the treeline into a broad mountain meadow, cradled by towering snow-capped mountains. The meadow was an ocean of yellow dried grasses, with the daisy-like speckles of late flowering fleabane woven through the shivering sea. The dried grassheads flicked and danced in the wind. The eponymous creek, which was really more of a river, flowed through the heart of the valley, shining like a scarred mirror in the sun. A ramshackle log building crouched on its banks, looking over a curved chokecherry tree, which had dropped all its leaves. Ellie noted the little fenced graveyard beneath the tree. Her heart gave a little dip at the sight of the wonky crosses. That was where Beau's mother and his sisters were. He'd dug those graves, Ellie thought, imagining the scene so vividly it seemed like it was playing out directly in front of her eyes.

Upriver, there was another cabin, modest in size, sitting in the shade of the woods like a tired child. The original cabin. Where once they'd almost starved, and where they regularly got snowed in so deep in winter that they had to dig themselves out. Between the two buildings was a little cookhouse close to the water, and around the edge of the meadow were other outbuildings: a stable and a barn and Kit's forge. And then the big house, a whitewashed farmhouse surrounded by orchard. Maddy and Kit's house. The kind of place Beau had said he'd build for his bride, only in place of Maddy's orchard, he'd plant roses, because his bride had said she liked them.

Ellie. Ellie had said she liked them.

Diana squeezed her hand. Ellie squeezed back, holding on for dear life, feeling like she just might float away on a wave of feeling.

He'd been going to propose to her. *Her.* Ellie Neale. Not beautiful Diana, not Nancy or Mabel or Kate or Frances or Flora. Beau McBride had fallen in love with Wallpaper Ellie, who might not be so wallpapery after all.

"Ahoy!" Junebug McBride came plunging through the dried meadowgrass towards them, sending chaff dancing in her wake. "Welcome to Buck's Creek!" Her dog yapped gleefully, invisible in the deep grass. "You can set up camp anywhere you like!"

Ellie couldn't see Beau, no matter where she looked.

There was a cookout set up in the lee of the stable, the fire leaping cheerfully, and poles with paper lanterns ringed the picnic area and a makeshift dance space of scythed grass, ready for darkness to fall. Delectable barbecue smells drifted in the air. She could see Kit and Morgan and Jonah; and Maddy and Pip and Pip's grandmother Martha were traversing the slope down to the cookout, carrying baskets of supplies. But no Beau.

"Diana," Ellie said, taking it all in, as though she was in a dream. "I have to tell you something."

"Yes, honey?"

"I don't want to live in Bitterroot with you," she blurted. She felt tears prickle. "I love you more than anyone in the whole wide world, but I can't live with you anymore."

Diana laughed. "I figured." She patted Ellie's hand. "We have to grow up sometime." She gave Ellie a fierce kiss. "And I'll only be four and a bit hours away."

Ellie watched as Diana slid from the wagon. "Diana!"

Diana turned, smiling.

Ellie took a deep breath. "I need you to know that even if you didn't like it, I'd still do it . . ."

Diana nodded. "And I need you to know that I'm happy if you're happy." She blew Ellie a kiss, and then grabbed a picnic blanket and headed out into the ocean of meadow grass.

She found him on the porch of the trading post. He was sitting in a rocking chair with his feet up on the railing, staring at the bright water tumbling by. The scent of water was heady on the cold breeze; it made Ellie's heart race. Or maybe that was just him. He did tend to have that effect on her.

Beau was deep in thought, looking more like a Bourbon prince than ever, his soulful dark gaze a million miles away.

But not so far away that he didn't hear her coming.

Ellie shivered as his liquid dark eyes caught her fast.

"You came," he said, his voice rough.

She felt terrible hearing the uncertainty in his voice. Ellie bit her lip and crept up the stairs to the porch. "I heard there was a party," she said nervously.

"Thought you didn't like parties." He turned back to the river.

He was going to punish her. Ellie lifted her chin. She could take a little punishment. But only because she had a good imagination and had thoroughly envisioned what it had been like for him. Not that it had been a picnic for her either, but she assumed she'd have plenty of time to describe it to him, in vivid detail. Then they could agree that they'd *both* had a perfectly horrid, terrible time of it. And none of it was exactly her fault.

"I've never really been to a party, so I wouldn't know if I like them or not," she said, easing herself into the rocking chair next to him. She tried to put her feet up too but her legs were too short to reach the rail. She shuffled the chair closer and from the corner of her eye she saw his lips twitch. "But I do like the look of all the food. And someone once told me I was a good dancer."

"I never said good."

"You said three-legged elks could be quite graceful."

He covered his mouth with his knuckles. She presumed to hide his smile.

"You know I thought you were a good letter writer," she said, finally managing to get her feet up next to his. She crossed her ankles.

He gave her a disgruntled look. "I am."

She shook her head. "I *thought* so. But then I got here and realized you didn't even begin to do this place justice."

He snorted.

"You never told me that your creek was actually a *river*. You'd need a boat to cross that thing."

"Yeah, well, you never told me it was you who went sniffing roses up at the Hill, not Diana. Or that you wrote all those letters, not her."

Oh. He knew. "She was there too," Ellie protested weakly. "I'm sure she gave an occasional sniff."

"You lied to me."

"I didn't. I told the truth. I just didn't sign my name to it." Her heart was pounding.

Beau rubbed his face, looking careworn. "My brother wants me to marry you. He's got his shotgun up there at the stable, and the pastor ready. I thought I'd better warn you."

Ellie's feet went thudding off the rail. "He what?"

"He's got some notion that I stole your innocence." Beau turned and fixed her with a withering look. "Now, where do you suppose he'd get an idea like that?"

"I never told him any such thing. In fact, I told him the opposite."

"You stole *my* innocence?" Beau's eyebrows shot up.

"I'll be giving that man a piece of my mind. He's too bossy by half."

"You're preaching to the converted on that one," Beau said dryly.

"I'm not marrying you in any shotgun wedding."

"And why not?" Beau bristled.

"There's no romance in it!"

"So, you're just going to steal my innocence and leave my reputation in tatters?" Beau seemed offended.

"Don't get me wrong, I'll be marrying you, but I'm not doing it at gunpoint."

He gave her an opaque look. "Morgan's hard to argue with."

"You can do it. I believe in you."

He snorted. "I don't know why." He went back to staring moodily at the creek. "Who says I want to marry you anyway."

"You do." Ellie dug around in her pocket and pulled out a letter. Her heart felt like it might beat out of her chest she was so nervous. "I have it in writing." She cleared her throat and then began to read. "'I wonder how it would feel to tell you all these things in person, rather than spilling them out in ink and sending them off. I'd like to watch your face, to see your thoughts happening, to know how you feel.'" Ellie heard the waver in her voice and cleared her throat. "'I was walking the woods the other day, not for any purpose, other than thinking about you away from people, where I could give it my full attention. And the fall color was in full riot, the leaves falling slow and spiraling, like gold and orange snowflakes, and I wanted with all my body for you to be here with me.'" Now she was here. Only all those gold and orange leaves had fallen. Their season was over.

Ellie's hands were shaking so much that the letter trembled in her fingers. She couldn't bring herself to look at him, for fear of what she might see. "This is the important bit," she warned him, and then she kept reading his words. "'I know this is rash and hasty, and my brothers will never understand it, but it's what I placed the ad for in the first place . . . Would you do me the honor of making me a happy man and becoming my wife?'" She tapped the page, trying to seem braver than she was. "See? It's a proposal."

He swore. "That was written to Diana."

Her heart pinched. "No," she disagreed, holding it out for him to take. "It was written to me; you just didn't know it yet."

"You're impossible." But there was a twitch and a twinkle. She was sure there was.

"Fortunately for you, I'm not. I'm very possible. In fact, I'm a sure thing." She dragged her chair closer to his, until her knees were touching his leg. She pulled his legs down from the post and tugged him around to face her.

"What are you doing?" He sighed. "Cain't you ever just speak plain?"

"I am! Hush and listen. You're ruining it." She smacked him on the knee. "I'm here, in person. You can watch my face, and see my thoughts happening—"

"Half the time all I see is you turning vacant and staring into space."

"Hush. When I read that letter, I wanted with all my body to be here with you too. I imagined walking through the fall woods with you so hard I thought it must have happened. And I'd like nothing more than to make you a happy man and accept your proposal of marriage."

"I ain't proposed to you yet!"

"You have. It's there in writing."

"I think if you put this in front of a judge—or even old Bascom—they'd tell you that the *Dear Diana* at the beginning would nullify your contract."

"Well, I'm not putting it in front of a judge or Mr. Bascom. I'm putting it in front of *you*."

"Is this your idea of romancing a man?"

"Oh, you want romance?" She perked up. Romance she could certainly do.

"What are you doing?" he asked, alarmed, as she began unbuttoning the neck of her rose-pink gown.

"Diana says I should show off my collarbones when I seduce you. She says they're my best asset." Ellie pulled her neckline back to show them off.

"Diana don't know what she's talking about," he said wryly. "And I never said anything about seduction. I said romance."

"In my experience, they're bedfellows," Ellie told him cheerfully. And then she slid over into his lap, making sure to keep her collarbones in his line of sight. Although she noticed his gaze dip down lower. She threaded her fingers through his dark hair. "Now close your eyes."

"Do I have to? I'm enjoying this." He tore his eyes regretfully from her cleavage.

"I need to paint a picture for you."

"No, Ellie, you don't." He leaned into the stroking of her fingers against his scalp, his eyelids heavy. "I like this. I don't want to leave it for any imaginings. This is all I've wanted." His voice was thick as his hands travelled up her spine. "So you can shut up now and kiss me."

"That doesn't seem very romantic."

"Trust me, it's all the romance I'll ever need." He pulled her down to him and as his lips touched hers, he melted back into the rocking chair. Ellie turned to press her full self against him, kissing him with every last shred of longing she'd hoarded.

And it was the most romantic thing that had ever happened to her, at least until Morgan showed up with his shotgun.

Twenty-one

Ellie and Beau's was a short wedding, as weddings under duress often are. It was held on the banks of the creek in front of the trading post. The bride wore rose pink and held a bouquet of swiftly picked seedy grasses, because the wild roses wouldn't bloom until June. The groom wore blue broadcloth and a rolled brim derby and was attended by his brothers, one of whom was armed. The bride was attended by her maid of honor, who wore watermelon pink and carried a posy of pine branches, and a flower girl who chose a nosegay of nettles. After the ceremony there was dancing under lanterns, and a party which ran late into the chilly night. Everybody who was anybody attended.

Aside from the nuisance of an unnecessary shotgun ruining the perfectly romantic wedding, the only other hitch was when a caravan of whores arrived in the meadow, causing the consternation of the shotgun-toting brother. The girls from the cathouse had been invited to join the party by one Junebug Everleigh McBride, who counted that day as one of the best days of her whole entire life. Not least because that was the day she knew for sure that she was going to see a circus . . .

Epilogue

"Boys, we've got a serious problem." Morgan had called a meeting of his brothers at the trading post. He pulled a bottle of whiskey out from his hiding place on the top shelf behind the ledgers and poured each of them a stiff drink.

He was aware of their unease. None of them liked talking about the problem of Junebug. Morgan sighed. He didn't either, but things were well out of hand.

"I think we need to admit that she's out of our control."

"Was she ever *in* our control?" Kit sighed, taking his whiskey and downing it in a single shot.

"She's not going to walk in while we're talking about her, is she?" Jonah asked nervously.

"No, she's gone down to Bitterroot with Pip and Ellie." Beau still got a blurry-happy look when he said his wife's name.

"We tried our best," Morgan grumbled. "*I* tried my best. But what do four backwoodsmen know about raising a girl like Junebug? And sure, we've got our womenfolk now—and I thought early on that a woman's influence would help. But I think we left it too late. She's . . ." Morgan tried to find the words. His heart got a bruised feeling when he thought about Junebug.

"Demonic?" Beau suggested.

"Stubborn," Kit sighed.

"Wild." Jonah drank his whiskey.

"Wild," Morgan agreed glumly. "All those things and more. She's got no sense of right and wrong. Ordering up one wife was bad—two was appalling. But *seven*?"

"Nine including Maddy and Pip," Beau corrected. "Oh no . . . actually eight. One of them was my doing."

"She gave no thought to the impact on the actual people involved. She has no empathy, or ability to imagine their experience . . ."

"She can," Kit protested, "when she puts her mind to it."

"But she *doesn't*. And she's getting too old for all her stunts. That time she ran off to Miles City with Pip. The gambling! She ain't a kid anymore and her stunts ain't child's play. She's going to end up tangling with the wrong people. And she's . . ." He cleared his throat. *"Developing."*

They all winced.

"She ain't far from adulthood. And what kind of adult is she going to be?" He hated this, but Morgan felt it was his duty to address it head on. "Is she going to be gambling with miners, getting herself into positions where they could . . ." He couldn't say it, but he could see by their faces that he didn't need to.

"I'd kill anyone who touched her," Kit swore.

"We all would. But we cain't kill every man under the sun—and she keeps throwing herself headlong into these dangerous situations."

"What are you suggesting, Morgan?"

Morgan felt sick about it. But he reached for the letter and handed it to Kit. "Boarding school," he admitted.

There was a stinging silence as they passed the letter around.

"She'll hate it," Jonah said miserably.

"Maybe. But maybe she won't." Morgan knew it was wishful thinking. "You know how she wants to travel. This Upcott place is in Chicago. That might interest her."

"It's like sending her to prison." Beau handed the letter back to Morgan.

"Better prison than assault. Or worse." Morgan looked down at the letter. "And she likes books, maybe she'll take to learning. She ain't never had much schooling, she might like it. Learning arithmetic and French and history and the like." He swore at the look on their faces. "Don't look at me like that. You know I hate this as much as you do."

They nodded.

"Can she at least go see her circus on the way?" Beau asked, consumed by guilt that his bet had led her to this.

"She'll be okay. And maybe she'll make friends. And you're right, she might learn to like it," Kit said, even though he didn't sound like he believed it.

"Sure. You're sending her off to a school full of girls. She'll probably enjoy spending her time trying to turn one of them into another bride," Jonah joked.

"Well good luck to her, since you're the last man standing."

Jonah shook his head. "She'd have better luck with Charlie."

Kit laughed wryly. "Maybe that's what we should do with her. Get her to find Charlie a bride. Maybe she could find *him* while she's at it."

"Well, if anyone could, it would be our Junebug." Morgan topped up their glasses. "Here's to Junebug. And the last of her brides."

"Don't jinx it," Beau warned. He'd learned enough to know not to bet against his sister.

She was a wild card. Every time.

Acknowledgments

I would like to acknowledge the Blackfoot, Crow and Bitterroot Salish people of Montana, and to recognize their spiritual connection to the country I write about in this book. I would also like to acknowledge that I write on the lands of the Kaurna people of the beautiful Adelaide plains, and I honor their living and ongoing traditions of storying and knowing, and pay my respects to elders, past and present.

This book is dedicated to my beloved cat, Lucy, who was my writing buddy for a golden fifteen years. This was the last book I wrote with her by my side, and while I'm heartbroken at her loss, I'm also deeply grateful for so many good years. I think part of the magic of the McBrides came from her—thank you, Lucy. I miss you.

Always I need to thank Jonny, who is all the McBride men wrapped into one very charming, complicated, grumpy but also sunshiny package. Thank you, cowboy. Although you really annoyed me five seconds before I wrote this and so I feel like putting 'grumpy' in bold. Screw it. I'll bold it and capitalise it: I love you, you **GRUMPY** ass. Thank you for all the ways you support me to write. I never take it for granted and everyone should have someone in their corner the way you're in mine.

Thanks to Kirby, for his quiet grace and for doing the dishes and taking out the garbage and being the calm in many storms. And thank you to Isaac, who is one of the inspirations for Junebug McBride—a person so beautifully, completely themselves that it makes the world a better place. Thank you to my parents, my brother, and all the family. Family time keeps my year grounded when things get wild, and I love you all enormously. Thanks to Lynn for morning discos and sanity; to Tully for rambling phone calls and more sanity; to the girls of SARA for their enduring friendship; and to my postgrads for constantly re-inspiring me to write.

I want to give a shout out to Alissandra Seelaus for the incredible covers for the McBride books. Their Technicolor joy always enhances my imagination. And to Eva Kaminsky for her vivid narration of the audiobooks—I can't imagine anyone else giving voice to Junebug and her world.

And with eternal gratitude, I say thank you to the dream team at Simon & Schuster for keeping the McBrides on this wild ride. Anthea, my queen; Bails—go Tigers; Dan and Ben and Anna for their support; Jasmine and Kelly for their calm and expert organization; Lizzie of the shiny cowboy boots for the edits; Gareth and Amy and Jade and all the sales team; and every single person who worked on the book and the audiobook. Thank you!

Sarah E. Younger, my warm, supportive and focussed agent—thank you for everything. Love working with you. And thank you to Kristine Swartz, without whom the McBrides would not exist.

Lastly, thanks to the McBride stans who DM me their love for these characters and their world—I promise there's more to come!

Photograph by Sia Duff

Amy Barry writes sweeping historical stories about love. She's fascinated with the landscapes of the American West and their complex long history, and she's even more fascinated with people in all their weird, tangled glory. Amy also writes under the names Amy Matthews and Tess LeSue and is senior lecturer in creative writing at Flinders University in Australia.

CONNECT ONLINE

Amy-Barry.com
AmyBarry.AmyBarry
AmyB_AmyM
AmyBarryAuthor

Ready for your next adventure in Buck's Creek?
Get back in the saddle with *Kit McBride Gets a Wife*
and *Marrying off Morgan McBride*.

Available now!

Available now!